TANGLED SOULS

Other Books
by Jana Oliver

Briar Rose

Young Adult novel
Macmillan Children's Books (U.K.)

Series

Time Rovers Series

Time Travel/Alternate History Romance

Sojourn

Virtual Evil

Madman's Dance

The Demon Trappers Series

Young Adult series
U.S. (U.K.)

The Demon Trapper's Daughter (Forsaken)

Soul Thief (Forbidden)

Forgiven

Foretold

Tangled Souls

Jana Oliver

 Nevermore Books

Published by
MageSpell LLC
P.O. Box 1126
Norcross, GA 30091

ISBN: 978-0-9704490-7-8

Tangled Souls

To Ireland,
her people and the rich heritage
they've so generously shared
with the rest of us.

Éirinn go brách

Acknowledgements

Many folks had a part in this story over the years and this is but a few of them to whom I owe my thanks.

My endless gratitude and hugs to Aiodhan, a dear friend and wise Wiccan who help me ensure Gavenia's magic was as it should be.

To my critique partners Nanette Littlestone, Dwain Herndon and Aarti Nayar for giving me sold solid input on the story. Also my thanks to Berta Platas, Carla Fredd, Maureen Hardegree and Michele Roper, my current critique partners, who came into this project later on, but contributed nonetheless.

My freelance editor, Kathryn Fernquist Hinds, is not only a copy editing genius but saved this author's butt when it came to Celtic goddesses and Irish folklore.

My thanks to artist Jeannie Ruesch created the amazing cover, and my spouse, Harold, for all the technical support behind the scenes.

Now, finally, TANGLED SOULS is ready!

"Miracles do not, in fact,
break the laws of nature."

— C. S. Lewis

Chapter One

In the midst of deep sorrow came a joyful giggle. A little boy, no more than four, gleefully captured raindrops sheeting off his parents' black umbrella. Blissfully unaware of the solemnity of the occasion, he toyed with the water running through his chubby fingers, grinning in childish wonder. Douglas O'Fallon winked in response. He'd been about that age when his mother died. It had rained the day of her funeral, too. A parental hand tapped the child's shoulder and the boy turned away, their moment of shared innocence interrupted.

As he watched the gray deluge shroud the mourners, O'Fallon thought of his grandmother. Now in her nineties, Gran claimed that when it rained, the angels wept. If that was true, copious celestial tears cascaded in unrelenting torrents. In many ways, O'Fallon found that reassuring. If the angelic host felt the need to acknowledge the loss of a single soul, even one as troubled as young Benjamin Callendar, every death had significance.

O'Fallon moved his gaze toward the funeral tent. It was packed with relatives, the family in the front row, as close as one could be to the hereafter without making the journey. The closed oak coffin lay draped in a blanket of flowers, a photograph of the deceased nestled among the blooms.

Despite the heavy rain, the resonant voice of Father Avery Elliot carried across the open ground. It was at odds with the voice O'Fallon knew from the squad room. Avery the homicide detective, Avery the priest—a man pulled in two directions. For twenty years after he quit his studies at the seminary, law enforcement had held him in thrall. Avery's sudden departure from the force had stunned many, but not his partner. He'd had been a good homicide detective. He made a better priest.

"Over the course of the last few days, we've sat vigil for Benjamin and celebrated the funeral mass in his honor," Avery said. "Now we return his body to the earth from which it came." He paused and then continued in a thicker voice. "Each of us carries a divine spark deep within our breast. Benjamin's spark glowed brighter than most and it will remain with us even as he dwells with the angels."

As Avery made the sign of the cross, he intoned, "In the name of the Father, the Son, and the Holy Spirit. Amen." He took a deep breath. "The family invites you to come forward and say farewell to their son, their brother, their beloved Benjamin."

Mourners filed tentatively toward the coffin. One young girl carried a tiny stuffed penguin, her face glistening with tears as she placed it next to the photograph with a quaking hand. O'Fallon looked away, memories crowding him. He'd put a small toy in his mother's coffin and a model airplane in his father's. Too many times he'd sat in that front row.

As time passed, the mourners departed, taking with them their grief and tears. The rain continued, though at a slower pace, for even the angels could not grieve forever.

O'Fallon folded his umbrella and leaned it against a tent pole.

"Avery," he said in a muted voice. His friend acknowledged his presence with a slight nod. The priest looked fit, his tanned face accented by graying sideburns and the white clerical collar.

"Thank you for coming," Avery replied.

O'Fallon held his silence; his friend would talk when he was ready. As he waited, he studied the framed photograph of the deceased. Benjamin Callendar wore a reserved expression; he had soft, powder-blue eyes and dark-brown hair. A former altar boy, he'd hung himself on the eve of his twenty-first birthday.

The smell of damp, fresh-turned earth struck O'Fallon's nose, followed by cigarette smoke. He hunted for the source of the latter and found two cemetery workers a short distance away, waiting in their truck. One smoked while the other tapped his hands on the steering wheel in time to a song on the radio.

Once the rain let up, Benjamin Callendar would go to ground.

"Did you ever meet Ben?" Avery asked, gesturing toward the photograph.

"No. I saw him at mass a couple of times. He seemed like a polite kid."

"He was. Polite and overly sensitive." The priest sat on a folding chair. "You read the police report?"

"It's a straightforward suicide, from what I could tell. The only thing that seemed odd was he went downtown to do it. Was he in the habit of hanging around Skid Row?"

A quick shake of the head.

"This isn't my usual sort of case," O'Fallon added.

Avery studied him for a moment. A deep frown creased the priest's forehead. "Ben's rosary is missing. It was his great-grandmother's, and the family desperately wants it found."

"They're hiring me just to find a rosary?" O'Fallon asked.

"Yes." More hesitation, and then, "Actually, I'm hiring you."

O'Fallon felt there was more. "Any PI can do that. Why me?"

"The family wants to know why Ben killed himself."

"You'd be more likely to know that than I would." Avery's sudden pained expression caught O'Fallon's notice. "You do know, don't you?"

Avery nodded solemnly. "I heard it in confession."

"Damn," O'Fallon swore. Most wouldn't curse in front of a priest, but he and Avery had too many years down the same road to worry about the minor infractions.

"I failed the boy, Doug. I didn't see it coming. I never should have let him leave the church that day."

"If you're seeking absolution, you'd best go to the bishop. That's not in my purview," O'Fallon said bluntly.

The priest winced as if he'd been slapped, then surged to his feet in a swift motion. "I don't expect absolution," he growled. "And I don't need your condescending tone, either."

O'Fallon blinked in astonishment and backed away a couple steps. "Okay; I'm sorry. Just tell me what you want me to do," he replied, unsettled by his friend's unusual outburst.

Avery's anger evaporated and he sank onto the chair. "Ben was having some serious difficulties."

That seemed obvious, given that the boy had committed suicide, but O'Fallon held his tongue in deference to his friend's grief. He reflexively reached for his pen and notebook, tugging them out of his suit-coat pocket. "That's not much. Is that all you can give me?"

"That's all. The rest I heard in the confessional."

"And it's off-limits," O'Fallon said, scribbling a couple of notes. He looked up. "The police report didn't mention a suicide note. Did he leave one with the family?" Avery shook his head. "Any way you can narrow this down for me?"

"Not really."

"Then what do you want, besides the rosary?"

There was a lengthy pause, as if the priest was weighing every word.

"I want to know if he was delusional. He believed something strange was happening to him, and it drove him to his death. That's why I need your gift."

"Is this one sanctioned by the church?" O'Fallon asked.

The priest shook his head. "The bishop doesn't know about this, and I'd prefer it remain that way."

O'Fallon examined his former partner's face, hunting for clues as to why Avery was playing this so close to the vest, but no answers emerged. He thought to ask about his fee but decided against it: Avery would see that he was paid, one way or another. O'Fallon replaced the pen and notebook in his pocket and took his place near the head of the coffin, preparing himself.

Some called his psychic ability a gift. His gran called it a blessed curse.

"You're blessed because the gift comes from God himself," she'd said in her lilting Irish accent. "And you're cursed because there are things that no man should ever see."

Puzzled, he'd asked her, "But is it God or the devil who works through me when I have these visions? How do I know the difference?"

"You won't," she'd said, and made the sign of the cross.

Closing his eyes, O'Fallon placed his hand on the coffin, the wood cool and damp under his palm. The heady scent of roses enveloped him. A young man's soft voice filled his mind, and he recognized the words, prayers particular to their faith. Slowly, an immense sense of sadness washed through him, smothering him like a thick cloud. He took a deep breath to steady himself.

Iron will had propelled Benjamin Callendar to take his life, as if he'd had no other choice. A prickle of unease seeped through O'Fallon's palm.

Why? he asked. No answer came forth.

O'Fallon turned to face his old friend. "What if I find he wasn't delusional?" he asked in a low voice.

Avery moved his dark eyes toward the casket and the gaping hole that awaited it. "Then may God help us both."

* * *

Given the trendy Bel Air address, the man standing near the rain-streaked window was younger than Gavenia Kingsgrave had expected.

In the world of international finance, Gregory Alliford was a mere fledgling.

"Sir, it's Miss Kingsgrave," the mocha-hued housekeeper announced in a heavily accented voice. When her employer did not reply the domestic left the study, quietly closing the door. Alliford gave no indication that he'd heard her.

As Gavenia waited, her eyes lit upon a large photograph on the wall above the marble mantel. Framed in finest walnut, it was a family tableau—Alliford, his wife, and their son, Bradley. The silence tore at her, and Gavenia took a tentative step forward using her cane for support.

"Mr. Alliford?" she said in a lowered voice, not wishing to startle the man. He turned with an embarrassed expression, as if he'd just realized he had a visitor. His tanned face was unshaven, with dark circles under bloodshot eyes, his expensive shirt wrinkled. She stepped forward and they solemnly shook hands. His were cool to the touch. She smelled liquor on his breath, though it was just past eleven in the morning.

"Ms. Kingsgrave. Thank you for coming." He gestured toward an expensive tan leather chair near the sofa. "Please make yourself comfortable."

As she sat, she noticed another picture, on an end table— Gregory Alliford and his son playing with a small black puppy. The little boy's smile was infectious.

"That was on his sixth birthday. I got him a dog," Alliford explained. He hesitated and then looked down at his hands where they sat in his lap. "It was only two months ago. . . ."

Gavenia cleared her throat. "How can I help you?"

"I called because I don't know what else to do. I thought of talking to our priest, but I don't think he'd understand."

"No doubt he can help you in other ways," she replied gently.

Alliford shook his head. "No, I don't think so." He sighed. "I thought it was just me, but my housekeeper, she's . . ." He trailed off.

"It happens sometimes."

Alliford cleared his throat. "Janet refused to be here today. She's staying with her mother in Palm Springs. We separated right after Bradley's birthday, and it was hard on him."

"I'm sorry to hear that. It usually works better if both parents are present." Gavenia paused a moment and then shifted tone. "Please, tell me more about your son."

She waited as the father returned to his post at the window, where raindrops pummeled against the glass with increasing intensity. A low growl of thunder echoed through the room, rattling the crystal in the wet bar.

Alliford began to shake, knotting the curtains in his fists, clutching the fabric until his knuckles bleached white.

"God help me, I don't know what to do anymore," he said, his voice quaking. Tears tumbled down his face as he struggled to maintain control. Gavenia rose from the chair, sensing his imminent collapse. "I can't take it any longer. Promise you'll help us."

Alliford fell into her arms, weeping uncontrollably. As she held him, her eyes tracked to the little boy's face in the picture above the mantel.

"I promise."

* * *

Gavenia placed her palm on the gaily painted nameplate that proudly proclaimed BRADLEY'S ROOM. She traced each letter with her index finger. Through the closed door she heard the characteristic sounds of a child at play. After a deep breath, she knocked and entered.

Gavenia's eyes swept the space and found it typical for a child of Bradley's age. The walls were festooned with clowns sporting big crimson noses, scrambling out of old jalopies and toting brightly colored umbrellas. A row of small teddy bears stood guard along a high shelf. Large paper stars hung from the ceiling on thin nylon threads, gently moving in the air above the twin bed.

"Bradley?" she called. The child was no longer playing, but curled up in a corner, his arms around a big brown teddy bear, observing her with wide, luminous eyes. With blond hair and brown eyes, Bradley was a carbon copy of his father. His jean cuffs were frayed, and one tennis shoe needed tying.

When he shrank backward as she approached, Gavenia maneuvered herself to the carpeted floor in an effort to appear less threatening. The movement made her wince at the discomfort in her left thigh. Placing the cane at her side, she tucked her long dress around her legs. All the while the child remained silent.

She closed her eyes and took a series of calming breaths. The faint scent of bubble gum caught her nose, and she smiled at that. When she opened her eyes, Bradley had not moved.

"I'm Gavenia." He did not reply, but peered around her as if expecting someone else. "Do you know what I am?" He seemed to think for a time and then gave her a barely perceptible nod. "I'm here to help you."

He straightened up and shouted, "I want Merlin!"

That puzzled her. Mr. Alliford hadn't mentioned someone named by that name. Gavenia searched around the room, wondering if one of the stuffed animals was named after the legendary wizard and the little boy couldn't see it from his place on the floor.

"Is he one of your bears?" she asked, pointing upward. The furry creatures were dressed in various outfits—one was a priest, another a ballplayer, a third an astronaut. She particularly liked that one. There didn't appear to be a magician.

"Merlin!" the little boy called, his voice sharp and high-pitched, evidence of his growing agitation.

The answer came to her in a flash, and she sighed in relief. "He's your dog."

The little boy nodded and then sank even farther into the stuffed animal, as if he could take on its skin.

"I didn't see him downstairs."

"Mama doesn't like him inside."

"Why not?"

"He chews stuff."

Gavenia chuckled. The image of a black puppy came into her mind, one with a lolling pink tongue and boundless energy. She could see the little boy and the dog rolling in the grass, squeals of laughter coming from the youngster as they played together.

"You really like him, don't you?"

The little boy loosened his grip on the bear and nodded.

"I'll ask about him. I'm sure he wants to see you."

"He isn't like me, is he?"

Gavenia hesitated, caught off guard by the innocent question. She closed her eyes for a second and let the impressions engulf her. "No, he isn't. Do you know what happened?"

The little boy nodded. "I got hurt."

Her heart tightened in anguish.

Leave it to a child to make death sound so simple.

Gavenia took a shuddering breath and fought for control. She had to help this innocent soul understand that something better awaited him on the other side.

"It's time for you to go home, to go see your grandmother."

Bradley's eyes widened. "Nana?"

"She is waiting for you," Gavenia said in a reassuring tone.

The little boy thought and then shook his head.

"Your grandmother misses you," she said.

"No!" he snapped, the force of his voice echoing in her mind. "I want to see Merlin!"

In the distance, beyond the misty veil, Gavenia could see Bradley's grandmother waiting for him, but the boy was oblivious to her loving presence, too anchored in the temporal plane. He had to make the final journey of his own volition.

Gavenia had only one choice. "I will find Merlin, and then you can go be with your nana."

The little boy blinked through fresh tears and nodded solemnly, as if they'd sealed a sacred pact. Then he gave the bear another intense hug and dissolved into nothingness, leaving Gavenia and the dancing clowns behind.

Chapter Two

The triple-belled chime announced Gavenia's entry as she crossed the threshold into the shop. Out of habit, she inhaled deeply, relishing the strong mélange of incense, dried herbs, and scented candles that enveloped her like an old friend. Crystal Horizons always evoked positive memories, from the weathered wood flooring to the aged tinplate ceiling. She and her sister, Ariana, had grown up playing with the magical ephemera while their Aunt Lucy served customers. Gavenia had been drawn to the same spiritual path as her aunt, embracing Wicca when she turned fifteen. Ari remained indifferent to anything metaphysical—yet another disparity between them.

The business had started as a bookshop with a small corner of magical curiosities. As the years passed, the books gradually disappeared under the relentless onslaught of the chain stores, and magical items took their place. Though Crystal Horizons still sold a few books, mostly metaphysical in nature, it was now a New Age shop. Gavenia found the term amusing, given that the store had existed for over thirty years.

She vividly remembered the day her aunt had sold the shop. Privately, she'd wept; it felt like a death in the family. Over the next decade the store had a number of owners, none of whom seemed to have a knack for commerce until Vivian. Though fairly new to the Craft, she had a deep wisdom that heralded an old soul. Applying her unique blend of financial acumen and the ability to relate to people on a personal level, Viv ensured that *Crystal Horizons* was a vibrant fixture of the Pagan community. While catering to the curiosity of the wannabes, she retained the crucial magical items needed by genuine witches. It was a difficult line to tread, but she'd proven adroit at the tightrope act.

As usual, Viv wore a shade of burgundy that accented her dark-brown hair, her dress a flowing number that rustled when she moved. At least today Gavenia didn't feel quite as dowdy in her presence—the long black dress she'd donned to meet Bradley's father remained in place; there'd been no time for her to retreat to the comfort of jeans. Still, there was no reason for Viv to know she'd borrowed it from Ari's clothes stash in the spare closet.

When Gavenia paused near the greeting-card rack, her friend acknowledged her and continued to wait on the portly customer at the counter. The woman was carrying on about the wonders of a particular psychic reader at the Cosmic Connection, a rival shop. The establishment was Crystal Horizons' leading competitor and located in a trendier neighborhood. It counted a number of celebrities as its patrons and never failed to capitalize on the association.

The customer gave one of the candles a cursory sniff, shook her head, put it down, and picked up another, then repeated the action eight more times as Gavenia watched in amusement. "I just don't know which one to choose," the woman said.

"Are you a Libra?" Viv asked.

"Why, yes. Triple-aspected," the woman announced. "How did you know?"

Viv nodded in understanding. "I thought so. Let me help you."

Gavenia struggled to keep a smile off her face. Most born under the sign of Libra were indecisive at the best of times, but a triple-aspected one was, well . . . triply inclined to dither. Though wonderful people, they often found decision making a problem, even when choosing something as simple as scented candles.

Knowing she had plenty of time, Gavenia headed for the bookcase and her personal ritual. To the casual observer, it appeared she was looking through the book stack, but she had another purpose. She removed two particular books from the shelf and set them aside, as the tomes held no interest—she was fairy hunting. And there *she* was, just like the day Gavenia had painted her.

Aunt Lucy had commissioned a wall mural, and the artist had

made the painting extra special, at least to Gavenia. Nestled in the middle of a pastoral scene depicting the God and Goddess holding court, her wee fairy was one of many fey hidden in trees and peeping around blades of grass. Gavenia's fey looked exactly like her: flowing blond hair, cobalt-blue eyes. In her hands, she held a tiny mouse sporting a gold crown.

Now it was all hidden behind the big bookcase, courtesy of a previous owner. Gavenia kissed her index finger and pressed it against the fairy for luck and then replaced the books, the ritual completed. She would continue to do so until the building no longer stood.

"Yes, these are perfect," the customer announced, and before she could change her mind, *again*, Viv rang up the candles. The woman trundled to the door, a beaming smile on her face. In the end she'd bought six candles instead of one.

Viv appeared at Gavenia's elbow. "Finding what you want?" she asked.

"I'm having trouble deciding between all these," Gavenia replied in a mischievous tone.

"Don't start with me!" Viv warned, and then grinned. "I love Libras, I really do. But sometimes . . ."

Gavenia picked up one packet each of Dragon's Blood and Temple Blend incense. She debated over the one labeled Tibetan Tiger. After another deep inhalation, she added it to her stack, as it claimed to provide clarity of thought. She doubted there was enough in existence to make a dent in her sluggish mental processes, but it was worth a gamble. "So how are things going?"

"It's slow today, but that's often the case on Thursdays," Viv replied, rearranging piles of incense on a spotless shelf.

"Is the homeless shelter affecting sales?" Gavenia asked. The shelter located next door was Lucy's baby, staffed by members of the Wiccan community, offering one meal a day to a minute fraction of the thousands who lived on LA's streets. In time they hoped to offer beds as well.

Viv shrugged at the question. "Most of my customers aren't upset. The ones that are I can live without." She collected the incense packets and headed toward the counter with Gavenia in tow. "Nice dress, by the way. Your blue jeans in the wash?" she teased.

"I didn't have time to change."

"Looks good on you. You should try real clothes more often." Gavenia shot her an irritated look. "So how's it going?"

"Okay."

Viv gestured, demanding more information.

"I have a particularly tough client right now," Gavenia explained.

As she leaned against the counter, her elbow jostled a plastic container. The sign on it described the plight of a fellow witch who had broken her leg and didn't have insurance. Gavenia fished a few dollars out of her purse, and dropped them inside the collection jar.

"So what's different? You used to enjoy doing Light work," Viv said, a serious note to her voice.

"It used to be easy. You'd show them the next stop and off they'd go. No problems."

"And now?" her friend prompted.

"I have a six-year-old boy, and he won't go anywhere until he sees his dog one last time."

"Sounds like a reasonable request."

Gavenia shook her head. "They're getting harder each time."

"You thought they'd always be easy?" Viv asked, deftly wrapping the incense in newspaper and securing the bundles with a Crystal Horizons sticker.

"There's so much I don't understand," Gavenia responded. She still wasn't being totally candid, even with Viv. Most folks didn't know about her ability, and those who did couldn't fathom the personal toll she paid for the ability to commune with the dead.

Some thought the souls just showed up every now and then, like uninvited house guests. They were everywhere: in the supermarket, standing in line at the post office, reading a book on a park bench, at the gas station. Some had crossed over and made the return journey, no doubt on some quest to aid a loved one or a friend. Others had never crossed, but remained on the temporal plane, stuck for whatever reason. Bartholomew Quickens, her ethereal

Guardian, said her job as a Shepherd would get better over time. She didn't believe him.

"Isn't Bart supposed to help you?" asked Viv, one of the few who knew of his existence.

Gavenia's eyes swept the store; *he* wasn't present, no doubt figuring she couldn't get into much trouble while inside the shop. Viv handed her a cup of hot tea without asking if she wanted any, and the lush scent reached Gavenia's nose in an instant.

"It's Moonbeam," she exclaimed. Moonbeam tea was one of her personal addictions, like fresh-baked cinnamon rolls and ice cream.

"I got Branwen over at Earth, Wind, and Fire to let me brew it here, providing I rebate a certain amount for each sale."

Gavenia grinned. "She can be as mercenary as you are."

"Worse."

As she inhaled the tea's aroma, allowing them to calm her mind, she belatedly remembered her friend's question. "No, Bart's not helping. He's pretty mum about things right now."

"So what's the plan?" Viv always had a plan, whether it was for the business or for her life.

"You know me, I don't have one."

"Then it's time you get one," was the swift reply.

Gavenia shrugged.

"Okay, then, if you could have anything, what do you really want?" Viv shot back.

Gavenia blinked in response. She'd not expected an inquisition during a routine incense run. Agitated, she downed the remainder of the tea in one big gulp. Regret crept through her for not having savored it for as long as possible.

"Someday I want *the Head Office*"—she paused and pointed upward—"to show me a copy of the script so I know what I'm supposed to do with my life."

Viv leaned over the counter. "You've been looking for your purpose, as you call it, for as long as I've known you. Have you ever thought that maybe you've already found it?"

Gavenia shrugged again, unwilling to commit to the idea. It sounded too easy.

"How much for the incense and the tea?"

Her friend took the hint and rang up the sale, dutifully deducting the Craft discount reserved for those who were genuine practitioners.

"Thanks, Viv," Gavenia said, handing over the cash. She glanced at her watch—two and a half hours before her sister's flight landed at LAX—and headed for the door, wishing she had time for another cup of tea.

"Bright blessings," Viv called, "and good luck."

"Thanks!"

The triple chime heralded Gavenia's reentry into the real world—the dirty streets, the graying sky. More rain was forecast, and that might delay Ari's plane.

"Another problem," she muttered. As she passed the shelter on the way to the car, she dropped coins into the foam coffee cups of three scruffy bums, whispering blessings as she did.

"Thanks, lady," one said. Their eyes met, and Gavenia glimpsed the humanity buried beneath the urban grime. Unsettled, she hurried down the street. Did she really want to read her life's script? What if the final scene found her living on a piece of discarded cardboard, clad in tattered clothes, begging for change?

"Goddess forbid," she whispered, and fumbled for her car keys.

* * *

O'Fallon leaned against the dirty, pockmarked wall to catch his breath as rivulets of sweat ran down his back, sticking his tan shirt to his skin. He was in a surly mood after the unexpected six-story hike from the hotel lobby. A tattered notice stuck to the elevator had announced its demise, and added to the note were misspelled obscenities, no doubt penned by the patrons of this half-star hotel in a futile attempt to vent their frustration. O'Fallon was less inclined to be poetic—a call to a building-inspector buddy was already on tomorrow's agenda.

The hallway was dimly lit, every other bare bulb illuminated, with cobwebs hanging from them in streaming gray trails like dusty curtains. A dark-brown mouse nosed its way down the hall, threading a path through the debris on the floor. It paused for a moment as if scenting danger and then continued to maneuver through the rubbish.

While making a mental note to get more exercise, O'Fallon mopped his forehead with a limp handkerchief. He'd been in fairly good shape when he'd been on the force, but the PI lifestyle hadn't proven to be so healthy with its late night stakeouts and too much fast food. It'd been bad enough when he'd been a cop.

While he waited for his heart rate to calm, he realized the hotel should be bustling with all sorts of illicit activity—dopers and winos and a few down-on-their-luck prostitutes working the halls. Instead, it was unusually quiet.

O'Fallon fished the tarnished brass room key out of his jacket pocket. That key had cost him a ten spot, and he'd still needed to bully the manager to get it. As he paused in front of the room denoted by the tattered crime-scene tape, it was easy to imagine the scene on the day Benjamin Callendar's body had been found. A couple of uniformed cops would have kept the curious at bay while the homicide detectives interviewed the tenants and traded dark humor. A suicide in a dive like the Hotel LeClaire didn't make for a compelling case, despite the fact that the kid was too middle-class to be here.

He slipped the key in, but before he could turn it the door fell open, the lock broken. He muttered an oath for the wasted ten bucks.

O'Fallon hesitated at the threshold and dug into an inner pocket to retrieve his rosary, his armor against that which was not of this world. He clutched it in his right hand and, after whispering a short prayer, he edged into the room. His pulse pounded in his neck. A streetlight cast a thin trail through a grimy window, one of its panes broken, the edge of the ragged glass glowing from the faint illumination. The buzzing whine of a mosquito echoed near O'Fallon's ear and he swatted at the insect in irritation.

A flick of the light switch yielded a harsh glow that did nothing to mitigate the squalidness of the surroundings. O'Fallon's eyes glanced around the room, taking inventory out of habit. The drapes were threadbare, the carpet of questionable pedigree, and a scratched table sat near the window. A dilapidated wooden chair was only inches away from the lumpy twin bed. His eyes settled on the tightly braided white rope and followed it from the ceiling down to where it had been severed, no doubt to remove the body. The chair sat beneath it, tiny bits of plaster flecked on the seat and the carpet beneath. The remnants of a shoe print remained, visible testimony to the victim's last moments.

He stepped closer and reached out his hand to touch the chair, the contact like a bolt of lightning through his body. O'Fallon felt the vision coming, though he had no real name for what would encompass him. Sweat sprang to his forehead and his temples pounded in time with his heart. His head burned, on fire from within. Vision and hearing collapsed, tunneling inward as if he were sitting in a darkened movie theater. He squeezed his eyes closed and tried to let go. To fight it meant failure.

He was entirely vulnerable during these moments, and that frightened him witless. As with a seizure, there was no control, no sense of what was happening around him, only the grand movie playing in his head. He saw images, heard voices, sounds on a scale that made a pin drop exquisitely painful. The film was not whole, but sliced into fragments and then thrown high into the air as if by a capricious child. He only saw the bits that floated by his eyes, and they were pitifully few. The rest streamed toward the dark cutting-room floor, untouched by his gift.

He'd never been able to explain it, even to another psychic, for the vision process seemed to be unique for each seer. Some came by the gift in a series of gradual revelations, each vision building on the next. Others hit the wall, hard. His had been the latter, the Morelli crime scene the trigger. He'd seen what no man was meant to see—the torture, violation, and slaughter of two innocents; the fragments in vivid color, no intimate detail spared. That was the hell of his gift, his curse.

As O'Fallon's mind grew dark, he closed his eyes and leaned back against the wall, hoping he'd be less likely to fall that way.

The first piece drifted by: murmured prayers for forgiveness. He saw the powder-blue eyes of the deceased, heard Hail Marys, and smelled greasy pizza. He felt the man's remorse, how he knew he would never grow old, never see his family again. Icy fear gripped O'Fallon's heart as voices tumbled over each other, calling the dead man's name.

He saw a flashing image of a rosary, intricately carved and of considerable age, clasped in pale, shaking hands. Then he saw Benjamin's face—tears washing down reddened cheeks, a thick strip of white at the neck.

O'Fallon struggled to pull himself away from what was to come, knowing that if he remained he'd share the victim's moment of death. He heard the protesting groan of the ceiling beam and then nothing. Mercifully, he'd been spared that final agony. A cold wind blew through him, chilling him to the marrow, as the screen went black. Silence enfolded him as he lost his ability to stand.

O'Fallon found himself on his knees, shivering intensely, his forehead nearly touching the muddy brown carpet. He shook his head, and a spray of sweat flew in an arc. A wizened face appeared within his field of vision, accompanied by strong, alcohol-laden breath.

"I thought I had it bad," the man said, his voice full of boozy concern. He offered a bottle wrapped in a paper bag. Without hesitation, O'Fallon took a swig and let the liquor burn down into his gut.

"Thanks," he said, handing back the bag. He looked into the old man's jaundiced eyes and felt reassured. This one wasn't a crazy.

"You okay now?" the wino asked, taking his own pull from the bottle.

"Yeah." His actions said otherwise: he rose unsteadily, using the wall for support.

The old man stood as well, his knees creaking. He gazed upward at the severed rope, and sadness came to his worn face.

"I'm sorry he's dead," he said, and shuffled into the hallway.

His words reverberated within O'Fallon's hazy brain. The old man seemed to care about what had happened in this room, and that might be a place to start. O'Fallon stared at the rope for a few moments more and then crossed himself, the final tribute of one member of his faith to another.

"*Kyrie eleison*, Benjamin," he intoned. "May God have mercy on your soul."

Chapter Three

Gavenia glanced at her watch, then tapped the dial as if that simple action would result in her sister's speedy appearance. She shifted positions to ease the cramp in her left thigh, her nerves bowstring tight. It was nearing seven in the evening and Ari's plane had landed half an hour ago. Immigration, Customs—it all chewed up time.

"Time I don't have." She took another long breath in a futile attempt to relax, gradually blowing it out through pursed lips. A sea of faces swept by her. Voices called out and reunions occurred, but her sibling was noticeably absent.

"You couldn't have waited until next week," she muttered in supreme irritation. The day had been difficult enough, and she still had another client to meet.

Where was she?

Gavenia knew the source of her impatience—Bradley Alliford. She'd encountered reluctant souls, but they'd always accepted the inevitable. Most were keen to move on, but Bradley was the exception. He was stalling, a classic child's ploy.

I have to find the mutt. That was the rub: Merlin was among the missing. For some unfathomable reason, Bradley's mother had spirited the dog off within hours of the boy's funeral. Gregory Alliford hadn't been much help, completely mystified as to his estranged wife's intent. He'd admitted that Janet had never liked the dog and had threatened to have him put down when he gnawed on one of the Oriental carpets.

No surprise that the little boy's spirit manifested the night of the funeral; the missing dog was the trigger.

"Weird," Gavenia muttered. She thought about the puppy as groups of passengers wandered past her. At least he was alive; that much she could sense. How long he'd remain that way was up for grabs given Janet Alliford's seemingly inexplicable behavior.

Gavenia wound a strand of her waist-length hair around an index finger and glanced at her watch. Seven ten, and another wave of passengers swept by. At times like this, her gift was a mixed blessing. She watched an older woman putter along with a walker, the essence of a man hovering beside her—the woman's husband. That was touching. He gave Gavenia a warm smile and she returned it.

Being a Shepherd was like wearing a neon sign, at least to the dead. The flip side was more disconcerting because she couldn't see all of them, nor could she sense some of the Guardians. That unnerved her and made her wonder what else ran under her radar.

It's not polite to stare, a voice said. She glanced sideways. Her own Guardian, Bartholomew Quickens, stood at her elbow. A quintessential thespian, he fussed with his garments as if in preparation for a curtain call. This time he was dressed as a Victorian dandy, with an engraved gold watch hanging from his elegant steel-gray waistcoat. She found that strange, given that the dead had no need for marking time.

"Channeling Oscar Wilde, are we?" she asked in a sarcastic tone. A woman close by gave her a confused look.

Bart chuckled, pulled out the pocket watch, popped it open, studied the dial, and then snapped it shut, tucking it back into his waistcoat with a decided flourish.

It was either this or something Native American. I had trouble deciding, he responded.

I thought once you were dead you didn't worry about things like that.

You're still upset about this morning.

She sighed and shifted her gaze back to the crowd. *There's more going on in that household than the death of the little boy. Something else is up, but I can't figure it out.*

Bart continued to fiddle with his clothes as if he hadn't heard her, disinclined to offer insight on the issue. At that moment a familiar face appeared in the crowd. Gavenia waved, and the figure waved back.

"She's still wearing black," she observed. It had been almost a year since her brother-in-law's death, and her younger sister still remained in full mourning. Ariana moved through the crowd, the gray ghost of Paul Hansford following just behind her. Gavenia groaned. This wasn't going to be easy.

Bart tut-tutted in consummate disapproval. *Ah, the widow Hansford and her very late husband. Some of them never understand the party's over.*

"Gavenia!" her sister called.

"Ari!" she called back, putting on a welcoming smile.

They fell into an awkward embrace. Ariana Hansford was a head taller than her older sister, her shoulder-length auburn hair contrasting with Gavenia's long honey-gold tresses. They'd always joked the fairies had left the wrong baby on the doorstep, though they'd never agreed as to which of them was the ringer.

Gavenia broke the hug first though she knew it should have lasted longer. Her eyes met those of her deceased brother-in-law and he returned a disdainful look. Ariana was unaware her sister could see Paul, and that worked fine.

She'll have to know someday, Bart commented, leaning against a pillar a discreet distance away. She ignored him.

"Come on, let's get you back to the condo," she said, and snagged up one of her sister's bags. "I've got something going tonight." Without waiting for a reply, she set off for the nearest exit at a ferocious pace despite her cane.

"Oh, sorry. I didn't know you were so busy. Maybe I should have stayed in England a bit longer," Ari called from behind.

"That would have helped," Gavenia replied without thinking, struggling to keep up the pace toward the far end of the terminal.

"I see."

The pathetic tone of Ari's voice caused Gavenia to halt midstride. Her sister deserved a warmer welcome. Dropping the heavy bag, she waited until Ari caught up, then she embraced her again, taking time with the hug. She brushed a light kiss on her sister's flushed cheek.

"I've missed you, Pooh," she said softly, using her pet name for Ari.

"You, too, Tinker Bell," Ari replied.

"I'm sorry, I'm a bit preoccupied."

"I understand." As they pulled out of the hug, Gavenia studied her sister's pale and weary face with concern.

"You look really tired."

"I am. I can't seem to sleep properly."

"You can rest in the car."

They hefted the suitcases and hiked through the busy terminal, the disapproving ghost of Paul Hansford trailing in their wake.

* * *

The man sitting across from Gavenia appeared remarkably alert, despite the late hour. Meeting a client at ten thirty in the evening wasn't the norm, but despite her hints that a more reasonable time might be considered, Bill Jones had insisted he had to see her *tonight*.

To mitigate her unease, Gavenia had chosen Earth, Wind, and Fire as the meeting place. A benign New Age café, it was an ideal location, despite the crime-infested neighborhood. She'd already talked to Branwen, the owner, and told her about the client's unusual request. If anything went wrong, she just had to raise the alarm.

Outside the psychic reading room, voices rose and fell in a soft cadence. The tantalizing scent of fresh-baked scones and Moonbeam tea wafted under the closed door. Gavenia had barely been able to drop Ari off at the condo before hurrying here. Supper had been lost in the shuffle.

She pulled her mind back to the moment, studying her client. Mr. Jones was an older man, nondescript; clean-shaven, wearing a white shirt, black-rimmed glasses, and gray pants. A paean to simplicity.

Too simple, Bart commented from his location nearby. He was watching with more interest than usual. Was that a warning? It was often hard to sort through his offhand remarks.

Where is his Guardian? she asked.

Doesn't want to be seen.

Why not?

He hitched a shoulder. Gavenia shifted in her chair, on edge. "How can I help you, Mr. Jones?" she asked.

He produced a smart phone in a scuffed case. "Do you mind if I record this?" he asked, pointing at it.

"I have no objections," Gavenia replied. Often what she told a client didn't make sense until they'd listened to the recording sometime down the line; then she'd receive a telephone call reaffirming that the session had been of value.

"I lost my brother last year," Jones announced after fiddling with the phone. He set it on the small table between them. It was scuffed and scarred as though it had a million frequent-flier miles.

"I'm sorry to hear that," Gavenia replied, as politely as she could given the late hour. A nascent yawn tried to sneak up on her, and she clenched her teeth to prevent its escape.

"I'd like to talk to him," he said as if ordering a glass of wine. His nonchalant attitude generated a prickle of apprehension, and she resisted the temptation to look at Bart. Instead, she lit a citrus candle and focused on the light.

"Please relax and take a few deep breaths. When you're ready, silently ask for assistance from your own personal source of Divinity, and I'll do the same." She disliked putting things in those terms, but given that she didn't know the religious affiliations of most of her clients, the generic reference was best. Gavenia closed her eyes and began her personal ritual: three deep breaths, a prayer for protection, another calming breath, and a prayer for guidance.

Let me speak for those who are no longer with us, those who still have great wisdom to share. Let this be a time of healing and of understanding. Use me as you see fit.

Gavenia sensed the presence immediately. The young woman stood near Jones's chair, clad in a fifties-style floral dress, her chestnut-brown hair in the soft waves typical of that era. She wore a small gold cross at her throat and a white apron, as if she'd just stepped from her kitchen. She twisted her hands together in an agitated manner, glancing right and left.

I am Gavenia. Do you wish to speak to Bill?

Yes.

Who are you?

I am his mother. My name is Linda.

"Mr. Jones, I have someone here, but it isn't your brother. She says her name is Linda. Does that mean anything to you?"

"No."

Gavenia hesitated and, after another look at the spirit, added, "She says she's your mother." The man's eyes narrowed, and a slight upward tilt appeared at the corner of his mouth. It almost resembled a smirk.

"What does she want to tell me?" he asked after a quick look at the phone. He was paying closer attention to it than to the actual session.

Bart shifted uncomfortably in his chair.

What's up here? Gavenia asked through their mental link.

I'm not sure.

She turned her attention to the waiting soul, hoping to find answers from that quarter. *What do you wish your son to know?*

That I love him and that he shouldn't blame his father. Donald was very angry. He thought I was having an affair. I wouldn't do that. The woman began to weep, dabbing at her eyes with the edge of the apron. *I'd never hurt little Billy like that.*

Gavenia explained to Jones, "She says she loves you and that you shouldn't blame your father, that he was very angry. Does that make sense to you?"

The man shook his head and flicked another downward glance at the phone. *Something's not right,* Bart said, rising from his chair. *I think you should end this session.*

Before Gavenia could react, images bulldozed into her mind, shoving aside any questions. She saw Linda in her pristine kitchen, a cake in the oven; its rich scent filled her nose. She heard the sounds of a screen door banging shut and angry words erupting.

Tears flowed, and then came a shrill scream as a bright flash of silver arced in the air. The screams continued, ricocheting through Gavenia as she crumpled forward. White-hot agony seared through her chest, burning as if someone had ignited an inferno within her heart. She clenched her hands together, burrowing her nails into her palms, oblivious to the pain. In her mind's eye, immense sprays of scarlet sailed heavenward, splashing the virginal white cabinets, raining downward onto the immaculate floor. Abrupt silence. Then the rhythmic chiming of the oven timer.

He killed me, the soul said in a hoarse whisper. *He killed me on Billy's second birthday.*

Gradually, the roaring in Gavenia's ears lessened, though the torment in her head and chest did not give way once the images ceased. Sweat dampened her forehead, and the meager light from the candle pierced her eyes like a torch.

Bart was near her now, kneeling, his face level with hers. *Just take a few deep breaths*, he advised. She did as instructed, and the pounding in her head diminished.

"Are you okay?" Jones asked. In contrast to Bart's anxious tone, his was indifferent.

Gavenia raised her head, confused by his attitude and was stunned to see he wore a jubilant smile. The expression vanished instantly.

"Your mother died violently," she said, struggling to keep her thoughts together.

A frown appeared. "Why do you say that?"

"She showed me her death. She was stabbed with one of the kitchen knives."

"So who killed her?" he asked. Again, the nonchalant tone.

"She said it was your father."

As if on cue, Jones surged to his feet. He started to chuckle, a low rumble in his chest as he pulled cash from his pants pocket. With a gesture of triumph, he tossed two twenties onto the table between them, a condescending smirk in place.

Gavenia shook her head, though it hurt to move. "I only charge twenty-five and donate—"

"Just so you know, my father is a used-car salesman in Bakers-field. He and my mom have been divorced for ten years, and she's very much alive," Jones gloated. He hesitated, as if he was going to add something else. Instead, he slipped off his glasses and dropped them into his shirt pocket, as if he was removing a disguise.

"You think I'm making this up?" Gavenia asked.

Jones nodded, his smile returning. "I know you are. Nice theat-rics, by the way."

His mother's ghost still wept. Linda was real, not some mind game one of the lower entities might play on an unsuspecting psychic. If she wasn't lying, then what was going on?

Gavenia made the supreme effort to rise to her feet, her balance unsteady. She leaned heavily on the cane as the room whirled.

"I only relate what I'm told. I see your mother as clearly as you see me. She has brown hair and is wearing a flowered dress and a white apron. She said she was killed on your birthday."

A peculiar grin crossed Jones's face, one that seemed at odds with the life-changing information she'd just revealed. It reminded her of a cat as it catches an elusive mouse, that moment of exulta-tion right before it begins to play with its prey.

"Thank you, Miss Kingsgrave; you've been fabulous, even better than I'd hoped," he said, scooping the phone off the table. He pointed toward the cane. "Great prop, by the way." He swept out the door as his mother's ghost wept harder.

He does not believe you, the soul said between heart-wrenching sobs.

"No, he doesn't," Gavenia said, a sickening sense of foreboding enveloping her. She massaged her temples to ease the pain, taking two deep breaths before sinking down onto the chair. "What did he think I was going to tell him?" she whispered.

Bart put his arm around the weeping soul in a comforting gesture. As Linda rested her head on his shoulder, he caught Gavenia's gaze.

I don't think he cared.

The ghost hadn't been much further help, too lost in her own grief. Gavenia bid her farewell, and the spirit vanished, still weeping and clutching her apron. To calm herself, Gavenia took some Moonbeam tea and a blueberry scone to go. Once in her car, she locked the doors in deference to the neighborhood, sipped the brew, and devoured the pastry. The headache eased, replaced by exhaustion and supreme irritation.

She'd been able to experience parts of a soul's life before, but never with such depth and intensity. Never had she felt the moment of death.

"Why did I . . . ?" She hesitated, ripples of the scene washing through her. She shivered and pushed the car's heater control higher into the red, as if that would solve the underlying problem.

You're getting more in tune with them, was the solemn reply. Bart was in the front seat staring out the passenger-side window like a kid who wished he could be anywhere else at that moment.

Gavenia finished up the scone and washed it down with a shot of the tea. "Anything else you want to tell me?" she asked.

A very long pause.

Jones wasn't what he said, Bart murmured in a reticent tone.

"Ya think?" she snapped back. "So why didn't you warn me?"

I didn't understand until it was too late, he said, lowering his chin as his cheeks flushed crimson.

Surprised at his uncharacteristic act of contrition, she elected not to chastise him further.

"So what is he?" she asked, and took another sip of tea, pleased to see her hands had finally stopped shaking.

A man who bends the truth to suit his fancy.

"Which means?"

We've been conned.

Chapter Four

O'Fallon hadn't intended to spend so much time with the old drunk, but there was just something about Bernie. Though grizzled with age and twisted with arthritis, he possessed a gentle nature, a graciousness the booze hadn't worn away. O'Fallon passed on tippling any more of whatever Bernie had in the bottle; his gut still burned from the first sip. Instead, they sat in the old man's dinky room, and he listened to him reminisce.

Bernie had had it all—a good job, a wife and kids. The wife had fallen ill, and his job vanished. Not knowing how to cope, he'd fled the field of battle. His children would be grown, and now his world revolved around the booze and his disability check.

They spoke at length about the dead man and how Benjamin had shared his pizza with Bernie the night he died. He and the old man had talked about their families and lost dreams. Not once did Benjamin indicate he intended to step off a chair into eternity.

O'Fallon knew not to ask Bernie if he'd taken the young man's rosary. That would have been an insult. When he asked about the hotel manager, the man spit on the floor in disgust.

"He's a bastard. You have to watch him all the time. He steals things."

"Even a rosary?"

"I wouldn't put it past him. I've seen him go into rooms and come out with stuff." Bernie hesitated and then added, "He was nervous that night."

"The manager?"

The wino shook his head. "No, the kid. He kept looking at his watch like he had a date or something."

"In a way he did," O'Fallon said. His companion nodded and then took another pull from the bottle.

In time, O'Fallon left the old man a twenty and trudged down the endless flights of stairs. His calf muscles twitched in complaint by the time he reached the lobby. He paused in the hallway and stared out the front door to find it was pouring rain. He'd left his umbrella in the car. A cloud of raw smoke drifted from a couple of bums huddled in the entryway; the pot they were toking was definitely subpar.

The manager fidgeted at his desk, higher than a chorus of angels. "You done lookin'?" he asked. O'Fallon recognized the telltale signs—the guy had a snort of coke up his nose.

He tossed the key across the desk, and the manager barely trapped it with a trembling hand as it careened toward the floor.

"The room was unlocked. You owe me ten bucks," O'Fallon observed, leaning over the desk.

"No kiddin'?" was the smug answer.

"I won't take it out of your ass if you answer a couple of questions." The guy yawned as if bored with the conversation. "Did you steal the kid's rosary?"

The fellow shook his head. "No man, I wouldn't do that. The nuns taught me better'n that." He grinned, exposing irregular teeth.

O'Fallon's practiced ear heard the lie. He leaned over and latched on to the man's sweat-stained T-shirt and hauled him across the desk with one forceful tug. Cigarette butts flew in all directions.

"Hey, let go!"

"Give me the rosary," O'Fallon barked into the unshaven face.

"I don't have it."

He tightened his grip. "Make me believe you."

"You can't do this," the fellow protested.

"Sure can. I'm not a cop . . . anymore." Out of habit, O'Fallon shot a quick look at the two men in the doorway. "This is between me and the loser. Any problem with that?" The bums shook their heads in unison and resumed taking puffs from the roach, talking in hushed tones.

Returning his attention to the manager, O'Fallon lowered his voice, adding a menacing undertone. "I want the rosary. If you don't tell me where it is . . ." He left the threat unspoken, knowing the doper would fill in his own worst fear.

"I didn't take it. I couldn't get it out of his hand."

O'Fallon heard the ring of truth and shoved him back across the desk. The manager landed on the filthy floor with a thud, spewing a string of expletives.

"Who took it?" O'Fallon asked, dusting his jacket with a flick of his fingers. "The maid?" She'd found the body, but he doubted she'd light-fingered the rosary.

The manager shook his head vehemently. "No, not her."

"Then who?"

The man rose to his feet and glanced around. The two bums at the door feigned indifference, the cloud of smoke thicker now.

The manager lowered his voice. "The fuckin' pigs, who else? They get all the good stuff down here."

O'Fallon straightened his jacket, buying time. The little prick could be lying, but he doubted it. He'd heard rumors about the local precinct, that some of the cops had sticky fingers. Over the years, he'd learned it was prudent to wear blinders when you carried a badge, at least for the minor offenses. Stealing off a dead man was another matter.

"I'll be back if you're lying, after I tell the cops what you said about them."

The manager's eyes widened and he licked his lips in a nervous gesture. "I ain't lying, man. They do it all the time."

It was O'Fallon's turn to act bored. "And you're a good Catholic boy, to be sure," he said, pushing his Irish accent to the max. "I bet the nuns would be pleased with how well you've turned out."

The two bums parted and allowed him to wade out into the torrential downpour. O'Fallon scurried in front of a honking taxi, water flooding into his shoes and down his collar. The rain only reminded him of angels and of lost innocence.

* * *

Gavenia leaned her elbows on the kitchen table, her chin in her hands, ignoring the bowl of cereal in front of her. After a night punctuated with dreams of energetic little boys cavorting with black puppies, she had no appetite.

This one is getting to you, a familiar voice observed. She levered open her eyes to find Bart sitting across from her as he meticulously polished a pair of antique spectacles with an embroidered handkerchief.

"You don't wear glasses," she observed.

I thought they went well with the outfit. He stood so she could get the full effect, executing a quick spin.

"Ben Franklin?" she guessed. He was far too thin to do Franklin justice, but the costume was impressive, right down to the lace at the cuffs. He nodded and sat opposite her, resting his chin in his hands, mirroring her posture. Through the round lenses, he batted his eyelashes in an attempt to annoy her.

It worked.

"Why are you bugging me? Don't you have a barmaid to proposition?" she grumbled.

You're ignoring your houseguest.

"Ari's not up yet."

I wasn't talking about her. You can ignore him, but that doesn't mean he's not there.

"If you mean—"

Bart vanished, and she found herself talking to the air. A moment later the sound of bare feet padded down the long hall.

"I figured you'd sleep later," Gavenia said as her sister appeared in the kitchen doorway, the gray presence of her dead husband right behind her. *Like he'd be anywhere else.* Gavenia put on her game face and headed for the coffeepot.

"Cream and two sugars, right?" she asked. Ari nodded and settled at the table. The dark circles under her eyes appeared a shade lighter than the previous evening. "Did you sleep at all?"

"A little," was her muffled answer. "My body is still on London time."

"Here, drink the coffee. You want some breakfast?"

"Yours will do," Ari said, pulling Gavenia's bowl toward her. She'd always grazed off her older sister's plate, even as a child, and remained tall and willowy. Another bone of contention between them.

"It might be a bit soggy," Gavenia warned.

"Easier to chew."

Gavenia poured herself more coffee and watched her sister eat. Bart reappeared by the sink, fussing with a bit of cuff lace. Ari's Guardian, Matilda, appeared next to him, and they spoke in hushed tones. She was positively drab compared to the flamboyant figure next to her. Given Paul's presence, the poor thing rarely had an opportunity to get close enough to Ari to do her work.

"Who were you talking to when I came in?" Ari asked between mushy bites.

"Myself," Gavenia said. It was a white lie, but her sister had never been comfortable with Bart hanging around. She shot a look at the ghostly form of her brother-in-law, and he pointedly ignored her. Not much different than when he was alive.

"So what's up?" Ari asked, unaware of the ethereal dynamics in the room. She pushed away the empty bowl and took a sip of the steaming coffee.

"The usual stuff."

"Still herding souls around?" Ari asked.

Gavenia frowned. "Yes, if you must call it that."

"Well, that's sort of what you do, isn't it?"

"Not really. You make me sound like a supernatural border collie." When her sister didn't object to that analogy, Gavenia's irritation rose.

"Any interesting clients at present?" Ari asked.

Gavenia thought for a moment and then shook her head. "Nope. Pretty boring." She had no desire to talk about Bradley or the Jones thing.

"So what's up today?" Ari asked. "I thought maybe we could have lunch and go shopping."

"I'm off to Palm Springs." Her sister's face brightened. "On business."

"Oh, I see." Ari rose, stretched, and trudged toward the doorway.

"How about dinner?" Gavenia asked, struggling to make amends.

Her sister's response was a loud yawn.

"I'm going back to bed," she announced. Gavenia winced at the rebuff. Ari wandered down the hall and then up the stairs, her astral entourage following her like dutiful servants.

Guilt nibbled at Gavenia, darkening her mood.

"Damn." No matter what she did, her sister felt like a stranger.

* * *

The drive to Palm Springs hadn't been a breeze. Usually it was a trip of a couple hours from LA, but an accident on I-10 ground traffic to a crawl and made the journey seem endless. Bart hadn't helped. Riding shotgun, he was dressed in a black suit and gunmetal-gray tie, like a mortician. That wasn't a positive sign. A quick sidelong glance told her he was off in his own world.

"How does a person become a Guardian? Was it something that happened right after you died, or did you have to earn that job?"

No comment, Bart replied.

"Someday you'll have to tell me."

But today is not that day.

Cut off from that line of thought, Gavenia fidgeted, her anxiety climbing. Acting as reluctant emissary between Gregory Alliford and his estranged wife wasn't her notion of a good plan, but they'd little else to go on. Alliford's attempts to talk to his wife had failed, circumvented by Janet's formidable mother, Augusta Pearce.

Now it was Gavenia's turn to exude charm and, hopefully, return with the missing puppy. Whether the marriage survived wasn't her problem.

"The guy on point always gets the bullets," she murmured.

Gavenia reached for the turn signal, intending to leave the highway an exit early.

Stay on the interstate, Bart advised.

Other folks felt vague impressions that they shouldn't do

something, but she got instructions piped directly into her mind in bold type.

"I'm tired of the traffic, Bart," she protested.

Remember Wales?

Her mind instantly conjured up the sound of grinding metal impacting stone.

"There are no flocks of sheep in LA," she said.

But there are cement trucks.

Her previous Guardian, Emma, a sixty-something grandmother with a thick British accent and a sweet sense of humor, had been a lot more flexible. She'd not known Emma existed until the accident.

Gavenia often ignored her intuition, like that morning in Wales. The end result was that it took the rescue crew three hours to cut her out of the remnants of the rental car. Given that it had been either the stone retaining wall or plow through the mass of woolies and hit their astonished shepherd, the choice was obvious. Gavenia had veered for the wall on her side of the car, leaving the rest up to the Goddess. She'd been spared. Her boyfriend, Winston, died instantly, his disdain for seat belts exacting the ultimate toll. His soul was the first she ever saw: he'd stood by the car, urging her to hurry so that they could still make their breakfast appointment with a friend. He didn't realize he was dead.

When she finally came to her senses in the hospital a few days later, the souls were still there. Some were in street clothes, others in hospital gowns parading through the halls pushing their IV poles. An elderly gentleman sat by her bed for the better part of a day, talking on and on about his wife and his Scottish terrier, Angus. That evening, when Gavenia mentioned him to her nurse, the doctor had promptly lowered the dosage of her pain medication. She soon realized that she was seeing and hearing things that others didn't.

You're a Shepherd, luv, Emma had explained when she manifested by Gavenia's hospital bed the following morning. *It's not such a bad thing, really.*

Now, nearly six months later, Gavenia still knew very little about her ability. It was a time of small, unsettling discoveries, like the mandate that didn't allow her to push a recalcitrant soul across. A particular six-year-old came to mind.

A thought popped into her head and she eyed Bart. "You still haven't told me why Emma isn't my Guardian anymore. Did she get a bad review or something?"

She needed a break.

"She did fine up until a few months ago, and suddenly there you were."

Can't say. Rules, you know.

Gavenia ground her teeth together. She made the turn at the required exit and studied the directions while she waited at a stoplight behind a car hauler full of Jeeps. "What are my chances that Bradley's mother is going to be helpful?"

Zip. She's got issues.

"You'd think that seeing her son's soul at rest would be her primary concern," Gavenia replied caustically. It wasn't fair to vent at Bart, but he was the only one present at the moment.

Lots of issues, was the reply. Her Guardian donned his wraparound sunglasses and leaned back in the seat as if he didn't need to watch her driving any longer. Gavenia knew the ploy. He was effectively shutting down their conversation so she'd stop asking questions he wasn't allowed to answer. She turned on the radio and cranked the volume. It did nothing to mitigate the anxiety bubbling in the pit of her stomach.

* * *

The woman sitting behind the massive black-walnut desk radiated authority. Her apricot silk suit complimented flawless skin and silver hair. Her fingernails were manicured to perfection, and the diamond ring on her left hand proclaimed an abundant bank account. A society matron? Someone's beloved cookie-baking grandmother?

O'Fallon knew better. Her eyes gave her away. Most men preferred to stare at a woman's breasts or legs. He was an eye man; if he didn't like what he saw inside, the rest was just wrapping paper.

Mrs. Pearce's eyes spoke of cold resolve, a lack of humanity.

She didn't move to shake his hand, and O'Fallon was grateful for that. He didn't relish any more contact than was required.

Like the Palm Springs matron, the room reflected a rigidly disciplined life. The desk was immaculate, not a mote of dust in sight, and a gold-rimmed china cup filled with steaming amber liquid sat in an equally exquisite saucer. Nearby a Montblanc pen and a manila folder rested on a leather blotter. The folder bore his name written in block letters. That unnerved him.

"Thank you for being prompt, Mr. O'Fallon. So many have forgotten the common courtesies," the woman said. Her voice was low and persuasive, like that of someone accustomed to having her words taken as gospel.

"Thank you." He waited for her to indicate that he should take a seat, but the gesture never came. Evidently the common courtesies only applied to those she perceived as her equals.

"Mrs. Samuelson recommended you. I have to admit, I'm not quite sure if you're the best choice, but she assures me that your street contacts are most valuable." He nodded politely at the backhanded compliment. "My son-in-law has recently become involved with a young woman."

"Are they lovers?" he asked as he pulled out his notebook and pen. He flipped to a new page and wrote *Pearce, Mrs. Augusta* and underlined it, adding date, time, and location. Old habits were hard to break.

"I would assume so. She appeared right after the death of my grandson. She claims to be a psychic. I don't hold with such nonsense."

A slow twitch crawled up O'Fallon's spine, like a troop of ants on safari.

Mrs. Pearce continued, oblivious to his unease. "Gregory and my daughter are separated. I want you to research this other woman and determine the nature of her relationship with my son-in-law. If she is his lover, I want photographs for the divorce proceedings. If she's intent on swindling him by claiming to talk to the dead, I want her stopped. It is, after all, my daughter's money as well."

"How did your grandson die?"

The woman hesitated, and for a moment he thought he saw a crack in her armor. It vanished in a nanosecond. "It was a hit-and-run accident."

"When did this happen?"

"Two weeks ago. Nonetheless, that is not the issue here, Mr. O'Fallon, and I do not want you sidetracked in an attempt to run up your fees."

He frowned in aggravation. "I don't pad my fees, Mrs. Pearce."

"Everyone inflates their fees. If you don't, then you're a fool." She paused and added, "Just don't attempt it with me."

"If you don't trust me, then you shouldn't hire me," he said bluntly.

"You have to earn my respect, Mr. O'Fallon."

"As you have to earn mine."

She studied him, a slight furrow between the thinly tweezed brows. "Mrs. Samuelson said you could be quite willful."

He spread his hands and delivered a wry grin, allowing the woman to believe she was the alpha in the room. They continued to analyze each other, like lawyers before a high-profile case. In the distance, the door chime sounded, followed by muffled voices.

A tap on the door interrupted the standoff.

"Come," she ordered. The maid hurried to Mrs. Pearce's side, offering her apology along the way. She whispered something that caused one of the matron's silver eyebrows to rise.

"Put her in the sunroom. Do not mention this gentleman's presence, do you understand?"

"Yes, madam. Serve her tea or—"

"No," Mrs. Pearce barked. "She doesn't deserve hospitality." Startled, the domestic nodded her understanding and, after a quick glance toward O'Fallon, hustled from the room, shutting the door.

Mrs. Pearce returned her cold gaze to him.

"Your timing is fortuitous, Mr. O'Fallon. The individual I wish investigated has arrived on my doorstep. Ms. Kingsgrave wants to talk to Janet, though I have no idea why."

He scribbled the young woman's name in his notebook,

followed by a question mark.

"Does your daughter know her?" he asked.

"Not that I am aware." She seemed on the verge of adding something. Instead, she responded, "Will you take the case?"

"Yes, as long as you understand I will work it my way."

Mrs. Pearce tapped a finely lacquered fingernail on the leather blotter and then nodded her approval.

"You have one week," she said.

"When you talk to Ms. Kingsgrave, is there some way I can overhear the conversation?"

A faint smile came his way. "I'll arrange it."

She handed him the file. Inside he found his retainer check, enough for one week at the going rate. She'd been so sure of herself she'd cut the check before he arrived.

As he riffled through the other papers, he found a picture of a woman in her late thirties, apparently the one currently waiting somewhere within the confines of the Pearce mansion. She was climbing out of a red sports car, her movement aided by a cane. Her honey-blond hair fell in waves to her waist. Despite the distance from the camera, he saw her eyes were a deep shade of sea blue.

"Is this the woman?" he asked, holding up the photo.

Mrs. Pearce nodded. "I have no idea how Gregory came in contact with such a person."

O'Fallon quickly skimmed the folder's contents. He found a credit report and the subject's vital statistics: full name, address, birth date, telephone number. All easily obtained if one was Internet savvy. He knew what he was seeing, and it aggravated him.

"I'm not the first investigator on this case, am I?"

Mrs. Pearce shook her head. "I've had my son-in-law watched for some time now. However, you're the first *licensed* investigator I've hired. Nevertheless, I assure you, you won't be the last if you don't deliver. Do we have an understanding?"

He slapped the folder closed, his Irish pride urging him to tell the self-centered bitch to go to hell. He hesitated and opened the folder again. Something about the case called to him.

"I'll do what I can," he said, pushing the check out of the way to study the face of his potential quarry.

Mrs. Pearce nodded and permitted herself a knowing smile. "Money always talks," she said smugly.

Not in this case, he thought.

This time it was the sea-blue eyes.

Chapter Five

The sunroom was pleasant, but isolated. By Gavenia's watch she'd been waiting for almost a quarter of an hour, her patience evaporating as the minutes crawled by. It appeared that Mr. Alliford had not smoothed the way. Only sheer stubbornness and the image of little Bradley hugging his bear kept her rooted in place.

To pass the time, she studied the exquisite Italian marble floor tiles, sampled the fragrances of the various potted roses set artfully around the room, then sat by the small fountain and let the water play off her fingers. Above her, the silken whoosh of twin ceiling fans generated a light breeze.

Nowhere during her long trek through the massive house did she encounter the telltale signs of a dog. Puppies made a great deal of racket and an equal amount of mess. Her heart told her Merlin wasn't here or, at best, was banished to an outside kennel.

As she thought this over, Bart appeared, sitting next to her on the long rattan couch as if they were waiting in a dentist's office.

"Is the dog here?" she asked.

No.

"Why didn't you tell me this was a wasted trip?"

You didn't ask.

"Yes, I did."

No, you asked if Bradley's mother was going to be helpful.

"And if I had asked about the dog?"

He shook his head. *It was your decision. It's not up to me to always tell you what to do.*

She glared. "You seem to do a damned good job of it when you choose."

He returned the glare and promptly vanished.

"Goddess," she muttered. First she'd pissed off her sister, and now her Guardian. The way things were going, her meeting with Janet Alliford was doomed.

She fell to self-grooming, selecting a long lock of her wavy hair for scrutiny. Its thick nature gave it a tendency to knot, especially at the back of her neck, and plucking apart the strands helped her relax. Some folks took medication or had psychotherapy; she unraveled her hair. Cheap and never-ending entertainment.

Bart reappeared, watching as she untangled one particularly stubborn clump.

"You're very quiet today," she observed.

Nothing much to say.

Gavenia frowned. Bartholomew Quickens was the master of banal banter. Why the sudden change?

"What's up?" she quizzed.

Bart was saved from a reply when the maid opened the door and beckoned. After another long hike, Gavenia found herself in the front foyer. Her temper flared. If they thought she was just going to leave . . .

The maid halted, gesturing for her to wait. "Mrs. Pearce come soon," the woman said.

"Thank you," Gavenia replied. The domestic was young, her eyes glancing up and down in a nervous fashion. "Have you worked here for very long?"

"No. She is . . ." The maid's eyes darted toward a closed door and fell silent.

Gavenia gave her a knowing smile. "*Comprendo.*" I understand.

The maid smiled in return, clearly pleased that Gavenia had used her native language. "It is . . . difficult—" She stopped short when a door opened and an older woman entered the foyer, marching toward them with firm steps. She appeared to be in her sixties. Her jewelry was gold, the real stuff, and her hair was a striking shade of silver. There was no welcome in her eyes as she approached.

Gavenia forced a polite smile.

"I'm Gavenia Kingsgrave," she said, extending her hand. It

trembled in midair, and she struggled for control. The tremors increased.

The woman ignored the outstretched hand. "I'm Mrs. Pearce," the woman said. "Janet's mother," she added as if it was an afterthought.

Gavenia dropped the arm to her side, hiding her fluttering fingers behind her long skirt. "I'm pleased to meet you. I'd like to talk to your daughter for a few minutes."

"She does not wish to see you."

"Well, perhaps you can help me. Mr. Alliford has asked me to pick up Merlin."

"Who is Merlin?"

Confused, Gavenia pressed on. "He's Bradley's dog. I would like to take him with me back to—"

"I don't keep a dog," was the solemn reply.

"Do you know where he is?"

"No."

Gavenia hesitated, disconcerted. When it appeared the woman didn't intend to add anything further, she asked, "Didn't Mr. Alliford call you?"

Mrs. Pearce adopted a stern expression. "He's called repeatedly, babbling some nonsense about ghosts and about you, in particular. I don't take what he says very seriously," she said, punctuating a dismissive gesture.

The rebuke struck home.

"I'm a . . . counselor, Mrs. Pearce, and I'm trying to help Mr. Alliford cope with the death of your grandson. It's very important that we—"

The woman's eyes narrowed. "Gregory said you were a psychic. I can only imagine what that means."

Gavenia felt warmth rise in her cheeks. "If you are suggesting that—"

"I shall be blunt—the last thing my son-in-law needs is someone like you. It would be better if he received professional treatment for his delusions and his juvenile craving for alcohol." The woman gestured toward the double doors. "I have no further time for you."

Gavenia opened her mouth to protest, but Bart overrode her.

Cut your losses. She doesn't care. He was leaning next to a large potted ficus, his sunglasses perched on the end of his nose.

Gavenia decided to give it one last shot. "Please ask your daughter about Merlin. It's very important we find him."

The matron gave her an icy glare. "I sincerely doubt that. If you have any sense, you'll stop troubling my son-in-law, or you will sincerely regret your interference." She turned toward the maid. "Ensure she leaves immediately."

Mrs. Pearce strode from the entryway, and the door closed soundly behind her, generating an echo in the cavernous foyer. The maid stood wide-eyed, breathing in little gasps.

Gavenia asked in a lowered voice, "*¿Hizo a Señora Alliford trae un perro con ella de Los Ángeles?*" Did Mrs. Alliford bring a dog with her from Los Angeles?

The domestic's eyes widened again as she gave a quick negative shake of her head.

On a hunch, Gavenia tried another query. "*¿Señora Alliford ha estado aquí en los últimos días?*" Has Mrs. Alliford been here in the last few days?

The maid looked toward the closed door. "No."

"*Muchas gracias,*" Gavenia said. A moment before she crossed the threshold into the bright sunshine, she added, "*Buena suerte.*" Good luck.

"*Gracias,*" the maid replied as she closed the doors behind Gavenia.

Bart was in the car waiting for her. Gavenia seethed as she negotiated the long circular drive, passing the greenhouse and then the carriage house.

"What is it with these people?" she demanded, glowering at her Guardian. "Why in the hell didn't that woman tell me her daughter wasn't there? Why act like everything is Gregory's problem?"

Bart shrugged, and Gavenia's anger exploded. "Why am I being stonewalled about a damned mutt?"

Her Guardian waited until they reached the first stoplight before he answered. *Because Merlin knows everything.*

* * *

O'Fallon bird-dogged the subject of his investigation through the dense traffic on the way back to LA. Fortunately, the red Miata was easy to track. Knowing he'd need a great deal more information on Ms. Kingsgrave than a credit report and a photograph, he put in a couple of phone calls to get the ball rolling. Once traffic settled down to a more tolerable flow, he popped in a worn CD and immersed himself in the stirring melodies of his favorite Celtic band. The songs always reminded him of home, of what he'd left behind when he'd immigrated to New York as a teenager. Now he was a hybrid, a true Irish-American. His accent had dulled around the edges, but his heart still straddled two countries. Increasingly, Ireland exhibited a stronger pull than California.

He was due a trip home; his gran was in her nineties and growing increasingly frail. Her time would come soon enough, though he couldn't imagine losing her. He called her every Sunday, flew home as often as possible, and made sure she had everything she needed, including a live-in companion. Guilt still gnawed at him. He allowed himself a long sigh. He'd go to Ireland when these two cases were finished. If he was lucky, he could be there in time for Easter.

O'Fallon shifted positions on the seat. He'd not taken the opportunity to doff his jacket before jumping into the car, worried he might lose his quarry, and now he regretted that haste. He shifted in his seat one last time and then accepted that he was going to be miserable, at least until he knew precisely where Ms. Kingsgrave was headed. If she took either of the next two exits, she was headed home. That he doubted; he'd already placed a mental bet it would be Bel Air and the grieving father's bed.

As if to mock him, the Miata's right turn signal flashed. A pang of disappointment shot through him.

Maybe they aren't lovers.

Time would tell. If the couple were scorching the sheets, getting a photo of them in the middle of a horizontal counseling session might prove difficult, despite the fact that most people were reckless during the throes of mindless lust. He'd caught one man with his teenage lover at the tenth hole of the golf course at three in the morning. In divorce court, the man swore he was just improving his putt. His practice session had cost him a hefty alimony.

What was that nonsense about a dog? The Kingsgrave woman seemed so fixated on it. Was the canine a pawn, a control issue between Alliford and his estranged wife? If so, why involve a third party? Didn't Alliford have the balls to confront his mother-in-law?

"Probably not," he muttered.

O'Fallon glanced at the dashboard clock—just after four. He had sufficient time to swing by the bank, deposit Mrs. Pearce's check, and then speak with Guadalupe Alvarez, the maid at the Hotel LeClaire. Perhaps she'd be able to narrow the field of potential rosary thieves. If he was lucky, it was the hotel manager. He'd cheerfully work over that loser.

When the red sports car vanished down the off ramp, he thumbed the button on his portable voice recorder and made note of the time. Ms. Kingsgrave would come under closer scrutiny tomorrow.

* * *

It was moments like these that O'Fallon deeply regretted he'd never learned much Spanish. Mrs. Alvarez peered at him nervously above the security chain, clutching a tissue in a thin hand. Two small boys peeked around her, staring upward in fear as if he might devour them at any moment. The instant the woman saw his PI license, her lip began to quiver. Belatedly, he realized how frightening he must appear: a gringo in a suit, an unknown menace who could crush this family's dreams in the name of bureaucracy. Trust came dear in the Hispanic community.

"I have . . . green card," she said haltingly.

"I'm sure you do. I wanted to talk to you about the Hotel LeClaire."

"I not work today. I am . . . fired," she said.

"Why?" he asked, frowning.

"The manager say to steal and give to him. I say no."

O'Fallon sighed. "You did right."

Mrs. Alvarez did not reply. Her worried expression told him she was at war with her decision, as honesty didn't always put food on the table.

"Did you see the rosary in the dead boy's hand?"

She nodded and then crossed herself. Her roughened fingers tore the tissue as she shifted it from one hand to the other. A thin silver wedding band graced her left ring finger.

"It's missing."

"Gone?" she asked. One of her small sons tugged on her skirt and asked a question in Spanish. The maid shook her head and he fell silent. "I did not take."

"I know you didn't. Do you think the manager did?" he asked.

"No."

"It was still there when the cops arrived?"

The woman bit her lip. She glanced down the hall and then slid back the security chain and beckoned him inside. The two boys scooted out of the way, watching his every move.

"Thank you."

She closed the door behind him. The apartment, small and sparsely decorated, was the antithesis of the Palm Springs mansion he'd visited earlier. A tiny fish tank sat in the corner with a solitary resident. Children's schoolbooks lay open on the kitchen table, tablets and pencils nearby. He'd already noted the pair of men's work boots by the front door and a small framed wedding picture on the wall. An immigrant family starting anew, like many of his relatives a century before.

O'Fallon sat in a threadbare chair and waited for his hostess to settle on the couch. Her sons huddled at her feet, still watching him with those dark eyes. "I know this is hard for you." More silence. "I won't say who told me, Mrs. Alvarez. I just want the boy's mother to have his rosary. I'm sure you understand."

The woman looked down at her children and smoothed the younger one's hair in a loving gesture. The little boy had a picture book at his feet filled with colorful dinosaurs.

"I've spoken to the manager. He's a . . ." O'Fallon hesitated. He couldn't use *that* word in front of the children. "He's not a good man."

The woman looked away, her eyes unreadable.

"It was there . . . in his hands, then gone," she admitted. Their eyes met and he knew he'd get nothing further. She was too frightened.

"I understand, Mrs. Alvarez." *All too well.*

O'Fallon rose and placed two twenty-dollar bills on the small kitchen table, twice his usual gratuity for information. He penciled a name and address on the back of one of his business cards, placing the card near the money. Tapping it with his finger, he said, "This is another hotel, one that will pay better. It's on a bus line, so you don't need a car. Talk to the housekeeper. Tell her I sent you."

Mrs. Alvarez looked stunned. "*Gracias a Dios,*" she murmured.

As he reached the apartment door, she intercepted him, lightly touching his forearm in gratitude. A soft smile graced her face. O'Fallon wondered how often that happened.

"Thank you for your help," he replied.

Three flights of stairs later he reached the street, where a couple of boys were playing basketball. It was so different from his childhood—big-city LA, small-town Ireland. He'd grown up innocent, believing that everyone loved him, that the world was a fair place. The bomb blast that killed his father had shattered those illusions, taught him the world was an unholy place filled with bastards who would murder you just because you were different from them.

Shaking off his melancholy, he hiked to the car, passing a pair of young Latinas in tight black capri pants and T-shirts. One giggled and said something to the other. He caught the word *pelirrojo*, "red," no doubt in reference to his hair. He hoped the rest was a compliment.

O'Fallon sat in his car for some time, watching the boys in the street. No matter how much he hoped, the trail of the missing rosary kept pointing toward the cops. He turned the key in the ignition.

"At least it's stopped raining."

* * *

Though Gavenia purposely chose her sister's favorite restaurant, seeking a neutral location that wouldn't add to the stress of the evening, unease sat between them like an unwanted dinner companion. She and Ari chatted about the weather and LA traffic. Then they moved on to the astronomical cost of British housing. Superficial social conversation, nothing that dug into the marrow of their private pain.

Gavenia toyed with her dinner, her appetite nonexistent. Ari had no such problem and tackled her rare steak with bravado. She wielded her eating utensils English style, cutting the meat with the knife held in the right hand and then using the fork in her left to bring the morsel to her mouth. An efficient food delivery system, no time wasted changing utensils from one hand to the other. Just what you'd expect from a woman with a scientific mind and a doctorate in archaeology.

"So why are you such a grump?" Ari asked between mouthfuls, tired of the social banter. She'd always been the more direct of the two.

Gavenia opened her mouth to retort and then let a low sigh escape. She couldn't really argue with that observation—she was a grump. "I've got a difficult case."

"I thought you said you didn't have anything interesting going on right now."

Oops, Bart chimed in as he appeared on the bench seat next to his charge. *She caught your little white lie.*

Gavenia paid him no heed. "I fibbed. I didn't want to talk about it."

Ari gave her a measured look and resumed her assault on the steak. The crimson juices oozed across the white china plate, making Gavenia queasy. She averted her eyes, studying her sister's clothes. As usual, Ari wore head-to-toe black.

The perpetual widow, Bart observed.

"So do you want to talk about it now?" Ari asked.

Gavenia pondered and then nodded. The way things were

headed, the Alliford case wasn't going to be resolved anytime soon and her grumpy mood would only get worse. Ari might as well be in the loop.

"It's a little boy," Gavenia began. As she buttered a warm roll, she related Bradley's tale. By the end of the story, Ari's eyes were misty, her dinner ignored.

"God, that's horrible. And his grandmother won't help?"

"Nope. Mrs. Pearce is a block of ice."

Ari frowned and took another sip of her red wine. "Is there anything I can do?"

Gavenia's first instinct was to refuse, but something held her in check. Her sister was taking a tiny step out of her all-encompassing widowhood. Why not foster that?

"Yes. I'd like to know more about Mrs. Pearce. Ask a few questions, see what you can find out about her. The Hansford name should open a few doors."

"It's not my name, it's the zeros behind it." Ari retrieved her knife and fork. "I'll see what I can find out for you."

"Thanks." Gavenia relaxed her posture. She'd been sitting so rigidly that her back cramped in protest.

Ari waved a hand in the air as if she'd suddenly remembered something important. "Oh, I didn't tell you. I've been asked to arrange a charity auction in London to benefit a museum exhibition."

"That sounds cool."

"I doubt they would have bothered with me before I married Paul."

"It's that hefty bank account again."

Ari nodded. "I still can't quite accept the fact I have *that* much money. I keep clipping coupons."

"So what's it up to nowadays?"

"Nineteen or twenty mil, the last I heard. It's ridiculous. Nobody needs that kind of money."

Gavenia chortled. "So are you going to do the charity gig?"

Ari frowned in thought. "I'm not sure. It's for a good cause, but—"

"Then do it. You can't mourn Paul forever." The second after the words tumbled out of Gavenia's mouth, she regretted them. They could easily ruin the evening. A quick look indicated that Ari hadn't taken the offhand comment negatively. In fact, she was nodding again.

"I know. It's just so hard. I've had to learn how to handle the Trust, and they're pushing me to join Hansford Technologies' board of directors."

Gavenia grinned. "Go for it. You have every right to be there."

"I'm not sure I want to be there." The waiter appeared and refilled their water and the basket of wheat rolls.

Gavenia snagged one. "I could live on these things."

"So I noticed."

"It's better than things that bleed," she said, pointing a butter knife at her sister's plate.

"Leave my steak alone." Ari sawed off another piece. "So what are you going to do while I'm checking out Mrs. Pearce?"

"Try to find Merlin, I guess. Maybe Bart will come up with a brilliant suggestion," Gavenia said. As if on cue, her Guardian studied the print on the wall above him as if it were a priceless antique—a tactic to avoid having to comment.

"Is he here now?" Ari asked, looking around as if he was lurking behind one of the potted palms.

"Yes." Gavenia angled her head toward her Guardian. "He's tuning me out at present. He does that fairly often." Her eyes rose to Paul where he hovered nearby.

"It must be weird to see them."

"It is. They're everywhere. I can't get away from them."

Ari eyed her, and Gavenia knew the next question before she asked it.

"Have you ever seen . . . Paul?"

"Yes," Gavenia said. There was no point in telling Ari her dead husband was in constant attendance. Now was not the time.

"Is he . . . okay?" Ari asked. The specter of her husband grew more solid, his sober eyes watching Gavenia intently. Perhaps he feared what she might reveal.

"He worries about you."

Ari bit her lip in an apparent attempt to control the tears. Gavenia reached across the table and grasped her sister's slim hand. It was so smooth to the touch, unlike when she'd been leading excavations full-time.

"You really didn't like him, did you?" Ari asked.

Gavenia blinked in surprise. This wasn't a topic they'd ever explored, at least not while Paul was alive.

"We never saw eye to eye."

"Why?"

Gavenia chose her words with precision. "I disliked how he made you give up your profession."

Ari jerked her hand away, narrowly missing her wine glass. "He didn't make me give up archaeology. I did that on my own." The waiter appeared at that moment, checked on them, then retreated as if sensing something amiss.

"You made the decision, but he laid the groundwork." As her sibling began to protest, Gavenia raised her hand for silence. "Let me finish. He pushed you to give up archaeology not because of envy or jealousy, but because he feared for your safety. It was his way of protecting you, the only way he could show you how much he loved you."

Well said, Bart whispered. In contrast, Paul's specter glowered.

Ari opened her mouth as if to argue and then gave a minute nod. "I still miss him," she said, hunting through her small purse for a tissue. Gavenia looked away, fearing her sister's tears would trigger her own. The restaurant suddenly seemed too open. She watched a young couple in the corner, sitting so close it was hard to tell they were separate people. He was feeding her slices of cheese and she was laughing between bites in a light, high voice.

Love and loss. Why do they always go hand in hand?

Gavenia grabbed the dessert menu and thumbed through it, desperate for a distraction.

"So what's it going to be—tiramisu or crème brûlée?" she asked.

Ari delivered a mock glare, accepting the diversion. "You didn't eat your dinner," she said, pointing at Gavenia's plate.

"You sound like Auntie Lu." Ari continued to point, shaking her head in disapproval. "Okay, so if I eat most of the pork chop, can I have some dessert?"

"It's a deal. We'll share some tiramisu."

Their eyes met, and Gavenia winked. Her sister winked back.

"I've missed this, Pooh. We've been apart too long," Gavenia said.

"I know. We've both lost a lot in the last year. It's hard to know what to say." After a sip of wine, Ari added, "Right before I flew home, I went to Wales. I stopped at the place where you had your accident."

Gavenia dropped her fork and it bounced to the floor. Her throat tightened as the sound of grinding metal slammed into her head and then receded. Unaware of the vivid memories her words had generated, her sister continued, "I left flowers for Winston. I thought he might like that."

Gavenia's eyes clouded. She pulled her napkin upward to stem the tide of tears. "It's been a hell of a year for both of us," she whispered.

Ari's warm hand touched her elbow in a loving gesture. "It'll get better. It can't possibly get any worse," she said.

Bart sighed, tented his fingers, and whispered, *Wanna bet?*

Chapter Six

Although O'Fallon hadn't served in this particular precinct, a surge of memories struck him the moment he entered the building. Typical of most squad rooms in the city, it was awash in piles of paper and binders, half-filled cups and soda bottles. The electronic chirp of telephones echoed off the faded tan walls. Two cops huddled in front of a computer terminal while another struggled with a copy machine. The fellow swore at the recalcitrant device, gave it a jarring bump with the heel of his hand, and it promptly spit out paper. The detective pumped his fist in the air as if he'd just won the lottery.

The pungent smell of overheated coffee hung in the air, perfume to O'Fallon's nose. He'd been part of this world for over ten years. Now he was the outsider, and that meant everything to those on the other side of the line.

If they're dirty . . . He shook his head at the thought and headed for the desk sergeant.

After explaining his purpose, O'Fallon wove his way through the desk jungle. A few of the detectives glanced up as he passed, but he didn't recognize any of them until a familiar face appeared in the distance—a young man studying a pile of papers.

It was impossible to see the young cop's trim figure and angular face without thinking of the first time O'Fallon had met his father. O'Fallon had been the nervous new detective, eager to prove himself, and Avery Elliot the old salt, the one with the sharp mind and a body of experience that kept O'Fallon from making a complete ass of himself. Too often it was a near thing. Now Adam Elliot was a homicide detective, just like his old man had been before Avery's wife had died and he'd become a priest.

Adam's partner slouched at an opposite desk, talking on the telephone, his feet in the aisle. He had graying hair and a bulldog look, in direct contrast to Adam's handsome features.

The young cop glanced up and his eyes flashed in surprise. A grin spread across his tanned face.

O'Fallon halted by the desk and stuck out his hand. "Your dad said you'd been transferred to this precinct. I didn't think I'd catch you in."

Adam rose and shook his hand, his grip strong. "It's been forever," he replied.

"Your father's retirement party, if I remember right."

Adam nodded in agreement. "What brings you here?"

"I'm doing some private work for the Callendar family. Their son was the kid who hung himself over at the LeClaire."

"Okay, that one. Bender and Coolidge were the investigating officers." Adam pointed toward two heavyset men.

"The family's missing a rosary; it's an heirloom and they'd like to try to track it down," O'Fallon said lightly. He watched the young detective's face. The only reaction was a quick double blink of his eyes.

Adam's partner hung up the phone and rose from his chair.

"This is Harve Glass, my partner," Adam said, beginning the introductions. "Harve, this is—"

"So just who are you?" Glass challenged. Adam started to speak, but his partner cut him off. "You stay quiet and let him answer." The younger detective's jaw tightened. It sounded like a rebuke delivered to a child.

O'Fallon's eyes narrowed. "I'm Doug O'Fallon, and once upon a time I wore a badge just like you. Except I was a lot more polite, especially to my own partner."

Glass's mouth twitched. "Private dicks aren't welcome here."

O'Fallon smirked. Tempting as it was, he decided not to make a scene. "Really? I'm shocked," he said in a joking tone. That generated a deep frown from the cop.

"I'm not in the mood for this."

"Funny, neither am I."

As the two men eyed each other, an unnatural stillness crept through the room. O'Fallon knew the other detectives were watching this confrontation with a wary eye. How often did someone challenge Glass?

"Doug's here to talk to Bender and Coolidge," Adam interjected. To his credit, he didn't rush the words, but made them sound nonchalant. O'Fallon gave him points for coolness under pressure.

"It's best you leave," Glass said, ignoring his partner.

"I will, when I'm finished."

The man's face reddened, and a twitch began at the corner of his mouth. "Now," he said, pointing toward the door with a beefy hand.

O'Fallon ignored the command and turned toward his best friend's son, letting his cold expression melt into a warm smile.

"Good to see you again, Adam." He paused and added, "I'm really sorry to see you're stuck with an asshole for a partner." As he turned away, an expletive exploded from Glass's mouth. O'Fallon didn't bother to answer, but headed like a heat-seeking missile toward the two cops in the corner.

As if Glass had set the tone for the room, they didn't look friendly either.

In five minutes O'Fallon was back in his car with little information to show for the time spent. Detectives Bender and Coolidge denied seeing the rosary, both blaming the hotel manager. Deep in his gut, O'Fallon knew they were lying.

* * *

"About damned time!" the voice shouted.

"Yeah, yeah, give me a break," O'Fallon grumbled as he hauled in his mail. "At least let me get in the door, will you?"

"No break, no break!" the voice shot back.

It belonged to a large African gray parrot marching along a heavy wooden pole in a sizable cage. It was a handsome bird with light-gray plumage, which terminated in magnificent red tail feathers. As O'Fallon locked the door and dumped his mail onto the spotless kitchen counter, he knew that Seamus's keen black eyes tracked his every movement.

"Yo, dude!"

"I hear you," he said as he scanned the pile of mail: two bills, a few catalogs, and his favorite Irish magazine. "Better than most days."

The light on the answering machine blinked repeatedly, but he paid it no heed. Until he'd seen to Seamus, there would be no chance to hear the messages. He shut off the television; today his housekeeper had left it on the History Channel.

"Spring me! Spring me!" Seamus called as O'Fallon headed for the bedroom. He ignored the bird and shucked his clothes, returning in a worn, dark-blue tracksuit. O'Fallon deftly worked the tumbler lock on the cage. Left to his own devices, the bird was a feathered Houdini.

"Seven . . . four . . . nine . . . one," Seamus instructed.

"Yeah, I know the number," he mumbled. Almost anything Seamus heard, he repeated. Having a bright bird wasn't always a good thing.

O'Fallon opened the cage and fished the parrot off his perch. He fluttered for a bit as he adjusted to his new position and then worked his way up O'Fallon's arm, one claw after the other.

"About damned time!" he shouted again.

"Yeah, yeah." O'Fallon put the bird on the top of the recliner and returned to the cage to dish out food and water. The parrot babbled on as he made his trek, claw after claw, down the armrest.

"Incoming!" Seamus called, and then imitated the sound of a mortar round with eerie accuracy.

O'Fallon flinched. "No more History Channel for you."

Chores complete, he settled into the chair, placing the magazine and the Kingsgrave folder on the end table for later scrutiny. A large bowl of cereal, his evening meal, was the final touch. Tonight it was one of those high-fiber sorts that he detested but his doctor insisted he eat. It balanced out the pancakes he'd devoured for breakfast.

"So, did you have a good day?" he asked the bird between crunchy mouthfuls. The parrot eyed him from the armrest, turning his head at an angle. In a claw was a bright orange carrot stub.

"Bor-ing!" the creature squawked back. It was one of his favorite lines.

"Mine wasn't. Not boring in the least." The moment O'Fallon put the empty bowl aside, Seamus settled into his hands for a bit of social grooming. It was their evening ritual—only now would the bird cease making an unholy racket.

O'Fallon tapped the *play* button for his messages. He deleted the first three, saved the next two, and then reached the one he'd hoped for.

Dr. Kathryn Bergstrom's melancholy voice filled the room, echoing slightly; no doubt she'd been calling from her office in the morgue. Working late again.

"Doug, I'm going to have to pass on tomorrow night. I have another meeting. Maybe we can get together later this week. Sorry."

"Bummer," Seamus squawked.

"Yeah, bummer." It was the third time Kathryn had canceled one of their nights together. They were drifting apart, an inevitable fate when the chemistry wasn't right.

"Dammit," he muttered.

For once Seamus had no reply.

When O'Fallon opened the folder to get his mind off his faltering love life, the witch's eyes snared him again. Gavenia Kingsgrave had moved into a new condo five months ago. Her credit report showed she paid her bills on time and had only one credit card, which carried a small balance. Her job as a translator must pay well.

"You're not strung out in debt," he murmured. "So why are you messing with Gregory Alliford? Cruising to be wife number two?" He stared at the woman's face a little longer and finally put the folder aside. It would do no good to obsess. The answers would come at their own speed.

His mind turned to his other case and his confrontation with Glass. How much should he tell Avery about his son's situation?

"Best not to meddle," he said, but somehow that didn't feel right. He looked toward the phone, wondering if the young man might call, perhaps drop him a hint as to where to find the rosary. It would save a lot of pawn-shop visits.

"Maybe the kid has his blinders on too tight," he said. "That would be a shame."

He opened the magazine and leaned back in the recliner, content to let things fall as they might.

* * *

"If you're on the make, Ms. Kingsgrave, you need some fashion tips," O'Fallon observed as his quarry caned her way to the front door of the Alliford house. Clothed in a long black skirt and a light-green blouse, she sported very little makeup, and her hair was in a long French braid. He personally thought she looked nice, but then he didn't socialize with the upper crust, where three-thousand-dollar designer dresses and five-hundred-dollar shoes were the norm. What did Gregory Alliford see in this woman? Was he slumming? Or was there something else?

As she was readily welcomed inside by the maid, O'Fallon popped open his notebook and made an entry, glancing at his watch to check the time. Nine fifty-eight. At nine ten she'd left her condo and stopped at a Starbucks, purchased two Grande coffees, and then made a beeline here. She'd drunk one on the way over and carried the other inside the house.

"Serious caffeine addiction," he said. He flipped open the subject's folder and riffled through the growing collection of documents he'd added to it this morning after an online search. Rising before dawn had its advantages. Not that there was a choice—once Seamus was awake, sleep was impossible. This morning it had been Gilbert and Sullivan opera tunes.

Better than artillery.

O'Fallon pulled out his voice recorder, a gleaming silver digital version he'd bought for his birthday. He still thought it looked cool, more high-tech than the one he'd carried before, although he hadn't figured out all the little bells and whistles. He clicked it on.

"Further notes on Gavenia Kingsgrave. She's thirty-seven years old, unmarried, a genuine card-carrying witch, and claims to be a psychic." He snorted at that and then read a bit farther, letting the machine run. "What, no one–eight hundred psychic hotline of your own?" he chided. "You're never going to get rich that way." A few more lines down. "Oh, you don't need the money because your family's rolling in it. Your aunt is the widow of Alexander Merin, of Merin Foundation fame, and your sister, also a widow, is co-owner of Hansford Technologies." He shuffled papers, doing a quick calculation of their combined net worth. "Ka-ching! Well, we'll never have to run a benefit for you, sister."

He clicked off the recorder and moved to the page he'd found most interesting—a newspaper account of his quarry's traffic accident overseas nearly six months earlier. The accompanying photo made him queasy. The car was mashed beyond recognition, crumpled into a stone wall like a flattened soda can. Apparently Ms. Kingsgrave had come damned close to meeting her pagan gods. Her boyfriend, a man named Winston Thomas, made the trip without her. O'Fallon scanned further in the article, but found no mention of drunk driving. According to the paper, it was just an early-morning encounter with a flock of woolies on a remote Welsh country road.

"Sheep happen," he said. He dug through more of the papers until he found the second article, a brief mention in the local Welsh newspaper from a month later, saying that the patient was returning to the States and that her aunt had contributed a sizable donation to the hospital in gratitude for the care her niece had received.

"Bor-ing," he muttered, unconsciously using Seamus's favorite word. Nothing screamed temptress or scam artist. "So if you're not screwing him, what's your game, sister?" he asked. He tossed the file onto the seat and huffed in irritation. The beginning of a case was always a hassle. Too little information, with no clue who was on the level.

"So how does this relate to the TE?" he grumbled, using Avery's shorthand for the "triggering event." In this case, the TE was the Alliford boy's death, the tragedy that had brought Gavenia Kingsgrave into Gregory Alliford's life.

"What's her angle?" No answer came bubbling forth. "'When in doubt, work both sides of the equation.'" Another Avery gem. It was time to learn more about the grieving parents. Perhaps they might provide clues to the lady with the sea-blue eyes.

He opened his notebook, flipped to a new page, and titled it *The Allifords*. It sounded like a third-rate sitcom. He dug out his cell phone and began a series of calls. He was one day into his seven-day timeline and needed answers.

Chapter Seven

"Augusta and I never got along because I encouraged Janet to stand up to her," Gregory admitted as he sank into a leather chair. Gavenia sat on the couch, averting her eyes from the picture of little Bradley on the end table. According to the maid, the child's ghost was increasingly restive.

The grieving father took a long sip of the strong coffee. He'd poured the steaming liquid from the Starbucks cup into his own and then added an overly generous helping of whiskey. Gavenia barely kept the exasperated expression off her face. His beard was filling in, adding years to his age. The bags under his eyes had a weight of their own, indicative of too much booze and too little sleep. Unfortunately, Gavenia didn't have good news.

"Your wife isn't staying in Palm Springs, despite what your mother-in-law told you."

Gregory gave her a puzzled look. "Then why did Augusta say she was?"

Gavenia shrugged. "Is she in the habit of running interference for Janet?"

A quick nod. "Mommie Dreadful always bailed her out of whatever mess she got into. Then she would lecture her about what a disappointment she was."

"That had to hurt."

Gregory's eyes softened. "It was hard for Janet. I think that's why she started taking drugs. Her way of trying to cope." He looked down at the cup of doctored coffee and held it aloft as if it were Exhibit A. "I'm not doing much better."

"You're in a rough patch. You'll get through it."

He shook his head. "I don't think so. Not without Bradley."

Gavenia didn't want to think about what that meant. "Where else might your wife be staying?"

"We have a beach house in Malibu, a cabin in Washington State, and a flat in London." He thought for a moment. "She's not in London; her passport's still in her desk."

"Could she have left the dog with someone—a friend perhaps?"

He took a big gulp of the coffee; his hands exhibited a fine tremor not unlike the one that plagued her.

"She has a friend named Paula." Another sip of coffee. "She lives in Glendale."

"If you have no objections, I'll give her a call," Gavenia said.

"Fine." He didn't move, staring at the contents of his coffee cup.

"Do you have her phone number?"

He blanked for a moment, then gestured. She followed him down the long hall into a bright room filled with light oak furniture.

As he rummaged through his wife's desk in search of the phone number, Gavenia inventoried the walls. She found a number of pictures of Janet and Bradley in loving poses, in contrast to Gregory's assertion that his wife was an indifferent mother. Then a framed piece made her gasp. It was an obituary. She reread the name, just in case she'd made a mistake.

"I see you found it," Gregory remarked as he thumbed through a leather-bound address book.

"I don't understand," Gavenia said, removing the frame from the wall to study the newspaper clipping in detail. "This says your mother-in-law died two years ago, but I talked with her yesterday."

"A screw-up. There was a private plane crash in Belgium and we were told Augusta was on the flight. The press jumped on it and ran the obituary before it was officially confirmed. Augusta was furious and sued the newspaper."

"I see." Gavenia skimmed the piece, the final testimony of a person's earthly accomplishments. Mrs. Pearce was respected, even feared, but not loved. The list of survivors held another revelation: Janet wasn't the only child. An older daughter, Emily, lived in the

Los Angeles area.

"I've got Paula's number," Gregory crowed, pointing to an entry in the address book. The reaction seemed overblown, as if he'd just discovered the Holy Grail.

He needs to feel useful, Bart's soft voice explained. He stood near the doorway, quietly observing the scene.

"That's great," Gavenia said, trying to sound supportive. "Do you have Emily's address as well?"

Gregory's face clouded. "Em? I can try to find it. We don't see that much of her; she's persona non grata in the family." He grinned. "She told Old Lady Pearce to shove it. It was a hell of a scene. Best Thanksgiving I've ever had."

Gavenia cracked a smile. "I can imagine."

"Em's out of the will; her independence cost her everything."

Gavenia puzzled over the framed obituary. Why would Janet keep such a thing, especially in such a prominent place?

Wishful thinking? Bart offered.

She gave him a subtle nod in agreement. Perhaps Emily's price for freedom was nothing compared to what her sister Janet was paying.

* * *

O'Fallon disliked stakeouts. You sat in your car; your butt got sore and your shoulders stiff while you waited for your quarry to do something interesting. Most of the time they never did. Except on one notable occasion when he and Avery were caught in the middle of an impromptu gang war, their car windows disintegrating in a blizzard of lead. His current situation was just the opposite; Gavenia Kingsgrave departed the Alliford residence about half an hour after she'd arrived, her clothes tidy and her hair in pristine condition.

"No quickie," O'Fallon observed. Somehow that pleased him, though he wasn't exactly sure why.

As he followed her on her daily rounds, she committed no untoward acts other than failing to come to a complete stop.

Nothing sinister at all, unless you counted the fact that she was currently inside a New Age shop.

"Low on eye of newt, no doubt," O'Fallon snorted.

He eagerly embraced his bias against all things New Age, and for that he blamed Shirley, his second wife. A seemingly sensible Catholic when they'd married, she'd hared off into the supernatural shortly after the honeymoon. Their small apartment became home to three stray cats—reincarnated souls, she called them—countless crystals, and enough incense to put the Vatican to shame. Seamus had rebelled, pulling feathers out of his tail in frustration until he resembled a bedraggled gray football.

O'Fallon took the hint; if Seamus wasn't happy, neither was he. He filed divorce papers at the six-month anniversary. Not quite a Hollywood record, but it left a scar nonetheless. The last he'd heard, Shirley was living with her lover—another New Age woman—in Portland. That was the ultimate blow to his male ego. O'Fallon had chosen his girlfriends with more care from that moment forward.

He sighed and poured more coffee from his thermos. Mrs. Pearce's fixation on the witch puzzled him. Why was she so sure that Ms. Kingsgrave was some sort of threat? So far she seemed pretty harmless.

"Everybody's got an agenda," he grumbled, clients included.

Parked down the street from the shop, he shifted his eyes from the entrance to the rearview mirror. It wasn't the best of neighborhoods, and it paid to be vigilant. He'd already fobbed a dollar into the dirt-smeared palm of an itinerant who'd cleaned his windshield. He suspected more dollars would part from his wallet in the near future; the nearby homeless shelter attracted a steady stream of patrons. One waved his hands in the air as if signaling the mother ship. Another waited while his scruffy dog urinated on a nearby fire hydrant, and then he followed suit.

O'Fallon chuckled. "It's pretty bad when a dog's got better aim that you do, buddy."

His cell phone rang. "O'Fallon. Yeah, hold on a sec." He wrestled his notebook and pen out of his jacket on the seat beside him, then hastily scribbled notes as he cradled the phone to his ear.

When his neck protested the unnatural position, he switched sides, nodding as the litany continued. One of the upsides of being a former cop was that his sources were always on the mark.

"Got it. Thanks, that helps," he said, smiling.

The female voice on the other end reminded him that the transaction would cost him dinner and a movie.

"I'm good for it. Just not a chick flick like the last time, okay?" A laugh was the answer.

He flipped the phone shut and tossed it onto the seat, reviewing the notes he'd made. Gregory Alliford's rap sheet was clean. His wife was another matter. Janet Pearce Alliford had a string of petty offenses: shoplifting along Rodeo Drive, speeding, tangles with authority figures ranging from tollbooth operators and cops to bouncers in upscale bars. Lots of citations, no convictions. The road map of a life off the rails, all smoothed over by Mommy's money and influence.

O'Fallon knew the pattern from his years on the force. When someone couldn't stand up to a bully, they found other ways to displace that aggression. *Boxing the man*, he called it. It was a no-win scenario. *The man* always won.

He cranked his attention back to the shop. By his watch, Ms. Kingsgrave had been in Crystal Horizons for over thirty minutes. It appeared that selecting the proper witchy supplies wasn't a slam dunk.

He tapped his foot in time to the radio as he balanced his checkbook, his gaze periodically bouncing from the numbers to the shop like a jack-in-the-box. Pleased with the balance he'd calculated, he tucked his checkbook away and started fiddling with the radio.

His cell phone rang and he snagged it off the seat, eager for the distraction. The caller ID gave him hope.

"O'Fallon."

"Doug, it's Kathryn."

A lusty smile crossed his face. "Changed your mind about tonight?" he asked. He crossed the fingers on his free hand.

"No."

Disappointment arced through him as the fingers snapped

apart. "You sure you can't drop by for a little while? That way you'll be nice and relaxed for your meeting."

A low chuckle, a moment's hesitation, and then, "No, I really can't. I'm sorry."

"Is he cute?" he asked perversely. Kathryn was too pretty not to attract other suitors, despite the fact she spent the majority of her time elbow deep in corpses.

"Sort of, but . . ." She sighed as if realizing she'd been mouse-trapped. "That's not the situation, Doug. It's just business."

He struggled to keep his voice mellow. "I understand. Just don't forget me, okay? Seamus misses you."

"Oh, right," she chuckled. "I'm headed out of town later this week, so it'll be some time before I can call again."

Now she's going out of town. Was it with the guy she was meeting tonight?

"Have a safe trip." He flipped the phone shut and shook his head. His lovers always came on strong and then faded long before the finish line. Only Seamus would be pleased when it ended. He wasn't fond of O'Fallon's paramours, Dr. Kathryn Bergstrom included. At least he hadn't bitten her.

A sharp rap on the window startled him, and he nearly dropped the phone. As he reached for another dollar in his front pocket, he hesitated. This wasn't a bum, not with that hair. His inattention had cost him the stakeout.

"Dammit," he muttered. He hauled himself out of the car and leaned on the open door. He noted she remained on the other side, using it as a shield. In the distance, a woman stood outside the New Age shop, phone in hand, watching the scene intently. Ms. Kingsgrave had come with backup.

Street savvy. Point for the witch.

The frown on his quarry's face appeared genuine, and she gripped the cane between her two hands like a weapon, her right hand exhibiting a coarse tremor. Her eyes were more vivid in person, with a depth he'd not anticipated. High cheeks—natural, not cosmetic—full lips, and honey-wheat hair. A striking young woman.

"Why are you following me?" she demanded.

He refocused on the question, away from those eyes.

"That's what I was hired to do. I'm a private detective."

"You have proof of that?" He politely handed over a business card. She took it in an unsteady hand and gave it a cursory glance. "Anyone can print a business card. I want to see your license." This one was cautious. He pulled out his wallet and displayed the license. She studied it and then nodded as if satisfied on that point.

"Who hired you?" she asked.

He shook his head. "Sorry, client confidentiality."

The frown deepened. He thought he could see the pale outline of a scar just above her left ear where it disappeared into her hair. A souvenir of the car accident?

"Why were you in Palm Springs?" she asked.

He hedged. "What makes you think I was in Palm Springs?"

"Because I saw your car at Mrs. Pearce's. It was back by the carriage house."

"There are a lot of beige Chevys in LA."

"Not with an *Irish Make Better Lovers* bumper sticker and a rusty dent on the left rear fender."

He mentally cursed. He'd been meaning to remove that sticker, a holdover from Shirley.

By his count the witch was two for two. He offered a conciliatory grin, hoping to disarm her anger. "You got me," he said, spreading his hands.

She returned the cane to the ground and then signaled to Viv. Her friend waved back and disappeared into the shop.

"A bit skittish, aren't we, Ms. Kingsgrave?" he asked.

When she glared at him, he made sure to smile back. He could tell she was assessing him, making note of his off-the-rack clothes, the lack of a ring on his left hand and the fact he wore a simple watch.

That's right. I'm not a threat.

That was exactly what he wanted her to believe.

"Why did Mrs. Pearce hire you?" she asked.

"Since you've tagged me, I might as well be honest. Mrs. Pearce has concerns that you might not be on the level."

"She's not helping the situation. All she needs to do is tell us where Merlin is."

"I find it hard to believe you drove all the way to Palm Springs looking for a dog."

"That's exactly what I did. Do you know where he is?"

He shook his head. "Why is the mutt so important?"

She delivered a smirk. "Sorry, client confidentiality, Mr."—she studied his business card—"O' . . . Fallon."

"It's a good Irish name," he said, frowning.

She gave him an astonished look. "Really? I never would have guessed."

They glowered at each other until a couple of bums began an argument, something to do with the rights to a particular patch of cracked pavement. Their voices grew more raucous, and a third transient intervened.

"Blessed are the peacemakers," O'Fallon commented, and gave a low sigh. Another check of those eyes; they were darker now, more intense, the sea at midnight.

"Are you going to keep following me?" she asked.

"That would be pointless. If you're trying to hide something, you'll just alter your routine. I'll do my research in other ways."

"Or you'll just change cars."

"You have a devious mind." *And a lot quicker than most.*

"I suspect that's a compliment coming from you," she snipped. "Why don't you just ask what you want to know?"

You called it. "What are you up to with Gregory Alliford? Are you two lovers?"

She blinked in what appeared to be genuine surprise. "No, we're not lovers. I don't sleep with my clients."

"So what is it you do for your clients?" he asked.

"I am a psychic. I read tarot cards and I'm a medium." Her expression turned guarded, as if she felt she'd revealed too much. "I promise I have their best interests at heart. I'll do nothing that will harm Mr. Alliford or his son."

She spoke of the child as if he were still alive. He furrowed his brow. "If you're scamming him, I'll find out."

"Is that what Mrs. Pearce thinks?"

"She thinks it's a possibility."

"I'm not surprised she'd see it that way. Mommie Dreadful views the world as her own private kingdom and Goddess help anyone who tells her 'no.'"

The witch had pegged his client precisely.

"So how much do you charge for conjuring up a spirit?" he asked.

"I don't conjure them. They come of their own free will. I only accept what my client wishes to pay, and that goes to charity. My psychic gift doesn't line my pockets."

"Your gift?" He leaned forward on the door, causing it to squeak in protest. "Don't you mean your imagination?"

His challenge seemed to threaten her. "We're done," she said, stepping back. Her left leg wobbled, and she had to lean against the car to regain her balance.

"That's from the accident, isn't it?"

Color flooded her cheeks and her breathing grew uneven, as though he'd invoked an ancient curse. He watched her struggle for control, seeking clues as to what hidden weakness he'd targeted.

"How did you—"

"I'm an investigator," he cut in, pressing the advantage. "It's my job to know things."

Her eyes shot brilliant blue. "You have no right digging into my life!"

"I have every right, especially if you're running a game on Gregory Alliford."

"I am not scamming him," she retorted. She took two quick breaths in an attempt to throttle down her anger. "You don't believe in psychics, do you?"

"Consider me . . . unconvinced."

"Then what will it take to convince you so you'll leave me alone and let me do my work?"

Gotcha. He barely kept the grin off his face.

"Let's see . . ." A thought leaped into his mind. "Tell me

about my father." That would settle it. She'd come up with some nonsensical patter, and he could report back to Mrs. Pearce that the woman was a flake. After he'd determined if she was working over Alliford's finances or his libido—or both.

As she stared over his left shoulder, he twitched, fighting the urge to turn. She nodded, more to herself than him.

"I see a short man with auburn hair standing next to you." She listened for a moment and then added, "He's got a thick Irish brogue."

O'Fallon shook his head. "That's easy enough to guess. I've got an accent, and the hair color is too obvious. You'll have to do better than that." He expected her to react in righteous indignation, but she didn't. She was fixated, as if listening to a voice he couldn't hear. Her pale eyebrows arched upward.

"He's smoking a carved pipe. His mustache is big and wide. He has a merry laugh." Her eyes reached his, and O'Fallon saw immense sadness. "He says his name is Patrick, and he's missing his left arm."

O'Fallon's heart beat double.

She took a shuddering breath. "He says he's thankful you didn't go to the pub that day, that you stayed home and worked on the model airplane. He says it turned out really nice and he liked it that you put it in the coffin for him."

O'Fallon's jaw went slack. He sucked in a deep breath, his heart pummeling inside his chest.

She continued, oblivious to his reaction. "He says he didn't feel anything; it was just over." A faint smile appeared on her face. "He loves you and is proud of what you do. He wants you to know."

O'Fallon reached into his pants pocket, fumbled for his rosary, and clutched it tightly, winding it around his right hand. The crucifix cut into his palm. How could she have known about the model airplane, the one he was building the morning his father died? Only his gran knew about the Corsair and that he'd placed it in the coffin.

"Blessed Mary," he murmured, and crossed himself, closing his eyes against the onslaught of memories.

A car bomb on Easter Sunday had cost his dad his left arm. Always in good humor, he'd joked that God was intending to take him home in bits and pieces. The explosion at the pub a year later ensured there wasn't enough of him left to bury, but they'd put what they could find in a coffin and sent him to ground, along with the Corsair.

By the time O'Fallon regained his senses, the witch was no longer in front of him. She hadn't taken the opportunity to gloat, to demand he drop his investigation—just delivered the bombshell and walked away as if she'd told him the time of day. His mind raced with questions, but he was rooted to the pavement. In truth, he feared what answers he might hear.

She paused by a cluster of bums, bending over, her golden braid swooping forward as she dropped coins into their cups. After sharing a few words with each one and darting a quick glance in his direction, she continued her journey to her car.

"My God, how did she know that?" He crossed himself again, his hand shaking, and kissed the crucifix.

As the red car pulled away from the curb and merged into traffic, he murmured, "Round One to the witch."

Chapter Eight

As she sat at the stoplight, Gavenia tried to relax the knot at the base of her skull, massaging it with her fingers. It tightened in response and shot a bolt of pain into her left temple. She abandoned the effort. The encounter with the red-haired private detective upset her on a number of levels. He seemed so sure she was the bad guy in this pathetic drama—yet another complication she didn't need.

A parade of pedestrians trudged in front of the car in response to the light, some dressed for business, others casual. Then the unexpected: a scruffy bum waltzed through the crosswalk, dancing to the music in his head, an invisible partner in his arms. He swirled around some of the pedestrians in the classic three-four rhythm of a Strauss waltz.

Fred Astaire lives, Bart observed.

"Actually, he's pretty good," Gavenia allowed, grinning. The bum's street theatrics were a welcome relief, a reminder that not everything in the world was complicated.

I'm a much better dancer.

She chuckled. "I bet you are." The transient reached the other side of the street, executed a courtly bow to his unseen partner, and then shuffled off into the crowd.

Show's over, Bart said, and shook his head in disappointment.

The light changed, and Gavenia moved forward through the crosswalk, avoiding a last-minute pedestrian.

"I'm wondering if it was wrong to unload on the PI like that."

He needed to hear it, Bart said.

"Maybe. What if he finds some way to keep me from helping

Bradley across?"

You must insure that doesn't happen. The little boy has to cross soon.

She gave her Guardian a penetrating look, sensing there was more behind his words.

He has to cross, Bart repeated.

"Why the urgency, other than for his father's peace of mind?"

Silence.

"You're hiding things from me."

More silence.

The anger welled up in her, seething from deep inside, fed by her insecurities and fanned by Bart's secretive manner. She wrenched the car toward the curb, angling into a parking place. As she slammed the brakes right before rear-ending the Blazer in front of them, another driver signaled his displeasure through a long blast of a horn and a raised finger.

She turned her full wrath on her Guardian.

"Bart, stop hiding things from me. Tell me what I need to do to help this kid."

His mouth formed a thin line, but he did not respond.

"Talk to me!"

He has to cross over because he's vulnerable on this side.

"What do you mean, vulnerable? He's dead. It doesn't get any safer than that."

You're not called a Shepherd just because it's quaint, he snapped.

"Meaning?"

What do shepherds do?

"You mean real ones?"

Yes.

She stammered. "They . . . herd sheep."

And?

"They keep them safe."

Safe from what? he pressed.

"Predators . . . like dogs and wolves."

His voice fell to a near whisper. *Your job isn't any different.*

Her breath hissed out in understanding. "You mean the souls are in danger on this side?"

He nodded. *The young ones, especially. They don't have any fear.*
"What happens to them?"
What does a pack of dogs do to a lamb?
"Goddess." She swallowed, but the knot in her throat didn't
vanish. She'd seen what a rogue pack of hounds could do to a flock
of sheep. Bits of wool, tangled sinews, and gnawed bits of bone.
"You're saying something might try to harm Bradley? But what
would happen to him?"
*The soul is mostly light, a kind of energy. Bradley's light is pure
because he's a child. It's like a beacon to some of the darker things out
there. The longer he stays on this side, the more likely something will
find him.*
"A lamb among the wolves."
Exactly. He has to cross—soon.
She closed her eyes as her hand fluttered in her lap like a
wounded bird, and she didn't try to control it. Weight pressed
down on her chest, the burden of being a Shepherd.
"Why didn't They just have you tell me all of it, right up front?"
*Not all Shepherds can handle who they are. Most end up like that
bum, waltzing to the voices in their head.*
"I'm not going to do that," she insisted.
I pray that's the case, he whispered.
His eyes spoke of deep concern, almost love. It was touching.
He wasn't the enemy; he was just stuck in the foxhole with her,
trying to figure out how to keep from being sprayed with shrapnel.
Gavenia stared out the driver's side window. The scene faded
from her view and she closed her eyes, thinking of that day she'd
hiked into the Welsh countryside alone. After going over a stile,
she'd found herself in the middle of a field of sheep, perhaps a
hundred or so of the woolies.
A pair of Border Collies had barked their warning and she'd
hesitated, unsure if she should proceed. A voice called to her, and
she found an old shepherd taking his tea under a broad-leafed tree.
She'd sat with him for some time, talking about the sheep, the
dogs, and life. He'd offered some of his tea, but she'd declined,
sipping from her water bottle instead. The day had been fine and

warm, the hike strenuous. Long before the car accident ended such simple pleasures.

"What is it you do, lass?" he'd asked.

"I translate documents from one language to another," she'd said. "It's not much fun. Not outside like this."

She watched as his old eyes swept the horizon, checking the locations of the dogs and the movements of the flock. He seemed at ease, but she knew he was looking for the nuances, the subtle shifts that meant something was amiss.

"What's it like to guard sheep all day?" she'd asked.

"Pretty quiet, most of the time."

"Do you ever think of doing something else?"

He shook his head. "I know there are other things I could put my hands to, but this is an old profession, an honorable one. God sent his angels to tell the shepherds of His newborn son. I like to think that means we're blessed, at least in the eyes of the Almighty."

"I have no doubt of it."

She watched the mass of moving animals. The low-pitched baas of the ewes were matched by the higher pitch of their offspring. The lambs bounced across the ground as if equipped with springs. Nearby, a small one butted his mother's distended udder, sucking hard. "It must be so peaceful to be a shepherd."

The old man's voice took on a serious tone. "A shepherd's duty is to the sheep. They come first. A shepherd protects the flock at all cost. It's what we do."

Now, as she felt the rumble of passing cars and the sounds of the city return, the old man's words burned into her heart.

A Shepherd protects the flock at all cost.

Bart observed her with solemn eyes, waiting, perhaps knowing what she intended to ask. She could not summon the courage to speak the words.

You will prevail, he said. *You're stronger than most.*

Gavenia leaned against the steering wheel, feeling the hard surface press into her forehead. After a few moments, she pulled the car out into traffic, feeling as alone as that night she'd awoken inside a nightmare.

* * *

Within the silence of the church, memories seized him. Gazing upward at Saint Bridget's loving face, O'Fallon traveled back to the day his dad died, reliving it. The morning had been quiet, no harbinger of the horror to follow. His father hiked to his pub, the Dragon's Forge. Doug decided to stay with his gran that day and work on a model airplane, a Corsair, his father's birthday present. He'd made it as far as the tail section and then decided to give it a rest. He'd go to the pub after all, have lunch with his dad, listen to the other men jest with one another, inhale the rich aroma of beer and whiskey. As he placed the model in an old shoe box, the house shook, rattling crockery in the kitchen. The muffled sound of an explosion reached his ears. His gran looked up from her knitting, her face unnaturally pale. Her hand trembled as she made the sign of the cross.

In that instant he knew his father was dead, felt it deep in his bones.

"Gran . . ." Tears wove their way down her face as she hugged the nearly completed sweater to her chest—a present her son would never wear.

"Sweet Jesus," she murmured, rocking back and forth. "How could they?"

He remembered running through the streets of his hometown, oblivious to everything but the need to prove himself wrong. The pub had vanished. Left in its place was a ruin of broken bricks, flaming rafters, and twisted metal. The stench of burned flesh filled his nose along with the acrid smell of thick, choking smoke. Sirens echoed around him.

He shoved his way through the gathering crowd, shouting his father's name over and over. A policeman caught him as he tried to rush into the fiery ruins, and he fought, kicking and swearing. Finally, he slumped to his knees in the broken glass and wept.

When he felt a hand on his shoulder, he jerked his eyes upward, a prayer of thanks on his lips—his father had survived. It was not his dad's face that looked down at him, but Father Murphy's. The old priest clutched a rosary to his chest, his eyes damp with tears. Fourteen men had died in the pub that day. One was Douglas O'Fallon's father.

Now, as he knelt before Saint Bridget, he couldn't prevent the tears from cascading down his cheeks. He squeezed his eyes shut and prayed harder. *How could that woman have known? How could she see his father's spirit and he could not?*

When he felt a reassuring hand on his shoulder, he half expected it to be Father Murphy.

"Doug?" Avery asked softly, his face covered in concern. "Are you okay?"

O'Fallon shook his head, scattering tears around him. "God, no, I'm not." He paused and then blurted, "I need to talk."

"I'll be in the courtyard when you're ready." As he turned, he hesitated. "Is this about Benjamin?"

"It's about me."

His friend's expression grew solemn. "I'll wait for you."

* * *

O'Fallon could only imagine what he looked like to his old friend, though Avery had seen him through every kind of hell, both on the job and off. Now, as they sat in the courtyard, his friend hadn't taken his eyes off him for a moment.

"You've been in the church a long time. I felt something was very wrong," Avery said. O'Fallon still didn't speak, unable to put the events of the day in any sensible order. "Doug, I can't help you if you don't talk to me. Something's shaken you to the core. For God's sake, let me help you," he said gently, putting his hand on O'Fallon's shoulder.

"It's because of the witch," he started.

Avery leaned forward, a puzzled look on his face. "Witch?"

"I have another case. . . ." He launched into the tale, explaining the trip to Palm Springs and Ms. Gavenia Kingsgrave. Then he revealed what she'd told him. Up to that point he'd kept his emotions in check, and then the dam burst. Words flooded out like a torrent, washing over both of them. Avery held his silence, listening intently.

When the torrent faded to a trickle, O'Fallon raised his face. "I don't know what to think," he whispered. "How could she have known about my father?"

"I find it rather remarkable. In all the time I've known you, you've never told me exactly how he died." Avery thought for a moment. "Is there any way she could have learned the details through a background check?"

O'Fallon frowned.

"You think she checked me out?" *God, let that be it.* The light bulb went on. *Of course, she's playing me. How could I be so stupid not to see it?*

"Is it possible?" Avery asked.

O'Fallon rose from the bench. The afternoon sun felt warm on his face, but it did little to mitigate the chill inside his breast. Above him, high in the trees, squirrels skittered, leaping from branch to branch.

Doubt returned. "This case doesn't seem that important. Why would she bother?" O'Fallon asked.

"Some folks are very adept at finding a weak spot. Your father's death is your Achilles' heel."

O'Fallon shook his head. "It doesn't make sense. She didn't know my name until that moment."

"Perhaps someone in the Alliford household found out about you and passed the information to her."

Is that what happened?

"The question stands—are the details available somewhere she could find them?" Avery pressed.

O'Fallon thought for a moment and then shook his head again, his mind in turmoil. "No. I put the plane in his coffin right before the funeral mass. Nobody but Gran knew I did it. Actually, she put it in there for me. She never let me look inside." He took a deep inhalation followed by a shuddering breath. "I never saw my dad after he died."

"That's a blessing, Doug. You remember him from that

morning, going out the door."

Tears threatened again and he struggled to push them down. "He gave me a big hug. He wasn't afraid to show his emotions."

"And, thank God, neither are you."

"All I feel is anger, even now. Our village priest said I should forgive the bastards who killed him. I never will." O'Fallon stared at the rosary in his hands and then held it up. Suspended from his fingertips, the heavy silver crucifix slowly turned in midair. "This was my father's. They found it in the rubble. They said it was a miracle it survived." He offered it to his friend.

Avery accepted the rosary as if it were a priceless relic. He studied it; the crucifix was discolored and bore signs of heat. Some of the beads were scorched.

O'Fallon explained, "My dad said beer didn't choose sides when it came to religion, and neither would he. Anyone was welcome at the pub as long as they parked their intolerance at the door."

"He sounds like a good man."

"He was. Some of the locals didn't like his attitude, so they vandalized the pub to warn him off. He ignored it. Then a couple came to work him over. They got the worst end of the deal." He sighed at the memory of his dad's arm in a cast and stitches across his forehead. Patrick O'Fallon had laughed it off in his usual style.

"Who planted the bomb?"

"The New IRA."

Avery's eyes flared. "Good God, they killed one of their own?"

"They'd kill the Holy Trinity if it served their purpose," O'Fallon replied, gall in his voice. "All the men in the pub that day were Catholic; not a one was a Protestant. It cost the bastards dearly. Some blamed my dad, but most felt the bombing was just plain murder."

Avery crossed himself and handed the rosary back. O'Fallon kissed it and dropped it into his inside jacket pocket. He thought for a time, allowing the stillness of the courtyard to cradle his sacred memories. His father would have loved Saint Bridget's just as much as his son did.

In time, he turned back toward the priest. "So what do I do?"

"It appears you have a choice. You can deny that this woman spoke of matters that only you and your grandmother know, or you can accept that God does indeed work in mysterious ways."

O'Fallon sputtered in protest. "But she's a pagan, Avery. You know what the church thinks about them."

The priest nodded. "I know what they think." He glanced around to insure they were alone. "Nevertheless, I know that there are cases in which the Almighty shares His gifts with those outside the fold, though Rome probably wouldn't like me saying that."

"You think she could be on the level?" O'Fallon asked.

"I'm saying you should give her the benefit of the doubt. Either she's a very clever fraud, or God reveals things to her that others do not see."

"But why would He do that?"

Avery gave him a gentle smile. "Why? Who better to teach you that your gift is a treasure than another psychic, even if she is a pagan?"

"Jesus," O'Fallon muttered. He shook his head. "I can't buy that."

"Being closed-minded isn't going to help."

O'Fallon shook his head more vehemently. "No, I'm not buying this. Somehow she's done her homework on me. God, she was smooth. I've never been played like that." A sense of righteous indignation filled his breast. He'd make her pay for playing that game.

Avery raised an eyebrow. "What was the first lesson I taught you as a detective?"

O'Fallon gave a quick smirk. "Don't call the captain a dickhead where he can hear you?"

"Besides that."

O'Fallon knew where this was headed, and even though it came from Avery, it pissed him off. "I'm not bringing my own bias to this case."

"Could have fooled me. You say you accept having your gift yet every chance you get you deny it exists. You will continue to deny it until hell becomes an ice skating rink, or you can just accept He has a reason you're that way."

"No, I'm not going there. She put a spell on me."

"God, you can be stubborn," Avery grumbled, shaking his head.

"Stubborn? I never expected to hear you defend a damned witch, Avery. We used to burn these people like kindling. Why the hell are you taking her side?"

Avery's eyebrow went higher, and his voice grew more intense. "*Her* side? Listen to yourself, Doug."

"That's what it sounds like."

His friend rose, a deep frown on his face. "Just to set the record straight, I only take *God's* side."

"Not in this case."

"Okay, then I ask you: Would your father have cared if this woman was a pagan? Would he have served her in his pub? I think you know the answer and I think you know you're not following in his footsteps, but being just as bigoted as the men who killed him."

O'Fallon stepped back, his face reddening. An oath sprang to his lips, but he slammed it down.

"I don't need this, not even from you," he growled, spinning on his heel and marching toward the arched gate that led to the street.

"Call me if you need to talk," he heard over his shoulder.

"Not damn likely," he muttered, storming through the old iron gate, resisting the urge to slam it behind him.

* * *

Gavenia inventoried her kitchen from the doorway: the counters gleamed, a Crock-Pot simmered, and the scent of baking cookies filled the room. Bart stood suspiciously close to the oven, as if intending to pounce on them the moment the timer chimed.

"I never pictured you as a domestic goddess," she said to Ari, who fussed with her laptop at the kitchen table. Gavenia's cat, Bastet, was curled up on her lap.

"I got bored," her sister replied, turning on the laptop.

Gavenia watched with mixed feelings. She found computers intriguing, but technology wasn't always her friend. She used it only when necessary, like when she had to do translations for a client.

"Okay, what do you want to know?" Ari asked, looking up. As usual she was in head-to-toe black.

Gavenia sat next to her and peered at the glowing screen.

"I want you to check out a guy for me." If the PI could dig up her past, why not do the same to him?

"Is he a hunk?"

Gavenia scrunched her face in thought. *O'Fallon a hunk?* "Well, yeah, at least when he's not smirking."

"But what about the rest of him?"

More thought. "I can't tell, he wears suits. He looks like an insurance salesman."

"Ew . . . What kind of car does he drive?" Ari asked, tapping on the keyboard as she spoke. Bastet took that opportunity to hop down and head for her food bowl.

"Why does that matter?"

"It tells you a lot about a guy. You are what you drive."

"So I'm a fast woman with no headroom?" she said, referring to her Miata. Ari didn't rise to the bait. "He drives a beige Chevy."

"Hmmm. A nondescript kind of fellow. Sensible. Stable. You know the kind." Without waiting for a reply, Ari asked, "Name?"

Gavenia pushed the PI's business card across the table.

"Lord, this connection is slow," Ari complained, tapping a fingernail in frustration. "How did you meet him?"

"He's been tailing me. Mrs. Pearce hired him to find out if I'm sleeping with her son-in-law."

"Are you?" Ari asked eagerly, leaning forward, typing again.

"Nooo! I don't sleep with clients."

"Whoa, this guy is definitely out on the Net." Her sister clicked links; opened, scanned, and closed pages in swift succession. It seemed a jumble to Gavenia. "Most of them are from the *LA Times*." More typing. "Okay. You're registered. I made your password *Tinker Bell*."

"Password?" Gavenia asked in all innocence, just to annoy her house guest.

Her sister gave her a sideways glance and then returned to the monitor. She flipped through more news articles and whistled when O'Fallon's photo appeared on the screen.

"Not bad. Not bad at all," Ari said. "Get him in a pair of blue jeans and you might have something."

Gavenia fidgeted in annoyance. "So what did you find?"

"Used to be a cop. He worked some real high-profile murder cases. This guy got around. Lots of press."

"What else?"

Ari read for a while and announced, "Oops . . . not good."

"What?" Gavenia pressed, leaning forward and peering at the screen.

"This article's about a week in the life of a homicide detective. It says your guy's got two divorces under his belt." Another pause. "He's got lots of commendations. Sounds like he's on the level, unless you intend to marry him."

Refusing to be sidetracked, Gavenia asked, "Can you check international news stories?"

"Sure." Ariana slid the mouse around and tapped a few keys. "Okay, now what?"

"You can change countries that fast?" Gavenia asked.

"Faster if you didn't have dial-up."

"Yeah, yeah. Same thing: check for O'Fallon."

Ari performed the search. "Well, there are a zillion of them. What are you looking for?"

"A pub bombing."

That earned her a strange expression. The oven timer chimed, and Gavenia rose to retrieve the cookies. As she slid them out of the oven, Bart eyed them hungrily.

"Keep your fingers out of them," she teased. She placed the cookie sheet on top of the oven, wondering if there was fresh milk in the refrigerator.

"What?" Ari asked.

"Sorry. Bart is coveting your cookies."

"He can have some if he wants," Ari replied.

"Guardians don't eat," Gavenia said.

"They can't eat cookies? That's awful."

Tell me about it, Bart said, inhaling deeply. After a deep sigh he vanished, as if the olfactory torture was too great.

Ari appeared by her side. "I didn't find a bombing connected to the name O'Fallon. What were you looking for?"

"Just wondering," Gavenia said, pulling two hot cookies off the sheet and placing them on a folded paper towel. She handed them to Ari; hopefully they'd distract her from asking further questions.

"Milk?" she asked, heading for the refrigerator.

"Please."

Gavenia poured their drinks, took them to the table, and then selected a couple cookies for herself. While munching, Ari clicked back to one of the main articles.

"This guy must be pretty smart," she said, taking a gulp of milk. "Right before he quit the force, he and his partner were tracking a pair of serial killers. They caught one of them, but the other got away."

Ari's seemingly innocuous comments caused the warm moment to evaporate. Unwelcome memories rose. In response, the tremors in Gavenia's right hand increased.

"My hip is bothering me. I'm going to take a shower," she said, desperate to be alone.

Her sister remained engrossed by the computer screen and murmured, "Okay. Dinner will be ready in a little bit."

* * *

The hot water rolling over her body granted little comfort. That wasn't the reason for the shower; in the midst of the pouring water she could cry and no one would hear her. She began her personal ritual, soaping every inch of her body and scrubbing hard with the rough washcloth, attempting to remove the taint, desperate to cleanse her internal agony. The ritual had begun the night after she was freed from the cage in the woods, pulled from the nest she had made within the cold steel trap.

Why had she lived? Why hadn't her captors murdered her?

They had killed the other girls, or so they claimed. Her right hand quivered violently now, as if *he* were still near, demanding she touch him again.

The soap slipped from her grasp and tumbled to the bottom of the tub, causing her to ease down and retrieve it with her left hand. Tears erupted, mixing with the hot water. Her personal ablution. She leaned against the cool tile wall, sobbing as the water carried her tears away. When would the past no longer hold claim to her future?

Chapter Nine

After hours of surfing, sucking down cup after cup of strong coffee, peace of mind eluded O'Fallon. While the Internet supplied reams of information about various branches of the O'Fallamhain family tree—some had even been transported to Australia at the behest of the Crown—there was scant detail regarding his father's death. It was as if history had decided the publican was just collateral damage.

The bottom line loomed: the witch might actually be on the level.

"Dammit." He glanced up at the wall clock. Two ten in the morning. Given the rocket fuel in his system, sleep wasn't an option. Seamus, on the other, snoozed quietly under his cage cover. After a long stretch to ease the cramps from his neck and shoulders, O'Fallon shut off the computer, sank into the recliner, and speed-dialed Ireland. Between his faith and his gran, he'd find the right path.

* * *

"You look like a Rodeo Drive pimp," O'Fallon observed.

The man across the table guffawed, exposing exquisitely capped teeth. Archie's deep tan bespoke considerable time at the beach. The gold link bracelet on his right wrist complimented the genuine Rolex on the left, accenting his mahogany skin.

"Coming from you, O'Fallon, that's a hell of a compliment."

"Hey, Archie, that's what I see. What's that tank you're driving?"

"A Hummer. Special edition. It's got my name imprinted on a

little gold plaque on the dashboard."

O'Fallon shook his head in bewilderment. "And to think you used to panhandle on the Boulevard. . . ."

The guy shrugged amiably. "I was just smarter than most and knew when to make the right moves."

"And when to get out?"

Archie's jovial mood evaporated. "Why are we here, O'Fallon? You're not a morning person, not even when you were walking beat."

"We're here because you know everything worth knowing."

Archie gave him a half nod, accepting the compliment, but his eyes remained leery. The waitress appeared, cleared the remnants of breakfast, and refilled the coffee.

Once she was out of the way, O'Fallon asked, "So why did you get out?"

Archie glanced around, lowering his voice. "When you gotta compete with the cops, it's time to hang it up. They don't play by the rules, and you can always count on getting fucked over."

O'Fallon leaned back and nonchalantly stirred his coffee. He knew Archie; if he left him alone, he'd vent. They'd sparred over the years, and never once had O'Fallon been able to tag the guy with anything more than a busted taillight, though Archie was one of the most ambitious bookies he'd ever met.

"So they're giving you grief?" O'Fallon hedged.

"Not yet, but it's coming."

"So what I hear is kosher, that downtown has sticky fingers?"

"Not all of them. Most are straight arrows. I pity those bastards. It'll only be a matter of time before the others pull 'em down in the mud." The man paused. "Why are you asking about this? You're not thinking of taking up the shield again, are you?"

O'Fallon shook his head. "Don't worry, our conversation won't go any further."

"Don't matter anyway. Me and the missus are driving to Mexico tomorrow night. Bought a condo down there. I can live like a king, and if I grease the right palms, I'll never have to come back, even if they prove I killed Kennedy."

O'Fallon chuckled. He'd always like Archie. Now he wished he'd listened to the bookie's stock tips over the years. If he had, he wouldn't be living in a one-bedroom apartment with a parrot. After another sip of coffee, he swept his eyes around the diner. It was early and most of the booths were still empty, and he'd made sure to choose a site well away from the precinct's stomping grounds. It never hurt to be cautious.

"Then if you're flying south, I need your help one last time," O'Fallon said.

"Gotta be something in it for me," Archie parried.

"Hell, you got more money than I'll ever have, and my client is a priest."

Archie's eyebrows furrowed. "Elliot?"

"That's the man."

Archie shook his head. "I still don't get that one. One minute the guy's a cop, and then he's sporting a collar." He paused for emphasis and asked, "What are you into?"

O'Fallon went for broke. "I'm trying to find a stolen rosary—it came up missing after a suicide at the LeClaire. I've tracked it as far as the investigating detectives. They say they never saw it."

Archie crossed himself reflexively. It was his turn to look around as he leaned over conspiratorially. "There are three pawnshops the cops use downtown. I'll give you the addresses. Just play it cool with them, okay?"

"Understood."

Archie removed a pen from his shirt pocket. It looked expensive, just like the rest of the man's accessories. He pulled a napkin over and started writing.

"You ever heard of a cop named Harve Glass?" O'Fallon said, pitching the name out like an ante into a poker game. Archie's eyes rose to check out the room again. Offering no answer, he returned to penning the addresses.

"Here," he said, pushing the napkin across the table. "Maybe that will help me get into heaven, you know?"

He stood, dropped a twenty on the table, and then flashed a gleaming smile at O'Fallon. "Be smart about this, okay? You made it too many years to not enjoy your retirement. I'll send you a postcard from Mexico. Come visit us . . . and I mean that." Without waiting for an answer, Archie turned and strode out of the diner.

O'Fallon scrutinized the napkin. Three pawnshop addresses were listed in a scrawling hand. Beneath the addresses was a single line, in block letters:

BEWARE OF GLASS.

* * *

Pawnshops always reminded O'Fallon of his two failed marriages—good intentions gone awry. He sneezed the moment he stepped inside the door, the dust irritating his nose. He was zero for two so far, and this was the last shop on Archie's list.

The Korean shop owner acted as if he didn't speak much English, though O'Fallon doubted that was the case given the *LA Times* on the counter. It was turned to the sports section. O'Fallon briefly glanced toward another customer, who seemed overly fascinated with the rack of guitars in the far corner.

O'Fallon systematically scanned the display cases. A vast array of merchandise presented itself: gold and silver necklaces, earrings, watches, a used camera, and a video recorder. Someone had even pawned a toaster. He wondered if it worked.

The hair on the back of his neck prickled. Leaning forward, he brushed some of the grime off the dirty glass counter for a better look. Shifting the *Times* out of the way, he pointed.

"Can I see that?"

"Nice." The owner grinned, exposing a gold tooth. Had someone pawned that as well? When the pawnbroker tried to hand the rosary to him, he shook his head.

"Put it on the counter," he ordered. The impressions he'd received in the hotel room had been devastating enough. The price tag said thirty-five dollars. The pawnshop owner clearly had no clue how much the antique rosary was worth.

"I'll take it," O'Fallon said. He extracted the money from his pants pocket, his wallet remaining out of sight, and slid two twenties across the counter. The pawnbroker held up each of the bills in turn to check the watermark. O'Fallon didn't know if he should be amused or offended. As he waited for the change, his attention wandered through the contents of the nearest case.

"I'd like to see that, as well," he said, pointing to a silver medallion. The owner placed it on the counter. O'Fallon began to reach for the object and then pulled his hand back immediately. "How much?"

"Fifteen." O'Fallon pulled out another Jackson and pushed it toward the pawnbroker. While the store owner verified the bill was genuine, O'Fallon wrapped the holy artifacts in his handkerchief, careful not to touch either one. He placed the handkerchief deep within his inside coat pocket.

"Thanks," he said.

"You come back," the owner said, his gold tooth gleaming as he handed over O'Fallon's change.

"Maybe I will. I might want a new toaster someday," O'Fallon said, shoving open the door. It chirped in response and then closed with a bang behind him.

Outside on the street, he tapped his coat pocket, a slow grin crossing his face. He'd found the rosary and the kid's Virgin Mary medallion.

But despite his success, he still had no notion why Benjamin Callendar had killed himself.

* * *

Avery appeared at ease in the paint-streaked jeans, his Palm Sunday obligations complete. His T-shirt proclaimed him a fan of the Dodgers and, minus his clerical collar, he might be any other guy in his mid-fifties. He was working on the church courtyard's fence, slapping on paint in broad strokes.

Despite their blowup the day before, O'Fallon adopted a light tone. "Not bad, van Gogh," he said, grinning.

Avery placed the brush on top of the paint can and wiped his hands with a cloth. He returned the grin. "Our new gardener has a case of shingles." He rose and dropped the cloth to the ground near the can of paint as his face changed from bemusement to concern. "How are you doing?"

"Better. I did as you suggested."

"And?"

"There's no mention of my father's name on the Internet, at least none that I can find."

"So that means—"

O'Fallon waved him off. He'd already had to listen to his gran give him an earful about his stubborn streak. Avery would only pour more salt into the wound.

He purposely changed subjects. "I found the kid's rosary."

The priest shook his head in apparent amazement. "I figured it was long gone." Avery pointed toward the fountain in the church courtyard. "Come on, I need a break," he said.

They sat on the same bench they'd occupied the afternoon before.

"I didn't see you at mass this morning," Avery said.

"Sorry, I was otherwise occupied." O'Fallon opened his jacket and extricated the handkerchief, placing it on the bench between them. He carefully flipped back the corners of the fabric, revealing the contents.

"That's it," his friend said. "I see you found the medallion, as well."

O'Fallon nodded. "You didn't mention it, but it was at the pawnshop." He hesitated and then added, "I sensed it was his."

Avery observed him with kind eyes. "Never apologize for your gift, Doug. Is it still like . . . how'd you put it? Like being sucked through a jet engine?" the priest asked.

"Yeah, most of the time. The hotel room . . . that was hell." O'Fallon looked away, studying the closest cherub to take his mind off the images trying to bulldoze into his brain. The fountain burbled in a reassuring tone as sprays of water jetted from the mouth of a dolphin. "Do you believe God forgave him?" O'Fallon asked, his question barely audible over the sound of the rushing water.

"I do. God knows what's in our heart even when we reject His most precious gift."

O'Fallon returned his gaze to the rosary. "I sensed so much sadness in that room, so much regret. I'd like to think the boy is at peace."

"He is."

O'Fallon raised his eyes to meet those of his old friend. "You say that with so much certainty."

"I have to believe that God is all-merciful. If not, what's the point?" the priest asked, spreading his hands.

"I suppose you're right. I just wish there was some way we could know for sure."

"You always were a skeptic," Avery gently chided. There was a lengthy pause, as if neither was sure where to go next. Avery changed subjects abruptly. "Adam said you were at the precinct the other day."

"I'm hearing that most of the cops in that precinct are dirty. I'd bet a month's pension the detectives ripped off the kid's rosary and pawned it."

Avery rose, shaking his head. He looked older in the sunlight, his face displaying a subtle undercurrent of anger. The expression remained in place for a few seconds and then vanished.

"I've heard the same. I've been pushing Adam to get out of there," he replied sternly.

"That would be for the best." O'Fallon slid the handkerchief and the medallion free of the rosary. "I'd like to keep Mary with me a little longer, if that's okay."

Avery nodded his approval. "Think it will help?"

"It can never hurt," O'Fallon said, tucking the cloth-wrapped Virgin into his breast pocket. "I'll let you know what I find."

"Be careful, Doug," the priest said, looking him full in the eyes.

O'Fallon didn't understand the nature of the warning, only that his friend felt the need to utter it. A spike of apprehension coiled up his spine and lodged at the base of his skull. He left the courtyard feeling alone despite Mary resting heavily against his left breast.

Chapter Ten

Gavenia noticed the car right off; the PI made no effort to hide himself, falling in behind her as she drove away from the condo.

"You Irish pain in the ass."

Maybe he can help you find the dog, Bart remarked.

"No way. I can't trust him not to sell me out to Mrs. Pearce."

Bart responded with a shrug.

"I should call the cops on the guy."

No reply. That usually indicated Bart's opposition to her plan.

"Okay, I'll ignore him. How's that?"

Your call, he said.

As Gavenia turned into the Allifords' driveway, she expected the PI to pull in right behind her. Instead, her shadow passed the entrance and parked up the street. The moment she pushed the doorbell, Bart appeared beside her, uncomfortably close, on the alert.

"What's up?" she asked.

Young Master Bradley has recently thrown a tantrum.

"So?"

Chaotic energy attracts interest, like chumming the water for sharks.

"I don't understand."

You will, he replied, his face solemn.

Gregory Alliford poked his head out, blinking furiously as if he hadn't been in the sunlight for months. When he recognized who it was, his eyes widened.

"Oh, thank God!" he said, waving her in. "I was going to call you, but I couldn't find your number, and Maria is off today."

The smell of whiskey flooded from his breath. He backed into the entryway, his erratic movements like those of a disjointed marionette. As she shut the door, a shattering cry rent the air, followed by a jarring thump. It came from the second floor.

Alliford looked up the stairs and pointed, his arm wavering in the air. "He's been doing that. I think he's angry because we can't find Merlin." He paused and ran a hand over his stubbly face. "I don't know what to do. I just don't—"

"I'll talk to him, settle him down," Gavenia said, taking hold of the father's arm to steady him. He lurched backward, despite her efforts. "Why don't you wait in the den? I'll talk to you after I'm done with Bradley."

He seemed relieved at the suggestion and staggered down the hall, using the walls for support.

Oh, boy, Bart whispered. *Serious meltdown.*

"Yeah," she muttered, shaking her head. Another thump, and she looked upward. "What is going on up there?"

Nothing good.

Gavenia paused outside the child's bedroom. This time the sounds were not of a little boy at play, but of something more sinister. An odd aroma filtered into the hall from behind the closed door. She gave her Guardian a bewildered look.

"Lavender?"

Bart didn't reply.

She touched the doorknob and cried out, jerking her hand back. It showed no damage, though it felt as if it had been seared to the bone.

"What is going on in there?" she demanded.

Before Bart could answer, from inside the room came a whimpering cry that wrenched at her heart. Gavenia took a deep breath and put her quaking hand on the doorknob. Once again it flamed as if immersed in molten steel. She turned the knob and pushed her way into the room. The door swept open, bulldozing a sea of stuffed animals. The room was in shambles—bedding scattered in all directions, toys upended, and books flung like leaves on the wind. The shelf of bears was completely empty, the occupants scattered on the floor. The scent of lavender redoubled, making her eyes water and her throat burn.

Searching through the debris, she spied Bradley in a corner clasping his big teddy bear to his heaving chest. A nervous whimper came from his lips. A fierce anger rose in her breast along with the overwhelming desire to protect the little boy, to hug him close and make the fear go away. Her eyes swept the room again, keen to find the source of this chaos and give her anger an outlet.

She found the entity hovering in the air as if suspended by wires. It wore a deep-purple cloak and had dark hair and unfathomable eyes. It wavered, a semisolid mist illuminated by the light coming through the window.

You have no business here, Shepherd, the phantom said in a low voice. It sounded female. *I shall take care of the little boy.*

Gavenia shook her head, grabbing the sun pendant that hung around her neck. The moment it touched her palm, heat and light shot through her, clearing the cobwebs of the enticing voice. The apparition revealed itself: a dark, slate-colored essence. It did not shimmer like a soul, but obscured the wallpaper behind it.

Make it go away, Bradley cried. He clung tighter to the bear, rocking back and forth, his eyes wide, dried tears on his cheeks.

"I will, Bradley," Gavenia said. She regarded the being. She knew its kind—an ethereal predator. "Time for you to leave."

I go where I will. The voice was no longer female, and the scent of lavender became the stench of decaying seaweed. Gavenia's stomach churned in response, threatening further involvement.

A book flew by her head, striking the far wall.

Leave, Shepherd. He is mine.

Gavenia ignored the order and began to collect the stuffed bears into a furry mound in her arms. The entity watched warily.

What are you doing?

Ignoring the question, Gavenia whispered into each of the bears' furry ears, instructing them on their duty.

What are you doing? the phantom asked again, shifting uncomfortably. The smell of rotten seaweed grew.

"I'm invoking an emotion you couldn't possibly understand,"

Gavenia replied. She formed a ring of fuzzy bodies around the little boy, a loving circle of protection. The fear in his face lessened.

"You will be fine," she said. "I promise."

The entity growled, realizing the boy was now safe beyond its reach. Gavenia smiled reassuringly, knowing what was about to happen. As she turned, Bart shouted a warning, but it was not needed. Gavenia brought her cane upward, separating the handle from the main section, exposing the sword within it. She dropped the scabbard to the floor, holding the blade heavenward.

"I am a Shepherd and I am of the Light. Depart, for you have no power here." A rill of light shot up the blade, and as the entity surged forward, fangs and claws extended, Gavenia plunged the sword deep inside its swirling mass.

"Light overwhelms Darkness," she intoned. "Leave this place and never return!" With a resounding pop, the dark-gray entity vanished into the air emitting a gurgling howl. The nauseating stench of seaweed and lavender immediately began to fade.

Deeply cool, Bart said from his place next to her. He gave her a lopsided grin and a thumbs-up.

"I note you didn't help."

I wasn't supposed to. At least, not unless things got really ugly.

Gavenia raised the sword upright again. "Thanks be to the God and Goddess." She bent to collect the cane's sheath and covered the sword.

A resounding giggle came from the corner, and then a childish laugh.

Bye-bye! Bradley called, waving. He bounced upward and danced inside the circle of bears. *Bad thing all gone.*

Gavenia grinned. She looked down at the ring of bears. "Thank you," she said, addressing them. They did not answer, but she knew they were pleased.

Shoving open a window, Gavenia leaned out and took a deep breath. The fresh air smelled so clean, even though this was LA. In the distance, she saw O'Fallon's car sitting by the curb like a cat awaiting a mouse. She laughed heartily. The PI was nothing compared to what she'd just faced down.

When she turned around, she found her Guardian observing her with a look of respect. She winked and he shook his head.

"You didn't think I could pull that off," she said.

I wasn't sure.

"It was a lower entity, nothing too nasty. I've had a couple of them show up when I'm doing magic. They're pretty harmless, providing you show them you're the boss."

There is worse out there.

"There's always something worse out there, Bart. That's the way things are." She looked over at Bradley. He was giving each of the tiny bears a hug in turn, his face wreathed in a broad smile. "That was just a coyote, and not a very bright one."

Still a danger to a lamb.

Gavenia nodded gravely. "Yes, but not this time." After another deep breath, she joined Bradley in the corner. She needed to convince the boy to keep his tantrums to a minimum and then place some magical wards on the doors and windows to keep other coyotes from finding this little lamb.

* * *

O'Fallon flipped closed the cell phone, gritting his teeth. Glancing around as if someone might see into his private hell, he swore for good measure. The instant he'd read the caller ID, he knew what Kathryn's call meant. To her credit, she'd let him down gently, telling him how much she'd enjoyed their time together, but the chemistry wasn't there, like always.

Sometimes blind hope gets in the way of cold reality.

He'd been polite about the whole thing, but all he really wanted to do was scream and throw things like a toddler having a royal tantrum. Instead, he'd kept his game voice in place, wishing her all the best while his heart raged in chaos.

He'd been naive to blame his problems on the job. Now that he wasn't a cop, the problems remained. That left only one other option. "It's me," he said, shaking his head. "Why am I so hard to live with?"

Another dream deflated.

O'Fallon glanced up at the sound of a car and watched the red Miata slowly exit onto the street. For a moment it looked as if she was going on past, then she veered in behind his car and came to a halt. His gut tightened. He didn't want another confrontation with that woman. Too many doubts swirled through his mind, and she only added to them.

As the witch walked toward his car, something about her appeared different.

What had happened inside the house?

He pulled himself out of the vehicle and leaned back against the rear quarter panel, arms crossed over his chest.

The witch halted about six feet away, her eyes wary. "Back for more?" she asked.

"Is there more?" he asked, hoping the answer was negative.

She peered over his shoulder in that unnerving fashion and then shook her head.

"No ghosts today?" he asked, secretly relieved.

"No. They come and go at will." She used her cane to point toward the rear of his car with the cane. "You took off the bumper sticker."

"I try not to make the same mistake twice."

She seemed on the verge of retorting but bit back the comment.

Sensing weakness, he asked, angling his head toward the house, "So how's Mr. A this morning? Was this a social call or just a quickie on the sofa?"

Her eyes narrowed as she rose to the bait. "Neither."

"Which means?"

"None of your damned business."

"Everything is my damned business, Ms. Kingsgrave. At least when it applies to you."

"You have one hell of a God complex."

The gloves were off.

"Does being a translator pay better than being a psychic?" he asked.

"Way better. Why?"

"So as a translator, you're familiar with things like foreign commerce and banking?"

"Meaning?" she shot back.

"That you'd know how to hide money offshore if needed."

The midnight-blue eyes signaled he was dangerously close to the line.

"Mousetrapping me into making incriminating statements isn't going to work, Mr. O'Fallon. You're not a cop; I'm not a felon. As soon as things are settled with Bradley and his father, I'm out of their lives."

"Then who's next on your hook?"

"You're fishing, and I'm not biting." She started to turn away and then halted. A distant look came to her face.

He knew the look. He'd seen it the day before. "Is it my father?" he blurted without thinking.

She shook her head. "No. This one is younger." She blinked and then sighed. "He's gone. He didn't want me to talk about him."

O'Fallon's fury surged, angered he'd fallen for her nonsense yet again. "Are you aware that head injuries can cause delusions?"

"Are you aware that being ignorant is curable?" she shot back.

"I'm not the issue here."

The woman glowered. "No, Bradley is, and until he's at peace you're in the way, Mr. PI, and I won't tolerate that. Once I find Merlin, I go away. Then you can plague some other innocent person."

"And Mr. Alliford?" he asked, watching her closely.

Her face grew grave. "Unless he gives up the booze, he's going to have a very short life."

"Are you in love with him?"

Her eyes jerked up, and he saw honest surprise. "No, I'm not. I'm just worried about him. Not everyone has ulterior motives, Mr. O'Fallon."

He rose from the hood and dusted off his jacket. "Not in my experience, lady."

"Then you must lead a pretty depressing life. No wonder both of your marriages failed."

His mouth fell open in astonishment. After delivering a triumphant smirk, the witch headed toward her car, the cane impacting the ground as she walked.

He shouted at the retreating form, "Did you know your boyfriend was already married?"

She abruptly halted and then continued on as if she hadn't heard him. Her steps were hesitant now, her right hand shaking each time she raised the cane from the ground. The car door slammed with incredible force and then the Miata spun gravel, pelting him with debris. Halfway down the street, the car blew a stop sign in a long screech of burning rubber.

O'Fallon's moment of gloating triumph faded instantly, replaced by cold remorse. Why had he lost control? Was it because she flogged him with his failed marriages? They were behind him, weren't they?

"Apparently not," he said, shaking his head, dusting his jacket and pants. He'd been cruel, even if she was aware that Winston Thomas had been a married man. From her reaction, it appeared she'd been clueless.

If not for an obscure Internet article penned by Thomas's bereaved wife, O'Fallon wouldn't have discovered his secret. The man had led a shadow life, girlfriends on the side, acting the dutiful husband when he was home. In the end, none of that deceit had mattered after his encounter with the stone wall in Wales.

O'Fallon swore under his breath. No wonder he couldn't get along with women.

Chapter Eleven

Gregory Alliford peered at the business card with a puzzled expression on his unshaven face.

"I'm sorry, but I don't quite understand why you're here, Mr. O'Fallon."

"I'm hoping you can give me a bit of information about Gavenia Kingsgrave."

"Gavenia? Why are you interested?"

"I have been hired to do a background check on her." Not quite a falsehood.

"Oh, like an employment check?" Alliford asked. He placed the business card next to a tumbler of whiskey. An empty fifth sat on the desk nearby.

"Sort of. What can you tell me about the woman?" O'Fallon asked, pulling out his notebook. He was sitting on a very nice leather sofa next to an end table. His eyes caught on the picture of a little boy and a dog. Bradley and the missing canine, no doubt.

"Gavenia came highly recommended by a friend of the family. She's very caring. She's trying to help us with Bradley."

"Your son?" O'Fallon asked, angling his head toward the picture.

"Yes. He's . . ." Alliford hesitated and took a sharp breath. "My son died two weeks ago."

O'Fallon played innocent. "I'm very sorry."

"Things will never be the same," the father said, more to himself than to his visitor.

"How is Ms. Kingsgrave helping your family?"

"She is a psychic. My son's soul hasn't gone to heaven like it should. She is trying to help him cross over, as she calls it."

Time to dig. "How is she trying to accomplish that?"

"By finding my son's dog."

"Why is that important?"

"My son refuses to cross over until he sees Merlin again. The dog was with him when . . . he was hit."

"I see. How did your son communicate this wish?"

"Through Ms. Kingsgrave. She sees him just like you can see me. It's rather creepy, actually, but I believe she actually does see the dead."

"And you don't?"

"No. But I've heard him. He plays in his room. It's like he's still alive."

Great. The man's a drunk and he thinks he's hearing his dead child. What a perfect setup.

"What sort of fee is Ms. Kingsgrave charging?"

"Fee? Oh . . . well. She gave me a piece of paper. Let me get it."

Bingo. A part of him felt regret. On some level O'Fallon hoped the witch wasn't like everyone else.

Alliford rose and dug through the unruly stack of papers on his desk. O'Fallon thought he could see unopened mail, bills and such—the fabric of a life unraveling thread by thread.

"Here is it." Alliford handed over the paper with a shaking hand and then retreated to his chair. Another sip of whiskey followed.

O'Fallon scanned the page. There had to be a mistake. This was a list of charitable organizations, complete with addresses, contact names, and phone numbers.

"Are you sure you gave me the right paper?"

Alliford nodded. "That's it."

"So how much is she charging?"

Alliford pointed. "It's explained on the back."

O'Fallon flipped the paper over expecting to see a sliding scale of outrageous expenses. Instead he found a paragraph of legal verbiage stating in lieu of direct payment, a charitable donation be made to any one of the organizations listed on the reverse side of the sheet. If a donation was beyond the recipient's financial abilities, that was acceptable. Ms. Kingsgrave's flowing signature was at the bottom. It was light, like a butterfly floating on the wind.

O'Fallon frowned. He turned the page over and studied the list: a battered-women's shelter, a literacy program, an inner-city day care, a library.

This had to be a scam. The organizations were probably just clever fronts to funnel money to the witch to keep her in bats' wings and bright-red sports cars.

"Is there any way I can have a copy of this?" he asked.

Alliford nodded and hoisted himself out of his chair. Each time it seemed more difficult. As he fed the paper through the fax machine, pressing the copy button, O'Fallon asked, "Has Ms. Kingsgrave made any other requests?"

Alliford frowned and then nodded. "She suggested I talk to my priest. She thought that might help me cope with . . ." His voice trailed off, and he returned his attention to the machine as if the words were too painful to speak aloud.

"And have you done that?"

Alliford shook his head. "Father Davidson wouldn't understand what is happening. He's a bit, well . . ."

"Old-fashioned?"

Alliford nodded. "He'd be upset if he found out that Gavenia was in the house."

Most priests would. O'Fallon closed the notebook and returned it to his suit-coat pocket. On impulse, he pulled out another one of his business cards and penciled a name and phone number on the back. When Alliford handed him the copy, he handed him the card in return.

"This is my priest. He's got an open mind."

Alliford took the card and nodded. He studied the name for a moment and then stuck the card into his shirt pocket. "Thanks."

O'Fallon folded the copy and tucked it away. "Thanks for your time."

"Have I helped you?" Alliford asked.

Guilt rose. Alliford was a genuinely nice guy. How much hurt would he feel when he learned that the witch was only after his money? That she'd lied about hearing his dead son?

"Yes, you have." O'Fallon hesitated, feeling the need to offer more. "Talk to Father Elliot. He's helped me more than once."

Alliford pulled the card out again and then nodded slowly. "I will."

As they walked to the front entryway, O'Fallon heard a distant thumping and then laughter, as if a child were bouncing a ball inside the house. The hair on his neck rose.

He gave Alliford a startled look.

"It's Bradley," the father explained.

O'Fallon swallowed. It didn't lessen the tightness in his throat. "Does he do that all the time?"

"No, only off and on." The man took a deep breath. "We just need to find Merlin."

O'Fallon thought for a moment and then asked, "Did you get the dog from the pound?"

"No, we bought him from a breeder. Why do you ask?"

"Does he have one of those microchips—you know, the kind they can scan if the animal gets lost?"

Alliford shook his head, an expression of deep regret covering his face. "He didn't have one of those."

"Well, maybe you'll get lucky."

"God, I hope so." They shook hands again.

Alliford opened the front door and then paused, transfixed.

"Janet?" He took a couple of steps outside the house. "Janet?" he repeated.

A cab sat near the front of the house, a vigorous argument in progress between the driver and the passenger. Something to do with the fare.

"I'll pay you," she shouted. "Just wait."

The man answered in broken English, gesturing wildly.

"Wait!" the woman said. "Just wait!"

Janet Alliford entered the house like it was the first time she'd visited, her gait uneven and her eyes darting in all directions. As she walked past O'Fallon, a frown appeared, as if she was trying to place him. Her hair was unkempt, her garments rumpled, her nail polish chipped. O'Fallon detected a fine body tremor. The tremor increased, and she hugged her arms across her chest in a protective gesture.

Coke or meth? O'Fallon pondered. It wasn't booze, though she probably had some of that in her system as well. He settled on cocaine as the addiction of choice.

"What are you doing here?" Alliford demanded. Outside the cabbie kept shouting in his native language, advancing toward the house, gesticulating wildly.

Janet hugged herself harder.

"I . . . need to talk to you, Greg," she said. Another look in O'Fallon's direction.

The cabbie was almost to the door. O'Fallon pulled a couple of twenties out of his wallet and intercepted the driver before he came inside. The couple stared at each other, oblivious, caught in their own private hell.

By the time he'd settled with the irate man and got a couple questions answered in the process, things were at a boil inside the house.

"That's why you're here? You need money? That's the only reason?" Alliford shouted.

Janet nodded, looking around nervously.

"You don't say hello, how are you; you just demand money. Well, I'll make a deal, Janet. Tell me where Merlin is, and I'll give you enough cash to pack your nose tonight. How's that?"

The woman blinked in surprise. "Merlin? Why do you care about him?" she asked.

"Because of our son. You do remember Bradley, don't you?"

Janet visibly flinched. "I don't know where the dog is."

"You took him!" Alliford advanced a step, and she staggered backward in response.

O'Fallon grew more uncomfortable. This had all the makings of a domestic brawl in the making.

"I just . . . wanted company. He . . . ran away," Janet said.

She wasn't a good liar.

"If you could give us a general idea where he got . . . lost," O'Fallon said, throwing his voice into the fray.

"Who are you?" she asked, squinting in his direction. He winced—he'd seen corpses with nicer eyes.

"Douglas O'Fallon," he said.

A strange look came to her face. "You're the investigator my mother hired, aren't you?" she charged.

O'Fallon gave a short nod. *Oh, damn.*

Alliford's fury refocused. "You lied to me," he fumed, pointing his finger at the PI.

"No, I just didn't tell you who my client was. The rest was on the money."

"Why the hell does she want to know about Gavenia?"

O'Fallon mentally tossed a coin and opted for the truth. "She thinks Ms. Kingsgrave's trying to run a scam on you using your son as the bait."

"That's ridiculous! Gavenia's not after my money."

"Then why is she here?" Janet demanded.

Alliford smirked at his wife. "Not for what you think, either. She's here to help Bradley."

"Then Mother needs to stay out of this," Janet said, switching sides with astonishing speed—no doubt a move designed to score some cash off her husband when the shouting ended.

O'Fallon felt the tide turning. *Just like a domestic. The battling couple unites against a common enemy, usually the cop.* In this case the enemy was Mrs. Pearce. But since she was safely in Palm Springs and he was her proxy . . .

As if on cue, Alliford turned on O'Fallon. "Get the hell out of my house before I have your license revoked."

O'Fallon accepted both his dismissal and the threat graciously. "Thank you for your help, Mr. Alliford."

He waited outside the house, leaning against the car. Janet Alliford appeared a few minutes later, shouting abuse. The front door slammed behind her, and he could hear the sound of locks engaging from twenty feet away. Janet stumbled into the driveway and then jerked her eyes around, bewildered. Apparently, she hadn't realized he'd dismissed the cab.

The shakes overwhelmed her as she teetered against a concrete planter, her face mottled and tear stained.

"I'll give you a ride," O'Fallon said.

"Why?"

"Because your husband's not going to change his mind."

"He's fucking crazy," she said.

"It must be going around." O'Fallon gestured, and she stumbled toward the car. He made no effort to help her.

As he pulled onto the street, she sniffled and rubbed her nose with the back of her hand. "I'm not that bad."

"You're that bad and then some." She hadn't specified a destination, but given what the cabbie had told him, it would be someplace downtown, the heart of Skid Row. He turned toward the freeway.

"I don't give a damn what you think," she retorted. He thought he could hear a bit of her mother's arrogance in the words.

"Fine by me." He stopped talking. People hated silence and often they'd babble just to fill the void. Janet Alliford didn't. For a time he thought she'd fallen asleep. She roused as he took the exit off the 110 toward the heart of LA.

"Where are we going?" she asked, staring out the passenger window.

"Downtown."

She eyed him. "Why?"

"Where else would you be? You can't go back to Palm Springs, and Gregory has cut you off. Skid Row knows your kind."

"It's because of . . ."

"Go on."

"Because of Bradley."

Righteous indignation flared within him. "That story might play with the other addicts, but not with me. You were coking up way before your son's death."

The blow on his arm surprised him, as did the second one. He was in no position to fend her off, so he drove on, sensing her anger would run out of steam. The third strike was lighter.

"I'm not a good substitute for your mother," he said.

"You son of a bitch."

He glared at her. "Leave my sainted mother out of this."

"If she's like mine, she's no saint." Janet's hands twisted in her lap, and her body twitched to its own rhythm.

"No, she was nothing like yours."

She gave him an odd expression. "Mother's to blame for this. I'm not strong, not like my sister, Emily. Mother always said so."

O'Fallon frowned. "Your mother is a coldhearted, self-centered bitch, Mrs. Alliford. That's the truth of it. Either you suck up and deal, or you're going to martyr yourself on her altar. And trust me, she'll guilt you every step of the way."

The woman's mouth fell open. He wondered if anyone had ever been that blunt about her mother. If she ratted him out to Mrs. Pierce his job would vanish.

So be it. "Your dead son needs your help. Where's Merlin?"

She shook her head. "I just . . . dumped him on the street."

He could hear the lie. "Try that again."

"I left him on the street," she insisted.

"How could you do that?"

Janet shook her head, refusing to answer.

"Why did you take him in the first place?" he probed.

"Like I said, I wanted—"

"No! Tell me the truth."

Janet bit her lip and then shook her head in a pathetic gesture. "I wanted somebody who liked me," she said in a childlike voice.

He drove the length of Main and, at her request, stopped in front of the old Los Angeles Children's Museum.

She stared out the window for a time.

"I always wanted to come here as a kid, but *she* would never bring me." A shuddering breath. "Now it's closed."

As the woman exited the car, he slipped her a twenty though it would, no doubt, go up her nose.

She gave him a wan smile. "Thank you."

"Good luck," he said. The words felt empty. Deep in his heart, he knew that luck had very little to do with Janet Alliford's future.

* * *

"How ya doing?" Viv asked, kneeling at Gavenia's side.

"Better," Gavenia replied, and then took another sip of Moonbeam tea. She'd retreated to Crystal Horizons seeking sanctuary. The moment she'd entered the building she'd headed for the hidden fairy behind the books. Touching her had helped.

"I can't believe he'd just say something like that," Viv muttered under her breath while keeping an eye on a browsing customer. "Was Winston . . . married?"

There was the problem. In the first few minutes after O'Fallon had unloaded on her, Gavenia fell into deep denial. By the time Bart had calmed her down, the truth had seeped into her pores like raw acid.

"It's possible," she said. Now that she thought about it, she remembered he had a roving eye and spent a lot of time on the phone to his "secretary." "Yeah, definitely possible."

Viv wisely didn't comment, but headed toward her customer. As she helped the lady pick out an appropriate quartz crystal, Bart appeared at Gavenia's side, concerned.

"Winston knew I wouldn't date married guys. Why did he lie to me?" she whispered.

You'll have to ask him.

Gavenia shook her head instantly. She took a sip of the tea and then asked, "Why did the PI tell me something like that?"

Because you hurt him.

"What do you mean?" she asked, furrowing her brows.

Think about it. He promptly vanished. She took a long sip of the tea, inhaling the aroma while Viv showed the customer her selection of amethyst clusters.

Gavenia replayed the encounter between her and O'Fallon and then groaned. She'd dinged him on his failed marriages—gloated about them—and then he'd struck back with Winston. They kept drawing blood each time they squared off.

"He's an ally, not an enemy," Viv said. The customer was gone, and now Gavenia vaguely remembered the sound of the cash register and then the triple chime of the front door. Apparently Viv had decided a tarot reading was in order. Sorry; I was off in my own world," Gavenia said.

"I figured." Viv held up a card. "Your PI is a questing knight, always in search of the truth. He's a good guy, despite his lack of manners."

Gavenia opened her mouth to protest and then abandoned the effort. Viv and the cards were right—O'Fallon wasn't the enemy.

"So what are we in for?"

Viv held up another card. Gavenia's mouth dropped open.

"Not a chance."

Viv ignored her protest. "The Lovers—either you two are going to become hot and heavy or you're going to form a partnership."

Gavenia scrunched her face. "Maybe a partnership, because I can't imagine . . ." She paused, thinking of what it would be like to kiss the Irish guy. Still, every time they'd met, he'd been an ass, and after the con game Winston had played on her . . . "Partnership," she announced firmly, as if that would settle the issue. "What else?"

Viv whistled and held up the Tower card—a horrific vision of lightning striking a tall tower as figures tumbled to their deaths on the rocks below.

"Looks like the crap is going to hit the fan and you'd better have a very large umbrella," Viv said, gathering the cards back into a single stack. "More tea?"

Despite the pounding in her temples, Gavenia nodded, holding out her cup in a quaking hand.

"Make it a double."

Chapter Twelve

Driven by some deep need, O'Fallon visited all six charities listed on the sheet within two hours, racing from one to the other like a man possessed. He'd come away from each laden with pamphlets and donation forms. They all had two things in common: all were legit, and Ms. Kingsgrave was not involved in their day-to-day operations. Four of them had never heard of the witch; the other two recognized her name solely because donors had mentioned her in passing.

Now, as he sat in his car staring blankly at the pile of brochures in his lap, he could hear Avery's voice as clearly as if the man were sitting next to him.

Epiphany, prove thyself.

If this had been a criminal investigation, O'Fallon would have crossed Ms. Kingsgrave off the suspect list long ago. Just as Avery had cautioned, he'd allowed personal bias to cloud his judgment. Her gift was genuine. If she had a weakness, it was her taste in men. Other than that, Gavenia Kingsgrave was on the level. Somehow he did not think Mommie Dreadful in Palm Springs would be pleased with the truth.

* * *

Gavenia shifted positions to ease the cramp in her back from leaning over the deep-sink. Nearby, Ari stacked pots on the wide shelves in the shelter's kitchen. They'd served fifty-three tonight, a new record. Cleanup wasn't a snap, at least from Gavenia's point of view.

"Am I done yet?" she asked, her hands pruned from the sudsy water.

"You're really close. Only one more," Ari replied.

"She's not whining, is she?" their Aunt Lucy asked from her place at a small desk in the corner, head bent over paperwork. Her short silver-gray hair stopped at her ears; reading glasses perched on the end of her nose. Bart leaned nearby, his face registering benign disinterest.

"Oh, no, I'm not whining," Gavenia said. "I'm too tired to whine."

"Here, Cinderella, this is the last one," Ari said, plunking an immense pot down on the counter next to the sink. Gavenia hoisted it into the water and scrubbed.

"I tangled with that PI again," she said as she worked on the pot's interior. She'd decided not to share Winston's secret, at least for the time being. Time would allow her to come to grips with that personal earthquake.

"You have a private investigator following you?" Lucy asked, her attention pulled away from the paperwork.

"Yup. He thinks I'm trying to scam one of my clients."

"Do you want me to have someone call him off?" her aunt offered.

Gavenia rinsed the pot and placed it on the countertop, pondering the offer. Lucy had enough clout that she could make that happen, but it didn't seem right. The guy was only doing his job, despite annoying the hell out of her in the process.

"No, he'll get bored and go away."

"You hope," Ari added. "Oh, I found out a bit about Janet Alliford."

"And?" Gavenia asked, drying her hands on a rough terry-cloth towel.

"You want the short or the long version?"

"Short."

"Married Gregory Alliford over her mother's objections, has a genuine affinity for cocaine, been in and out of rehab a number of times, and is overly concerned about her mother's goodwill."

No surprises there, Bart murmured.

Gavenia nodded. "That fits what her sister, Emily, told me on the phone. Anything on Mrs. Pearce?"

Lucy's head came up from the papers. "Augusta Pearce?" she asked.

"That's the one," Gavenia replied. An ice-cream bar would hit the spot right now, but the shelter appeared woefully lacking in those necessities of life. She made a mental note to bring down a few cases.

"Be careful of that one. She's got a ruthless streak," Lucy advised.

"Tangled with her before?"

"Oh, definitely. Nasty piece of work under those designer clothes. Heart of absolute granite."

"I noticed. We met a few days back."

Her aunt eyed her. "I'm impressed. You have fewer scars than I would anticipate."

"We mutually agreed to loathe each other."

"She'll keep pushing until she gets what she wants."

Ari nodded in agreement and leaned against a counter. "Word is that Mrs. Pearce intends to hire a detective to find Janet. She wants her locked up so she doesn't embarrass the family."

"What if Janet doesn't want to be locked up?"

Ari's face grew solemn. "That isn't Mrs. Pearce's concern."

"Is O'Fallon the guy she hired to do the deed?" Gavenia asked.

"I don't know."

Gavenia frowned in thought. "Nobody has a clue where Merlin is?"

"Nope," Ari replied. "It's like he doesn't exist."

"Unreal." Gavenia looked around the kitchen. "Am I done?"

"You're done," Ari reported. "Same time tomorrow night."

"Okay, I'll bring my spare pair of hands and some ice-cream bars." After brushing a kiss on her aunt's cheek, she exited into the back parking lot, Bart at her side.

Staring up into the night sky, she asked, "Where art thou, Merlin?" When no comet blazed in the heavens to light the way, she dragged herself into the car, weary. She knew what she had to do, and it irked her.

"O'Fallon is the key," she said. "He knows how to work an investigation. I have to convince him to help me."

And just how do you intend to do that? Bart asked from the passenger seat. He was now dressed in the saffron robes of a Buddhist monk, and she decided not to call him on it.

"I will have to turn on the charm," she said.

Now we're in trouble.

* * *

It wasn't O'Fallon's first gay bar, but this time he wasn't toting a badge and in the midst of an official investigation. The Out-Rageous Onion certainly wasn't one of the more over-the-top queer bars in LA; in fact, it had a reputation for being quite tame. He still felt out of his depth.

He took a deep breath, exhaled loudly, locked the car, and straightened his jacket. It was on the chilly side now that night had fallen, and the jacket was his personal favorite, one that made him feel comfortable no matter the situation. Tonight it wasn't working its magic.

It made sense that Adam had chosen this particular bar: the Out-Rageous Onion was his home turf, and it was very unlikely that any of the cops from his precinct would be within ten miles of the place. A perfect location to meet with someone you didn't want to be seen with.

"But still," O'Fallon muttered, straightening his jacket once again in a self-conscious gesture. With another long sigh, he strode toward the door.

The bar's interior was rather chic, with sky-blue decor, low lighting, and music subtle enough to permit conversation. Once his eyes adjusted, he found he rather liked the place. It wasn't smoky or loud and, though most of the couples were of the same sex, it seemed quite pleasant. O'Fallon blew air through pursed lips, realizing he just couldn't stand near the door like a wooden Indian. Right before he moved farther into the bar, a young man in a royal-blue silk shirt and tight leather pants paused in front of him, grinned, and announced, "Flamin'!"

O'Fallon frowned. "Pardon?"

"Your hair," the man said, pointing upward at O'Fallon's locks. "Flamin' red. Cool color." After a thumbs-up, the fellow rejoined his companion in a nearby booth.

"Apparently, I'm a hit," O'Fallon mumbled under his breath. He made his way through the crowd to the bar, ordered an overpriced beer, and surveyed the situation. A familiar face caught his attention. To his chagrin it wasn't Adam, but Frank Dunston, one of the cops O'Fallon used to work with in West Hollywood. He sat at a table with another young man, and they were holding hands. Dunston's eyes widened, and then a knowing smile appeared on his face. He raised his beer bottle in salute.

Dammit. He'd never known Dunston was homosexual. He gave a quick nod, silently cursing his luck. Telling Dunston he wasn't gay would sound lame; it was best to let the moment pass. Keen to avoid awkward conversation, he moved toward the back of the building, wiggling through the couples. No sign of Avery's son. He fidgeted, trying to keep his face neutral so as not to attract unwanted interest.

Two men were kissing in the corner, cuddling close, deeply in lust. He averted his eyes. Nothing about the scene aroused him— not like a woman with pretty eyes and a well-turned behind.

As it should be. When his last therapist had told him that Seamus was acting as an "outward manifestation" of O'Fallon's "inward hostility toward the female sex" and that he might be gay, he'd put a prompt end to those therapy sessions.

"Psycho bullshit," he grumbled. "I just haven't met the right woman yet."

As if on cue, a lady with long blond hair walked by, hand in hand with a young man. Her eyes were nice, but nothing to compare with Gavenia Kingsgrave's sapphire gems. He thought about the witch for a moment and then shook his head. No matter how gorgeous her blue eyes, her body was forbidden fruit. Still, his mind tugged at him, pulling forward an image of the witch lying nude on his bed and all the untold delights that might be in store.

He bulldozed those erotic thoughts out of his brain.

Pagans pave the road to hell.

A discreet tap on his shoulder. He prepared himself for the come-on. Instead, he found himself scrutinized by a tall, goateed individual in impeccable clothes. The jacket alone would have cost most of O'Fallon's monthly pension.

"You O'Fallon?"

He nodded in response.

The guy beckoned. "This way."

O'Fallon trailed behind, weaving through the mélange of couples, some male, some female, and some heterosexual. His apprehension dropped a couple of notches despite the encounter with Dunston.

Avery Elliot's only son sat in a private room in the back of the club, a beer at his elbow. Once the goateed escort dropped O'Fallon in the designated place, he shut the door, insuring private conversation. In some ways, it felt like an illicit meeting right out of a dime detective novel, except Adam wasn't rolling a coin across his knuckles.

The young cop gestured to a chair. Buying time, O'Fallon took a swig of his own beer and then sat down. Adam had called this meeting; it was up to him to set the agenda.

"Ever been to a gay bar before?" the young detective asked.

"More than once. But always on duty."

"Did you get hit on tonight?"

"No. But one guy liked my hair."

"Disappointed?" Adam challenged, as if spoiling for a fight.

O'Fallon grinned, not willing to take the bait. "Not really. My taste swings toward uptight Catholic matrons." The witch flittered through his mind again. To distract himself, he took another sip of beer. "So what's up?"

Adam leaped right in, as if he'd had trouble keeping his emotions bottled up. "I don't appreciate you talking to Dad about the precinct. He's got enough on his mind without worrying about me."

"Avery already knew the situation. Old cops never completely unplug from the network."

"I can handle this on my own," the young man retorted, his face marred by a deep frown.

"I have no doubt you can, but sometimes you just have to look at a situation and decide if it's worth the hassle."

"It'll work out." Adam's voice sounded unsure, despite the patina of bravado.

"Cops can be the best of angels or the worst of devils. You're in a dangerous situation. Sometimes your own can be the enemy."

"I'm going to stay. I'm not a quitter," the young man insisted. His body tensed, his knuckles white where they gripped the beer bottle.

"That's obvious. I'm just saying it would be better if you go somewhere you don't have to fight the bastards you work with."

"Not all of them are dirty."

"No, but your partner is, and if he goes down, you'll have a hell of a time proving you weren't in on the take."

Adam's eyes shifted down to the green tablecloth, and he studied it for a time. O'Fallon pressed on, sensing a breach in the young man's defenses.

"Internal Affairs will ream you just to get to him. They won't care if you're clean. And believe me, your name and sexual orientation will be in the papers when it goes to trial. You'll hurt your career, your father, and your . . . fellows all at the same time. Is this really worth all that?"

The young cop shifted the beer bottle, creating new rings on the tablecloth, deep in thought.

O'Fallon continued. "I've seen what can happen in your situation. I don't want you eating your gun someday just because of those bastards. You're too good of a cop."

The young man's eyes raised, and O'Fallon thought he saw a glimmer of gratitude.

"I used to be."

"You still are. You've got a chance to be every bit as good as your father. Just the get the hell out of there."

The young man's eyes narrowed. "You really think they'd hurt one of their own?"

O'Fallon took a long swig of his beer to let the tension play out. "I'd bet on it. Glass is a malicious SOB. I saw it in his eyes. He'd tear you apart and enjoy every moment of it."

Adam seemed to ponder this observation while shredding the label on his beer bottle with a fingernail.

"Dad said you found the kid's rosary. This evening, I overheard one of detectives saying you'd bought it at a pawnshop near the precinct."

"Those guys are more plugged in than I had realized." A disturbing thought arose. "I hope they don't think you fed that to me." He tried to remember what the other customer examining the pawnshop's guitars had looked like. Had he been an off-duty cop?

Adam shrugged. "I don't know what they think. Glass doesn't tell me anything, just treats me like I'm a moron."

"Keep your head down and get the hell out of there."

"Carey's been saying the same thing."

"Carey?"

Adam gave a faint smile. "He's my . . . significant other."

"I see. Your father didn't mention him."

"Dad's still dealing with the whole gay thing. It's even harder now that he's a priest."

O'Fallon nodded. "I understand. How long have you been together?"

"Six years."

He snorted. "God, that's longer than either one of my marriages."

That elicited a raised eyebrow. Unconsciously, the young man had copied some of his father's trademark gestures.

"Carey doesn't like me being a cop, but I can't leave the force. I've wanted to be a police officer from the moment I saw Dad in dress blues."

"Then do what is important to you, but just do it in another precinct."

"That might not be enough."

"Ah, I see," O'Fallon said. Irony twisted in his gut. He'd had this same conversation with Avery as his two marriages failed. Now he was on the receiving end.

"I wonder if we'll be able to hold it together," was the young man's solemn admission.

"Keep talking. That was my mistake. I held it all inside, and it killed any chance we had."

Adam gave a resigned nod. He pointed at O'Fallon's empty bottle. "Want another one?"

"Yeah, I do." After Adam left the room, O'Fallon gave a low whistle. Apparently it didn't matter if you were gay or straight—carrying the shield shredded lives.

There had been more talk than beer. In two hours O'Fallon learned a great deal about Adam Elliot: he idolized his father, loved the Dodgers, and had always wanted to sail around the world. His stint in the navy had only deepened that desire. His lover was a hard-charging civil rights attorney, and they lived on a boat. A young man with dreams, not unlike O'Fallon when he was thirty.

They paused their discussion in the middle of the Onion's parking lot. Adam clicked his remote, and an SUV two rows away flashed its lights and gave a welcoming chirp.

"My car's that way," O'Fallon said, gesturing in the opposite direction. "Keep in touch. I'm willing to be a sounding board, if you need one."

The young cop offered a sad smile. "Thanks, I appreciate it. Dad's good at listening, but he's got enough hassles with the church and all that."

O'Fallon leaned against a nearby car, studying his companion. "Don't ever doubt that you're the most important thing in his life. The church owns a big piece of him, but you're his son. You come first."

The smile grew brighter. "That's good to hear. I've always wanted to make him proud."

"You already have. You had the guts to let the world know you're gay."

There was a moment of hesitation, and Adam then asked, "What was it like when he told you?"

O'Fallon rummaged through his memory. "We were at breakfast. He was really tense, and I knew it didn't have anything to do with our current case. He just came out and said, 'Adam's gay.' He asked me what I thought he should do."

"What did you tell him?"

"I told he might not want to plan on any grandkids, but everything else would be the same. You're still his son, no matter what."

Adam looked away, and O'Fallon thought he saw a mist in the young man's eyes. "I always wondered how much it hurt him. He never said."

"It did in some ways, but it didn't in others."

"It's the way I am," the detective said, looking back.

O'Fallon nodded. "God fashions us to His own ends." A subtle beep from his watch announced the top of the hour—midnight. "I'd best be going."

"Thanks for the conversation."

"Not a problem. Call if you want to talk. Or you can come over and meet my roommate, Seamus." O'Fallon waited a moment before he delivered the punch line. "He's a parrot."

"Oh . . ." A quick smile flashed, one that reminded O'Fallon of Avery. "Does he speak Irish?"

"Sure does. And swears like a cop."

"I'd like to meet him."

"That can be arranged."

Adam stuck out his hand and they shook firmly.

"Watch your back," O'Fallon advised.

"I will." Adam turned and trudged across the parking lot toward the SUV, his shoulders hunched as if he was deep in thought.

O'Fallon wove his way through the cars until he reached his Chevy. It seemed like a wreck compared to the newer ones around to it. As he put the key in the lock, he heard a slight crunching sound. On instinct, he lurched sideways. A dark object flew past his head, impacting the roof with a solid thump. The driver's-side rear window exploded in a hailstorm of glass.

Before he could react, a fist caught him in the gut, and as he doubled over, another shot into his ribs. He swung blindly and connected with someone's midsection. Someone shouted, and then an impact in the center of his back sent him to his knees.

"Stay the fuck out of it, asshole. This is your wake-up call. You got it?" a voice snarled near his ear. A kick to his right ribs made him cry out. He slumped to the ground.

O'Fallon's stomach rebelled. He rolled to his side and lost the expensive beer. Through the roaring in his head he heard the sound of a car peeling onto the street. A pair of shoes came within his vision.

"Holy shit, O'Fallon, what the hell was that?"

Dunston. O'Fallon inwardly groaned. *Of all people.* With the man's aid, he made it to his knees and then to his feet. He leaned against his car, sucking in deep swallows of air to keep the rest of the beer down. Dunston hovered a short distance away, his date a few steps back sporting a wide-eyed expression.

"What the hell happened?" his rescuer demanded.

"Just a warning," O'Fallon said, wiping the blood from the corner of his mouth. "Teaches me to play it straight."

Chapter Thirteen

Gavenia hung up the phone, stared at the handwritten list, and drew a fat red line through one of the names. Now that she'd completed the translation of a complex employment contract from English into German for a corporate client, the hunt for Merlin was in full force. Her fingers were rapidly growing tired from tapping out the animal-shelter phone numbers.

"Any luck?" Ari asked, flying into the kitchen, her dead husband and her Guardian right behind.

"Not really. Lots of black puppies, but most came in before Bradley died."

"Oh, bother. How about some breakfast?" Ari asked, and then noticed the discarded ice-cream wrapper on the table. "Forget I asked."

"I'm screwing up my courage to call the Irish guy."

"Going to eat crow?"

"Hoping not to. I just need his expertise, not his goodwill."

"What if he refuses?"

Gavenia sighed, looking down at the long list in front of her. "Then life is really going to suck." Her cell phone began to vibrate and she snatched it up right before it launched itself off the tabletop.

The caller didn't even wait for her to say hello.

"Gavenia, it's Branwen. We got a problem."

When Gavenia absentmindedly liberated another ice-cream bar from the freezer, Ari glanced up and shook her head in disapproval. Gavenia stuck her tongue out in response. All the while Branwen rattled on at supersonic speed.

"Slow down; I can hardly understand you."

Gavenia wandered toward the room she'd designated as her temple, listening as Branwen continued on in a breathless voice. She stopped and gave Bastet a scratch. The cat was curled up on her plush cushion between two statues of her Egyptian goddess namesake.

"What are we going to do?" Branwen demanded, and then sucked in a deep breath. Belatedly, Gavenia realized she'd only been marginally paying attention. Most of the time you just let Branwen vent, and then she was fine. This morning appeared to be an exception.

"Why do we have to do anything?" Gavenia asked.

"But you did a reading for him."

"Who?"

A sigh echoed down the line. "Bill Jones. You know, the columnist guy."

"Columnist guy?" Gavenia stopped dead in her tracks, casting her eyes around the room. No Bart. That wasn't a good sign.

"Didn't you see the paper?" Branwen asked.

A thick knot of dread formed in her chest. "No, I've been busy with other things."

"The first article is a teaser, how *so-called* psychics trick the defenseless public by telling them all sorts of lies and bilking them out of their Social Security checks."

"Does it name anyone?" Gavenia asked, sinking into an armchair. She licked at the ice cream before it trailed down her wrist.

"Not in this article, but tomorrow he promises to relate his experience with Dazie Mazie."

Gavenia snorted. Miss Mazeline was one of LA's more infamous psychics—infamous because of her A-list Hollywood clients and her complete lack of anything resembling a psychic gift. What she lacked in true psychic expertise, she made up with impressive high-tech gimmickry.

"She deserves to get nailed," Gavenia said. "I went to one of her séances. What a show." Bart had collapsed on the floor, rolling in laughter. It had been nearly impossible to get him to leave, he'd found the evening so hilarious.

"It won't matter. They'll lump all of us together."

Gavenia's chest tightened. "I told him something he didn't like."

"Jones?"

"Yeah. Damn, this isn't good. Lucy doesn't want anything to cast doubt on the shelter."

"You don't think this will affect that, do you?" Branwen asked.

Gavenia sank further into the chair, leaning back, ice cream forgotten. "I hope not."

"Do you think Lady Lucinda knows?"

Gavenia heard the unspoken plea behind the question. The majority of the Wiccan community regarded her aunt with unabashed awe and always referred to her as Lady Lucinda. Gavenia held the inside edge as the elder's niece. Bad news should come from her.

She sighed. "I'll let her know."

"Thanks!" Branwen didn't bother to conceal her relief.

Gavenia disconnected the phone and resumed her ice-cream fix. Her aunt would want a straightforward assessment of the situation. She glanced at her watch. It was almost ten. She'd grab another ice-cream bar and make the trip to the Wiccan shelter.

Some things were better done in person.

* * *

Mrs. Pearce's maid opened the front door and stared at O'Fallon with wide eyes and an open mouth. O'Fallon knew how he looked—he'd seen himself in the mirror this morning. His right cheek was bruised and swollen, and his lip had split open. Fortunately, the rest of the damage was under his clothes. On the way to Palm Springs, he'd dropped his favorite suit at the cleaners, who'd assured him the bloodstains could be removed. It was a pity his ribs couldn't be repaired so easily.

"Douglas O'Fallon to see Mrs. Pearce," he said in a strong voice.

It was time to end this nonsense and focus on more important things.

Mrs. Pearce raised a thin eyebrow at his appearance. "I trust you weren't involved in some petty brawl that will find its way into the papers."

"No, I somehow forgot to make a police report."

She seemed mollified by that. "I wish to assign you another task, Mr. O'Fallon. I want you to find my daughter."

"What about Ms. Kingsgrave?"

"I suspect you will find that both matters are interrelated, that my son-in-law and that woman are behind my daughter's disappearance."

"Disappearance? I just saw Janet yesterday."

"What?" the woman sputtered, rising from behind that fortress of a desk. Grim satisfaction spread within him—he'd actually surprised the old dragon.

"She was at the Alliford place trying to shake money out of her husband for drugs."

Mrs. Pearce's eyes grew cold. "My daughter does not have a drug habit, Mr. O'Fallon."

He shook his head, not allowing her the delusion. "She was strung out."

"No, she wasn't. Is she still in Bel Air?"

"I dropped her in Skid Row."

"Why would you let her go there?" the woman fumed.

"That's where she wanted to go."

Mrs. Pierce shuddered and sank back into her leather chair.

"I want you to bring her here. I do not care how you accomplish it. I have a facility willing to take her."

There it was—a royal edict: find the wayward princess, drag her back to the castle, and we'll lock her in the turret for her own good.

"Are you suggesting I kidnap her?" O'Fallon asked.

"If that's what it takes."

"Kidnapping is a federal offense," he observed, wondering how far this woman would go to get her own way.

"You will have the best lawyers and a healthy bonus, if it comes to that."

O'Fallon grinned. "How wonderful. I'll be rich. Of course, I'll be in prison with some folks who'd love to settle scores, but hey, you just can't have everything."

Mrs. Pearce glared. "I want my daughter off the streets. This time I'll have her committed. It's the best way to get her treatment."

Apparently the princess-in-the-turret analogy wasn't too far-fetched. He wondered if a stray prince might show up to rescue her someday. But first, he'd have to slay the dragon. . . .

"Will you bring her here?" Mrs. Pearce asked, rising from her chair.

"Not unless she asks me to."

"Then you're off this case."

He nodded, pleased at how this had fallen out.

"Actually, I wrote you off yesterday. Ms. Kingsgrave's totally on the level." His former client seemed bewildered. "Surprises you, doesn't it? Well, that's two of us." He marched to the door. "Oh," he said, turning, "the one-week retainer is nonrefundable. I'll let myself out."

The woman didn't reply as she reached for her telephone, her face shading into a dark crimson. It wasn't her best color.

* * *

Lucy slowly removed her glasses and pushed the morning's paper across the table toward Gavenia. They were sitting in the shelter's dining room. The enticing scent of roast turkey drifted in the air as pans rattled in the kitchen.

"You already knew," Gavenia said. She shouldn't be surprised; little got past her aunt.

"I always read the morning paper, unlike you."

"So what do we do?"

Lucy scrutinized her with those serious brown eyes. "Was the reading you gave this Jones person on the mark?"

"Yes," Gavenia snapped, more forcefully than she wanted. "Sorry. I'm worried about this."

Lucy nodded. She seemed weary, as if the news was one more weight she couldn't afford to carry. The shelter was her baby, a means for the Pagan community to become more proactive, more mainstream. Bad publicity could dynamite the whole project.

"Let's hope it blows over. I prefer not to stir things up, but if the article proves libelous, you might consider a lawsuit. If so, call Llewellyn and he can file the papers."

Llewellyn, her aunt's boyfriend, was a top-rated attorney. For some reason she hadn't thought of asking him for help.

Lucy continued, "I'll let the community know Mr. Jones is off-limits, magicwise. There will be an uproar, I'm sure. It'll take some time to repair the damage."

"I had no idea he wasn't on the level."

"Bart didn't warn you?" her aunt asked.

Gavenia shook her head. "He was as blind to it as I was."

"Hmm . . . that's interesting," Lucy said. She tapped an index finger on her upper lip in thought. "Well, what's done is done. Keep your cool and we'll make it through this." She reached across the table and took Gavenia's quaking hand in hers. "You didn't do anything wrong."

The words hung between them and called forth memories. Her aunt had said those very words after the kidnapping. Said them over and over to try to reassure Gavenia it hadn't been her fault that a young girl had been spirited away, held captive, and threatened by two human monsters.

You didn't do anything wrong.

"Gavenia?"

She pulled herself back to the present. "I just didn't want to bring any harm to the shelter. It's too important."

"It'll work out." Lucy leaned forward and embraced her niece. "Tonight, seven o'clock. And no whining this time."

Gavenia smiled in return. "No whining."

As she cleared the back door of the shelter, her cell phone rang. The caller ID made her do a double take. *O'Fallon.* Maybe she wouldn't have to eat crow after all.

Chapter Fourteen

O'Fallon found the witch in a booth toward the back of Earth, Wind, and Fire, intently studying a newspaper article. Her hair hung loose, draping over her shoulders, cascading in deep waves. The paper quivered in her right hand, and she bit her lip in concentration. He made a slight noise so as not to startle her, and her eyes went from sea blue to deep midnight in a heartbeat. Her mouth fell open just like the maid's in Palm Springs.

"Good Goddess. What happened to you?"

"Slipped in the shower," he said. He took a deep breath. The smell of incense jostled in the air with the scent of fresh baked goods.

"Looks like a lot more than a close encounter with a bar of Irish Spring."

He tried to smile. It hurt. "All in the line of duty."

"Something to do with the Alliford case?" she asked.

He'd already run that notion through his brain and discarded it. "No, doesn't feel right." He slowly slid into the booth, his right side protesting the movement. The pain pills were wearing off.

"Are you still working for Mrs. Pearce?"

"No. She fired me this morning."

"Why?" Gavenia blurted.

"Because I let her know that you were legit."

A brief smile crossed her lips and then vanished. She glanced down at the paper, quickly folded it, and slid it to the side of the table as if it held some dark secret.

She eyed him. "I have damn little reason to trust you, O'Fallon."

That was blunt. "Ditto." He pointed at her cup. "What is that stuff?"

"Moonbeam tea. You want some?" He gingerly nodded. "Did you see a doctor?"

"Yes. Lots of bruises, nothing broken."

"Thank the Goddess." She slid out of the booth and caned her way to the counter. He took the opportunity to try to ease a cramp out of his back. It didn't work, but only made his ribs ache more.

At least we're not shouting at each other.

Gavenia returned with cups of tea and cranberry scones. She pushed one of each toward him.

The PI gave her a faint smile. "I owe you an apology, Ms. Kingsgrave. It wasn't right for me to use your boyfriend's marital status as a weapon."

Gavenia bit her lip in response and her hand trembled where it sat on top of the table. She put it in her lap. His eyes followed its descent, and she thought she saw pity.

His voice lowered. "You didn't know he was married?"

She gave a sharp intake of breath and then a quick shake of her head. She stared at the far wall of the café, focusing on a large poster touting an upcoming Celtic concert to keep the tears at bay. "All the signs were there. I was just ignoring them."

"I'm sorry I was the one to tell you."

Gavenia pressed on. "Why did you call me, Mr. O'Fallon?"

"I want to help you find Merlin."

"Why?"

"Then I'll know that at least one member of the Alliford household is at peace."

That sounded reasonable. She took a long sip of tea to work it through. No crow eating required, yet she hesitated. She owed him something.

"I want to apologize as well. I shouldn't have . . . it wasn't right to mention your . . . marital history, either."

Their eyes met. "We both have scars, Ms. Kingsgrave."

Gavenia gave him a wan smile. "Yeah, we do." She dug in her purse and pulled out the list and handed it to him. "I've just started to weed through the animal shelters. There's a ton of them. If we could find Janet Alliford—"

"I talked to her yesterday when I drove her to Skid Row. She's no help. She says she dropped the dog off downtown, but that sounded false."

Gavenia's estimation of the PI rose. "Is there anything we can do for her?"

"Not to sound cold, Ms. Kingsgrave, but she's too far gone. Unless she can deal with the mommy hatred, she's headed for the grave."

"How can you be so sure of that?" she challenged.

"I've seen it too many times."

She involuntarily shivered. "You're right, it is cold."

His eyes grew sad. "I know," he said. "It's how I cope."

"It hurts you," she murmured.

"Pardon?"

"Never mind." She glanced at her watch. "Okay, what do we do?"

"I think we should go back to my place, lay out a map, and start working a grid pattern. We'll check the animal shelters' websites based on the map."

Gavenia's mind stuck on the first part of the plan. "Your place?"

He nodded. "I figured after the stalker problem you had a couple years back, you'd not want to go to your condo."

"What don't you know about me?" she demanded.

He leaned forward in response, a slightly roguish grin on his face. "Well, I don't know your favorite wine or if you wear pajamas to bed."

"Fumé Blanc, and I sleep in the nude."

They eyed each other, neither giving an inch. "See, now you're no longer an enigma," he said, spreading his hands. "Well, I'll just have to think up more questions."

Gavenia allowed herself a grin that matched his. The Irish guy had style. "So where do you live?" she asked.

He pulled out a notebook, ripped out a page, and penned directions in between sips of the Moonbeam. She noted he hadn't complained about the tea. Another point in his column.

"I should warn you I have a rather unique roommate," he said, his eyes flickering up to hers.

"Is this roomie as unpleasant as you are?" she asked, dismantling the cranberry scone into manageable pieces.

"Yes, he can be. Seamus is a bit of a character." He laid the paper next to her cup.

"Seamus? Oh, give me a break."

"Pardon?"

Gavenia pointed at him. "Your last name's O'Fallon; you've got red hair, an Irish brogue, a Saint Christopher medal in your car, a roommate named Seamus; and you used to be a cop. Goddess, you're a walking stereotype."

His jaw tightened. "I'm not the one who sees ghosts, sister."

They eyed each other warily.

Gavenia raised her hands in surrender. "Okay, I give up. Anything to get Merlin and Bradley together. Then you can go away, and I can get back to my life."

"Works for me."

"So is Seamus your lover?" she asked, with a hint of mischief.

He answered with an irritated shake of his head. "Seamus is a parrot."

"What kind?"

"An African gray." His tone sounded as if he was waiting for her to challenge him about having a bird for a pet.

"That's cool." She studied the directions. The writing was amazingly legible for a guy's. "Give me an hour or so. I've got an errand to run."

He nodded. "Let's meet there at"—he studied his watch—"three. Have you eaten?"

"Nothing substantial but this scone." *Plus a couple ice-cream bars.*

"I'll pick up a pizza. You aren't one of the vegetable people, are you?" he asked.

"You mean . . . vegan?"

"Yeah, one of those who won't eat something if it used to have big brown eyes."

"Not a problem."

"Thank God." He rose. "At three, then." O'Fallon dropped a ten on the table, rolled his cranberry scone in a couple of napkins, and made his way out of the café without another word.

Gavenia started to snicker, not able to help herself. The snickering grew to muted laughter after the Irish guy exited the front door.

"Goddess, he's a piece of work."

* * *

O'Fallon's apartment building was nondescript, a two-story complex. Apparently, a cop's pension wasn't that bountiful, or the PI was the frugal sort. A crew of painters attacked the exposed wood trim like hyperactive monkeys from a forest of ladders and scaffolding. Animated conversation flowed downward from the scaffolding in a variety of languages. Two painters were debating, in Russian, whether Gavenia's breasts were real or otherwise. One of them claimed only women from their home country had real breasts. The other disagreed.

Gavenia pulled open the front door to the complex and paused as the debate continued above her. She couldn't resist.

"They are real," she announced in flawless Russian. One of the painters dropped his brush in astonishment and it hit his boot, splashing white around his ankles. Trickles splattered the ground near Gavenia's cane. The other painter laughed heartily, slapping him on the back.

"Very nice!" he called down in a thick accent.

"You're welcome," she replied.

* * *

O'Fallon found his guest sitting on the floor outside his apartment, relaxing against the wall, her eyes closed. When she heard him, she gave him a wry smile.

"Had to stop for some hair dye?" she teased.

"No. Actually, it increases my mojo to have women lined up outside my apartment door."

She chuckled, reached for her cane, and levered herself into a standing position. He saw a brief flash of discomfort. Belatedly he realized he should have offered to help.

"You could have waited in the car," he noted as he shifted the pizza box and cola to unlock the door.

"And run the testosterone gauntlet again?" she said, angling her head toward the parking lot. "Thanks, but once was enough."

"They give you a rough time?" he asked, frowning.

"Not really, unless you consider having your breasts critiqued a hard time."

"Don't know, I've never had that happen."

She scrutinized his chest. "I can see why."

He swung the door open and headed for the wailing alarm. Four quick jabs at the keypad disarmed it, but the noise continued. Gavenia turned in the direction of the sound: a large gray parrot.

"Ah, the infamous Seamus," she said.

The siren abruptly ceased. "About damned time!" the bird shouted.

"Give me a break, will you?" O'Fallon replied.

"No break, no break!"

Gavenia quirked a smile. The parrot marched back and forth on his perch, watching them intently. She headed for the cage, leaning over to inspect its occupant.

"Hi there, Seamus," she said. "I've heard about you."

"Woo-hoo. Fresh meat!" the bird called.

"Seamus, behave yourself," O'Fallon scolded.

The bird appeared to think that through and then spouted, "Woo-hoo. Pretty lady, pretty lady."

"That's better," O'Fallon replied, nodding his approval.

"He's gorgeous," Gavenia said. "I've never see an African gray in person."

"Spring me, spring me!" the bird called.

"He wants out to say hi to you. Are you okay with that?"

"Sure."

"If he frightens you, let me know," O'Fallon cautioned.

"He's not as scary as some people I know," she said, giving her host a knowing look.

O'Fallon ignored the jibe. "Let me stick this stuff in the kitchen first."

"Spring me, judge!" the bird called.

"He will. Give him a minute," Gavenia replied.

"Seamus," the bird said, clawing his way up the side of the cage, apparently in an effort to get a closer look at her.

"I know."

"Seamus," the bird repeated a bit louder, as if she'd not heard him the first time.

It dawned on her what he wanted and she knew her actual name would be too difficult. "I'm Tinker." He tilted his head. "Tinker," she repeated.

"Tink . . . er?"

"Yes. Tinker. Glad to meet you, Seamus."

"Tinker!" the bird proclaimed.

"You got it." She held up a small plastic bag. "I brought something for you."

"Yo, Tinker! Spring me!"

She chuckled and wandered away from the cage, much to Seamus's annoyance. A faint rustling sound came from the kitchen; followed by the oven door opening and closing, and then the refrigerator. All the while the bird kept up a litany of pleas for clemency.

The apartment was a surprise. She'd expected a typical bachelor pad replete with dirty plates and half-eaten food. This was the opposite; everything seemed to have its place. The previous day's newspaper was in a box by the front door, ready to recycle. The small dining table was immaculate, and pictures were artfully displayed on one wall.

Her eyes grazed through the photos—this man's life in retrospect. She recognized his father immediately. The photo of O'Fallon as a baby with his mother reminded her of a Madonna and Child. His mother radiated a benevolent grace. More photos, including that of an older woman, probably a grandmother. A wedding photo of her host, in a tux, with a very pretty young woman. Another wedding photo. This wife was blond and heavier than the first. He seemed more careworn that time around. Gavenia found that intriguing. Most guys wouldn't have pictures of their exes in plain sight.

Then came the cop photos: O'Fallon in uniform, O'Fallon receiving some sort of award. The series abruptly ended with a framed invitation to Detective Third Grade Douglas O'Fallon's retirement party, dated nearly two years earlier.

But nothing since. Another look toward the kitchen where the noises continued. *As if his life ended the day he retired.*

Impressive, don't you think? Bart said as he appeared next to her.

"Not bad," she said, unwilling to give an inch.

I wonder what your wall would look like? Before she could answer, he faded out of view.

"Damn you," she whispered.

I heard that.

O'Fallon found his guest studying the photographs. "Not many people ever look at those," he said, placing two glasses of cola on an end table near the couch.

"I like to. They tell me about the person who chose them."

"So what's the verdict?" he asked.

She looked back at the wall and pointed toward a photo. "Your mother had a bright heart. That comes through, even in a photo."

He nodded. "She was a very good woman. She died too young."

"They always do," she said in a softer voice.

"I'm sorry, that was tactless. You lost your mom when you were nine," he said.

A nod. "Breast cancer."

"And your dad?"

"Gone. He packed up and left Mom when she told him about her illness." A long inhalation. "If Aunt Lucy hadn't taken us in . . ."

What kind of man deserts his wife and kids? "You've never seen him since?" O'Fallon asked.

"No. It's best I never do," she said, her tone bitter.

"What about the two wives?" he asked, gesturing toward the photos in an effort to change the subject.

"The first looks like she was sure of what she was doing."

"That would be right. Martha and I married young. My work tore us apart."

"And the second one?"

"Shirley . . ." He sighed. "She decided to go all New Age on me."

"Oops."

"Yeah. That's a mistake I won't make again." In some perverse way, he hoped she'd argue with him.

"I see," she said, not offering anything more.

"Hey, dying here!" the parrot called.

Gavenia turned toward the cage, a wide smile brightening her face. "Parrots and two-year-olds have a lot in common," she observed.

"Tell me about it," O'Fallon replied. He opened the cage and removed the bird, apprehensive. This could end up with his guest requiring stitches. He set the parrot on the sofa and motioned for Gavenia to have a seat.

Seamus made a beeline for the Gavenia, his usual way of vetting newcomers. If the visitor freaked, he'd retreat to his cage and sulk. If it looked like he was going to be tolerated, he'd test the newcomer. He was relentless when it came to doing his duty.

After his guest and the bird settled on the couch, O'Fallon fussed around the room, trying not to telegraph his nervousness. Maybe if they were lucky, Seamus would give this one a pass.

He heard the rustle of a plastic sack. "You're a very fine parrot, Seamus. I suspect your reputation has been a bit overblown." A second later, O'Fallon heard, "Hey! Ouch!"

Seamus had latched on to her left index finger with his powerful beak. With a bit more pressure he could snap the bone.

The parrot waited as if to judge Gavenia's reaction.

O'Fallon started across the room, aggravated. "Don't move, I'll get him to—," he began.

Gavenia shook her head and waved him off with her free hand.

"No problem. We just need to come to an understanding." He could tell the beak was inflicting pain, but blood wasn't dripping, at least not yet.

She leaned over and addressed the bird directly. "Seamus, if you crunch down on my finger, I will have to go to the ER, and you will not be able to eat these blueberries." She rustled the sack that sat next to her and fished out a single blue orb, holding it in such a way that the bird could see it. "You let go, I'll feed you the berries. So what's it going to be?" O'Fallon saw her bit her inside lip after she spoke, evidence that the bird's bite was increasing in pressure.

Seamus kept his beak in place for a time as if thinking through his options.

"Well, gee, I wonder if there are any *nice* parrots around that might like these," she said. She popped a berry into her mouth and then cooed, "Oh, boy, was that good."

Seamus unclamped his beak and called, "Yo! Berries!"

"That's better," Gavenia said, pulling a couple more out of the bag and placing them on her palm. Seamus dove in. Her index finger sported a red mark, but there didn't seem to be any permanent damage.

O'Fallon's jaw fell slack. Gavenia hadn't screamed and tried to fling the parrot away like a Frisbee. Instead she'd bribed the rascal with fruit. *I'll be damned.*

The answer was obvious. "You've been around parrots before," he said.

She nodded, watching the bird gnaw on a berry while balancing on one foot. "I worked in an animal lab during college. We had a macaw named Tommy, a monkey named Bill, a very shy hedgehog called Hermione, and a bunch of snakes."

"More, Tinker!" Seamus commanded. "Berries."

"Tinker?" O'Fallon asked, grinning. "How'd you get that nickname?"

"It's Tinker Bell, courtesy of my sister." She grinned. "I call her Pooh, so it's only fair."

He chortled. In truth, she did look a bit like a fairy.

"Hey, you had to have a nickname with hair like that," she

countered.

He ignored her, not about to share that bit of personal information. "Seamus will get bored here pretty soon and stop plaguing you."

"Not going to tell me, huh?"

He gave a quick shake of his head.

"I'll just have to figure it out." She fed the bird another berry. "He's a kick. How long has he been with you?"

O'Fallon's smile widened even more. She'd not asked how long he'd *owned* Seamus. She understood.

"Twelve years, two marriages, and a number of girlfriends."

"Hard on women, is he?" she joked.

"Both of us are, I think. You, however, seem to be a hit."

"It's the berries, not me," she said wistfully.

Don't be so sure. What had Avery said? *Find a woman who passes muster with Seamus, and you got it made.*

It was just his luck the woman was a card-carrying witch.

Chapter Fifteen

Seamus kept an eye out from his perch on the top of a kitchen chair as Gavenia and O'Fallon ate their pizza. He'd been nearly mute since she'd stuffed him full of berries.

O'Fallon cleaned his greasy hands on a napkin and unfolded a ragged LA map. Once it lay flat on the table, he took his empty paper plate and traced around it with a marker, using Bel Air as the central point.

"High-tech," Gavenia said around a mouthful of pizza.

O'Fallon shot her a boyish grin. He detected her unique scent—a blend of strawberries and jasmine, he thought. It suited her.

"Okay, we know that the day of Bradley's funeral the dog was here, in Bel Air, and then Janet took off with him." He pointed toward the Allifords' address with a plastic fork tine. He paused and frowned. "Did she leave in her own car or call a cab?"

Gavenia shook her head. "I don't know." She tugged her cell phone out of her voluminous purse and punched in a number.

"Gregory Alliford, please. It's Gavenia Kingsgrave."

She sprinkled a few more red pepper flakes on her pizza while she waited. When Alliford picked up the phone, she posed the question. A long torrent of words flooded down the line.

"Yes, I know about the private investigator Mrs. Pearce hired. We've tangled a couple of times." She gave O'Fallon a look. "I have it on good authority he's no longer on the case."

More words. O'Fallon mimed someone taking a drink, and Gavenia nodded in response.

"Okay, that's good. I'm glad Emily called." More words.

"Bradley's quiet? Oh, good. We're going to work through all the shelters and see if we can find the dog." A question. "We?" She looked up, and O'Fallon shook his head. "Ah, my sister is helping me."

She nervously pushed a stray piece of cheese back in place on top of a slice of pizza. Lying clearly wasn't her forte.

"Thanks, Gregory; I'll be in touch."

Gavenia sighed and flipped the phone shut. "Janet took her own car."

O'Fallon sipped his cola and then tapped his finger on the map. "Damn. I'd hoped it was a cab."

"Why would that help?"

"I could call the dispatcher to see where she was dropped. That would narrow the field to something a bit smaller than metropolitan LA."

"You can do that?" Gavenia asked.

"I can." O'Fallon gave a knowing smile. "See, having a PI on your side isn't a bad thing."

"I'll withhold judgment on that," she said.

"Not going to give me an inch, are you?" he asked. She had warmed considerably since entering his apartment, and he wanted to keep the good vibes coming.

"Nope. You're still on that line between 'total nuisance' and 'might be a good guy.'"

"What will it take to push me over to the 'good guy' side?"

"Finding Merlin." She returned to her task of paging through the animal shelters' websites. Scores of black dogs appeared in front of her. Rosco, Bert, Blackie . . . but no wizard.

"I never had any idea of how many black dogs there are in LA," she mused.

"Start with the shelters at the far end of the circle," he said, pointing to the map.

"Why not near Bel Air?"

"Because if she really wanted the dog to be lost, she'd not let it loose anywhere near her house. It might find its way back home like in one of those movies."

"What if she wasn't trying to lose it?"

He only shrugged.

"Great, just great," she muttered.

Bart faded back in view and cleared his throat. Gavenia looked over at him. *Rather domestic scene, don't you think?* he asked. *A man, a woman, a bird. All you need is a couple of kids and—*

"Stop it," she said, and then realized O'Fallon had heard her. "Sorry; some issues with the mouse," she said, pointing at the object.

Fortunately he didn't question her and instead picked up his portable phone and headed for the living room, dialing as he walked. She thought she heard the words *DMV* and *license plate number.*

Tabbing down through the pictures reminded Gavenia of playing the slots in Vegas; one hit and they had the jackpot, providing Lady Luck sat at her elbow.

"Boring," Seamus observed from his perch on the chair, and dug under a wing with his beak.

Gavenia gave him a knowing nod. "You got that right, Seamus me lad."

They called it a night at about seven after letting Ari know Gavenia would be late for her shift at the shelter's bottomless sink.

"Eight in the morning at Red's?" he repeated.

"I heard you the first two times," she said. "So what are we going to do?"

"I'll come up with a plan by then."

She gave him a dubious look. "Is this kind of thing always so frustrating? Investigations, I mean?"

"Usually," he admitted. "Lots of blind alleys until you find the right one. Sometimes you never do."

"When you talked to Janet, did she say why she took the dog in the first place?" Gavenia asked, leaning on her cane near the open door.

"She claims she wanted company. I don't buy it."

Gavenia shifted her weight to the doorjamb. "You know, that actually might be the truth. Animals love you no matter your vices," she said softly. "Unlike her mother. I think all Janet wants is someone who loves her for who she is."

"Isn't that what all of us want?" he said softly.

Gavenia gazed upward into his brown eyes and saw the sadness within.

"Yes," she said. She hesitated at the door for a moment and then looked over at the parrot, resting inside his cage.

"Bye, Seamus."

"Tinker," was the reply.

"Gavenia?"

She jarred out of her stupor, surprised at the use of her first name. "Yes?"

O'Fallon held out a piece of paper. "Directions to Red's Diner."

"Thanks." An insulated mug appeared in her field of vision.

"Fresh coffee. You look too tired to drive safely."

"Thanks." She took the sealed mug and headed for her car. Much to her amusement he escorted her, waiting until she was inside the vehicle and the doors locked.

Well, well, old-fashioned manners, Bart remarked. *Winston didn't even do that.*

"See you in the morning," O'Fallon called, and walked back toward the apartment building. As she pulled out onto the street, he waved. She returned it. Bart had been right: it felt so damned domestic.

"Don't start with me," she said.

Her Guardian stuck out his tongue and vanished.

As she drove back toward the shelter, the mug's contents steaming up the interior of the car, she had to admit two things: Douglas O'Fallon could be a really nice guy when he wanted to, and he made a great cup of coffee.

* * *

The call came at three in the morning. O'Fallon's years as a cop worked in his favor—he was awake and coherent before the second ring.

"Doug, it's Avery."

"What's wrong?"

"It's Adam. He's been hurt."

O'Fallon didn't ask for any more details than the basics, then flew into his clothes and headed for the hospital. His friend's worried face was easy to spot among the crowd in the emergency room. Since Avery didn't have his rosary in his hands, and that gave O'Fallon hope. If things were really bad, he'd be bent over in prayer.

The priest rose at his approach.

"How is he?" O'Fallon asked.

"They're still doing X-rays." The priest frowned. "What happened to you?"

O'Fallon scanned the room. He didn't see any cops, at least none he recognized. He beckoned to Avery, and the pair moved to a discreet corner.

"I met Adam at the Onion the other night. He wanted to talk about what's going on. . . ." He paused and looked around again for good measure. "After he left, I got jumped in the parking lot. It was a warning to back off."

"Did you file a police report?"

"No, and I didn't tell your son, either." O'Fallon rubbed a hand over his face in weariness.

Avery shot another look toward the double doors that led to the treatment bays. "They're supposed to come for me after they finish the X-rays."

"What exactly happened?" O'Fallon asked, unconsciously reaching for his pen and pad. The moment the pad came out of his jacket, he felt foolish. A wan smile appeared on his friend's face.

"Old habits . . . ," Avery said.

"Yeah." He opened the pad and waited for the details.

Avery turned toward the large window in thought. Outside, the insistent beeping of a vehicle motion alarm announced the arrival of an ambulance.

"Adam's partner told him to meet him near the Alexandria Hotel at two, but Glass wasn't there when he arrived. Adam heard screams coming from a nearby alley and he went in without backup."

"And walked into what?" O'Fallon asked, eyes narrowing.

"He found two guys roughing up a woman. Then they jumped him."

"A setup?"

"He's not sure. I don't think he wants to admit his own partner would do that to him. They beat him up pretty bad. One had an iron pipe."

O'Fallon's attention popped up from his notes. "That sounds familiar. One of the guys who went after me used the same thing. Did Glass ever show up?"

"Eventually. He said he'd been held up in traffic."

"At two in the morning?" O'Fallon snorted.

A dark glare from Avery, at odds with his clerical collar. "They're chalking it up as a random assault."

"What's your gut say?"

"He got set up."

O'Fallon nodded, tucking away the notepad and pen. "My gut agrees."

"Father Elliot?" a voice called. They turned to see a worried young man walking toward them. He looked about thirty, tanned, tall, well-built, clad in a jeans and a blast jacket.

Adam's lover?

"Carey," Avery said. The two men stared at each other for a moment and then awkwardly shook hands.

"Doug O'Fallon," he said, offering his hand. The man reciprocated, and O'Fallon received a strong handshake, not unlike Adam's.

"How is he?" Carey asked, exhibiting that haunted look so common to loved ones waiting for bad news.

"They're still checking him out," Avery reported after another look toward the double doors.

"He just can't keep doing this," Carey said, jamming his hands into the pockets of his jacket, his brows knit together.

"He'll be out on medical for a while. Let him stew on what's happened, and maybe it'll help him make the decision," O'Fallon advised. "Just don't push him."

"That's hard to do when you know he could get himself killed," the young man retorted.

"Part of the territory," O'Fallon said.

"Doesn't have to be," was the tight response. "It's not worth his life."

"If someone told you to quit being a lawyer, would you go for that?" O'Fallon asked, testing the waters.

Carey frowned and looked away. "No, I probably wouldn't," the man admitted.

"Then the best thing is to let him be a cop somewhere else than downtown. Somewhere they'll appreciate his abilities and not care that he's gay."

Carey stared at him as if O'Fallon had just admitted to still believing in Santa Claus. "You think such a place exists?"

O'Fallon shrugged and sighed. "I don't know, but if he gets himself a mentor like I did"—he paused and looked over at Avery—"he'll do okay."

"Father Elliot?" a voice called. The priest hustled toward the white-coated figure, Carey and O'Fallon right behind.

"I'm Dr. Liao. We're finished with your son. You can see him now," the doctor advised. She appeared to be Chinese or Taiwanese, and petite. The lab coat dwarfed her.

"So what's the verdict?" the priest asked, his voice barely under control.

"Broken arm, cracked ribs, lots of bruising. I want to keep him until this afternoon to make sure everything remains stable, and then he can go home," the woman replied.

"Thank God," Avery said, crossing himself as Carey out let a whoosh of air in relief.

"Go on, I'll wait. You two are family," O'Fallon said. He retreated to a far bench and lowered himself into the seat. Though his own ribs ached in sympathy, he knew that Adam's disillusionment would be far worse than the actual wounds.

He looked around the room and realized somebody was missing. *Where the hell is Glass?*

* * *

A couple hours later, Adam was propped up in a bed, his right arm in a cast, his face swollen like a prizefighter's. He was trying to work a pencil with his left hand and it kept slipping out of his grasp. He wasn't a southpaw.

"Can I help?" O'Fallon asked.

Adam took his time focusing on who stood next to the bed and then nodded in slow motion. Apparently they'd been very liberal with the pain medication.

"They want me to fill out the menu. Do I look like I want to eat?" he grumbled. He blinked at his guest as if just realizing O'Fallon had a few skid marks of his own. "Heavy date with one of those Catholic matrons?"

O'Fallon grinned; the kid was going to be just fine.

"Yeah, they're a kinky bunch." He took the pencil and scanned the offering. "From what I can see here, I wouldn't stay too long or you're going to starve to death."

"I'll have Carey smuggle in food." Adam worked his jaw gingerly. "Soft food." He thought for a moment and then added, "Just mark what you want. I really don't care."

O'Fallon heard the depression behind the words. The young cop was coming to grips with the truth—he'd been sold out by one of his own.

"Okay, just don't bitch at me when they bring you the soft-boiled eggs," he joked. He put marks next to the best options, waiting Adam out. The detective needed to vent to someone besides his father or his lover. Someone who would be objective.

The wait wasn't long. "Why the–" Adam looked over toward his roommate, an older gentleman with salt-and-pepper hair; he was snoring. Adam lowered his voice. "Why the hell did *my partner* hang me out to dry?"

"I do believe we've had this conversation before," O'Fallon said, though he knew that might kindle some anger. He ignored the chipped beef on toast and opting for the chicken surprise. "Did you know the goons?"

"No, but I swear one of them sounded familiar."

"Someone Glass knows?"

"Might be."

"What did they look like?"

A long sigh. "One was five seven, stocky, brown hair, thick muscles. The other was taller, more wiry. He sounded like he was from Jersey."

O'Fallon put mental check marks by both the descriptions—he'd tangled with the pair in the Onion parking lot.

"And the woman?" he asked.

"Brown hair, scraggly build. I barely saw her before they turned on me. She took off like a frightened rabbit."

"What did Glass say when he showed up?"

Adam's face darkened beneath the cuts and the nascent bruises. He shot another glance toward his neighbor and then back again. His voice dropped to a barely audible whisper.

"He leaned over me as I'm puking up my guts and says, 'I shoulda known a fag would get in trouble. What ya do, drop your pants for the wrong guy?'"

The pencil snapped in O'Fallon's hand. He discarded the useless end in the wastebasket and continued to mark the food choices with the remaining stub. In his mind, he'd just broken Glass in half.

"So why did he want to meet down there?" he asked, keeping his voice level.

"He had a snitch who wanted to talk to him. Glass said he wanted me down there so we could follow up any leads."

"Is that the way you guys operate?"

"No. He usually meets his snitches alone, doesn't like me along."

O'Fallon's analytical mind kneaded through the information, forming a couple of theories. "There, I've picked the least-ghastly choices. You'll have to let me know what the chicken surprise is like."

Adam ignored his attempt at humor. "Dad and Carey want me out of there."

"Make it three for three. Take your medical leave, file for a transfer to cover your ass, and keep your head low. Let Glass think he's won."

"If I leave, how do I nail the bastard?"

"You don't. I will, because I intend to get personally involved."

A gradual, painkiller-enhanced grin appeared on the young man's face. "Dad always said you had a ruthless streak."

"Never piss off an Irishman," O'Fallon retorted. "We carry a grudge until the end of time."

Adam sighed and leaned back in bed. "Just leave me a piece of Glass when you get done."

O'Fallon winked. "It's a deal." He waved the menu. "I'll drop this by the nurses' station."

"That's what I was afraid of," Adam replied, and then closed his eyes. O'Fallon watched him for a moment more and left the room, closing the door behind him. Avery's son had paid a heavy price for his naïveté. Fortunately, the price didn't involve a funeral.

As O'Fallon exited the hospital, he paused to tie a shoe, allowing himself the opportunity to study two men talking to the Asian doctor. They smelled like Internal Affairs. One of them caught his eye. O'Fallon gave a polite nod but only received a no-nonsense stare in return.

As he exited through the automatic doors to the driveway, he smirked. The sharks were circling, and it was his job to make sure that Glass was the main course.

Chapter Sixteen

Red's Diner proved to be Gavenia's kind of place, especially when she'd discovered the sandwich-plate-sized cinnamon rolls fresh out of the oven. Add a mug of hot chocolate, and she was set. Caffeine and sugar, always the best antidotes to bad news—and there was plenty of the latter. The article on Dazie Mazie, Hollywood's favorite psychic, proved scathingly accurate. Jones had pulled no punches.

HIGH-TECH CHARLATAN BILKS
GULLIBLE HOLLYWOOD ELITE

"Oh, Goddess," she muttered. On the table next to her plate, her cell phone buzzed continually like a trapped wasp, countless calls from the community's worried and outraged psychics.

It was close to eight thirty when she realized the Irish guy was late. That wasn't his style. She dug in her purse for his card and dialed the number; it instantly rolled over to voice mail. She flipped the phone shut.

"Not good." Drumming her fingers, she worked through her options. One resonated more than the others, so she waved down the waitress, put in another order, and asked for the check.

* * *

O'Fallon answered the door in his jeans, shirtless, unshaven; it made him look like a regular guy. Almost hunk-calendar material, except for the cluster of ugly bruises scattered along his torso in deepening shades of blue and black.

"Good morning," she said. He just stared at her as if trying to figure out why she was at his door. "Since you stood me up, I brought you breakfast." She hoisted the bag with a Red's Diner logo on the side. "Just supply the coffee."

A look of chagrin appeared and then he waved her in, yawning widely in the process.

"Woo-hoo, Tinker!" Seamus called. The cover was partially off the cage. Apparently, she'd caught both the bird and his roomie just out of bed.

"Late night. The coffee's made," was the barely audible response. She couldn't tell if he was groggy or pissed. He shuffled toward the parrot's cage, leaving her at the door to fend for herself.

Apparently no further explanation of his bad manners would be forthcoming. As she hunted through kitchen cupboards for plates, she could hear the sounds of the parrot's breakfast being served in the living room. Seamus was his usual animated self, the Irish guy unnaturally quiet.

O'Fallon finally sat at the kitchen table. He yawned again and rubbed his eyes just like a small child. It was endearing, at odds with his tough, no-nonsense image.

"Nice outfit, by the way," she said, sipping from a Styrofoam cup of hot chocolate. "You should wear jeans more often."

O'Fallon shot her a glare that said he'd rather wear a negligee and high heels. He took a sip of coffee, stared as if trying to remember what he should do next, then pulled the plate of eggs, bacon, hash browns and pancakes his direction.

"Thanks," he said. His voice had a low, throaty sort of sound. Coupled with the accent, it was sexy. Did he sound like that every morning?

"You're rather monosyllabic."

"Haven't had my coffee . . . or a shower."

"I'm on my third cup of caffeine."

"So I hear."

She pulled out her second breakfast of the morning, another Paul Bunyan–sized cinnamon roll.

"You eat those things?" he asked between bites of egg. She nodded. "Explains a lot."

Gavenia watched him pack away the food, wondering why he didn't weigh twice what he did. His chest gave her the answer; apparently the Irish guy wasn't adverse to lifting weights. Despite a small roll over the top of his jeans, he looked darned good. She pulled herself back to the problem.

"We need to settle this Bradley thing. I can't handle much more of this."

O'Fallon pushed the bacon strips to the far side of the plate as if they were an abomination, and started in on the hash browns. Once they were gone, he went after the pancakes. It was a methodical, clockwise assault around the plate, consuming one type of food at a time before proceeding to the next. Gavenia wondered if he was aware of it.

"Why didn't you eat the bacon?" she asked, curious.

"I gave it up for Lent."

"Sorry, didn't know." A grunt was his only response.

O'Fallon perked up about halfway through the pancakes.

"Since the dog isn't at any of the shelters, we're going to have to broaden our search."

"You were the one who was going to have a plan by this morning."

His frowned grew. "I was busy last night."

"Repo'ing cars?" she chided, knowing that would piss him off.

It did. He stopped eating, dropping his fork on the plate with a jarring clatter.

"You're the damned psychic, or is all that just voodoo?"

She resisted the temptation to throw the remnants of her hot chocolate at him. He was back to normal—abrasive. Her cell phone buzzed, and she reached for it out of habit. As she dug into the depths of her purse, her hand brushed the embroidered bag that carried her tarot deck. She hesitated and then pulled it out, ignoring the phone call.

Why not? Bart's voice asked from the other room. He was loitering near Seamus's cage, studying the occupant with a great deal of interest. Seamus was returning the interest, trying to introduce himself. Apparently, animals saw Guardians. She made a note of that. Extricating the deck from the bag, she dropped it on the table with a thump. She made room in front of her and began to shuffle the cards.

O'Fallon's eyes widened. "I'm not so sure that's what I had in mind."

"Hey, you called it. Let's see if it's all voodoo, shall we?" She took a deep breath to calm her irritation. "Besides, as I see it, we're running out of options. You can call the DMV and get info on cars, I can ask the Head Office to help us out."

"Head Office?" he puzzled until she pointed upward. "Oh." He still looked unsure.

"I'm just going to lay out the cards and see what they tell me."

"'The safest road to Hell is the gradual one—the gentle slope, soft underfoot,'" he quoted, collecting his fork and returning to the pancakes.

"Who said that?" Gavenia asked, continuing the shuffling process while visualizing a bouncy black puppy.

"C. S. Lewis. *The Screwtape Letters*. It's about two devils who compare notes on how to tempt souls."

She ignored the message. "The guy who wrote *Chronicles of Narnia*. I really liked those books."

He cocked his head. "As I remember, the witch dies in the first one."

"Yup, but she wasn't one of the good guys, was she?" Gavenia said, laying out the cards one at a time, facedown.

"Ante up!" she heard from the other room. She gave O'Fallon a puzzled look.

"Seamus heard the cards shuffling; he thinks it's poker night."

* * *

O'Fallon rose and refilled his coffee. He'd been caught off guard when he'd found her on his doorstep after a short night's sleep. Now that the coffee and food had done its job, he was more intrigued than upset.

His visitor turned the first card, and an annoyed expression appeared on her face. He peered over her shoulder and then gave a low whistle.

"The Lovers," he said, reading the flowing script at the bottom of the card. He pointed to the nude couple reclining in a bower, embracing ardently, only a step away from consummation.

"It also means forming a new partnership," Gavenia added hastily, her explanation sounding forced.

He picked up the card and studied it. "Pretty intense partnership from what I can see. And anatomically correct, as well."

She snatched it out of his hand and put it back on the table. "For our purposes, it means a new partnership."

"Okay; you're the psychic," he said, grinning. This might be more fun than he thought. He pulled his chair over as she turned the next card. "What kind of deck is that?"

The witch shot him a confused look. "I thought you didn't know anything about this stuff."

"I've seen tarot decks before. Sometimes we'd get a card left at a murder scene, but they looked different from these."

"This is my own personal deck. I painted each one myself." He heard pride in her voice, and it was well deserved. Every card was a masterpiece of color and design.

"They're really nice. Must have taken forever."

"Over a year," she said, returning her attention to the latest card. "The King of Swords. A man who sits in judgment, someone involved in the law or in authority." She looked toward him. "I'd say that's you."

"I can buy that."

"I'm going to modify it by placing another card on top. It'll give us a bit more information." The new card depicted a pallid moon in a coal-black sky. Below it, in a forest, glowing eyes watched intently. "Not good," she muttered.

"How so?"

"The Moon card usually means hidden enemies or deception."

He pondered for a moment and then nodded. "That fits with

the other case I'm working."

She turned those brilliant blue eyes toward him. "Is that how you got your ribs worked over?" He nodded. "Then watch yourself," she said. "The danger hasn't diminished. If anything, it's grown."

No surprise there.

The next card was rather strange: a petite fairy with golden hair and a mouse wearing a crown. The fairy looked somehow familiar.

"That's my card," she said, smiling brightly.

Bingo. "Are you the fairy or the mouse?" he teased.

She gave him a sidelong glance. "I'll modify it."

A slight intake of breath came when she turned the new card, and he shivered unconsciously. A stark metal cage sat in the middle of a forest clearing. Inside was a young girl, peering out, trying to pick the massive lock that held her prisoner. In the distance he could see the backs of two figures. They had shovels and were digging what appeared to be a grave. Next to them on the ground was a shrouded figure—a body.

"Whoa," he said, shivering involuntarily. "God, that's . . ." The witch just stared, the blue in her eyes dulled.

Her voice came so quietly that he had to strain to hear her.

"The Entrapment card. The feeling of being ensnared, caught in a situation in which one has no control. Fear of the unknown, fear of . . . death."

She'd intoned the words as if it were a personal litany.

"Bradley?" he asked, watching her closely.

Gavenia opened her mouth as if to immediately agree and then sighed. "I'm not sure."

The witch flipped another card. Her left hand was shaking now with almost as much intensity as the right. The Entrapment card had clearly frightened her.

"The Water card," she said, pointing toward a scene with a blue expanse of ocean, seabirds, and tiny boats. "It could mean a number of things."

"And in relation to the dog?"

She didn't answer, but modified the card. An elderly woman in a rocking chair looking expectantly at the door, as if hoping for visitors. His gran came to mind and, along with the thought of her, a twinge of guilt.

"The Patience card," she said. This time her sigh sounded exasperated. "One more." A young man and woman, standing under an archway. He was handing her a bunch of ripe purple grapes, she offering him a full goblet of wine. They gazed at each other with unabashed adoration.

"The Bounty or Sharing card. He offers his beloved the fruits of life, and she returns them in a new form. For barren couples I tell them this means they will have children. For lovers, I tell them to learn to give and receive of each other, to enjoy the bounty that love can bring."

"What does that mean to us in this case?"

For a moment she looked disconcerted, and then he watched her shields fall into place like solid steel doors.

She sputtered, "I think . . . I think it means we will be successful in our search for Merlin. We're each contributing something to the case and—" She stopped abruptly. "At least I think that's what it means."

Can't lie to save your soul, can you?

In some ways, he found that refreshing. To ease the awkward moment, he asked, "So what did we learn here, other than that both of us need to be careful?"

Gavenia appeared grateful for his change of subject.

"Water," she said, tapping the relevant card. "Janet loved the ocean; at least that's what her sister said. Don't the Allifords have a beach house in Malibu?"

He nodded. "You think we should check it out?"

"Why not? It's a nice day; it'll be a road trip."

He rose, moving his chair back in place. "While I take my shower, give Alliford a call. We'll need a key and a security code."

The witch instantly perked up, as if having a plan allowed her to submerge the disturbing reading.

"Need someone to wash your back?" she jested, the shields lowering again.

He eyed her, tempted to play along. What would it be like to make love to a pagan? His ribs throbbed in response, reminding him of the impossibility of the notion. There was far more to Gavenia Kingsgrave than her bio indicated, and until he knew the meaning of the Entrapment card, he'd best be cautious.

"I'll take a rain check on it," he said, pointing to the bruises.

"Good point." She gathered the cards, returning them to the embroidered bag. In the living room, Seamus began a series of catcalls worthy of a longshoreman.

"He's paging you," O'Fallon said.

Gavenia just rolled her eyes.

* * *

When O'Fallon appeared in the doorway to his bedroom after his shower, she stared. Self-consciously he straightened his shirt and dusted off his pants, his suit jacket draped over his right arm.

"You're wearing that?" she blurted. "Oh, no, not happening. I refuse to go to a beach with a guy in suit. You look . . ." She waved her arms in the air, struggling for the proper word.

"Professional?" he suggested, frowning.

"No, type A. Nobody goes to the beach dressed like that, O'Fallon."

"I like my suits. They're nice ones. I'm fussy about them," he retorted.

"Yes, you are, but they're not right for the beach," Gavenia said, rising from the couch, hands on her hips.

"Bar fight, bar fight!" Seamus crowed.

"Don't you start," O'Fallon cautioned. The parrot edged toward Gavenia as if taking her side.

"See, even Seamus agrees. No suit," she said.

When O'Fallon mumbled under his breath and retreated to the bedroom, Gavenia winked at the parrot and fed him another carrot.

When the Irish guy reappeared, Gavenia let loose a wolf whistle and delivered a thumbs-up. Seamus promptly duplicated the whistle with uncanny accuracy. She waved the PI into the center of the room and circled around him, nodding her approval.

Oh yeah, now that's nice. O'Fallon's broad chest worked wonders on the LAPD T-shirt, and the faded blue jeans filled out nicely. The tan boat shoes were an added bonus. He looked good. Amazing what a change of wardrobe could do for a guy.

"Lookin' hot, Mr. PI," she said, and grinned.

"Lookin' stupid," he muttered. "I feel like a . . ." He struggled for a word.

"Like a normal person?"

"No, like a geek."

"You don't look like a geek. Besides, you're not meeting a client; we're dog hunting at the beach."

"I might see someone I know," he hedged.

"And they'll be astounded how cool you look."

He shook his head, a scowl on his face. After a couple more muttered words, he headed for the kitchen counter, scooping up his wallet and keys. "Did you talk to Alliford?"

"Nope. He's sleeping it off. The maid said she'd have the key ready for me."

"Good. Who knows, maybe we'll get lucky."

"Hey . . . in those blue jeans . . ." She waggled her eyebrows, and that earned her a sharp look.

"Get lucky, get lucky!" Seamus chimed in from his place on the sofa.

"You be quiet." O'Fallon scooped him up and deposited him in his cage.

"Yo, baby! Nice buns!" the parrot shouted.

Gavenia leered from the door. "I couldn't have said it better, Seamus."

O'Fallon pointed toward the door. "Outside!" He turned the television to the shopping channel. "See if you like that all day, old buddy." As he locked up, Seamus issued a series of piercing wolf whistles.

The negotiations continued when they reached the parking lot. Feeling testy, O'Fallon refused to allow the *sugar junkie*, as he'd dubbed her, to get behind the wheel of a car. He predicted dire results when the substance evaporated from her system, leaving her without a working brain.

"Well, I'm not driving to Malibu in a car that has a broken window," Gavenia said, pointing to the duct-tape-and-cardboard substitute he'd fashioned for the Chevy.

He pointed at her car. "No back seat. If you're okay with having the mutt sit on your lap all the way home..."

"Got it. Your car, you're driving. Let's cruise!"

Chapter Seventeen

O'Fallon watched as Gavenia crawled back into the car at the Allifords'. She was moving slower now. A long yawn followed.

"Sugar high winding down?" he asked with a knowing grin.

She nodded, buckling her seat belt. "It always does."

"I, however, am in good shape."

"Hurrah for you," she said, yawning again.

He knew she'd not be with him for very much longer.

"Go ahead, take a nap. It'll be a while until we get there."

Gavenia cranked back the seat and tugged her light jacket around her shoulders, pushing her voluminous hair out of the way. In a very short time, she was asleep.

Lucky you. O'Fallon's brain was in overdrive. Adam's assault and the IAD sharks had ratcheted up his nerves. Part of his brain told him he shouldn't be going to Malibu on some doggie hunt. Still, he'd heard the child's ghost for himself, and if the witch was on the level, the kid needed to cross. Once that happened, O'Fallon could focus on Glass full-time.

Waiting at a stoplight, he glanced over at his passenger. She looked peaceful, as if sleep was the only respite she received. His mind skipped back to the tarot reading. He'd seen the terror in her eyes when she'd pulled that Entrapment card. What did that mean to her? If she'd created the tarot deck, then each card had to have significance. He made a mental note to do a bit more research into the witch's past.

Then there were the Lovers card and the Bounty card. Did they mean what he thought, or was he trying to read something into them? Another look at the sleeping woman. Her hair draped around her like a golden cape, her soft breath making her full breasts rise and fall.

We have nothing in common. Except Seamus.

As he passed Castellammare on the Pacific Coast Highway, he nudged the witch back into wakefulness.

"Rise and shine, Sleeping Beauty," he said, feeling the appellation fit. He pointed toward the side pocket stuffed with maps. "Grab one of those and tell me how to get to this place."

"Oh, Goddess, you have to be kidding. I'm directionally challenged."

"You can't read a map?" he asked in disbelief.

"I'm okay with maps, I'm just not really great with directions. Maybe I could drive and you could navigate."

He was shaking his head before she finished.

"No way." He pointed toward the map again. "Work it out."

Muttering under her breath, Gavenia unfolded it, flipped it around a couple of times, and then asked, "Okay, which side is the ocean supposed to be on?"

"What?" he sputtered.

Gotcha. "Just kidding. I think you need to go about"—she did the math—"four more miles and turn . . ." She thought it through, staring at her hands. "Watch, I mean . . ."

"Watch?"

"Hey, give me a break. I can't remember left from right, so I go by *watch* or *bracelet*," she said, pointing to each in turn.

"What if you're not wearing them?" O'Fallon asked, apparently intrigued by her mental acrobatics.

"Then I'm screwed." She paused and added, "But I'm really good with up and down."

"I'll remember that if we're ever in a submarine."

When she laughed, he joined in. For a brief moment, the day seemed brighter.

Once O'Fallon made the required turn, Gavenia hunted around for Bart. She found him in the backseat wearing a set of wraparound sunglasses, jeans, and a T-shirt that said *Whaddaya*

Mean This Isn't Heaven? He had a folded beach towel on his lap and a tube of sunscreen.

"Over the top," she said, without thinking. That earned her a puzzled look from O'Fallon. "Sorry, just regrouping my brains."

"I warned you about all that sugar."

If that were my only problem . . .

* * *

In her mind's eye, Gavenia figured the beach house would be a two-bedroom affair with a broad porch facing the ocean, sort of an upscale cabin. Instead they were confronted with a large two-story house with a wraparound porch, hot tub, massive glass windows, and a broad expanse of beach.

"Some serious bucks here," she muttered, leaning against the deck rail, gazing at the ocean. "You know, maybe I should start trading out my services for a few weekends at a place like this."

"I doubt anyone would fault you," O'Fallon remarked, taking his place next to her. He leaned forward, hands on the railing, almost relaxed. She wondered if he ever really let loose.

As another wave rolled in to shore, Gavenia took a deep breath, inhaling the heavy salt air. "It's so beautiful here."

"And quiet."

"Yes."

"Which isn't good."

"Pardon?" she asked. That didn't make much sense.

"It means no Merlin."

Gavenia groaned, jerked back to reality like a puppy on a short leash.

"I'll check out the house," O'Fallon suggested, resuming his usual uptight posture. It seemed at odds with his casual clothes.

Gavenia wasn't ready to return to the moment. "Give me a few minutes here. I'm . . . recharging."

He chuckled and extended his palm. She dug in her purse and extracted the key and the security code.

"I could have hacked this," he said, waving the paper in the air.

"It's Alliford's birthday."

She turned her attention to the call of the ocean as he marched around the side of the house. She heard a door open, a series of beeps, then silence.

Gavenia closed her eyes and took deep, cleansing breaths, allowing the sea air to flow into her lungs. She imagined the seabirds in the air over the water, wheeling in the wind with a freedom she envied. Sunlight rippled off their wings; their shrill cries filled the air. Beneath them the rumbling waves were a counterpoint, like the deep breaths.

When she opened her eyes, O'Fallon was back, standing quietly, respecting her moment of peace. Without thinking, she gave him a soft smile, and he returned it. In the sunlight he appeared years younger.

"I could live here," he said, gazing toward the moving water. "But I like Ireland better."

"I've never been there. Is it as beautiful as they say?"

His eyes returned to study her. "More."

"Then I'll go there someday."

"I'd be happy to show you around. You could meet my gran. She's an amazing old lady."

Did he just invite you home to meet his grandmother? Bart chirped, grinning like a two-year-old.

Gavenia switched subjects. "So what did you find inside?"

For a second O'Fallon looked chagrined, as if he'd been caught shirking his duty.

She put her hand on his arm. "It's okay to unwind every now and then. That's why you retired, wasn't it?"

He put on his cop face. "I found a dog's bowl and some drug paraphernalia."

"So Janet and Merlin were here."

"Looks like it."

"How long ago?"

"It's been a while. The food in the bowl is rock hard."

"Patience," she whispered. He gave her a curious look. "The Patience card. Sometimes things don't reveal themselves until the proper moment."

She could see he understood. Probably part of his detective DNA. She swept her eyes the length of the deck and found Bart reclining on a chaise lounge at the far end, mellow to the extreme.

He delivered a knowing grin. *I'd stay and enjoy the scenery. I hear the ocean is gorgeous at night.*

The sunglasses flapped back down. End of conversation.

Gavenia announced her decision. "We're staying, at least for the time being."

O'Fallon's mouth fell open. "Why?"

"Merlin is here, somewhere. I feel him. So we might as well enjoy the beach house, get some food, and"—she gestured toward the ocean—"watch the sunset."

"I . . . uh . . ."

She scrutinized him, amused by his flustered behavior.

"You got a hot date?"

He frowned at the question. "How late are we going to stay?"

"As long as it takes."

He processed that and then consulted his watch. "I have to make arrangements for Seamus," he said, pulling his cell phone off the belt clip attached to his jeans. He walked farther down the deck and stopped just short of Bart's chaise.

"I better call Ari, or I'm in deep trouble," Gavenia said, digging in her purse for her own phone. Someone else was going to man the shelter's sink tonight.

* * *

At the bottom of the stairs leading from the deck onto the beach, O'Fallon kicked off his deck shoes and rolled the legs of his jeans to his knees. Gavenia did the same, revealing two jagged white scars on her left calf. Her legs were pale, proving she wasn't a sun bunny.

"Welsh skid marks," she said, pointing at her calf.

He rolled the right leg of his jeans up a bit farther and pointed to a long white scar.

"We're a matched set."

"Bar fight with a midget?" she joked.

He shook his head. "Drunken stupidity. I got wasted after a girl dumped me, jumped on my motorcycle, and ran it off the road."

"They nail you for DUI?" she asked.

"Nope, but it was the last straw for my gran. She shipped me to the States to live with my great-aunt."

"How old were you?"

"Just seventeen."

"Ugly lesson."

"Most of 'em are."

Three steps into the sand and Gavenia halted, wavering on her feet. "This isn't going to work," she said. The cane was useless.

"You're right. Give it to me and I'll leave it on the deck."

She shook her head instantly. "I can't walk without it."

"With my help you can." She didn't move, reminding O'Fallon of a doe blinded by an 18-wheeler's headlights.

"Ah, I don't know about this." She wavered on her feet again.

He extended his hand, palm up. "Trust me." Her brow furrowed. "We're burning daylight here," he urged.

The frown deepened, but she relinquished the cane—with great reluctance. By the time he returned to her side, she was edging forward in the sand like a toddler taking her first tentative steps. He slipped his left hand around her waist. She stiffened and then relaxed. They took a few cautious steps forward, hips bumping.

"How's that?" he asked.

"I'd feel safer with the cane." He gave her a hurt look and she shrugged in response.

"See, it works," he said, pleased with the results as they matched strides. "You walk pretty well without that thing. Why do you use it?"

She abruptly halted, putting him off-balance. "I don't see that's any of your business."

"Okay, it's none of my business. Why do you use it?"

The frown returned. He pulled her back into place and they continued along the beach while he waited for an answer.

"Because it makes me feel safe."

"Safe?"

"It just does."

He felt there was more, but he wasn't likely to hear it. After a quarter mile or so of tandem trudging, she stopped and rubbed her left thigh.

"Great exercise," she said. "Hurts like hell."

"Time to go back?" he asked.

She looked up the stretch of beach and hesitated.

"What are you sensing?"

She shook her head. "I don't know. It's all a jumble."

While he waited for her to make a decision, O'Fallon stared at his pale feet. "I forgot how weird sand feels between your toes," he admitted.

She laughed, mashing the stuff between her own toes. "So did I."

"Why do we rush to become adults and then forget how to be kids?" he asked.

She looked up, blue eyes deep in thought. "Maybe because kids act on impulse, and adults think everything through."

Testing the notion of acting on impulse, he pulled her into his arms and hugged her. To his surprise, she didn't resist him.

"Then let's vow to visit the beach every now and then," he said as he pulled out of the embrace.

Her eyebrows rose. "Separately or together?"

"Either way." He sucked in a lungful of air. "I feel so much . . . stronger here, like after a good night's sleep."

"You're just getting in touch with Mother Nature."

"Whatever it is, I like it."

"Then do it more often, O'Fallon."

He nodded. "You got a deal."

They walked back toward the beach house, talking about inconsequential things. After only a short distance, Gavenia halted and looked over her shoulder as if trying to hear a faint sound on the wind.

"What is it?" he asked.

She listened a little longer. "Spirits," she said.

"Are they playing on the beach?"

"No." Her answer sent a shiver up his spine, and he hugged her closer.

* * *

They walked in silence for a time, listening to the birds. They passed two children building a sand castle with brightly colored spades.

"My gran's psychic," O'Fallon said.

Gavenia studied him with renewed interest. "In what way?"

"She knows things before they happen. Do you?"

"No. Just vague warnings about stuff, but nothing specific," Gavenia said.

"I get those, too. Most of time I ignore them."

Oh great, another one, Bart said as he trailed behind them, dragging his beach towel and kicking sand in the air like a bored child. O'Fallon's Guardian hovered nearby, a pint-size ball of light. A Twinkle, as Bart called them. He claimed he couldn't see them any better than she could.

"From my experience," she said, "it's best to listen to those little voices. I wouldn't have played tag with that wall in Wales if I'd listened."

"I saw the photo in the paper. I'm surprised you survived."

"Aunt Lucy says I'm like a cat, that I have nine lives. That was life number two."

He opened his mouth as if to ask what had cost life number one, but she shook her head.

"Don't ask."

He did anyway. "Does it have something to do with the Entrapment card?"

A tremor coursed through her.

He cursed under his breath. "I'm sorry," he said. "I won't mention it again."

"That would be best."

He abruptly switched topics. "The beach house has one of those tropical-rainforest showers with all the jets and the fancy panel that lets you set the temperature."

Gavenia looked up at him in wonder. "You cops don't miss a thing." She visualized what the shower might look like, tried to imagine how wonderful it would feel. Cascades of water, all at the perfect temperature. Heaven.

"Of course, I'll need someone to wash my back," O'Fallon added with a hint of mischief.

She dropped her mouth, her brain rampaging for a snappy retort. Instead her rebellious mind conjured up the image of the Irish guy, nude, as she lathered soap from his neck, over his broad shoulders and down to his well-rounded—

"Earth to witch."

"Oh, sorry," she said, chagrined she'd been caught daydreaming.

Blush alert! Bart advised, chortling at her embarrassment.

Gavenia stammered. "Ah . . . what . . . were we talking about?"

O'Fallon's face told her he wasn't buying the act. "Showering . . . together."

"We have to find Merlin first."

"Now who's being all business?"

"Just learning from the best."

She paused at the bottom of the stairs that led to the deck. He handed her the cane.

"You do better without this."

"You won't always be around to help me," she shot back.

He opened his mouth to reply and then closed it as if he'd thought better. They judged each other for a moment.

"So what next?" he said, removing his arm from around her waist. She missed it immediately.

"Let's raid the cupboards."

For folks with eight-figure incomes, the Allifords' pantry was painfully thin. Apparently, they brought food each time they visited. When O'Fallon found a jar of spaghetti sauce and some wheat pasta, he announced their problems were solved.

"I cook, you shower," she offered.

"But you can't wash my back if you're cooking."

"Shoo," she said, pushing him away with her hands. "Just don't stay in there forever, or I'll have to come get you."

His leering grin told her he was considering the notion.

Chapter Eighteen

Gavenia glanced at her watch as she stirred the sauce, adjusting the burner to the lowest setting. The Irish guy had been in the shower fifteen minutes.

"And they think women take forever."

He just wants you to come fetch him, Bart said. He sat on the counter watching her cook, feet swinging to and fro.

"I'm not going there," she replied.

You don't trust him.

"Not entirely." Gavenia fidgeted with a strand of hair. "What do you think of him?"

He's got about as many issues as you do; maybe more.

"That's not what I asked."

If he were a cowboy, he'd be wearing a white hat.

"And?" she said. She felt like a teenager quizzing her dad about his reaction to her prom date.

I like him. Bart jumped down from the counter and headed for the leather recliner.

"Were you ever in love?" she asked.

He stopped midstride and turned toward her, his face solemn. *Yes. She was . . . everything.*

"Where you married?"

He slowly shook his head. *No, we never had a chance. Someone came between us.*

Gavenia's heart tightened. Why had she never asked about that before? Why hadn't she realized he'd left an entire life behind, perhaps even someone he loved?

The Shepherd always takes precedence over the Guardian, Bart intoned, as if citing some celestial rule. Before Gavenia could ask what that meant, O'Fallon sauntered into the kitchen, clad in his jeans and T-shirt.

"About damned time," Gavenia said, mimicking Seamus. "A few minutes longer and I would have called the cops."

A hearty laugh answered her. "That shower's a religious experience. You have to try it."

"I might." She gave the sauce another stir as he joined her at the stove. "This is ready."

"Good; I'm starved." He glanced toward the blazing hearth. "You built a fire?"

"You sound surprised. We Pagans are good with wood. All those human sacrifices, you know."

He quirked an eyebrow. "I'll keep that in mind." He carried the bottle of wine to the table and poured two hearty glasses. After helping her with the spaghetti-laden plates, he sat and bowed his head. After a moment he looked up, as if unsure of how to proceed.

"I usually offer a blessing before my meals," he explained.

"Go ahead, and then I'll offer mine."

He took a deep breath. "Dear Father, thank you for another day of life, one filled with"—he paused and looked toward his dinner companion—"unexpected surprises. Thank you for reminding me to take time to enjoy the beauty of your creation and those who share it. Bless this meal and those who prepared it. In the name of the Father, and of the Son, and of the Holy Spirit. Amen," he said, crossing himself.

Gavenia closed her eyes, raising her palms heavenward.

"To the God and Goddess I ask a blessing on this food for the health of those present. Give us wisdom to see your Light and to magnify it in this dark world. So mote it be."

O'Fallon sighed in contentment. After the meal, they'd curled up on the couch like they'd known each other for years, Gavenia tucked up against his side. They'd talked about their lives, sharing stories, learning about each other. Her work, his work.

The courtship dance. He knew it well. New beginnings were so pure; the endings, so sad.

He pushed a strand of hair from her face. When had they crossed the line between working on the case to the promise of something more? *The walk on the beach.* She'd begun to open up from that moment forward, as if he'd connected with her on some deeper level.

"I'm sorry I got you out here for nothing," she said.

He tipped her chin up and studied those twin blue oceans.

"It wasn't a wasted day. I enjoyed myself, and it's been a long time since I could say that." He bent over and placed a kiss on her nose. Gavenia didn't pull away. The second kiss fell on her cheek. She leaned into him. The third was on her mouth. She was warm, and the kiss burned into his lips. When they broke apart, he found her eyes watching him with an intensity that caused his heart to pound.

"I'm going to take a shower." Gavenia reluctantly pulled out his arms. O'Fallon watched as she made her way down the long hall toward the cavernous bathroom and her own religious experience.

"I think I'd best stay right here," he said with a sigh. *Dammit.*

By the time Gavenia returned from the shower, O'Fallon was asleep in front of the fireplace. He'd unfolded the sofa bed, despite his injured ribs, and now snoozed under a blanket, his hair tousled. She banked the fire, checked that the doors were locked, and then counted the stairs to the second floor. The circular stairway was just too daunting for her and the cane.

"Not happening," she murmured. Stripping off her shoes, she lay next to the Irish guy, who murmured in his sleep but didn't wake. He smelled of expensive soap, a strangely erotic scent. She impulsively deposited a kiss on his cheek and tucked the blanket around them.

As she drifted to sleep, she caught Bart's subtle glow coming from the leather recliner. O'Fallon's Guardian hung next to Bart as if they were having a conversation.

I wonder why I can't see it, she thought, and then drifted to sleep.

* * *

O'Fallon woke to the sound of running water, which aggravated his full bladder. Swinging his feet over the edge of the sofa bed, he rubbed his eyes and got his bearings. He was at the Allifords' beach house and he was there with a witch. He looked over at the other side of the bed. Gavenia was gone, but the pillow next to him looked like she'd shared his bed. He half remembered that, the warmth of her next to him. It had felt good.

Steady there. They needed to gain some space between them, give themselves time to think this out before it went too far.

He hiked across the cool wood floors to the bathroom and took care of business. By the time he entered the kitchen, the running water had stopped.

Finding fresh java in a coffeemaker, he poured himself a cup and savored the silence. If he were at home, Seamus would be entertaining him with a cacophony of songs and sound effects. On the beach there was just the gentle murmuring of the ocean, the call of seabirds, and . . .

Waaaoof!

The clatter of claws on wooden flooring made him swing his head around. A black blur rocketed toward him, leaping upward. He maneuvered at the last minute to avoid full-body contact in an area that wouldn't tolerate that sort of enthusiasm.

"Merlin?" he asked.

Waaaooof! was the answer.

The puppy danced around his feet, shaking like an earthquake. Cascades of water splattered the length of O'Fallon's torso and he shielded his coffee cup and waited for the droplets to settle to earth. A boisterous laugh came from the doorway as Gavenia leaned against the doorjamb.

"Irish guy, meet Merlin. He's had his bath. It's up to you to dry him," she said, pointing toward a sizable navy bath towel draped over one of the kitchen chairs. As she turned to go outside, O'Fallon called, "Wait! Where'd he come from?"

"He found me on the deck this morning. I was meditating and then next thing I know, I get a wet nose in my face—a nose attached to a very stinky dog."

"I'll be damned," he said, squatting to pet the energetic hound.

"The Patience card was right on—all we had to do was wait him out. If we'd given up and gone home last night . . ."

O'Fallon shook his head in amazement. Merlin looked pretty bright for someone who'd been living on his own for two weeks. "Does he need to be fed?"

"Already done. I decided not to wake you."

He gave her an appreciative nod. "I owe you one."

"I'll remember that," she said, winking.

He pulled the towel off the chair, intending to do his part. Merlin reacted instantly, grabbing the towel in his teeth and backing away, a playful growl in his throat. A tug-of-war ensued.

"Grrrrr . . ."

They struggled for control of the towel as Merlin dug in his toenails and pulled. The dog wrenched the towel out of his hand and headed for the door, O'Fallon jogging after him.

"God, you're worse than Seamus."

* * *

The drive to LA was quiet, as if both of them knew the case was nearing an end. Merlin snoozed in the backseat.

O'Fallon broke the silence. "Do you want to go to Alliford's now?"

Gavenia shook her heard. "No, let me call and get things set up first. This is going to be really hard on Gregory."

"Like burying his son a second time?"

"Exactly."

"I'll call Avery. Maybe Alliford will agree to have him there."

"Is your friend okay with Pagans?" she asked. He heard the uncertainty.

"Yeah, he's cool." *Or at least I hope so.*

She gave a slight huff of air. "I just want Bradley to be at peace." Merlin raised his head at that. She reached back and patted him. "Yes, you'll see him soon." The dog put his head back on his paw and dispensed a long canine sigh. It mirrored O'Fallon's mood perfectly.

"Call me when it's over, okay?" he said. "I want to know how it goes."

"I will."

* * *

O'Fallon gave her a light kiss on the cheek before walking toward his apartment. As Gavenia watched him, she regretted that something more hadn't happened during their time at the beach.

"Whoa," she said, shaking her head. Things were moving too fast.

As she climbed into her car, she found Bart in the passenger seat, Merlin in his lap.

"Do animals see all the Guardians?" she asked. Bart nodded. "But I can't."

That's the breaks.

She sighed and pulled the car out of the parking lot. It never got any easier.

When she arrived home, Merlin rose from his nap a virtual tornado. He surged into the condo at warp speed and engaged in a brief skirmish with Bastet. The cat clawed her way to the highest level of the bookshelf in the temple room, hair bristling as she glowered at the intruder. Gavenia herded the dog into the kitchen, out of harm's way.

Unlimited puppy energy overwhelmed Ari as she stirred a pot of vegetable soup at the stove.

"You found him!" she said, kneeling to pet the cavorting dog.

"Yeah, we did."

Ari beamed and then commanded, "Sit, Merlin." The puppy gave her a puzzled look. "Sit!" she repeated.

The dog eased into a squat.

Gavenia blinked in astonishment. "You're good," she said.

"Men and dogs—same thing. Give them a command, and they'll behave."

Gavenia angled her eyes toward Paul's ghost as she fished an ice-cream bar out of the freezer. He was frowning at his widow's remarks.

"I've never found men or dogs like that," Gavenia said.

"Wrong men, wrong dogs," Ari said, crossing to the sink. "So what's the plan?"

"I need to call Gregory to get things going and then I need a nap before we do this."

"So what happened at the beach house?" Ari asked in the midst of drying her hands.

"Nothing."

Her sister gave her a skeptical look. "Nothing? You spend the day with a good-looking guy and nothing happens? Sorry, I don't buy that."

"We walked on the beach and talked a lot. We cuddled on the couch in front of the fireplace. End of story."

Ari looked crestfallen. "That's it? Damn. I'd hoped someone was having more fun that I was."

"Nope. Just finding Merlin." Gavenia headed for the kitchen door.

"By the way, you've got a bazillion calls from lots of nervous witches. I made a list and left it by phone," Ari said, pointing toward a sheet of paper filled with names and numbers.

"I'll deal with those tonight. Bradley comes first."

Ari tasted the soup and shook her head, adding more chopped basil. "I'm going out for dinner with some friends. This soup is for you so you don't eat your weight in ice-cream bars."

Gavenia wrinkled her nose at her sister. "Cute, Pooh."

As she turned away, Ari called, "Tinker Bell?"

"Yeah?"

"Nice work with the dog." Ari pointed down at Merlin, who sat at her feet, pawing at her shoelaces. "Now take him somewhere else, will you?"

"Come on, Mr. Wizard," Gavenia called, slapping her thigh. "Let's go find a cat to piss off."

Bastet made the mistake of appearing in the doorway at that very moment, whiskers twitching in agitation. The dog thundered after her and they flew down the hall in a blast of noise and swirling hair. Tempting as it was to intervene, Gavenia decided to let them sort it out. Once Merlin was home with the Allifords, she'd do penance with the feline.

Chapter Nineteen

Merlin began bouncing around the car the moment Gavenia pulled into the Allifords' circle driveway.

"How does he know this is home?" she muttered, shaking her head in amazement. Merlin responded with a loud bark and another acrobatic bounce from the front seat to the floor and back. "We're almost there." Her Guardian, on the other hand, was noticeably missing. "Hey, Bart, you going to miss this?"

He appeared next to her, dressed in a solemn black suit.

Just trying to stay out of Hurricane Merlin's way.

"Yeah, he's a handful." She pulled up behind another vehicle, one she didn't recognize. It had a bumper sticker that read, MY OTHER CAR IS A CONFESSIONAL.

"The priest," she said. Hopefully he was as open-minded as O'Fallon claimed. She looked toward her Guardian for reassurance, but he was staring out the window, deep in thought. Bart exited the car, through the door. It was still odd to watch him move through solid objects. He seemed so much like a real person.

I am a real person.

"You know what I mean."

I'm real and I'm dead. A real dead person. Get over it.

His snappish behavior caught her off guard. He looked as if he was fighting tears.

"Let's get this done. I don't think any of us can take much more."

Maria was instantly set upon the moment she opened the front doors. Merlin lunged at her, snagged one of her stockings, and then bounded past her at a gallop.

She laughed and beckoned. "Come, come," she said.

Gavenia followed the excited barking and found Gregory on the hallway floor playing with the puppy. He grinned at her, and the expression reminded her of Bradley.

"He looks good," Gregory said. The dog danced around him, tail impacting the wall with solid thumps.

Standing behind the pair was a man in a clerical collar who was older than O'Fallon, but blessed with that same steady self-assurance. The priest stepped around Alliford and offered his hand.

"I'm Father Elliot," he said. His voice flowed like smooth whiskey.

"Gavenia Kingsgrave." They shook solemnly. Pushing down her apprehension, she said, "I'm pleased you're here."

"I'm pleased Mr. Alliford has allowed me the privilege."

The expression on Gregory's face withered. He rose to his feet and took a deep breath. "It's best we get this done."

"Your son will soon be at peace," Gavenia said. Her words felt inadequate, no match to the father's endless grief.

"I think of him every day," Alliford said. "Something triggers a memory. Will it ever get better?" he asked, his eyes pleading.

Gavenia shot a quick glance at the priest. She saw the truth in the cleric's eyes. She had no choice; she lied.

"You'll never forget him, but your . . . grief . . . will fade . . . in time." An approving nod came from Father Elliot.

Gregory accepted her falsehood. He looked down at the puppy waiting at his feet. "Come on, Merlin; Bradley wants to see you."

The dog gave an enthusiastic bark, skittered down the hall, and headed for the stairs to the second floor. No one attempted to catch him. They knew where he'd be. Riotous sounds erupted from Bradley's room: Merlin barking and the little boy's laughter. The boy's father hesitated at the doorway, his eyes misty and his bottom lip quivering.

"It'll be fine," Gavenia said, taking his hand and squeezing it.

"I want him to know I love him," he said.

"You can tell him yourself. He can hear you."

There was a movement behind her. She turned to find the

priest draping a stole around his neck, one with the Tree of Life embroidered on it. It seemed appropriate. He gave a short nod to indicate he was ready.

"Let's send Bradley home," she said, fighting down the tears.

She found Merlin lying on his back, paws in the air, wriggling as Bradley scratched his tummy. The child giggled and scratched harder.

"Bradley?" Gavenia called. He looked up, and his smile blossomed.

Merlin's back! the little boy crowed, his eyes twinkling.

Gregory lightly touched Gavenia's elbow. "He can see the dog?"

"Oh, yes, and he's very happy."

She shifted her gaze toward the priest. So far Father Elliot had been supportive, a calm presence, precisely what Gregory needed. More of her apprehension melted away.

"Will Merlin be with him . . . when the time comes?" Gregory asked.

It was Father Elliot who answered. "Your son has a special bond with Merlin, and that will exist long after death."

"Then Bradley won't be alone," Gregory said, his voice breaking at the end. "Thank God."

"We're never alone, Mr. Alliford, not in this life or the next," the cleric replied in a soft voice.

When Gavenia moved a few steps forward, Merlin ran over to her. She scratched his chest as he licked her hand, his tail swooshing in broad swipes. She looked into the boy's eyes, caught by the power she saw within them.

Children understand love better than adults, Bart said quietly. *They don't know how to shield their emotions.*

"It's time, Bradley," she whispered.

The little boy's face saddened. When a matronly voice called to him, he turned and smiled in recognition.

"He can see your mother," Gavenia said to Gregory. "Now would be the time to tell him what you'd like him to know."

Gregory stepped forward and dropped to his knees only a few feet from his son's spirit. The little boy watched him intently.

Daddy's sad.

"He misses you, Bradley," Gavenia said.

Gregory cleared his throat, wiping tears from his cheek. "I . . . love you, Son. I . . . am . . . so lonely without you," Alliford murmured. "Every day without you is . . ."

The little boy walked to his father and crawled within his arms, embracing him, like he would have if still alive.

Gregory's sobs lessened for a moment. He gave Gavenia a startled look.

"My God, I think I can feel him!"

She nodded. "He's in your arms, hugging you."

"Oh, God, it'll be all right, won't it?" he said. He embraced the ethereal form and then let go.

Bradley pointed over the top of his father's arm toward the priest and gave Gavenia a quizzical look. *Who's that?*

"That's Father Elliot. He's here to help your dad."

Bradley extricated himself from his father's arms and stood in front of the cleric. Elliot continued to intone prayers, unaware of the spirit's scrutiny. A little boy to the end, Bradley mischievously tugged on one end of the priest's stole and then giggled.

As the garment shifted, Elliot's eyes popped open in surprise.

Gavenia couldn't help but smile.

"Come on, Bradley; it's time for you go," she said, ushering the soul back toward the wall.

Can Merlin come with me? the boy asked.

"No, not yet," Gavenia said as tears welled in her eyes.

Can Mama and Daddy come?

"No, but someday they'll be there with you."

The little boy's face clouded.

The bad man won't find me, will he?

Gavenia felt a sharp twinge of pain in her chest. "You mean the man who hit you?"

The boy nodded vigorously. *He tried to take me away.*

Gavenia frowned. That didn't make sense.

"Is there something wrong?" Gregory asked.

Gavenia took a deep breath and shook her head, not eager to

prolong the father's agony.

"Bradley, it's time. You see your grandmother?" she asked, pointing in the distance toward the shadowy figure. The boy nodded. "Then say good-bye to Merlin and go to your nana," Gavenia said, her voice shaking.

Bye-bye, Merlin! the boy called. Bradley shuffled toward the wall as though he'd been sent to bed early. Beyond the veil, Nana Alliford waited. She knelt, arms held open in welcome, her spirit glowing like a brilliant sun on a frigid winter's day.

Come to me, Bradley, she said.

The boy took one last look toward his father and then ran forward with outswept arms and buried himself in his nana's embrace. She spoke quietly in his ear, and after a time, he nodded. She tied his shoelace, rose, and took his hand. Without a backward glance, she walked into the mist. At the very last minute, Bradley turned and flashed that innocent smile of his. He waved and then vanished.

The dog issued a mournful howl, one that set Gavenia's teeth on edge and made the hair on her arms rise.

"Dwell in the sunshine, Bradley," she whispered. She set her tears free and they rolled down her cheeks, wetting her shirt. Behind her, Father Elliot prayed in a voice made strong with faith.

Gregory Alliford's grief overwhelmed him, and deep, aching sobs rolled from his chest. Gavenia knelt beside him, placing her arm around his waist. The priest knelt on the other side of the stricken man, a reassuring hand on his shoulder.

"He is with the angels now; he's safe," Elliot said. His eyes met hers, and she saw he was barely holding his own grief in check.

"What will I do? There's nothing left," Gregory said, looking from Gavenia's face to that of the priest.

"You have to go on, Gregory," Gavenia said. A wet nose nuzzled her hand. She pulled Merlin closer to them. "Merlin needs you."

The bereft father sought her eyes and then gave a quick nod, petting the dog. "I'll watch over him. I won't let anything happen to him," he promised. "I'll do it for Bradley."

Gavenia rose with considerable difficulty and moved to where

Bradley had crossed over. The wall was solid now, showing no evidence that he'd passed across. Resting her forehead against the wallpaper, she let her grief rain down on the clowns and their jaunty umbrellas.

Her task was complete; Bradley Alliford's soul was safe.

Then why do I feel so empty?

Relief warred with an aching sense of loss. Though Gavenia had held it together for Gregory's sake, it was a near thing.

As if understanding her tenuous state, Father Elliot offered to escort her to her car.

"Thank you," she said. "This one has been so hard."

"How many others have you helped?" the priest asked.

"Bradley's the twenty-third. The others were . . . well, mostly older, ready to go on to something better. Bradley was my first child."

Elliot's hand lightly touched her shoulder. "You did very well. I can only imagine how hard it is."

"It doesn't seem to get easier."

"Bradley tugged on my stole, didn't he?"

She looked up immediately. "Yes. Does that sound weird to you?"

"Not any weirder than having Doug tell me you spoke to his father's ghost."

Doug? It took her a bit to connect the dots. "O'Fallon is a hard man to convince."

The priest scrutinized her closely. "It's the truth that matters to him." He looked toward the house. "My faith has been reinforced today." His head swiveled back toward her with a curious expression. "Have you see it? Heaven, I mean?"

"No, I'm not allowed across, at least not while I'm alive. I'm not in any hurry to make that journey."

He nodded his understanding. "Neither am I." He pulled a business card out of a pocket and handed it to her. "Let's keep in touch, Ms. Kingsgrave."

"Gavenia," she said, offering her hand.

"Avery," he replied, and they shook.

"Thanks for being so understanding, Avery."

Gavenia watched him walk back up the stairs into the massive house. She didn't envy him his task.

* * *

O'Fallon rang Gavenia's doorbell twice but got no response. He turned to leave, then hesitated. Despite the positive report from Avery, he really couldn't leave. *I just want to make sure she's okay.*

He tried the knob—the door was unlocked. A ball of anxiety formed in his gut. He knocked again and then shoved open the door, hoping he'd not be met with a loaded firearm. Instead he found himself challenged by a sleek cat with big green eyes. A black one.

"And I'm a walking stereotype?" he muttered, shaking his head. The hallway proved mundane—no inverted crosses, bat skulls, or the like. Even the photographs of the witch's family looked normal.

"Gavenia?" he called. Silence. He raised his voice. "Gavenia?"

A low meow came from the floor as the cat sauntered down the hall ahead of him. Not having any other option, he closed the door and followed the feline. It paused outside a room, sat down, and groomed a paw in a casual manner.

"Is she in there?" he asked, and then felt ridiculous. He was talking to the cat just like he did Seamus. Only lonely people talked to their animals.

He peered inside the room, where a smattering of candles provided the only illumination, their light twinkling off pale-yellow walls. What appeared to be an altar stood at the far end of the room, low to the ground. Incense hung heavy in the air, and it made his eyes sting.

Must be some sort of sanctuary. "Gavenia?" he called again.

"I'm here."

He hunted through the semidarkness until he found her sitting in a corner, her knees drawn up to her chin, her hair draped around her like a golden blanket. He removed his jacket, hung it over a chair, and sat on the floor next to her.

"He would have been such a great person," she said in a raw voice, one thick with grief.

O'Fallon gently wiped away a tear as it trickled down her puffy cheek. "He's at peace now."

He pulled her into his arms, holding her tight despite the twinge in his ribs. She curled into him like a child seeking respite from a hideous nightmare. "You didn't call. I got worried," he murmured.

A slight nod against his chest. "I only made it as far the temple. I just couldn't go any farther."

They huddled together for a time, neither speaking. He could feel her heartbeat through his fingers. The incense plagued his nose, threatening a sneeze, and he gritted his teeth to hold it back.

"Would you like some tea?" she asked. She wiggled out of his embrace and sat upright. He helped her stand, earning him both a grateful look and a kiss on the cheek.

"You're a good guy, you know that?"

He shrugged. "I'm okay."

As she left the room, he noted she was leaning more heavily on the cane. It seemed to be a barometer of her mood.

With nothing else to do, he wandered around and found the cat. It sat on a shelf in the bookcase, curled up on a thick pillow, watching him with those dark-green eyes. He studied the statues flanking the beast and rummaged through his memory for the Egyptian goddess they represented. The name wouldn't come. He moved closer and found it engraved at the base of the statues.

"'Bastet,'" he read. The cat trilled in response. "Must be your name, too."

The cat rose from the cushion and allowed him to scratch her head, purring appreciatively.

"You're rather friendly for the devil's minion."

He heard a low chuckle from the doorway.

"Trademark of a good minion," his hostess observed. She handed him a steaming cup of tea.

"Just trying to figure out if my mortal soul is in danger," he joked, testing the waters.

"Not from us. We only like virgins," she bantered back. "You wouldn't know any, would you?"

"No, not a one." He delivered a few more scratches under Bastet's chin, and the cat ratcheted up her purring.

"Is she your . . . what do you call them . . . ?"

"Familiar? Nope, just a cat. She appeared on my doorstep about eight months ago."

"A black cat just came to your door?"

"All sorts of strays find their way to my door, O'Fallon," she jested with a glint of mischief. "Come on, sit down and enjoy the tea."

He settled into an overstuffed chair and sighed appreciatively. The chair was comfortable, just like the room. It felt like the sanctuary at Saint Bridget's, safe and sacred—as though the outside world didn't exist.

He eyed the witch as she perched on a cushion she'd positioned next to the wall. She seemed to like to sit on the floor.

"What?" she asked. He'd been caught staring.

"Just wondering why you sit on the floor all the time."

"Makes me feel connected to the earth."

"No other reason?"

"My hip seems to be less cranky down here."

He shifted gears. "What kind of room is this?"

"It's my temple, my magic room."

"It feels like a church."

Gavenia nodded. "It's a similar kind of energy. If the worship you offer is positive and loving, the energy will feel the same."

"The only witches I've encountered have been the scary ones, the Satanists."

She shook her head immediately, her hair shifting in time to the movement. "Satanists aren't Wiccans. They cultivate the darkness, revel in it."

"And you?" O'Fallon came right back.

For some reason the question seemed vital, as if a bridge needed to be crossed, even if just in his own mind. She studied him with those deep eyes. Did she sense the doubts raging within him?

"There's enough evil in the world. It doesn't need any more power. I only do Light work."

He took a sip of the tea and pondered her comment.

"So if someone was threatening your family, you wouldn't slap a spell on them?"

A reflective expression appeared. "Ah, that old question. I'll turn it back at you. If someone threatened Seamus or your grandmother, would you shoot them?"

"In a heartbeat."

She didn't seem surprised at his reply, but nodded as if she'd expected it.

"I won't use dark magic, but I will use offensive magic if someone I love is threatened."

"How dangerous is this offensive stuff?"

"Just as nasty as a gun."

"Really." He took another sip of the tea. It was licorice, some sort of herbal blend. "Needs sugar," he muttered, and set the cup on the table next to him.

Gavenia rose to her feet, using the wall as support. Realizing she'd heard the comment, he shook his head. "No, no, it'll be fine. I didn't mean for you to get up."

"It's not a problem. I should have brought the sugar anyway."

She disappeared out the door. As he waited, he noticed a small penknife on the end table. Curious, he picked it up. It felt cool within his palm. He flipped it over with a thumb. It was engraved—*Bradley.*

His hostess returned, bearing a sugar bowl.

When she saw him holding the knife, she explained, "Gregory gave it to me as a remembrance along with one of Bradley's bears," she added, pointing toward a furry astronaut located on the shelf one level lower than the cat.

O'Fallon closed his palm without thinking.

The moment his hand encircled the knife, he knew he'd made a mistake. Sweat burst on his forehead and his eyes burned as if sprayed with acid. He tried to pry open his fist, but failed. It clenched convulsively, as if the knife refused to be set free. He opened his mouth to beg for help. No words came.

O'Fallon thought he heard the witch call his name, felt her touch him, but he wasn't sure. As a black abyss opened in front of him, he fell out of the chair, onto his knees. The darkness pulled on him, swirling, hauling him down into its gaping maw.

Images tumbled: the little boy playing, his brown eyes twinkling in the sunlight, his baseball hat crooked at an angle, one of his shoelaces untied and dragging on the pavement. Merlin bounded around him, barking in excited tones. A man's voice called the boy by name. Bradley answered, the smile still on his face.

"No, don't," O'Fallon shouted, as if he could stop the drama playing out in his mind.

Hands grabbed at Bradley, pulling hard. The boy struggled and cried out. There was deep snarling and then an oath followed by a high-pitched howl of pain.

"Run," O'Fallon called. "Run!"

The boy broke free and dashed away in blind panic. The images accelerated, streaming before O'Fallon's eyes like torrential raindrops: the little boy running, the limping dog, the SUV accelerating in an effort to catch the fleeing pair.

"Oh, God, no!" he bellowed.

He felt the blinding moment of impact, the crushing blow to the chest, the sensation of weightlessness as the small body arced into the air and careened off the side mirror in an explosion of glass.

The body tumbled over and over like a leaf and crumpled to the pavement. The stench of burning rubber stung O'Fallon's nose. A low, mournful howl filled his head. The scene abruptly disintegrated like a sand castle in a heavy wave.

O'Fallon slumped to his left side, despite the injury to his ribs, curling into a fetal position. Tears burned down his cheeks.

He sucked incense-laden air deep into his lungs in thick gulps, choking in the process. With each hammer beat of his heart, his head roared like a jet engine.

Hands touched him and he fought them, striking, connecting. The darkness returned, and he welcomed its embrace.

Chapter Twenty

O'Fallon felt a hand on his shoulder and heard comforting words in his ear. He had no idea what they meant, but the roaring in his head decreased and he was able to breathe again. He lay on his back, the first few buttons of his shirt open. A cool cloth mopped his face. His rosary was clenched in his left hand. When had he pulled it from his pocket? Or had he?

"Doug?" the voice called, and he nodded slowly to acknowledge it. The cloth made another pass over his forehead, and this time he forced opened his eyes. He found Gavenia's deep-blue ones riveted on him, wide in concern.

"Do you need me to call a doctor?" she asked. Her voice sounded steady, but he heard the edge of panic in every word.

"No." He gingerly rolled to his right side, taking slow, measured breaths. His mind wasn't quite whole yet, thoughts still disjointed. She helped him sit upright and propped him against the overstuffed chair, adding pillows behind him for comfort.

The boy must have been carrying the knife when he died—that was the only way the sensations would have been that strong. Did the witch know that? Was this some sort of a cruel test?

A cup of water appeared in front of him, and he took hesitant sips. The cool liquid flowed down his parched throat, soothing it. Once it was empty, he handed it back to her and she set it aside. Taking one of his hands, she held it between her warm palms.

"What happened to you?" she asked.

He couldn't hide it any longer, had no wish to. "I get sensations from things. The knife . . . I saw . . . Bradley's death."

Gavenia's mouth dropped open. "You're psychometric?"

O'Fallon felt a hand on his shoulder and heard comforting words in his ear. He had no idea what they meant, but the roaring in his head decreased and he was able to breathe again. He lay on his back, the first few buttons of his shirt open. A cool cloth mopped his face. His rosary was clenched in his left hand. When had he pulled it from his pocket? Or had he?

"Doug?" the voice called, and he nodded slowly to acknowledge it. The cloth made another pass over his forehead, and this time he forced opened his eyes. He found Gavenia's deep-blue ones riveted on him, wide in concern.

"Do you need me to call a doctor?" she asked. Her voice sounded steady, but he heard the edge of panic in every word.

"No." He gingerly rolled to his right side, taking slow, measured breaths. His mind wasn't quite whole yet, thoughts still disjointed. She helped him sit upright and propped him against the overstuffed chair, adding pillows behind him for comfort.

The boy must have been carrying the knife when he died—that was the only way the sensations would have been that strong. Did the witch know that? Was this some sort of a cruel test?

A cup of water appeared in front of him, and he took hesitant sips. The cool liquid flowed down his parched throat, soothing it. Once it was empty, he handed it back to her and she set it aside. Taking one of his hands, she held it between her warm palms.

"What happened to you?" she asked.

He couldn't hide it any longer, had no wish to. "I get sensations from things. The knife . . . I saw . . . Bradley's death."

Gavenia's mouth dropped open. "You're psychometric?"

He looked deep into her eyes and then nodded.

"Why in the hell didn't you tell me? Good Goddess, I never would have let you touch anything of his," she said, furious.

The sound of squealing tires ricocheted through his mind, and O'Fallon shivered. "He died instantly."

Gavenia looked down and then gently kissed his hand.

"Thank the Goddess," she whispered. As if realizing the penknife still posed a threat, she scooped it up off the floor and stuck it in her pants pocket.

"I need to go home," he said, trying to rise.

"No, no, you've had a major psychic experience. You need time to adjust to all this. Stay here for a while, let things settle down, then I'll drive you home."

"No, I need to go," he insisted, lurching to his feet.

He heard a phone ring; Gavenia ignored it for a time, but finally rose. "Just stay put. I'll explain everything in a moment." She hurried out the door.

O'Fallon didn't want an explanation. He wanted to be out of here, safe, where nothing would trigger the horrific visions.

"I have to get home," he said, grabbing his jacket where it sat on the chair. He moved with great care, fearful of touching anything that wasn't his.

As O'Fallon walked by the bookcase, Bastet meowed at him, but he shied away as if she was a threat, forgetting he'd petted her earlier. He paused in the hallway and stared toward the kitchen. Gavenia paced, phone to her ear, talking rapidly.

No, can't stay. He pulled open the front door and plunged outside into the chill evening air. It burrowed into his lungs, rapidly displacing the incense. His disorientation increased.

The moment he reached his car, he felt the panic rising in his gut, choking him, as his heartbeat sped up. His skin crawled, millions of unseen ants pricking at his flesh, slowly consuming him.

O'Fallon swung in an arc, hunting for the danger—no one near, no reason to feel threatened. Still, he felt vulnerable, as if surrounded by unseen predators. He unlocked the car door with a shaking hand.

He'd barely got the key into the ignition when the witch appeared at his door, knocking on the windshield. He locked the doors. He had to run away. The witch had planned this whole thing, suckered him inside her lair and then incapacitated him, just like a spider bound an insect before sucking it dry. Why hadn't he seen it sooner? Why hadn't he realized she was after his immortal soul?

"Don't go!" Gavenia called. She sounded frantic, but that had to be an act. He turned the key. More knocking on the windshield.

"You don't see them. It's not safe! Stay here!" she insisted.

He threw the car into gear and veered into the roadway, narrowly missing his frantic hostess as she scurried out of his way. He heard her shouting a name as he gunned the motor. It sounded familiar, but it didn't matter. *Escape* was the only word he understood.

"Dammit!" Gavenia swore, stamping her foot in frustration. She paced in the driveway in an erratic circle, her cane forgotten in the rush. Bart stood nearby, his arms folded over his chest, eyeing their surroundings warily. He glowed as if sending a warning of some sort.

"You saw them?" she asked.

Oh, yeah. Worse yet, they saw him.

"I think there were three, maybe four earthbounds."

At least.

Gavenia rubbed the bridge of her nose in thought.

"I'll call him on his cell phone. Maybe he'll settle down once he's away from here. He's got to go someplace safe."

It's time you went inside. He's attracted too much interest, Bart said, his arms dropping to his side in a defiant pose. His glow increased.

Her eyes scanned around them, picking out at least five entities hovering in the shadows waiting for her to lower her guard. Their brittle voices called to her, earthbound entities keen to feed on the Light. Gavenia ignored them and hurried back to the condo, murmuring a spell of protection.

Bart took one last look at the dark forms and followed his Shepherd. *Gee, General Custer, just how many Indians can there be?*

* * *

When O'Fallon halted at a stoplight a few blocks away from the condo, he leaned his forehead against the cold steering wheel. A ringing sound assaulted his ears. In time, he realized it was his cell phone, so he dug into his jacket and squinted at the caller ID. It was *her*. He dropped the phone onto the seat next to him as the call rolled over to voice mail.

His obsessive need to get home had evaporated, shoved aside by thoughts that made no sense. Voices whispered on the edge of his hearing, their words overlapping one another. They called his name over and over, and each time felt like the blade of a razor dragging along his skin.

A man appeared in the road in front him. O'Fallon swung the steering wheel hard, narrowly missing him.

"Crazy bastard," he growled. Again the man appeared, and O'Fallon swerved like a drunk, causing another car to honk at his erratic behavior. When the figure appeared once again, too quickly to avoid a collision, O'Fallon cried out as the Chevy ploughed through him. He waited for the scream of agony, the thump as the body impacted the grille. They never came. He'd struck a ghost.

"Oh dear God," he said, and a coarse shiver shot through him. Shrill beeps bounced off the car's interior. A new voice-mail message. "Go away! Leave me alone," he shouted. "I'm not listening to you."

The phantom chorus in his head rose in volume as if in response to his command. He hunched forward, his hands clawing into the steering wheel, his shirt soaked in sweat. In the car's dark interior, the cell phone's face ignited with an eerie glow, but it didn't ring. Puzzled, he picked it up in a shaking hand. The text message said, *Go to your church.*

"Saint Bridget's."

Avery would know what to do. He tried to dial his old friend, but he couldn't remember all the numbers. The cacophony in his head grew as if ten thousand demons were bellowing all at once. Oblivious to his driving, he blew through a stoplight, incurring the wrath of a taxi driver, who flipped him off.

"Go to the church," he repeated like a mantra. O'Fallon dug in his pocket for his rosary, and when it emerged, he kissed it and wrapped it around his right hand.

"Sweet Saint Bridget, help me," he prayed.

The din in his mind retreated, like the tide flowing outward from the beach. The voices were still there, calling to him, and he swore he could feel flames dancing along his skin.

Then there was another voice, different from the dark ones.

This one was calm, as if there was no threat it could not face. A soft glow filled the car. A glance at the passenger seat made him gasp: Benjamin Callendar sat next to him, powder-blue eyes etched with concern.

Go to Saint Bridget's. Father Elliot will help you, the spirit said.

O'Fallon screeched to a halt at a green light causing drivers to honk their horns behind him. He veered around the corner and stopped in a bus lane; a quick scan of his surroundings told him he was lost. Nothing looked familiar.

The voices rose again, taunting him.

"I don't know how to get there," he cried, wiping sweat from his forehead.

Go straight.

"What?"

Go straight. I'll guide you.

He studied the ghostly face, fearing to trust the apparition. What if it was a spell? *The witch could do that, couldn't she?*

If you stay here, you are lost, Benjamin's shade replied. O'Fallon looked into the eyes, searching. In them he saw compassion, understanding. A desire to help him.

"God help me if I'm wrong."

O'Fallon followed the dead man's directions as if they'd come from the Almighty himself. By the time he turned in to the church parking lot and parked under one of the security lights, tears of relief bathed his cheeks and rolled under his shirt collar. He turned to thank his guide, but the ghost was gone.

The voices surged stronger now, no doubt realizing they might lose him once he stepped inside the sanctuary. O'Fallon heaved himself out of the car and sprinted for the church as if the devil's hounds were on his heels, for indeed he felt they were.

He skidded to a halt at the side door and hammered on it, then pushed the bell repeatedly. Shooting a panicked look over his shoulder, he swore he saw dark figures near his car, moving toward him across the parking lot.

The rectory door flung open with a crash.

"Oh, thank God," Avery exclaimed, pulling him inside with a

ferocious tug to his collar. The security door slammed behind them and then the priest bolted it.

The voices abruptly vanished, and O'Fallon heaved a body-trembling sigh of relief.

Avery swept his gaze over his old friend. "You look like hell."

O'Fallon gave a short nod, trying to catch his breath.

They moved to the private chapel, where his friend set about lighting candles. As each one flamed into being, portions of the saint's statue came into focus: first the right side of her benevolent face, then the left side, and finally her gentle hands. Her kind eyes called to O'Fallon, offering him solace, soothing away the nightmare that had encompassed him.

"Thank you, Bridget," he whispered, crossing himself. "I knew you'd help me."

Avery settled on the pew next to him, observing him with intense eyes.

"Gavenia called me," he began.

"What? But she was . . ." O'Fallon's mind cleared enough for him to remember her words. *Go to your church*—that's what she'd shouted. He issued a long sigh. "She was trying to help me."

Avery nodded. "She said you'd be safe here." One of the candles sputtered and then flamed brighter. "What happened, Doug?"

O'Fallon leaned forward, resting his elbows on his knees. Now that his coat was off, his damp shirt felt clammy in the cool air of the chapel.

"I touched the Alliford kid's penknife. I saw how he died. It wasn't an accident. He was run down on purpose."

"Oh, my God." The priest crossed himself then placed a comforting hand on O'Fallon's shoulder. "But why would someone kill the boy?"

"It was a botched kidnapping and Bradley knew the guy. I think the dog interfered, and that's when things went wrong."

"Oh, God, this is going to destroy what's left of Gregory Alliford's world."

O'Fallon nodded. "There's more. . . ." He kept his eyes on the rosary in his hands. "While I was driving, I heard voices. They were

. . ." He shivered in remembrance. "They were so loud I couldn't think. Then I saw the Callendar kid's ghost."

The priest rocked back in shock. "Ben?"

"I couldn't remember how to get to the church; I couldn't even remember your phone number. I wouldn't have made it here if he hadn't helped me."

The priest rubbed his face in weariness and blew out a long breath. "It looks like God's been working overtime tonight."

O'Fallon allowed himself to smile. "Yes, He has. I thought the witch was trying to . . ."

He hesitated—now it sounded silly. Why had it seemed so logical only a short time before? "I thought she was trying to put a spell on me."

"No, I don't think so. Gavenia was frightened; I could hear it in her voice. She said you were attracting . . . entities, whatever that means. It didn't make much sense to me at the time, at least not until I saw you."

"I look that bad?"

A solemn nod. "Stay here tonight. You can use the guest room."

O'Fallon felt safe here, like he had in the witch's house.

Why had he left? Why hadn't he trusted her?

Too many questions.

Avery patted his shoulder and rose. "I'll be in my office. You promise you'll stay here tonight?"

"I promise."

Weight seemed to fall from his friend's shoulders. The moment the priest's footsteps echoed down the hallway, O'Fallon felt the presence. Benjamin Callendar's ghost appeared in the pew next to him as if the young man were still alive and they were at mass.

He carries too much guilt for my death, Ben said.

O'Fallon pushed his disbelief aside. "Why can I see you? I don't see other . . . ghosts."

The apparition pointed toward O'Fallon's shirt pocket. "The medallion."

O'Fallon had forgotten it was there.

We are very much alike. That's why Father Elliot asked you to find my rosary.

"Why did you go to the Hotel LeClaire?" O'Fallon asked.

I didn't want my family to find me. Down there, I'd be just another body. Nobody would care.

"Well, Bernie was upset you died."

The young man looked puzzled and then appeared to connect the name. *He's a nice old guy. We had pizza that night. He didn't know I was going to kill myself.*

"You said we are very much alike. How?"

We both resisted God's gift. The young man gave a gentle smile. *Or at least, I used to.*

O'Fallon pondered on that. "Are . . . were you psychic?"

Not like you or the Shepherd, but I sensed things.

"Did you kill yourself because you heard voices?"

Yes.

O'Fallon's mouth fell open. "But how could you . . ." He searched his heart and knew the bitter truth: he'd have done anything to stop those voices sucking at his very marrow, even commit suicide. He raised his eyes, and Ben's ghost smiled faintly.

Now you understand.

"That's why Avery wanted me on the case, so I'd make the connection. I doubt he figured I'd be meeting you in person."

The ghost nodded. *He couldn't tell you directly, so he did it in the only way he knew how.*

"Thank you for being there tonight," O'Fallon said. "I wouldn't have made it on my own. I'm sorry there wasn't someone there for you."

There was someone, but I was too blind to accept their help. That was my mistake.

Overwhelmed, O'Fallon placed his head in his hands. After some time, he leaned back in the pew, blinking his eyes in the dim candlelight. The dead man was gone, his task apparently complete.

O'Fallon crossed himself, rose, and fell on his knees in front of Saint Bridget's statue. "Bless you for watching out for this stubborn Irishman," he whispered. "And thank you for giving me friends who know when I need help."

Chapter Twenty-One

"Thank the Goddess," Gavenia murmured as she hung up the phone. She jammed her lips together to keep the tears from falling.

Is he safe? Bart asked from his place next to her. He was clad in the blue robe, a contrast to her bright-white robe. They were in the temple room, inside a consecrated circle, one Gavenia had created with unseemly haste.

"Yes. He's staying at the church tonight."

Bart gave a nod of approval. *His vulnerability will be lessened by morning*, he advised. *I'm glad he made it.*

"So am I." She examined the Brigit's cross in her hand, twisting it so the candlelight played across the interwoven rushes, each rush rendered in finest silver. She hadn't had any real rushes to create a cross from scratch. This one, a gift from a friend, would have to do. Using it as a focus, she would weave a spell of protection, asking for divine assistance in keeping Douglas Patrick O'Fallon safe.

"He has no idea what he's facing," she said. The irony of the statement struck her. "Like I'm much better."

Bart eyed her with a worried expression. *You understand the danger*, he said.

"Do I? Do I really know what it takes to be a Shepherd? Or if you told me everything, would I dive into the closest bottle of vodka and stay there?"

His gaze met hers. *There is more, and I'll tell when I'm allowed to. But stay away from the alcohol.*

"Oh, are tipsy Shepherds hard to keep track of?" she joked.

He looked away now, averting his eyes as if they'd reveal some dark secret.

"One of the homeless guys told me he drank so he couldn't hear the voices."

Bart jerked his head back in her direction. She'd hit home.

"If I drink too much, I won't be able to see or hear the spirits, will I?"

No.

"Will I be able to see you?"

No.

So there it was—become a lush, and it all went away.

Nothing is that easy.

"What's the downside? A rotten liver? An early grave?" she taunted.

He didn't reply, but vanished in an instant with a distinct snap. She took that as supreme disapproval.

"So there is a way out."

Gavenia smoothed a finger over the uneven surface of the cross. Now was not the time to make that decision; O'Fallon came first. She closed her eyes, cleared her mind, and began the ritual. At least the Irishman would be safe.

* * *

Avery's eyebrows ascended at record speed. There was a witch on the church's doorstep, clad in an emerald-green Kinsale cloak.

"Sorry, we don't have midnight mass," he joked, trying to lessen the tension.

Gavenia chuckled nervously. "And I'm sorry for coming so late, but . . ." She glanced behind her as if uneasy. "I don't want O'Fallon to know I'm here."

He's turned in for the night. *Collapsed* was closer to the truth.

"Good. He needs to rest after . . ." She seemed to be struggling for words. The blue eyes reached his. "I have a rather unusual request to make."

"Well, it's been a rather unusual night." He welcomed her inside and then locked the door behind them. "We can talk in the library."

As they negotiated their way through the church's hallways, Avery took a quick glance at his watch, pressing the button to illuminate the dial. It was nearing midnight—his joke had been closer to the mark than he'd realized. Sleep was going to be at a premium the way folks were lining up at his door.

As they sat in the library's two armchairs, flanked by walls of books, Avery scrutinized his visitor closely. His first impression of her at the Alliford's had been correct—she had intelligent eyes and a bearing that spoke of an old soul. *No wonder Doug is intrigued by her.*

Gavenia gingerly rearranged her position in the armchair, apparently trying to get comfortable.

"Sorry, the chairs here aren't very well padded, even for a library," Avery apologized.

"No, it's okay. My hip gives me problems every now and then."

"Old football injury?" he joked, testing the waters.

She smiled instantly. "No, a wayward broom."

He returned the grin, pleased she was beginning to loosen up. "I was hoping you could explain what happened to Doug tonight."

The witch nodded. "He touched Bradley's penknife and collapsed. I thought he was having a heart attack. He never told me he was psychic."

"He's very uncomfortable with that."

She chuffed. "No kidding." Gavenia hesitated, and then continued, "I'm trying to figure out how to explain this you." She gave a wan smile. "It's . . . rather strange."

"I'll try to follow along," Avery offered.

"By experiencing such an intense a vision, O'Fallon opened himself up psychically. Suddenly he sensed all sorts of stuff that scared the hell out him. Worse yet, all sorts of things noticed him."

Avery leaned forward. "What sorts of things? Do you mean devils?"

She shook her head again. "Nothing to do with Satan or demons or anything like that. These are earthbound forms. Some are souls that haven't crossed over and others are, well . . . just entities. They haven't been enveloped by the Light. They don't belong here and so they seek energy to feed on."

"So Doug has the kind of energy they want?"

"Yes. His gift attracts them. Tonight he glowed like a lighthouse after the penknife incident. That's the only reason I didn't call the paramedics."

"Do you appear the same to these . . . entities?"

"Not as much anymore. I've learned how to shield my gift from them, but they're still out there and I consider them a threat."

Avery sighed and studied his hands. "None of my professors at the seminary ever got into this sort of thing."

"I suppose not."

"Did one these things come after Bradley in his room?"

She stilled. "Yes. Gregory told you about that?"

Avery nodded. "I thought maybe he'd had too much to drink, but now . . . How would you know if you were being targeted by these things?"

"You'd feel paranoid; you'd see visions and hear voices."

Avery shifted awkwardly. "What happens if you try to ignore them?"

"They keep working on you like termites on a log, sucking energy, draining you, taking over your thoughts."

"Could it lead you to consider suicide?"

"Perhaps."

"Good God," he said. "Did you tell Doug all this?"

Gavenia shook her head. "He wasn't listening. He was too afraid of what'd he'd seen. I know how that is." She lowered her eyes and with a slight movement she placed her left hand over its quivering mate.

"You said you had an unusual request for me?" Avery asked.

Gavenia reached into a pocket, pulled out a satin pouch, and handed it to him.

"Doug needs some sort of talisman, something tied to his faith that will shield him. His rosary will help, but he needs a bit more than that."

Pulling open the drawstrings, Avery slid the pouch's contents onto his palm and blinked in surprise. It wasn't what he had expected. "It's a Saint Bridget's Cross," he said, looking at the witch in astonishment.

Gavenia gave him a nod. "Our two faiths have her in common, even though we spell her name differently. Since O'Fallon's Irish, I asked Brigit to empower the cross, to protect him as a Celtic goddess would one of her own."

"What do you want me to do with it?" Avery asked, intrigued.

"As O'Fallon's Catholic, I'd like you to ask your Saint Bridget to do the same. By combining our strengths, maybe we can keep him safe."

Avery puzzled over the unusual proposal; it definitely wasn't in line with church doctrine.

They gauged each other for a moment.

"Doug and I have argued about his psychometric ability for the last five years. He's fought me all the way," he said, buying time.

"Apparently they did cover some of this in seminary."

Avery gave a shrug. "I'm an avid reader."

The witch exhaled deeply. "I made a vow to Brigit that I will not compromise Doug's faith in any way." She gestured toward a statue of the saint that sat in the corner of the library in a lighted niche. "*She* is his strength. I have no right to interfere." Gavenia abruptly rose, as if she'd run out of arguments. "I leave the decision in your hands, Father," she said, indicating the cross.

"I'll pray on it," Avery said, slipping the item into the pouch and tucking it into his shirt pocket.

After locking the rectory door behind her, he felt in his pocket for the cross. How would he reconcile the witch's request with his faith? With a low sigh, Avery headed toward the private chapel. He had a number of hours of prayer ahead of him, and only God and Saint Bridget could show him the way.

* * *

The smell of fresh coffee beckoned to Gavenia only a moment before Ari drew open the curtains and flooded the bedroom in brilliant, burning light.

"Goddess, what are you doing?" Gavenia mumbled, pulling a pillow over her head.

"Time to get up."

She raised the pillow sufficiently to see that it was just past seven. Ari always started the day at the crack of dawn. "Go away," Gavenia ordered.

A heavy plop made the bed shake.

"Page ten, left-hand column. The picture sucks."

Gavenia slowly maneuvered herself upright and tugged the morning paper closer. She flipped to the designated page, sought out the article, and swore at the headline: QUEEN OF THE PSYCHIC CHARLATANS.

She skimmed the article, praying it wasn't as bad as she feared. It proved worse. Bill Jones had faithfully transcribed every word and added a few dramatic embellishments. His summary of her *performance*, as he called it, was scathing.

> **In a spectacle unworthy of a B-movie actress, Ms. Kingsgrave hysterically spouted a blood-soaked tale about my mother's brutal murder. While I admit this is Hollywood and some poetic license is allowed, my mother is alive and approaching her sixty-fifth birthday. I didn't hang around long enough for the hook, but I knew it was coming. Charlatans like this want money. Despite her protestations, I knew the scam was in play the moment she channeled my dead mom.**

"You lying bastard," Gavenia growled, slinging the paper across the room, where it descended in a flurry at her sister's feet. Ari adopted their aunt's favorite stance, leaning on the doorjamb, her arms crossed over her chest.

"So, what do you intend to do?" she demanded.

"What can I do? By tonight Letterman will be doing a Top Ten list with my name on it."

"Fight back."

"With what?" Gavenia snarled, rising out of bed. Her left thigh immediately cramped, and she rubbed it furiously.

"With whatever it takes," Ari replied, straightening up and dropping her hands to her sides. "Talk to Llewellyn. He'll help you."

"Suing the paper isn't going to make this go away. I just have to ignore it, and in a few weeks—"

"Stop it! Just stop it!" Ari gave the papers at her feet a furious kick, and they hurtled into the air, then settled to the floor like massive leaves. "Don't you see what you're doing?" she challenged.

"I'm admitting there's nothing I can do."

"No, you're playing the victim, *again*. You used to be the strong one, the one who stood up to bullies, the one who always kept me safe. Now you're—" Ari waved a hand and gave the papers at her feet another vicious boot. "Now you duck and run." She grabbed Gavenia's cane from the door handle and held it up. "This is a prime example. There is no reason you need this. I know your leg hurts, but you've refused physical therapy and you hobble around like an old woman. Hell, even Lucy walks better than you do, and she's had her hip replaced."

Gavenia's mouth dropped open. "What is this, Pooh?"

"Don't play innocent. You're doing all this on purpose. Look at your hand!"

Gavenia refused to look down. She knew the hand was quaking.

"You wear it like a badge of honor. Don't you know how that makes me feel?" Ari didn't wait for an answer, but plunged ahead. "Guilty, that's how I feel. Is that what you want? Well, you've got it."

"Why would I want you to feel guilty?" Gavenia snapped, grabbing on to the bedpost for support.

"Because you kept me from being taken by those perverts. I never would have survived in that steel cage. I never would have had the guts to escape. They would have . . ." She faltered and stepped backward, unsteadily. "You fought those guys off and gave me time to escape. If not, I'd be dead."

"Ari, I never—"

"No, you've never said it, but I feel it every day of my life. My sister could have died because of me. If you hadn't told me to run . . ." She looked away, wiping tears from her eyes.

"They needed two girls for their plans," Gavenia said solemnly.

"What?"

"Two. That's why they didn't kill me right off. They were trying to find another girl."

"You never told me that!" Ari said, stunned.

"There was a lot I didn't tell you."

Her sister's face twisted from confusion back to anger. "Well, we're a pair, aren't we? We switched places all those years ago. Now you're too scared to do anything, too frightened to defend yourself even when you're in the right."

"And you're too blind to see you married a man who ran you like a top, who remade you in his own image," she shouted, gall in her voice.

Ari's eyes flared. "Damn you!" She swung out the room, her feet pounding down the stairs followed by the crashing slam of the front door. Paul hadn't been at her side during the entire confrontation; Ari's seething anger had driven him away.

Gavenia sat on the bed with a trembling breath. She clenched her fists but it didn't keep the memories at bay.

They'd been in the park next to their aunt's house, always a safe place. Gavenia was five years older than Ari and had been assigned the task of keeping her ten-year-old sister safe. As Ari ran to catch an errant Frisbee, a van had pulled up along the curb and a man had stepped out. Something about him had frightened Gavenia, and the moment he moved toward her sister, she'd shouted for Ari to run. In the end, it had been Gavenia who'd been kidnapped.

She'd spent three days in a cage in the woods. Once she'd escaped, but had been caught almost immediately and returned to her prison. Her captors, one old and one young, hadn't raped her, but she knew they would once they found another girl that fit their specifications, however sick those might be. She also knew this wasn't the first time they'd committed this hideous crime.

Seventy-two hours later she'd been found in that cage courtesy of Llewellyn, who had never given up hope. She could still remember him crying as he helped her to freedom. Despite that joy, her tormentors had escaped and continued to kidnap and kill. They'd never been caught.

Her sister was right—from the moment Gavenia was freed, she'd collapsed into herself. If she took no risks, nothing bad would happen every again. She'd carefully constructed her life, choice by choice, all with one thing in mind: staying safe. The accident in Wales had proven her theory didn't hold water. Life was dangerous no matter how hard you tried to hide from it.

Welcome to the real world, Bart whispered from his place near the window.

"Did you hear all that?"

He nodded. *So did most of LA.*

"Is she right? Am I an emotional cripple because of . . . ?" Gavenia couldn't say the words.

Do you think you're an emotional cripple?

"Don't answer a question with another question," she said. "I know that tactic. It's called reflection. Lucy uses it on her patients."

Really?

She opened her mouth to protest and then let it go. Her hand continued to flutter in her lap. The trembling had begun the day after she'd been pulled from the cage. The older man had made her hold hands with him while he talked to her. He'd made her do other things as well, always with that hand and it was now a permanent reminder of that horror.

She'd prayed it would rot off, and her prayers had been ignored. Lucy said she needed to exorcise her demons, and then it would stop shaking.

But you haven't. Isn't twenty-two years long enough? Bart asked, watching her closely.

"Eternity isn't long enough."

Then you'll be forced to deal with this in the next life. Gavenia's eyes widened in astonishment. *That shouldn't surprise you. It's the way it works.*

"Goddess," she said, and rubbed her face wearily. *One thing at a time.* "So what do you think I should do about . . . that," she asked, pointing to the pile of newsprint on the floor.

A coward dies a thousand deaths. . . .

"Meaning?"

What have you got to lose?

"It could get worse."

You didn't think that the night you broke out of that cage and escaped into the woods. You fought back.

"That was different."

Was it? Bart challenged, moving a few steps closer to her. *Life is a series of tests, Gavenia. Some are bigger than others, but all are important.*

"What about you? Do you get tested?" she growled.

Her Guardian nodded. *Sometimes I pass them.* He faded from view, leaving behind the sunlight streaming through the window in long, airy shafts.

Gavenia limped into the bathroom and tried to turn the faucet in the shower. Her jittery hand made the task difficult. Angered, she slammed it against the tile with a loud thump; pain catapulted into her shoulder. The hand convulsed into a fist, the nails digging into her palm like barbed wire.

"I hate you!" she shouted, sinking to her knees on the chilly tile floor. "I hate you!"

The words echoed in the small room. As she leaned against the shower door, she thought she could hear her captor's brutal laughter. He didn't care if she hated him or the mark he'd left on her body. He'd had all the power.

"Just like Jones," she whispered.

Chapter Twenty-Two

"I want you to be careful," Avery said as they shared breakfast in the rectory's kitchen after mass.

"I'm fine now," O'Fallon said for the third time, amused.

"Bullshit," Avery replied, followed by a belated glance toward the door, most likely to ascertain whether the rectory's housekeeper was within earshot.

O'Fallon nearly choked on his orange juice. "Don't do that," he said, coughing again. "Priests don't use that word."

"This one does when he knows he's being lied to. You're not fine. You're in trouble, and we both know it."

"I don't know what you mean."

Avery glowered; it wasn't an attractive look when mixed with the clerical collar. "You're denying everything that happened last night?"

O'Fallon shook his head. "No. I'm . . . embracing it."

The priest's face screwed up in confusion. "What? I don't understand."

"You've been too busy warning me to realize the situation has changed. I spent some more time talking to Ben's ghost last night. I know why you put me on that case." Avery slowly lowered his fork, never once removing his eyes from his guest.

O'Fallon continued, "You hoped that if I found out why he killed himself, maybe I'd get the hint that I could end up the same way."

"Are you upset I used you like that?"

"Somewhat, but I'll get over it," O'Fallon replied, watching his friend closely.

The priest speared a sausage. "It was the only way I could tell you."

"It worked."

Avery frowned. "I figured you'd be really pissed at me."

O'Fallon shrugged. "After last night . . ." A deep inhalation. "I can't be angry with you, my friend."

The priest chewed on the sausage and followed it with a sip of coffee. "You need to be careful." He extracted a pouch from his shirt pocket and slid it across the table. "This will help."

O'Fallon cleaned his fingers on a napkin and took possession of the pouch. A silver Saint Bridget's cross dropped into his palm, and he looked up in surprise.

Before he could comment, Avery explained, "I want you to wear it at all times, even when you're sleeping. Do you understand?"

His friend's tone of voice generated a shiver, one O'Fallon barely repressed. "I assume you've blessed it."

The priest hesitated and then nodded. "Yes. It's been . . . thoroughly blessed."

Odd way to put it. O'Fallon closed his palm around the cross and listened to what it had to say to him. Love, warmth, security, the voices of monks, the clear blue skies of Ireland . . . No . . . not skies . . .

He opened his hand to find Avery studying him. "Gavenia's touched this, hasn't she?"

The priest nodded. "She brought it to me last night. She had her . . . deity . . . bless it and asked me to have Saint Bridget do the same."

"I see." O'Fallon mulled that over. Was he comfortable wearing something the witch's goddess had blessed?

As if knowing his dilemma, Avery added, "I anointed it with holy water, and it spent the night in Saint Bridget's hands."

If Avery's okay with it . . . "I bet Rome would just love this."

A glare. "I know what's best for my flock."

O'Fallon raised his hands in surrender.

Hell hath no fury like a pissed-off priest. Dropping his hands, he kissed the cross and placed it over his head, letting it fall under his shirt. It tingled against his skin.

"Thank you, Avery," he said quietly.

"Just be careful."

"Oh, I will."

"You sound very sure of yourself."

"I am. I intend to find Bradley's killer and I want Glass behind bars."

Avery grew pensive. "As your confessor, I would remind you that vengeance is the Lord's purview."

"And as Adam's father?" O'Fallon asked.

"As Adam's father?" The priest rose from his seat and dabbed his mouth with a napkin. "Nail the bastard."

A fine, crisp morning greeted O'Fallon as he stepped outside the church, and he took a deep inhalation, savoring the moment. He listened for the voices, though in his heart he knew they wouldn't be there. Instead of the horror of the night before, he was welcomed by the reassuring sounds of car horns, chirping birds, and a driver trying to cajole a traffic officer out of a ticket. Rubbing his fingers over the top of the cross, he whispered, "Thank you, Lord."

* * *

"What do you mean I can't sue him?" Gavenia demanded, a scowl on her face. "He's lying, Llewellyn; we both know that."

"Yes, but that means jack in court." Llewellyn inserted a neat stack of papers inside a folder and placed it on the side of his broad desk. "What sort of evidence do you have?" he asked.

"Well, nothing but—"

He waved her off. "Come on; you worked in this office—you know what you need to present a case. Do you have anything that proves his mother was murdered and that he knew of it before he ran the article?" Llewellyn challenged.

"Well, no . . ."

"If you can prove prior knowledge, then we can go for libel. If not, you're out of luck."

She opened and closed her mouth in rapid succession. "Damn."

"Precisely."

"What if I find the proof?" she asked, her hand gripping the cane so tightly her fingers blanched.

"Then that bastard's balls are mine."

Gavenia cracked a grin and he followed suit.

"Let me see what I can find out," she said.

He swung himself around the desk and unexpectedly gave her a big hug. His aftershave brought back memories of the night he'd pulled her out of that death trap, taken her away from those who would have ended her life. Her own father had abandoned her and her sister when she was nine, but Llewellyn had always been there.

Had she ever thanked him?

Gavenia hugged him hard. "I've always thought of you as my father," she said. He pulled back, and the expression on his face was priceless.

Llewellyn placed a peck on her cheek and his eyes grew moist. "You have no idea how much that means to me."

"I never thanked you for finding me. I—"

He placed his finger on her lips, gently silencing her. "No need; I understand." They broke apart when his intercom reminded him the next client was waiting.

She paused at the door, sad the tender moment had passed so quickly.

"I'll be waiting to hear from you," he said. "Now go get what I need to file suit."

* * *

The newspaper receptionist had a well-practiced monotone.

"Mr. Jones is in a meeting. You'll need to wait here," she said. In front of her was the accursed paper, turned to the page with *the* article. The woman studied the picture and then looked up at the original. A sneer lit her face.

"How long do you think it will be?" Gavenia asked, resisting the urge to snatch the paper and grind it into pulp on the exquisitely polished marble floor.

"I have no idea." The woman's sneer grew. "You're the so-called psychic, aren't you?"

Gavenia ground her teeth and parked herself on a sofa. Bart sat nearby, dressed in a fifties-style suit and black-rimmed glasses. She leaned over to catch the name on the tag above his breast pocket: Kent.

Got a pair of tights and a cape under that suit, mister? she asked, repressing a chuckle.

Wouldn't you like to know? he replied, waggling his eyebrows suggestively.

Gavenia's patience proved nonexistent. "Enough of this," she said, and headed toward the bank of elevators. After scanning the directory, she pushed the button and waited. The elevator arrived quickly.

She shot a quick look at the gatekeeper. The gate dragon was too engrossed with a UPS delivery man to notice the psychic was on the loose. "So far so good," Gavenia said, entering the elevator.

Bart only gave her a wink in reply and pushed his glasses up on his nose.

After the elevator doors closed, she whispered, "Why are you the only Guardian I've seen who wears costumes?"

Once a thespian, always a thespian.

"That's not an answer."

He gestured graciously as the doors opened. *Your floor, madam.*

Gavenia hesitated at the newsroom doorway, and despite the initial rush of adrenalin, nerves took over. At best she'd have a chance to confront Bill Jones, demand he retract that ridiculous story. The worst-case scenario involved a trip with the cops and a call to Llew to make bail.

That would play really well for Jones, Bart advised.

"Then we won't do that," she whispered. She wove her way through the desk maze, trying to blend in, which proved difficult given the fact that her photo was in today's edition.

Jones's desk sported a gold nameplate. As predicted by the receptionist, he was absent.

Gavenia eased herself into a chair next to the desk. As she sat, loose papers fluttered to the floor at her feet. She collected them with difficulty, her hip protesting. As she placed them back on the desk, she caught sight of a valet parking stub from the Mirage in Vegas. It was dated only a few days earlier.

Bart leaned over to inspect the stub. *Hmmm . . . now that's interesting.*

Before she had an opportunity to ponder that discovery, the noise level around her increased. Reporters streamed back toward their respective desks. Jones appeared a few moments later. He stopped in midstride, glanced at top of the desk, and then continued toward her in an arrogant strut.

"Here for another séance?" he asked in a derisive tone.

"No, I'm here for a retraction."

"Really? You must not be very psychic, then, because there's no retraction in my future."

"Perhaps you can explain why you feel the need to make my life a living hell."

Jones dropped into his chair and swiveled around until he faced her. Lacing his hands behind his head, he propped his feet on the desk, grinning. "It's what I do. Besides, if you weren't good for it—"

"I know what I saw, Mr. Jones."

"I already have an article filed for tomorrow—about one of your people, in fact—but I can change that."

"'My people'? You make that sound like we're the enemy," she said, her voice rising.

"You all are."

"I told you the truth."

Another reporter stopped by the desk. "You need me to call security, Bill?"

"No, not yet."

Gavenia took the hint. She stood, pressing heavily on her cane for support.

When in doubt, bluff. "You're on notice that if you don't print a retraction, I'll be filing suit against you and the paper."

The laugh that issued from Jones's mouth sent shivers up her spine. "Go for it. We have lawyers sitting around with nothing to do but move paper clips from one side of their desk to the other. They'd love to earn their retainer."

She shook her head. "You're racking up a lot of very negative karma, Mr. Jones. Trust me, it always comes around."

"Is that a threat?" he asked, leaning forward. "Are you going to put a spell on me?" The other reporter took a step backward as if she intended to do something nasty to him as well.

Gavenia shook her head. "I wouldn't bother. You're not worth it."

"There's where you're wrong. I'm the best there is because there are no boundaries. I *make* the news, Ms. Kingsgrave. People will remember me for years to come because of what I do."

Another shiver coursed along Gavenia's spine. She shot Bart a look, and he gave a low whistle.

Oh boy . . . he's named his own fate.

Gavenia repressed her answering nod. "So be it, Mr. Jones. It's your karma, not mine."

Jones blinked for a moment as if suddenly unsure. He gave a quick glance toward the desk and then back to her.

"I stand by my article," he said.

"And I stand by my gift." As Gavenia strode out of the office, patches of conversation filtered around her. No one had missed the scene. When she passed one desk, a young man smiled up at her. She nodded in return, disconcerted by his overly friendly demeanor. It seemed almost treasonous.

As she descended to the lobby, the elevator paused at the third floor. Much to Gavenia's relief, a heavyset woman enveloped in floral perfume exited, unfortunately leaving most of her scent behind. At the last minute, a man got on. She recognized him: he was the one from the newsroom, the guy who'd smiled at her.

He was breathing heavily, as though he'd sprinted a marathon. Now they were the only two in the elevator as it continued downward. She brought her cane up and held it between her two hands, ready to separate the two halves if he proved a threat. A glance toward Bart netted her a shrug. She was being too paranoid.

She put the cane back in its place.

The young man turned toward her, gave her another smile, took a deep breath, and said in a lowered voice, "Merry meet!"

Gavenia stared. She'd just received a Pagan greeting from a most unlikely source.

"Merry meet as well," she replied. *What the hell is this?*

The winded man continued, "A responsible reporter would conduct research"—a breath—"before he submits an article." Another deep breath. "If everything pans out, then he submits it. If not, he shelves it."

Sensing an ally, Gavenia asked, "Even after the article is submitted?"

"You can always pull a piece before it goes to press," the young man observed. The elevator gave a slight bump as it reached the first floor.

"What about Bill Jones?"

"He flew to Vegas *after* he submitted the article."

As the doors began to open, she asked, "To do research or to play the slots?"

"That's for you to find out. Merry part!" he said, and then swam through the group waiting for the elevator. By the time she'd escaped the throng, he was gone.

"And Merry meet again," she said to herself, shaking her head at the improbability of encountering a sympathetic soul in the middle of Jones's ink-stained world.

* * *

As Gavenia waited for Ari to come to the phone at the homeless shelter, she watched people roll their grocery carts to their cars, kids in tow. She'd pulled into the store's parking lot after Bart warned her not to talk and drive at the same time.

While she waited, Gavenia pondered on O'Fallon. How was he doing this morning? Would he blame her for last night? Had Avery gone along with her plan for the Brigit's cross?

"The world's shortest nonaffair," she said, shaking her head as a surge of sadness pushed through her. He'd looked so hot in those blue jeans. Who knew how it might have turned out? "Double damn."

"Cursing me already?" her sister asked in her ear.

"No, O'Fallon."

"What'd he do this time?"

"I'll tell you later. I need your help on the computer."

"The Jones thing?"

"Yup."

"Name it."

"I need to figure out why Bill Jones went to Vegas a couple days ago."

"Okay, can do. Go to that Starbucks near the condo. I need caffeine. I'll meet you there in about . . . thirty minutes."

Gavenia sighed in relief and ended the call. Ari would help her. They often had spats, but they never held grudges. Pity the Irish guy wouldn't be there to see her take Bill Jones down.

Before she had the opportunity to turn off her phone, "Dance of the Sugar Plum Fairy" announced an incoming call. She scrutinized the caller ID.

Speak of the leprechaun. "Hello?"

"So where have you been?" O'Fallon grumbled. She heard the clatter of dishes in the background, so he was probably at the diner. "I've called three times this morning. If you're trying to blow me off . . ."

Three times? "No, it's just been an ugly morning. I turned off the phone. So how are you doing?"

"Fine." A pause, and then, "I owe you for last night."

Gavenia blinked in surprise. "I'm sorry you went through that hell."

"Yeah, it was hell all right. Avery gave me a Saint Bridget's cross. It's done the trick. No more voices."

Did he know the origin of cross? Was that an attempt to feel her out?

Best not go there. "I'm very glad to hear that."

"Can you meet me this afternoon? I have some questions about last night."

"No, it's not a good time." She heard a sharp intake of breath and realized she'd been a bit abrupt. By way of explanation, she added, "I'm willing to talk to you some other time, but not right now."

"What's wrong?"

He'd read between the lines. "Did you see this morning's paper?"

"No, too busy ducking demons. What's in there I'd care about?"

"An article about psychic charlatans."

"Hold on, there's a copy on the counter." She heard the phone clunk on a hard surface and a few words in the distance, then the PI was back. "Okay, I got the paper. What page?"

"Ten. Ari says the picture sucks."

Gavenia heard the flipping of pages, another intake of breath, and then, "That son of a . . . Who the hell is this bastard?"

She couldn't help but grin that the Irish guy was rising to her defense. That felt good.

"I did a reading for him. I didn't realize he wasn't legit until after the fact."

"Do you want me to check him out for you?"

The offer was genuine, and Gavenia knew O'Fallon would turn Jones's life inside out by the time he got done with him. She thought about it and then shook her head. "No, this one's mine. You have other things to worry about."

"This isn't right, Gavenia, and you shouldn't take the heat like this. Let me know if you need help."

"Thanks, O'Fallon. That means a lot to me."

"Hey, we psychic charlatans should stick together, you know?" he joked.

Gavenia's eyes widened. *He's made a lot of progress in one night.*

"Your sister's right: the photo does suck."

She chuckled. He'd just made the dark morning a little brighter. "I may end up in Vegas running down a lead, but I'll let you know one way or another."

"Just be careful, Gavenia."

"You too, O'Fallon."

She disconnected the call and leaned back in the seat.

"Talk about change of heart . . . ," she murmured.

Sounds like the Irish guy is on our team, Bart observed.

"Oh, yeah," Gavenia said. She looked over at her Guardian. "Let's cruise, dude. We've got work to do."

He flipped down his sunglasses and mimed buckling his seat belt. "Let 'er rip, lady."

Chapter Twenty-Three

The mystery Pagan's tip about Vegas sent Ari's nimble fingers dancing over the keyboard with the sort of enthusiasm she used to exhibit at an archaeological dig. By the time they'd downed their second cup of Arabian Mocha Sanani, Ari had unearthed why Jones went to Sin City: the reporter's mother lived there. That bit of news triggered an avalanche of uncertainty. Whose ghost had Gavenia seen? Had she fallen for an elaborate ethereal trick? The only way to put her doubts to rest was to meet June Jones.

Four hours later, Las Vegas greeted them with temperatures in the mid-seventies, a vast blue sky, distant snow-clad mountains, and just a hint of smog. As anxiety formed a knot in her stomach, Gavenia pressed the doorbell and waited. Ari stood next to her, twisting the strap of her purse in subtle agitation.

The person who answered the door had a strong resemblance to the dead woman, probably in her early seventies, her hair turning silver. At her ankles a Yorkie yapped a shrill warning.

"If you're here to proselytize—," she started, no doubt in reaction to Ari's somber black garb.

"Are you Mrs. Jones?" Gavenia asked.

"Yes," the woman answered warily. She studied Gavenia's face as if trying to place it.

"I'm Gavenia Kingsgrave. This is my sister, Dr. Ariana Hansford."

The woman's eyes noticeably widened, and she took an unsteady step backward.

"Quiet, Bootsie," she said, pushing the canine aside with a sweep of her foot. "You're the one Billy wrote about, aren't you?"

"Yes, I am," Gavenia replied, waiting for the door to be slammed in their faces.

"You really believe you saw Linda's ghost?"

A surge of hope. "Yes."

Mrs. Jones appeared to be wrestling with her conscience. Finally, she beckoned them inside and ushered them down a dimly lit hallway, the dog prancing at her side. The living room was sixties-style, with a broad window that overlooked the xeriscape yard. As she and Ari sat on the plaid couch, Gavenia kept her right hand firmly anchored underneath the other, her heart pounding.

"What is it you want of me?" Mrs. Jones asked, her eyes moving nervously from one visitor to the other. The Yorkie docked at her feet, gnawing a miniature chew bone with sharp crunches.

"I need to try to understand some things," Gavenia said. "You are Mr. Jones's mother, right?"

"Yes."

Gavenia frowned. Why had the ghost claimed Billy was her child? *Did I read this all wrong?*

"What relation are you to Linda?" Gavenia asked.

"She was my older sister."

Gavenia shifted uncomfortably, wondering how to proceed.

Ari jumped in. "We need to know the circumstances of her death."

Gavenia inwardly winced—her sister was too keen sometimes.

"Billy's article said you knew," Mrs. Jones replied, a slight frown on her brow.

Gavenia found her voice. "I clearly saw your sister's death, Mrs. Jones. Your son says I'm lying. We're here to learn the truth."

The woman studied her for a moment. Rising, she fetched a photograph from a nearby hutch and handed it to Gavenia with a trembling hand.

"That's Billy and my sister when he was about a year old." The photo showed a little boy perched in Linda's lap, clutching a toy train. His smile was wide, carefree. The man Gavenia had met at Earth, Wind, and Fire physically resembled the child, but his soul was different—darker, more angry.

"When did he change?" Gavenia asked, looking back up.

Mrs. Jones appeared surprised, as if she had divined a great secret.

"After his mother died. The doctor said Billy wouldn't remember her, but he did. He started throwing tantrums, demanding to see her."

"Then Linda was his mother," Gavenia said quietly.

"Yes. After her death, my husband and I adopted him and moved to Vegas to get away from the gossiping neighbors."

"You never told him about his mother's death?" Ari asked.

"No. The doctor said we shouldn't."

"The doctor was wrong, though I'm sure he meant well," Gavenia said, handing the framed photograph back to Mrs. Jones. "Children sense more than we realize."

A pensive look flowed over the woman's face as she returned the photo to its place, rearranging it just so. Without a word she made her way down the hall.

"So now what?" Ari whispered.

"We wait," Gavenia replied. Her initial apprehension was wearing off, replaced by a vague impression she'd been sent to Vegas other than to clear her name.

A quick glance around proved that Bart was nowhere to be seen and Paul's shadow loitered near his wife, a faint mist at the far end of the couch. A slight noise caught Gavenia's attention. A young man in a private's uniform stood near the hutch, holding a rifle. Gavenia gave him a slight nod to acknowledge his presence. He nodded back.

Mrs. Jones returned bearing a red-leather photo album. She settled into her chair as if in some discomfort, caressed the top of the album in a loving gesture, and then set the book on the coffee table between them.

"Your answers are in there," she said. She tapped the side of the chair, and the Yorkie vaulted upward onto her lap.

As Ari squeezed her arm in a reassuring gesture, Gavenia lowered her eyes to the photo album. After a deep inhalation, she picked up the book. Tempted as she was to flip rapidly through the pages, that would be disrespectful; the album contained the sacred memories of Linda's short life.

Ari scooted closer as Gavenia opened the front cover.

She read from the first page. "Linda Amber Stilton, 1937 to 1959."

"So young," Ari murmured.

As with most albums, it was chronological: baby photos, first day of kindergarten, first bicycle, cheerleading, high school graduation, and then the wedding photo. Linda was dressed in white, a true blushing bride, her eyes gazing in adoration at the man standing next to her in the church.

Gavenia bit the inside of her lip. Her eyes sought those of Mrs. Jones.

"This isn't the man I saw in the vision," Gavenia said. Ari gave her a sharp look. In contrast, their hostess issued a short nod, as if she'd passed some test.

"That is Linda's first husband, Albert. He died only a few months after their marriage."

A revelation struck home. "Your nephew is this man's son, isn't he?"

Mrs. Jones nodded. "After Albert's death, Linda remarried. It was a mistake that cost her everything."

Gavenia flipped the page and found another wedding photo. This time Linda's face was subdued, her expression one of uncertainty. Clad in a tailored navy suit, she clutched a bouquet of flowers strategically placed in an attempt to hide her bulging stomach. The groom's eyes were haughty. Gavenia shivered at the memory of the carnage his jealous rage had caused.

She continued on, finding the birth announcement of a son, William Albert, four months after the wedding. Then she found the police report.

Don't read it, Bart commanded. *It'll bring back the vision.*

Gavenia shoved the book toward her sister, bile rising in her throat. "I . . . can't." She took a series of cleansing breaths and kept her eyes riveted on their hostess.

There was the sound of flipping pages as Ari scanned the

pages. "It's all here," her sister said. "The police report, newspaper clippings, death certificate . . ."

Gavenia took a deep breath, praying her voice wouldn't betray her. "If I owe Mrs. Jones an apology, tell me."

Their hostess shook her head. "No apology needed, Miss Kingsgrave. You saw my sister's death as if you were in the same room. You saw things that weren't reported in the newspapers."

A single tear escaped down Gavenia's cheek. She bit her lip, tasting blood, in an attempt to keep Linda's dying shrieks from overwhelming her. "I'm so sorry," she whispered.

There was an awkward silence. Ari kept glancing back and forth between Gavenia and their hostess, as if waiting for something else to happen.

"Is Linda here now?" Mrs. Jones asked.

Startled by the question, Gavenia wiped away the tear and looked around. Only Paul and the soldier. The man gave her a nod, granting permission to speak of him.

"No, but there is someone else here. A young man in a soldier's uniform. He has dark-brown hair and thick eyebrows." Gavenia paused and added, "He says his name is Christopher."

"Oh, my God." Mrs. Jones's hands flew to her mouth, startling the Yorkie. "Chris?" Her eyes filled with tears, and she dug in a sweater pocket for a tissue. "I . . ." She paused and then asked, "Can you tell him that I miss him?"

Gavenia gave her a gentle smile. "You just did." The specter was speaking now, and she relayed the message. "He says he will be waiting for you when you come across and that it won't be long now. He says you understand what that means."

The woman dabbed at her tears and then sighed expressively.

"I do. I look forward to that day, Chris." She dabbed at her nose with the tissues and explained, "He died in Vietnam. We were going to be married."

"I'm so sorry," Gavenia said, stunned by the losses this woman had endured. "Does your . . . son know about your condition?"

"Yes. He was here a few days ago and I told him then. I also showed him those papers," she said, pointing to the album on Ari's lap. She halted and looked away, blinking at the tears that flowed freely down her cheeks. "He was very angry. I can't blame him. We should have told him a long time ago."

"Then he knew about his mother when he submitted the article?" Ari pressed.

"Yes. I told him he should write the truth, but he refused."

Time to go, Bart whispered as he appeared at Gavenia's elbow.

She agreed. Gavenia stood, steadying herself with her cane. "We won't take any more of your time."

Ari stared at her in disbelief. "But what about the article?" she demanded.

Gavenia ignored her. "Thank you, Mrs. Jones. You've put me at ease. I'm sorry to have brought back such painful memories."

As she paused at the front door, the woman took Gavenia's hands in hers. They were cold, as if her life was ebbing away even as they touched.

The woman cleared her throat. "I have an extra copy of the police report. You can take it to the newspaper. They'll know what to do with it."

Gavenia thought for a moment and then shook her head.

"No, thank you. That's not what's important right now. You've told me what I needed to know."

Mrs. Jones studied her a moment. "It wasn't about money, was it?" she asked.

"No. I thought I was helping him."

The woman nodded her understanding. "My son shouldn't have done this. That's not what Linda would have wanted."

Gavenia gave the woman a long embrace, enveloping her within a calming spell, and then retreated down the front stairs. She heard Ari politely saying farewell, but her words were clipped and tense. To her credit, she wasn't making a scene.

Gavenia hesitated before opening the rental car's door. She took a last look toward the house where Mrs. Jones was framed in the doorway, the Yorkie at her feet. Standing beside her was the ghost of her fiancé. He gave Gavenia a solemn wave.

Thank you, he said. *I will watch over her.*

I know you will.

Ari waited until Mrs. Jones was inside the house, the door closed, before she exploded in frustration.

"What in the hell was that?" she exclaimed in a lowered voice. "Why didn't you take the police report? Why did we come all the way over here just to back down?"

Gavenia climbed into the car and buckled her seat belt. Her sister's anger was understandable and she was touched that it was on her behalf. She waited until Ari shut the door and engaged her own seat belt.

"Mrs. Jones is dying of colon cancer. Her fiancé told me she has very little time."

Ari looked toward the house and back again, her mouth open. "I . . . I thought . . ."

"You thought I was wimping out?" Gavenia asked as she started the car. Her sister nodded in admission. "Well, I am, in a way. I realized I was brought here to prepare Mrs. Jones for her death, not to clear my name."

"Good God."

"Yeah, good Goddess."

"At least now we know the truth," Ari whispered.

"Yeah, there is that." She started the car and backed out of the driveway. "Let's see if we can catch an earlier flight. I want to go home."

Chapter Twenty-Four

"You have a guest," Ari announced from the kitchen doorway. Gavenia shook her head, her hands gripping a cup of coffee. Her sister was far too perky the morning after the trip, already dressed and with her makeup on. Of course, she'd slept the entire flight back to LA and during the drive from the airport. Gavenia, on the other hand, had managed just four hours of sleep once she crawled into bed, her mind refusing to shut down until exhaustion overtook her.

She raised her eyes to the wall clock. *Eight ten.*

"Earth to Tinker Bell! You have a guest," Ari tried again.

Gavenia glared at her. "I heard you, and no, I don't have a guest. I'm not dressed yet."

"I think the robe looks fetching. I'm sure the Irish guy at the door will think so too."

Gavenia's glare increased. "O'Fallon?" A twinge of guilt. She'd not called him as she'd promised, and with her cell phone off . . . No, she didn't need the hassle. "Tell him to go away and come back at a civilized hour," she said.

Bart tsk-tsked in the background. *Temper, temper*, he whispered.

"Leave me be," she muttered, and gulped the scalding coffee. It immediately retaliated, burning her tongue.

Ari vanished down the hallway, and Gavenia heard the murmur of conversation.

Her sister reappeared. "He says it is a civilized hour, and if it helps, he's wearing jeans and he brought a peace offering."

Jeans? "Tough."

Ari stepped out of the doorway and O'Fallon entered the kitchen. Gavenia opened her mouth to protest, but her sister held her hand up for silence.

"You two talk it out. I'm not a diplomatic secretary." She gestured for their guest to take a seat and O'Fallon obliged, placing a Red's Diner bag on the table.

"Glad to finally meet the infamous Irishman," Ari said, then headed toward the front door, Paul's ghost right behind.

Gavenia inwardly groaned. The last thing she wanted was to be left alone with *him*. She needed peace and quiet and at least a half dozen more ice-cream bars.

As she took another sip of her coffee, she eyed her guest: jeans, T-shirt, and denim jacket. Knowing he was genetically hardwired for suits, O'Fallon was pulling out all the stops.

He returned her disgruntled look. "Aren't you going to be polite and ask if I want some coffee?"

"No. If you wanted some, you should have brought your own."

"Are you usually this bitchy in the morning?" he grumbled.

"No. Only when I get four hours of sleep."

"Midnight orgy with the nymphs and satyrs?" he chided.

She frowned. "No, that trip to Las Vegas." When he opened his mouth to ask the inevitable question, she waved a finger in the direction of the bag. "Someone mentioned a peace offering?"

He pushed the bag toward her and when she dug inside, she found heaven: a cinnamon roll. She inhaled its scent and let out a soulful sigh.

O'Fallon watched her, a knowing grin on his face. The guy was trying.

"Okay, you win. Tell me why you're here at this hideous hour."

"I need to talk to Gregory Alliford."

"Why?"

"I prefer not to say at this point."

She stared at him. "Oh, right. You want me to help you but you're not going to tell me why. Doesn't that strike you as a bit one-sided?"

O'Fallon flared right back. "You not telling me why you made a quickie trip to Vegas is different?"

"I went to Vegas because of the article in the paper."

"They don't have cell phone service in Vegas? I was worried, you know."

He was worried? Gavenia licked the frosting off her fingers. "I'm sorry about that. It was . . . not an easy trip."

His ire faded instantly. "Something you want to talk about?"

She shook her head. "Not until I get it straightened out in my own mind."

"Did you find what you were looking for?" he asked, heading toward the coffeepot on his own.

"Yes . . . and no."

"Ah, one of those." He selected a MAGIC RULES mug and poured himself some coffee. Once he returned to the table, he shifted back to the original topic.

"Alliford won't talk to me because he knows I used to work for Mommie Dreadful. I need you to run interference so I can ask him a few questions."

"About Bradley?"

"Yes, and that's as much as I'm willing to reveal."

Gavenia gave another low sigh and took a tentative sip of her coffee. It had cooled enough to be drinkable. "Let me get a shower, and then I'll try to get you in to see Gregory—providing he's sober, of course."

"Thanks." He hesitated and then grinned boyishly. "Was it the cinnamon roll or the blue jeans? I'd like to know for future reference."

"Both. But the jeans pushed you over the top."

"Got it."

* * *

When she came downstairs after her shower, O'Fallon wasn't in the kitchen. She found him in the temple, was sitting on the floor on one of the oversized cushions, eyes closed. His expression made her pause in the doorway; he appeared less careworn, as if years had melted off during the time it took her to shower. She knew the room held positive, healing energy, but he was soaking it up like a starving man would a rich broth. Bastet sat near him, purring contentedly. If the cat liked the Irish guy, he had to be okay.

O'Fallon opened his eyes and gave her a warm smile, like that day on the beach. "I hope you don't mind that I'm in here," he said in a softer voice than usual. Like a person would use in church.

He respects my faith. That's neat. She shook her head. "It's a good room for recharging."

He pondered and then nodded. "You're right; it feels like I've plugged into a wall socket and I'm blinking away."

"Well, hate to tell you but your blink appears broken," she jested.

"I'll have to work on that."

She took her place next to him, lowering herself gingerly to the ground.

"Have you ever had therapy for your leg?" he asked.

Caught off guard by the question, she stammered, "No . . . I . . . don't know if it will help."

"It can't hurt."

"I'm not sure," she said, uncomfortable.

"Then perhaps the problem isn't the old injury," he said.

She opened her mouth to retort and then thought better of it. He'd hit the issue head-on. "Bart says I'm doing penance for Winston's death."

"Bart?" O'Fallon asked, his forehead wrinkling in confusion.

Oops. The lack of sleep was affecting her tongue. A quick glance around revealed her Guardian sitting near the altar in a lotus pose.

It's time he knows, he said.

"Okay," she said. Turning her attention back to the PI, she explained, "Bartholomew Quickens is my ethereal Guardian."

"You mean, like a guardian angel?" O'Fallon asked, his face betraying his confusion.

"Sort of, except he doesn't have wings; at least, he's never acted like he does. His job is to keep me out of trouble. He gives me advice when he's in the mood to be helpful."

Bart stuck out his tongue. She chuckled at the sight and pointed for O'Fallon's benefit. "He's over there," she said, "but you'll have to take my word for that."

O'Fallon stared and shook his head. "You're right, I'll have to take your word. Do I have one of these . . . guardians?"

She nodded and pointed just over his right shoulder. "I only see it as twinkle of light. Some of them I can't see at all."

"Doesn't that bother you?" he asked, leaning forward, staring in the general direction where Bart sat. "It'd creep me out."

"You're being a lot more open than you were a couple of days ago."

"A lot of stuff has hit the fan. I've seen things that . . . well . . . Let's just say I've seen a ghost of my own, so either I'm crazy or I'm psychic. I've decided to go with the latter."

"Sounds familiar." Suddenly ill at ease, she struggled to her feet. He rose to help her up. "Thanks." She felt his hand on her cheek, and with the merest hint of pressure, he turned her face toward him. The kiss caught her by surprise. It wasn't demanding, just a gentle buss on the lips.

"You have the most gorgeous eyes," he said, gazing at them as if they were fine gems.

"Yours aren't bad, either," she said. She could smell his after-shave now, a citrus blend.

The second kiss was longer, more insistent. The Irish guy knew how kiss. She found herself putting her hands around his waist, careful not to touch his sore ribs. He returned the gesture and pulled her in to his warm body. It was impossible not to notice his growing arousal.

"I wish we had more time," he said, nuzzling her cheek.

The next kiss was more insistent, and Gavenia began to wonder if he'd forgotten about Alliford. The sound of an opening door jarred them apart, followed by Ari's voice calling Gavenia's name from the front entryway.

"In the temple," she replied. O'Fallon's eyes reflected hers— regret. He gave her a wink as he moved a discreet distance away, pulling his T-shirt back into place.

"Oh, hi; I see you're still in one piece," Ari said, flashing O'Fallon a brilliant smile. "That's a good sign."

Something about Ari's smile irritated Gavenia. "We were just leaving," she said.

"Really? Okay . . . I'm going to lunch with a friend, so I'll see you this afternoon at the shelter."

"Oh, Goddess, I forgot," Gavenia said, tapping her forehead with her finger as if that would help her remember. "What time?"

"Four will do. I'm off to Portland tonight, so you get the dishes."

Clearly she'd missed something. "Portland?"

An exasperated frown replaced Ari's smile. "Remember, I told you about that when we were on the flight to Vegas?"

"Oh, yeah, sorry. I'm not really with it right now."

"Par for the course," Ari murmured, and then turned her attention back to the PI. The smile returned. "Glad to meet you, Mr. O'Fallon."

"You as well, Dr. Hansford."

The use of her title made the smile broader. She headed down the hallway, Bastet trailing behind.

"Ready?" Gavenia asked, keen to leave. She didn't think she could take too much more of Ari's fawning.

Oh . . . jealous? Bart piped up.

"Be quiet!" she snapped.

"Pardon?" O'Fallon asked, startled.

"Sorry. Bart's doing Bart-like things," she said, glaring in her Guardian's direction.

"Perhaps it's best I drive," O'Fallon offered diplomatically.

Gavenia didn't bother to argue.

* * *

As they drove toward Bel Air, O'Fallon talked about Seamus and how the bird missed her. He announced he was going to Ireland once his cases were complete, and then asked if Gavenia liked Chinese, as he knew a place on the other side of town that did excellent dim sum.

A virtual chatterbox, Bart observed from the backseat.

He's working up to something, Gavenia replied.

Her prediction was correct. O'Fallon cleared his throat and then leaped into the fray.

"After this case is over and I get back from Ireland . . . I'd like to spend time with you, at the beach, if that's okay."

Aww, isn't that sweet? Bart whispered.

O'Fallon shot her a worried expression and then returned his attention to the traffic.

Bart chimed in, *He's taking this pretty seriously. I suggest you do the same.*

It's not like he's asked me to marry him or anything. It's just a damned date, Gavenia grumbled through the mental link.

It's more than that to him.

Gavenia puzzled on that comment. Her silence was interpreted differently by the private eye.

"If you're not comfortable with the idea, just tell me," O'Fallon said, blessedly unaware of the unspoken conversation flowing around him. "I know I don't have a . . . great track record . . . not with two divorces behind me."

Honesty. How refreshing, Bart observed.

Gavenia gave her Guardian a sidelong glance and then addressed the Irish guy.

"Okay, on one condition."

"Which is?" O'Fallon asked in a cautious tone.

"You wear those blue jeans."

A grin blossomed. "Like them, do you?"

She gave a nod and a low sigh and let a slow stream of air out her lips. "On you, oh yeah."

"Okay, it's a deal. I know a great Irish pub. We can get lunch, listen to some good music and drink some fine Irish beer, and then head out to the beach. Sound like an option?"

She nodded enthusiastically. "You're on, O'Fallon. I might even learn a few words in the mother tongue just for the occasion."

He fell silent, as if he'd accomplished his goal. In the backseat Gavenia could hear Bart humming to himself. To her horror, it sounded like Mendelssohn's "Bridal Chorus".

The wedding march.

Chapter Twenty-Five

Gregory Alliford appeared surprisingly well. His shirt was ironed, his face clean-shaven, and a glass of water sat next to him instead of something 100 proof. He eyed O'Fallon while consuming a sizable stack of vitamins of various kinds and colors.

"You're lucky I let you back in the house," Gregory announced.

Gavenia kept the smile from her face. She heard control in his voice, giving a hint of the kind of man he'd been before Bradley's death. Maybe this whole thing wouldn't end like a Shakespearean tragedy.

"Augusta actually fired you?" Gregory continued, still eyeing the PI.

"Yes."

"Why?"

"Because Mrs. Pearce isn't good with the truth."

One of the vitamins tumbled out of Gregory's fingers and landed in front of Gavenia's shoe. She retrieved it and handed it back.

"Sounds like Augusta." Gregory took another swallow of water. He looked over at Gavenia. "Emily's staying with me, helping me . . . deal with all this. She took me to an AA meeting last night. She's been sober for almost two years now." He rolled the vitamins around his palm in thought.

"Janet's sister?" O'Fallon asked. Their host nodded.

"That's great news, Gregory," Gavenia said.

"God, some of those guys are way worse than I am. I saw where I was headed." He shook his head and popped down another vitamin.

"Just do it one day at a time," O'Fallon observed.

"That's what they said. Are you an alcoholic?"

"No, but I've had partners who were."

Gregory washed the last vitamin down with a gulp of water. "Doesn't have the same kick as whiskey," he observed, and grinned like a child.

A furry blur hurtled into the room and pounced on one of O'Fallon's shoes, attacking the shoelace with a vengeance.

"I hope you can handle cats," Gregory said. "This is TJ. He's Emily's. He's a whirling dervish. He even wears Merlin out."

O'Fallon disentangled the kitten from the laces and held him in his lap, instigating a loud purr of contentment. The kitten snuggled up close, grooming O'Fallon's thumb in short swipes with his abrasive tongue.

"You've got a way with animals, O'Fallon," Gavenia remarked.

"Not only cats." He gave her a libidinous grin.

Whoa, a genuine come-on! Bart observed.

Gavenia decided to ignore both of them and addressed Gregory instead. "O'Fallon needs to ask you a few questions. Do you feel you're up to that?"

"If you say he's on the level."

Gavenia shot a quick glance at the Irishman. She just had to trust him. "He is."

"Okay, then ask away."

O'Fallon handed the kitten to Gavenia and pulled out his notepad and pen. "I'm sorry to bring this up, but I need to know more about your son's death."

"Why? The police ruled it an accident."

"I know, but not everything is clear to me."

"You read the police report?"

O'Fallon gave a nod.

"Then what confuses you?" Gregory asked, straightening up. He gave Gavenia a quick glance, and she shrugged. This wasn't what she'd expected. Why hadn't O'Fallon warned her?

"The police report said your maid had car trouble at the grocery store and that she called the school to let them know to keep

Bradley there until she got a ride arranged."

"Yes. Maria called the neighbor's maid, Lupina. She said she'd bring Bradley home and make sure he got inside safely."

"Why didn't that happen?"

"Bradley left before Lupina could find him. He walked home with Julianne." Gregory paused, a sad expression covering his face. "Julianne was Bradley's best friend."

"Julianne Foster?" O'Fallon asked, pulling the name off his notes from the police report.

"Yes. She lives three blocks from here. They played together all the time."

"Had Lupina picked him up before?"

"Yes. Bradley knew she was okay."

"Was anyone else 'okay'?"

"Only Maria and myself."

"Not your wife?"

Gregory's voice grew stern. "No. She wasn't reliable."

"But she knew the routine?"

"Yes."

O'Fallon scribbled a note and underlined it. Gavenia wondered what he'd heard that had caught his notice.

Gregory continued, "If I was in town, I'd walk home with him. We'd talk about his day and——" The father abruptly halted and jammed his lips together. His eyes glistened with tears.

"Maybe now isn't a good time for this," Gavenia said, placing the kitten on the floor, where it launched its second attack on O'Fallon's shoelaces, then flew out of the room in search of new prey. "I'll see if I can find you some juice, Gregory." As she left the room, she gave O'Fallon a stern look that counseled against pressing much further.

He ignored the unspoken warning. "Was Merlin usually outside?"

"Yes. He has a kennel."

"Could Bradley let him out?"

"Yes."

"Could your son could get into the house if he needed to?"

Gregory nodded. "We taught him the security code and he had a little step stool so he could reach the alarm panel."

"A bright little boy," O'Fallon observed. "So he came home, let Merlin out, and then walked with Julianne to her house. Then what happened?"

Gregory leaned forward, placing his head in his hands. "Dear God, he was only a few blocks from home. . . ."

Gavenia returned at that moment, bearing a glass of orange juice.

"Here. Drink this," she said, setting it next to the distraught father. "Emily says it'll help." She glared at O'Fallon, but he disregarded her.

Gregory downed the juice like it was pure vodka, his hands clutching the glass so tightly that O'Fallon thought it would shatter into a thousand tiny missiles.

Though he hated what he had to do, he pressed on. "Would your son have accepted a ride from a stranger?"

That earned him another brilliant blue glare from the witch. "I think he's had enough for—," she started.

Gregory answered over her. "No. We taught him it wasn't safe."

"Was Merlin protective of him?"

"It depended on the person. With most people he's just a big lovable lump."

O'Fallon paused and then shifted directions. "Does your wife owe anyone money?"

"What are you suggesting?" Gregory asked, setting the glass down with a clunk on the end table. He leaned forward, more in control now. "I really don't understand what you're after."

"I'm just covering a few bases, Mr. Alliford."

"I need know why you're asking these questions," the father said, his frown returning.

Stalemate. O'Fallon shifted his eyes toward the witch. She was going to be pissed, but he had no choice.

"I think your son died during a botched kidnapping attempt."

"Jesus," the father exclaimed as he lurched back in his chair. Gavenia's mouth formed a thin line. Her eyes flashed dark blue.

Had she made the connection to the penknife?

Gregory's expression dulled. "You think Janet's involved?"

"I'm not sure."

"But he was her son," Gregory protested. "I can't imagine—"

O'Fallon didn't pull the punch. "She needs cash to feed her drug habit, and you're the one with the deep pockets. Mrs. Pearce certainly wasn't going to pony up the cash."

The father massaged his temples in slow motion. "Ask me anything you want," he said in a raw whisper.

Treading a fine line around what the vision had revealed, O'Fallon probed into the relationship between Alliford and his estranged wife. It proved an ugly tale: as Gregory descended into the bottle, Janet found her nirvana in the snowy lines of cocaine. The only good thing between them was Bradley.

Now he's dead. "What about Maria? Is she on the level?" O'Fallon asked.

Gregory seemed startled by the question. "She's been with us for five years. She's as devastated as we are."

"Is she here today?"

"No, it's her day off."

"I'll need her home address. I'd like to ask her a few questions about her routine."

Gregory nodded and finished off the last of the juice.

"Can you think of anyone who might want to extort money from you?" O'Fallon asked.

"No; no one," Gregory replied. The answer was too quick, too forced. The truth burned deep in the father's bloodshot eyes— Alliford feared his wife had caused the death of their only son. "I want to hire you," he blurted. "Money isn't important now."

O'Fallon shook his head, tucking his notebook away.

"This one's on the house."

* * *

Though his instincts told him to cut and run, O'Fallon stood by his car, waiting for the witch. Gavenia was going to barbecue him. He should have told her what the vision had revealed, shared the burden, but he hadn't trusted her. She couldn't tumble from the pedestal if he never gave her a reason to betray him.

The shrinks had been right about that—trust wasn't something he gave lightly. Doubly so, when it came to a woman.

"No wonder I live with a damned parrot."

He rubbed his hand across his face, exhausted though it was only midday. Turning his mind to the case only yielded a dozen questions: Why did the maid's car decide to malfunction on that particular day? Was it just bad luck or something else at work? Why did the boy collect Merlin and go to the girl's house only to walk back alone?

O'Fallon leaned against the car, crossing his arms over his chest despite a sharp note of protest from the bruised ribs. The moment Bradley's killer knew he was being hunted, all bets were off—O'Fallon would become a target, as would Our Lady of the Azure Eyes. His gut pretzeled into a knot as emotions waged war within him. He would have liked to believe he didn't care for Gavenia Kingsgrave; that would be the safest course. He'd never been ruled by his libido, yet there was something about the witch that unnerved him, an exotic attraction he couldn't deny.

O'Fallon heard the front door close and then the sound of Gavenia's metal-tipped cane on the stone steps. He steeled himself and met her eyes. They broadcast a merger of boiling blue anger and deep hurt. The hurt he hadn't expected. Guilt stabbed at him, but he forced it down. He had two tasks: find Bradley's killer and keep the lady out of the line of fire.

Gavenia halted on the second step down.

"Just what did you see when you touched Bradley's knife?" she demanded.

Damn, she made the connection. "What I told Alliford—someone tried to kidnap him."

"No, that's not everything." He didn't reply, and that only seemed to infuriate her more. "Out with it, O'Fallon!"

He took a long, slow inhalation and then released it through pursed lips. "Bradley's death wasn't an accident. He was killed when the kidnapping went bad."

"Good Goddess," she whispered.

"I don't want Alliford to know, at least not yet. I need to talk to the investigating detectives."

"I'll come with you," she said, moving a step down.

"No, this is something I have to do on my own," he insisted.

"No, we do this together." Another step down.

"You're out of this, Gavenia. It's too dangerous. I don't want you hurt," he said, straightening up. She wasn't listening. "Stop being stubborn. If this guy will kill a kid, he'll be happy to off you if you get in his way."

"That's the breaks," she said, taking another step down the stairs. Only two to go and she'd be on ground level and able to move quicker. "I'm in this no matter what happens."

O'Fallon had hoped it wouldn't come to this, but he had no choice. He strode around to the driver's side and crawled into the car.

"Dammit, woman, I wish you'd listen," he said, turning the key in the ignition. He heard her calling to him as she struggled down the remaining steps.

O'Fallon put the car in gear and drove away before Gavenia made the driveway. In the rearview mirror he watched her expression move from incredulity to stern resolve. His heart told him she wasn't going to back down.

* * *

If Gavenia expected sympathy in equal proportion to the Moonbeam tea, her friend Viv wasn't serving any. Much to her dismay, Viv had thoroughly enjoyed the tale of O'Fallon abandoning her on Gregory's doorstep.

"He has the nerve to ask me out on a date and then strands me? Damned arrogant son of a leprechaun," Gavenia grumbled.

"He's just watching out for you," Viv said, puttering around her shop.

"We'll have to disagree on that one." Another sip of tea. *Time to move on.* "So how do I find someone down . . . here?" she asked, waving her free hand to encompass downtown LA.

"Check over at the shelter. One of those guys might be able to help," Viv recommended as she dusted under the crystal pyramids.

"Good idea. Why didn't I think of that?"

"Maybe your brain's a little clouded by this PI guy?"

"Not a chance," Gavenia shot back, shaking her head vehemently.

"You've mentioned he looks good in blue jeans twice, hon. That's a clue you've got the hots for him."

Gavenia frowned and shook her head again. "No, that just means I'm missing out in the sex department."

"Then why not give him a whirl? Maybe his bumper sticker was kosher and Irish do make better lovers. Either way, it'd do wonders for your attitude."

"My attitude is just fine," Gavenia growled.

"Providing you're another mongoose with PMS."

Gavenia pointed at the pyramids. "Shut up and dust."

She took a deep inhalation of the tea's fragrance to steady her nerves. Somewhere O'Fallon had his nose to the ground, hunting for Bradley's killer. Part of her was pleased he was on the case; the other part wanted to find Bradley's killer first and make the Irishman eat crow.

Tsk-tsk, so competitive, Bart remarked from his place by the kids' fairy wands. He pointed. *You should get one of these. They're pretty cool.*

"No, I don't think so."

"Pardon?" Viv asked, looking up from her dusting.

"Sorry. Talking to Bart."

"Is he heckling you again?"

"Of course," Gavenia replied. She stared out the window in thought.

Viv replaced a large amethyst crystal on a nearby shelf. "I'd say he cares for you or he wouldn't bother to keep you out of the way."

Gavenia was momentarily confused. "Bart?"

"No, the PI." Viv shook her head. "You *do* need to get laid."

"Change the subject, please," Gavenia demanded.

"Oooh . . . kay. Word is that some of our fellow witches are pissed that Lucy won't let them nail that Jones jerk. You know, like rain spells on his head until he glows in the dark."

"Real tempting. No, his karma will catch up with him."

"That's what your aunt said. Though there's a lot of grumbling, they won't cross a Wiccan elder."

"Sensible plan. Lucy doesn't tolerate insurrection very well." Her Guardian still stood by the fairy wands, blowing on the feather on the top of one. Why he was so fascinated with the thing? "And ring up one of those wands. Bart seems to think he wants one."

Thanks, Mom.

Gavenia rolled her eyes and paid the tab. She selected the appropriate wand and Bart grinned. As she reached the door and pushed it open, the triple-belled chime caught her by surprise, as if it were the first time she'd been in the shop. Glancing back toward the bookshelf, she realized she'd not completed her ritual. She'd been too riled when she'd arrived to think of it.

It was a childish thing to do anyway.

Rituals have reasons, Bart urged. He stood near the bookcase.

"Okay, whatever you want." She crossed to the bookshelf, uncovered the fairy, and touched the little being with the wand, just to be cute.

"Happy?" she asked.

Blissfully, Bart responded.

"At least someone is."

Chapter Twenty-Six

O'Fallon's time with Alliford's maid, Maria, hadn't revealed any information that was earthshaking. The Volvo had been fine until she parked it at the grocery store. When she returned, it wouldn't start. She'd called road service and they'd towed the vehicle to a nearby shop. The car had been forgotten for a few days in the aftermath of Bradley's death.

O'Fallon's trip to the auto-repair place netted the Chevy an oil change, a warning about his brake pads, and an interview with the guy who'd fixed the Volvo. Irv, the repair guy, said the car's starter fuse had been missing, but it wasn't uncommon for them to fall out every now and then.

Once it was replaced, the car started instantly.

"Too simple," O'Fallon muttered. Especially in the light of a potential kidnapping. If Maria's car had worked perfectly, there would have been no opportunity to snatch the kid.

O'Fallon's next stop was to visit Bradley's friend, Julianne. Her house was even bigger than Alliford's, and that was saying something for Bel Air. The maid was Slavic, with a heavy accent and a frigid, no-nonsense attitude. She scrutinized O'Fallon as if he were KGB rather than a private detective. It took a phone call to Gregory to smooth his way inside the fortress.

Bradley's friend sat in an armchair swinging her legs back and forth. Her dark-brown hair was in pigtails. Although Julianne wore a dress, from the way she acted O'Fallon suspected she'd rather be in jeans and playing in the dirt. Her mother hovered nearby, an anxious look on her face. He'd already had to promise the moon to talk to this kid, and now he had to earn the little girl's trust.

"Bradley's father wanted me to ask you some questions. Is that okay?" The girl fiddled with a pigtail. It reminded him of Gavenia when she was nervous. "I need to know some things about Bradley." More braid fidgeting, then a quick nod.

"Why did he walk home with you that day?"

When the girl gave her a mom a worried look, Mrs. Foster returned a reassuring nod.

"He wanted his picture, the one he painted," Julianne said.

"What picture?" O'Fallon asked, confused.

"Maria's picture."

"Why was the picture here?"

"It was a surp'ise."

Kid logic. O'Fallon addressed the girl's mother. "Did you know about this?"

"It's the first I heard of it. When Bradley was here, they would go to the playhouse. Sometimes they'd paint."

"Why didn't you tell your mom about the picture?"

The little girl dropped her gaze to her shoes. "I forgot."

"To tell her?"

A shake of the head. "To take it to school."

Mrs. Foster read between the lines. "Sweetie, it's not your fault Bradley got hurt. It's nobody's fault."

Except the bastard who killed him. "What did the picture look like, Julianne?" O'Fallon asked.

"Blue and red flowers," the girl said. "I got him a . . ." She frowned as if unsure of the word and then twirled her hand in a circle. "You know, Mommy."

"No, I don't, sweetie."

"What Daddy does with his drawings," the girl insisted. She made the hand circle again.

Mrs. Foster thought for a moment. "Oh, you mean one of the tubes?"

The child nodded vigorously. "We put it in there so it wouldn't get hurt.

"Tube?" O'Fallon asked, not quite following.

Mrs. Foster explained. "My husband's an architect. He stores his blueprints in those cardboard packing tubes. Apparently Julianne gave one to Bradley."

O'Fallon jotted down a note.

"Did Bradley take the picture with him?"

A nod.

"So what happened to the picture?" O'Fallon mused.

The girl shook her head and shrugged. Then she frowned and said, "Maybe the man took it."

O'Fallon and the child's mother traded looks.

"What man, sweetie?" Mrs. Foster asked.

"The man," the girl insisted. "He followed us."

Before her mother could react, O'Fallon raised a hand, gesturing for her to let him resume the questioning. He made sure to keep his voice level and calm. "What did this man look like?"

"I dunno. He was in a big car. He drove by us."

"More than once?"

A nod.

"What kind of car?"

A shrug. "Big. Like Mrs. Elton's."

Before he could ask, Mrs. Foster replied, "She means an SUV."

"What color was the big car, Julianne?" O'Fallon asked, his heart picking up speed.

"Black."

Mrs. Foster's mouth opened in surprise. She'd just made the connection between the car cited in the little boy's accident and the man who'd followed the children.

"Did Bradley know the man?" O'Fallon asked.

Another shrug.

"Did he stop and talk to Bradley."

"No."

"Have you seen the car before?"

"No."

He was running out of questions. "Is there anything else you can tell me?" he asked gently.

The girl nodded. "Merlin growled at him."

"Did Merlin do that a lot?"

"No. Just at him."

O'Fallon rubbed his chin. *Why would the dog react like that?* Another puzzle.

"Thank you, Julianne. You've been very helpful," he said, standing. He hesitated and then added, "Do you like cats?"

The little girl nodded and her face brightened.

"Mr. Alliford has a new kitten at his house. His name is TJ. I bet he'd love to meet you."

The girl gave her mother a hopeful look. "Can we see him, Mommy?"

"Sure, sweetie. We can do that. You can play with TJ and I can see how Bradley's father is doing."

Mrs. Foster didn't speak again until they reached the front door. Right before he stepped outside, she caught his arm. Her voice dropped low. "You don't think this was a hit-and-run, do you?"

Perceptive lady. "No, but I'd appreciate it if you didn't spread that around."

"Do you think it was some sort of pervert?"

He felt her fear: *What if this bastard comes after my daughter?*

"I don't think so. I think this was an attempt to extort money from Mr. Alliford. But, to be on the safe side, I'd be extra cautious for the next little while."

She seemed to think that over and then offered, "I only met Janet Alliford once. She was flying high that day, barely coherent. That's why I encouraged Bradley to come here to play, so he could have some time away from that."

"That was good of you," O'Fallon said.

The woman sighed and shifted her gaze back toward the interior of the house. "I'm not sure how Julianne is going to deal with this, especially if it wasn't an accident. She'll have to know that someday."

"Children are very resilient," O'Fallon said. "They always surprise you."

"I hope so. Let me know if I can be of any further help."

"I will."

"Oh, Mr. O'Fallon?"

He stopped in midturn. "Yes?"

"If it wasn't an accident . . ." Another look inside and then back. "Crucify the bastard, will you?"

He crooked a smile at the matron's ruthless streak.

"I'll be pleased to do just that, ma'am."

* * *

Red's Diner was only half full, a breather before the supper hour. A businessman was ensconced in one of the booths, wired every way technologically possible. O'Fallon kept the smirk to himself, knowing one poorly placed cup of coffee would ruin the guy's day.

He chose his usual booth, ordered some coffee, and tried to calm himself by scanning his notes. The list of potential suspects was growing exponentially, since a Bel Air household resembled a fiefdom. With the window washers, trash haulers, gardeners, pool people, security folks, painters, dog groomers, and so on, the possibilities were nearly endless.

O'Fallon sighed. "Too many unknowns," he muttered. He could waste a lifetime trying to narrow the field. He flipped back a few pages, tapping his pen against an underlined name. "Weakest link first," he said. "Janet Alliford."

The diner's door swung open and two men entered, engaged in an animated conversation. From the cut of their clothes he pegged them as the homicide detectives who'd investigated Bradley's death: Detectives Zimansky and Larsen. The news he had for them wasn't going to be an icebreaker. Cops never liked to hear they'd overlooked clues that turned an accident into a full-blown homicide. Especially when the victim was a six-year-old child.

Zimansky resembled a bedraggled bloodhound, ready to hang up his badge and call it a career. Larsen was the younger of the two.

"O'Fallon?" the older cop asked.

He gave an acknowledging nod and the pair slid into the seat opposite him. The waitress appeared, took the drink order, and returned with the beverages in record time.

"If I hadn't heard of you," Zimansky drawled lazily, his accent closer to Tennessee than California, "I'd tell you to go to hell and enjoy the ride."

O'Fallon offered a benign grunt. At least he had the veteran cop's attention. "I didn't like folks second-guessing my work, either."

Zimansky gave a slow nod. "So what's this about?"

Time to dangle a bit of bait. "I have a . . . source . . . that says the Alliford kid's hit-and-run wasn't accidental."

A snort of derision came from Larsen. Zimansky, on the other hand, nonchalantly stirred more sugar into his glass of iced tea. By O'Fallon's count, he was up to three packets; a true Southerner.

"Why hasn't this source come forward?" Larsen demanded.

"It's an odd situation. You're just going to have to trust me that it's worth your time."

The younger cop shook his head. "We don't owe you jack."

Zimansky reached for another packet of sugar, tore it open, and dropped the contents into his tea. The granules sheeted downward and then spun in a leisurely clockwise swirl as he blended the concoction. It was a subtle indication he was willing to listen, if only for a brief period of time.

Zimansky glanced up from his mixing. "Why'd you pull the pin?"

O'Fallon should have expected the question. Cops always wanted to know why one of their own took early retirement.

"The work got to me," he replied honestly.

"Scuttlebutt said you starting seeing things, things that weren't there," Zimansky replied, his dark-brown eyes intense. He took a sip of the tea and nodded his approval. Apparently he'd found the proper proportion of colored water and sugar.

"I took some leave to get my head straight, then decided to make it permanent, if that's what you mean."

"You were on the Morelli killings, weren't you?" the senior detective asked.

"Yes." O'Fallon took a sip of his coffee. It was vastly superior to the stuff at the car-repair shop. "That's when I started having problems."

"Did the shrinks help?" the bloodhound asked.

"No. They talked a lot of bullshit about how I should get a life outside the force."

Zimansky huffed in derision. "They've got no clue what's it like. I've been that way myself. They said I talk slow because I don't have any self-esteem."

"You seem fine in that department," O'Fallon observed. He'd already made Zimansky's type: the quiet cop who studied everything before drawing a conclusion. Like Avery. Slow speech rarely meant a slow mind.

"Okay, you got five minutes," the detective said. "After that, we're gone and you're paying for the drinks."

"Fair enough." O'Fallon took another jolt of his coffee, playing it nonchalant. He didn't want to sound desperate, though that was exactly how he felt. The cops had to sign back onto the case, or Bradley's killer might never be found.

He pulled his mind back to the task at hand. "I believe it was someone the kid knew; that's why they had to kill him when the kidnapping went south."

"How can you be sure?" Zimansky asked, leaning across the table. "Did you have one of those . . . visions?"

Larsen snorted. It appeared to be his favorite response. As the waitress sailed by, the junior cop elevated his cup for a refill.

Play it cool. "You'll have to take my word; it was someone who knew the kid." They eyed each other, and then the bloodhound leaned back.

"Go on."

"The kidnapper knew the Alliford family routine, knew the maid bought groceries on Tuesdays. By insuring she had car trouble while she was at the store, the kidnapper could pick up the kid and vanish before anyone was the wiser."

"Why do you think the car was tampered with?" Larsen asked.

"I spoke with the guy who serviced it. He said the starter fuse was missing. Sometimes they fall out of their own accord—and sometimes, they have help."

Zimansky tapped his chin in thought. "Interesting."

"Bradley walked home, then to Julianne Foster's house."

"Yeah, we know that. He took the dog with him," Larsen interjected. "None of this is news."

O'Fallon ignored the naysayer. "Do you know why he walked to his friend's house?"

"Why would we care?" Larsen asked. "Either way, he ended up dead."

"Go on," Zimansky pressed.

"Bradley went to Julianne Foster's to get a painting he'd made for the Allifords' maid. On the way back, he meets up with the man in an SUV."

"How do you know it was a guy?" Zimansky asked.

"I spoke with Julianne today. She said that a man in a big car followed them from her house, passed by them a couple of times. She said the vehicle was black."

"A car, not an SUV," Larsen said. "There's a difference."

"To a kid, maybe not," Zimansky said. "So the boy gets his painting and starts home. What do you think happened?"

"I think the kidnapper made his move once the little girl wasn't around. He offered Bradley a ride, maybe even told him that Maria said it was okay."

"So what went wrong?" the senior detective asked.

"I'm guessing the dog interfered, and Bradley panicked and ran for it."

"Then the asshole ran him down?" Zimansky asked after another hit of tea syrup.

"Yeah."

"So what do you want from us?"

O'Fallon barely kept the wave of relief from showing on his face. "Has the SUV surfaced yet?" he asked.

"No, and it hasn't been reported stolen. The only reason we know it's a Cadillac Escalade is the paint they found embedded in the victim."

"Your report doesn't mention the picture."

"So? Why is that so damned important?" Larsen demanded, his voice rising.

Zimansky swirled the glass again, took a long sip, and then swore under his breath. "It's important because the picture wasn't where it should have been."

Larsen waved a dismissive hand. "The kid could have dropped it along the way."

O'Fallon shook his head. "No; I'm willing to bet it's in the SUV."

Larsen perked up. "How much?"

O'Fallon blinked. *What the hell?* "Fifty bucks . . . to the Benevolent Association."

Larsen gave a shark grin. "You're on."

"This goddamned case never felt right to me," Zimansky grumbled. "No matter which way we went, we never got any traction." He raised a stubby finger. "We checked vehicle registrations within twenty miles of the crime scene; every black Caddy Escalade was accounted for." Another finger. "No skid marks." Third digit. "No witnesses, except the mutt." Fourth and fifth fingers. "Now you say the girl claims they were followed and that the maid's car might have been tampered with."

"And there's the missing picture," O'Fallon added.

"Shit," Zimansky muttered. "Too many holes."

"You're buying this?" Larsen asked warily.

"I'm considering it. There is a difference," Zimansky replied, folding his fingers back in place and resting his hands on the table on either side of his iced tea. "How reliable is this source?" the older cop quizzed.

"As reliable as the grave."

That earned O'Fallon a penetrating look.

"Will their testimony stand up in court?"

"No, it won't. That's the problem."

Zimansky swirled his glass for a moment and then set it down. "Do you have a suspect in mind?"

"Not in specific. But I think it's someone connected to the dead boy's mother. Maybe her dealer or a loan shark. She's got a hell of a coke habit, and Alliford closed down her credit cards, so she needs cash to keep the blow flowing."

"You think she planned this?" Larsen asked.

"I'm not sure yet."

As Zimansky sipped his tea, O'Fallon could almost hear the wheels turning. Had he given them enough to chew on?

The bloodhound nodded. "Okay, you got my interest. We'll have the grocery store where the maid shopped pull the security tapes, see what we find, and we'll talk to the little girl."

"Alliford is pulling together a list of people who knew their routine—gardeners, pool people, folks like that," O'Fallon advised. He pushed a business card across the table. "Here's the car-repair place. Ask for Irv."

"You figured you'd hook us, didn't you?"

O'Fallon gave a conciliatory shrug. "I hoped I would. I just want to watch that bastard sweat when they sentence him to meet his Maker."

Zimansky's eyes narrowed. "That's two of us."

"Three," Larsen added. O'Fallon nodded in his direction, accepting the man's unspoken apology.

"So who's your source?" Zimansky asked, leaning forward.

O'Fallon hesitated, then decided against ruining the moment. "I'll tell you when it's absolutely necessary. I don't want it to taint your enthusiasm."

"Playing this one close, aren't you?"

"I have no choice."

Zimansky rose, dug in his wallet, and threw a five onto the table. "The next time you see Avery, say hi for me."

O'Fallon was at a loss. "You know him?"

"We used to play poker every Wednesday night when we were walking a beat. I hear he's lugging a cross now."

"So why did you bust my balls on this?" O'Fallon asked.

"Just because I could," Zimansky replied. "Besides, it'll make a great story the next time I see the man."

As the two detectives exited the diner, O'Fallon waved down the waitress for more coffee and a piece of apple pie. The cops were back on the case. Now it was time for him to deliver the goods.

Chapter Twenty-Seven

"Work your white ass somewheres else!"

Gavenia raised her hands in surrender and retreated, not keen to tangle with the statuesque black woman in the shiny vinyl boots and the abundant gold glitter eye shadow. This was the second time she'd been ordered off someone's turf.

"You're too good-looking," her escort explained. "They think you're going to steal their tricks."

Bernie leaned on a lamppost, taking a nip out of a paper-bag-wrapped bottle. Lucy had paired them up, saying that the old guy knew pretty much everything that went on in Skid Row. As usual, her aunt had it right. The bum had been very adept at taking Gavenia to places where no sensible person would tread. The entire time, Bart muttered under his breath and fidgeted. She could only imagine what O'Fallon would be saying if he knew she was down here.

He wouldn't be saying anything; he'd be shouting, Bart grumbled. He looked over his shoulder for what had to be the four hundredth time. *Can we go now?* he whined.

Her Guardian was right; it was time to call it a night. There was no sign of Janet, which made her wonder if O'Fallon had been wrong about Bradley's mom being down in Skid Row.

Besides, she couldn't take much more of this part of town. Apparently it was the "in" place to be if you were dead, pure hell on her gift. *They* were everywhere, the ghosts of two different centuries. She'd turn a corner, and there would be someone clad in a raccoon coat tippling out of a flask or one in top hat and tails. Then there were those of this era: the lost ones, ones who'd died in the streets, forgotten and alone.

They're not used to seeing someone as bright as you, Bart explained. *Down here there isn't much light.*

No matter how nonchalant her Guardian was about her shadows, it still creeped her out. She'd never had them follow her before, like a pack of hungry cops trailing after a Krispy Kreme truck. An entourage, except all her groupies were dead.

A quick glance over her shoulder proved the pack was holding firm some fifteen paces behind. A thin wraith led them, a girl of about fourteen with dull eyes and dark needle tracks down her bare arms. Another dead child. Gavenia shivered and pulled her jacket tighter around her shoulders.

Heads up! Bart shouted. It took her a moment to recognize the problem. Bernie caught on immediately.

"This way," he advised, tugging on her arm. They hurried down a side street as fast as Gavenia's pace would allow. The car turned the corner, following them, illuminating them in the glare of its headlamps. Wolf whistles came from the vehicle's occupants.

Not good, Bart said.

"Just keep walking and don't look at them. They want to see if they can spook you—make you run," Bernie said, keeping hold of her elbow.

"No problem there," she replied, resolutely putting one foot in front of the other. Behind her she could hear the slow crunch of tires on gritty pavement. Car doors opened and then slammed one by one. Gavenia's blood chilled.

Really not good, her Guardian warned.

In the distance, the Miata sat under a dim streetlight, a red lily pad in a swamp filled with alligators. All its tires were in place and Gavenia thanked the Goddess for that.

"Keep walking," Bernie said. "They're gangbangers. They're looking for fun. I'll try to distract 'em." He started to turn, and she grabbed his arm.

"No, stay with me. We'll be okay."

"You got some secret weapon?" he asked, the smell of booze filling her nose.

A thought flew into her mind. "Yeah, I just might. You have any matches?"

He blinked. "No. I gave up smoking. It was bad for my health."

"Now there's irony for you," she said. So much for crafting a makeshift Molotov cocktail out of Bernie's bottle and slinging it at the gangbangers' car to buy some time.

Three of the hunters were on foot now, jiving in front of the car. The driver cranked the stereo, the bass ricocheting off the nearby buildings like musical artillery. The dead hovered around the edges of the scene, watching and whispering to one another.

Gavenia halted, turned, and put her hands on her hips. "Stop following us," she shouted to the live threat.

Oh, there's a plan, Bart observed. *Confront the crazies.*

The answer she received was laced with expletives. One of the guys cupped his crotch and then pointed at her, making a lewd gesture impossible to misinterpret.

"Well, that didn't work. How far are we from the car?" she asked her companion in a low voice.

"About a hundred, hundred fifty feet," he said without looking back. She envied his cool behavior. There was more to Bernie that met the eye.

Suggestions? she asked her Guardian.

Not be here, was the reply.

Not helpful. You're my Guardian—give me an idea how to survive this.

If you'd listened to me in the first place—

SUGGESTIONS? Gavenia shouted through the mental link.

Distraction.

Such as?

Act like a Shepherd.

She frowned. That only worked if the guys were dead. Given that the three outside the car had guns tucked into the waistbands of their oversized pants, she'd be needing a Shepherd sooner than they would.

The trio held their ground, joking with one another about the situation—one old man and a crippled woman. Out of the corner of her eye, Gavenia saw one of the ghosts detach itself from the entourage and step forward. He was a black youth clad in gang colors.

Tell them you can see me, he said.

Who are you?

Antwoine. That's Jerome, my cousin, he said, pointing to the apparent leader of the trio. He's called Easy J.

Gavenia stood taller and called out, "Hey, Easy J, why are you hassling us?"

That got the trio's attention, and the one she'd addressed signaled for the driver to turn off the radio. The resulting silence was eerie, the thunderous bass replaced by the booming of Gavenia's heartbeat in her chest.

"How you know my name, bitch?"

"I know a lot of things," she said, pushing the bravado.

The kid snorted. "You don't know dick."

"I can talk to your cousin."

"The fuck you can. No one can talk to him. He's dead."

"I know. Antwoine's here, but you can't see him," she said, gesturing toward the young ghost.

"You lie." Easy J flicked open a switchblade in a fluid motion, as if it were an extension of his hand. "I'm gonna cut your motherfu—"

"Antwoine says you shouldn't jump up Deon." The words pouring out of her mouth made little sense, but apparently they did to Easy J. He stared.

"How you know that?"

"Simple. Your cousin's here, talking to me."

"I'll jump up Deon if I want to," he said, puffing up. A couple of the other guys traded uneasy looks.

Gavenia gingerly liberated her car keys from a pocket and passed them behind her back to Bernie. She whispered, "Walk to the car nice and slow, like you're wandering off. Press the button twice. It'll unlock the doors."

"But—"

"Just do it. I've got an edge right now and I'm not sure how long it'll last."

Bernie nodded, took a drink from his bottle, either for show or for courage, and shuffled down the street as though they'd amicably parted ways.

"Where's he goin'?" Easy J asked, frowning.

Gavenia shrugged as if she didn't care. "So what do you want to know from Antwoine?" she demanded in a loud voice. "I got things to do, and standing around talking to your sorry ass isn't one of them."

Behind her she heard the sound of Bernie trudging to the car, one shuffling footstep at a time. He was humming to himself, like a drunk would.

"We gonna do you," Easy J said, moving forward, waving the switchblade back and forth like a conductor's baton.

Antwoine, I need some help here, Gavenia called.

The ghost moved in front of her, waving his hands in an apparent attempt to stop his cousin.

"He can't see you," she said, not realizing she spoke aloud. The other ghosts filed in front of her, facing the menace, forming a supernatural barrier.

"I wonder. . . ." Gavenia popped open the cane, drew the sword, and tucked the scabbard into the back of her jeans. Holding the sword upright, she let the pale streetlight illuminate it, as if she were a great warrior facing the ultimate battle. In some ways she was. It was a hell of a bluff—one that would either save her or make her death really messy.

The sword stopped her hunters in their tracks.

"Look at that, it's like that *Star Wars* dude," one said, and then elbowed the other.

Easy J wasn't buying it.

Fake it, Bart advised.

She gave him a sharp look as she rampaged through her brain for something awesome to say.

"I am a Shepherd. I walk with the Dead; I hear Them and Speak for Them." She paused and then eyed the hunters. "Fear me."

For a second she thought they'd bought it, and then loud guffaws of laughter erupted. Behind her she caught the telltale click of the remote control which meant Bernie was at the car. Fortunately, Easy J didn't appear to hear it.

"This isn't working," she whispered. Bart wiped his brow with a shaking hand, his face pale even for a ghost.

"I don't fear no dead people," Easy J said, swaggering forward.

Gavenia dropped the sword to waist level. "You get much closer, you'll be able to talk to Antwoine in person." She looked over at the young ghost. "Now would be a good time to show these guys you're here."

A quick movement of the ghost's hand sent his cousin's cap flying.

"How'd you do that?" Easy J demanded.

"I didn't. That was Antwoine."

"You lie, bitch," he said, moving forward, knife in hand.

The ghosts shifted, closing ranks in front of her.

Bart whispered, *What does a Shepherd do?*

"Protects the flock," she shot back reflexively. A thought popped into her head. A Shepherd watched over the flock. But in some ways, the flock protected the Shepherd. It acted as a barrier between the predators and their protector.

Guys, she said, addressing the spirits, I can't do my job if I'm dead. Can you help me here?

The ghosts didn't move, just looked at her expectantly. She gave a sharp glance at Bart. Like the other ghosts, he seemed to be waiting for her to do something.

"Suggestions?" she asked under her breath.

No reply. She could tell he wanted to say something but held back. He glanced upward as if asking a question and then bit his lip. Apparently, the answer had been a cosmic no.

Panic edged into anger. Turning toward the line of ghosts, she commanded, "Keep them away from me!"

Antwoine gave a quick nod, flashed a toothy smile, and launched toward the car. A headlight disintegrated in a hail of glass, followed shortly by its twin. Her three hunters whirled around, mouths agape as the windshield shattered in a spiderweb pattern first on one side and then the other.

Yes! Bart crowed, pumping his fists in the air.

Astonished, Gavenia stared, barely following the ghosts' movements as they surrounded the vehicle, pummeling it with their kinetic energy. A taillight exploded in a volley of red plastic, then a door sheared off its hinges with a grinding sound, skidding across the pavement, trailing brilliant sparks.

Ah, Gavenia. . . , Bart started.

She ignored him, astounded by the level of destruction. One of the gang hurtled backward onto the sidewalk. He pulled his gun, shouting, searching for something to shoot. Another doubled over in pain, hit in the gut by an unseen hand. Two ghosts pried up the hood, ripping it off and hurtling it over the top of the car. It landed fifteen feet away with a tremendous grating crash.

Time to leave, Bart urged.

Antwoine's spirit turned toward her and delivered a thumbs-up. Gavenia sheathed her sword and returned the gesture.

"Thanks." She pointed toward a glowing patch of light down a pitch-black alley. "You see that?" The spirit nodded. "That's where home is when you decide you want to rest." The spirit nodded again. "Take the others with you if they want to go."

The young man's face turned from triumph to sadness in a second. Standing next to his bewildered cousin, Antwoine sadly shook his head. *He'll join me soon.*

"No doubt, unless he gets smart," Gavenia agreed. "But that's his choice."

With a solemn nod that made him look twice his age, Antwoine slowly pivoted and set off for the alley. Most of the ghosts followed.

Be at peace, Gavenia said. A couple waved at her. Only the young girl stayed behind.

The hike to the car was a quick one, for Bernie had moved the vehicle closer in cautious increments. He hefted himself out of the driver's seat and limped for the other side, the car's engine still running.

"What the hell was all that?" he asked, pointing toward the wrecked vehicle.

As Gavenia started to answer, shots split the air and the side mirror disintegrated, spraying glass and plastic into her face. She cried out and slung herself into the car. Bernie burrowed into the floorboard, wrenching his door shut.

She gunned the car forward, burning rubber. Three staccato shots impacted the vehicle.

"Not the gas tank," she prayed, taking the corner at an impossible rate of speed only to find a stumbling drunk in the middle of the street. He stopped, pinned by the headlights like the proverbial deer.

"Hold on," she cried, veering away from the bum and coming perilously close to a light pole. She wrenched the wheel back toward the right and the center of the street. Prayers poured from Bernie's mouth as he huddled in a ball, still on the floorboard. Part of her wanted to be down there with him.

The gang didn't follow them, but considering their car was minus a couple of tires and a few doors, and didn't have much glass left to speak of, that wasn't surprising. A few blocks away Gavenia pulled to the curb, locked the doors, and leaned against the steering wheel, her stomach pitching around like an overturned turtle trying to right itself. She swallowed repeatedly, hoping to keep dinner in place.

"You okay?" Bernie asked, climbing up into the seat in an awkward series of arthritic movements.

She took a deep breath, and some of the nausea subsided.

"Yeah, just great."

Chapter Twenty-Eight

By the time she dropped Bernie off at the Hotel LeClaire, they were joking about the evening's events, trading dark humor, indulging in maximum stress release. Gavenia hadn't explained precisely what had happened, fobbing off the car's destruction as witchcraft rather than the handiwork of the dead. Oddly enough, Bernie seemed to accept that explanation, and after she handed him forty dollars and her business card, he was even happier.

"I'll call if I find this Janet lady for you," he said, stuffing the two twenties into his shirt pocket.

"Hey, thanks for saving my butt."

"No sweat. You got serious stones, lady," he said with a grizzled grin.

"So do you, Bernie."

He winked at her and shuffled toward the hotel.

As her nerves settled, the cuts on her face began to register, stinging as though someone had dumped salt in each one of them. Bart settled into the passenger seat, the glower on his face telling he was supremely pissed.

She counted out ten blocks before she asked the question uppermost in her mind. "Why did the dead protect me?"

Because you asked.

"That's weird. It's not like I'm a necromancer or anything." No reply. "What else can I do?"

Bart looked out the side window, studied a street sign, and then vanished. Gavenia shot a burst of air between pursed lips.

"Situation normal, clueless as hell."

* * *

After seeing to Seamus and having to listen to a running series of requests for Tinker, O'Fallon knew he was screwed. Tempting as it was to apologize over the phone, it would be best to see those blue eyes in person. He would not grovel, but if he made her aware of the case's progress, maybe she'd be more inclined to remain on the sidelines. Either way, he suspected their date was history.

A sweep past her condo didn't reveal a red Miata. He drove down to the homeless shelter—no car. He swung by her other haunts: the New Age café, the Alliford house. Zip.

"Where is she?" he muttered. Now he felt like a stalker. His cell phone rang, and a hope encompassed him. Maybe she'd thought about what he'd said and decided to initiate contact. That would make the whole situation easier. A check of the caller ID revealed a number he didn't recognize.

"O'Fallon."

"It's Adam. We need to talk." Behind the young cop's voice he heard traffic noise and then the whine of a power window.

"I pick the bar this time," O'Fallon replied.

"Where?"

"Flannery's. You know the place?"

"Too many cops."

O'Fallon cursed himself for not thinking. The witch was burning up too many of his brain cells at the moment.

"How about McCrea's then?"

"Over by the kosher deli?"

"That's the one."

"Okay." A pause, and then, "I'll be there in about a half hour."

"I'll be in a back booth," O'Fallon replied. He flipped his phone shut and dropped it into his jacket pocket. At the light, he made a right. This would be his second trip to a bar in a little over a week; his social schedule was picking up.

* * *

The pub wasn't that packed—just the regulars, and none of them were cops as far as O'Fallon knew. McCrea's was favored more by the expat crowd. No Union Jack on these walls, only the Irish tricolor and pictures of immigrant families who'd made good in America. All sons of the sod, to be sure.

"*Dia duit*, Finney." Good day. "Pint of Beamish, please," O'Fallon said, leaning against the bar. The publican, a man with hair nearly the color of his own, gave him a knowing nod.

"Ah, O'Fallon. Good evenin' ta ye. I see the divil's not got ye yet," the man said, grinning, his accent far thicker than his patron's.

"Always one step ahead, Finney."

"Ye'll outwit him; ye always do. So how's that gran of yours?"

"Old and bitchin' at me about a visit."

"Well, ye don't have much choice, now do ye?" the publican replied.

O'Fallon shook his head. "I'm headed home shortly." The Beamish appeared, and he turned and raised the pint in honor of the flag. "*Éirinn go brách*," he intoned. *Ireland forever.*

He took a deep sip of the brew and headed for a booth. McCrea's always stirred vivid memories, for in many ways it was his father's pub come alive again. With the lilting Irish voices, the deep rumble of laughter, and the rich balm of the beer, it felt like home.

Yet something was missing. He took another sip of the rich Beamish, and the loneliness struck him like lightning. Too long he'd been skirting the issues of the heart. He'd prayed for a woman who would understand him, love him. After so many false starts, now he was confronted with another opportunity. *Could God really mean for Gavenia to be the one?*

He tried to shake off the thought. She wasn't Catholic, not even Christian. Surely she was just another temptation on the long road of life. He stared down into the beer, the sounds of the pub fading away. Her eyes had told him the truth: Gavenia Kingsgrave had the power to reach his very soul.

Was he brave enough to let her inside?

"Be careful what you ask for," he muttered.

To his relief, Adam Elliot appeared at the front door, pulling

O'Fallon's mind back to the present. The young cop bought a pint of Harp and slid into the booth opposite him.

"Interesting ambience," Adam said, glancing around at the pictures on the wall. The one of the coal miners seemed to captivate him the most.

"They serve good Irish stew, if you're interested," O'Fallon said, testing the waters. If the kid had his gut in a knot, the food would be the last thing he'd be thinking of.

"No, can't eat. Too much on my mind."

Bingo. "How are you feeling?" he asked, pointing toward the young cop's arm. It was in a navy fiberglass cast, suspended in a sling.

"It's getting better." Adam looked around nervously. "I'm being followed. I think my phone's been tapped."

O'Fallon nodded and took a sip of his stout, savoring its taste. "That surprises you?" he asked.

The young cop blinked and then shook his head. "I guess not."

"Has IAD talked to you?" Another shake of Adam's head. "They're hoping you'll trip up and give them Glass," O'Fallon said.

"Yeah, that's the way it looks."

"Your job is to make sure they get him but to not get caught in the fallout. He chose to be dirty, and if IAD wants to fry his ass, that's righteous. You're clean, and that's what they need to know."

"Should I go to them?" the young cop asked.

O'Fallon bought time by taking another sip of the Beamish. That was a tough call. *If any of the others find out Adam helped with the investigation . . .*

"If it was me, I'd keep my distance from IAD. You know how it is with cops who help them out."

Adam pushed his empty pint away, nodding slowly.

"I'll go get us another round and we'll work on a strategy," O'Fallon offered.

The detective's face filled with gratitude. "Thanks."

As O'Fallon rose, he asked, "How dirty is Glass?"

"Like an oil slick. But he's not the only one. I think it goes higher."

"Well, that's one place where physics is wrong: shit does flow uphill."

It was close to ten by the time they'd talked it out. Adam agreed to request a transfer and start chronicling everything he could remember that seemed out of place—names, conversations, anything that could be used against his partner when IAD finally flushed Glass down the toilet.

"Be careful," O'Fallon warned.

"I will." The young man turned and then hesitated. "Call my cell number. I'm not at the boat right now."

O'Fallon frowned at that. "What happened?"

"Carey and I are . . . well, we're taking some time apart to think things through."

"Damn," O'Fallon said. "I hope you can hold it together."

A wan smile returned. "I hope so, too."

"Just be honest with each other."

Adam delivered a quick nod and headed for his car. O'Fallon waited and then climbed into his own vehicle, mindful of anyone who looked out of place. Other than a couple making out against the hood of a car, lustfully oblivious to his presence, everything was kosher.

He headed for Gavenia's condo by instinct. Until the matter with the witch was settled, he'd have no peace, either in his heart or at home.

* * *

Gavenia's damaged side mirror proved a handicap as she parked. Once she got the vehicle in place, she pulled herself out and then leaned on the car for a moment, her left hip throbbing. Bart was nowhere in sight, and the condo was dark. Then she remembered—Ari was in Portland for the next couple of days. How had she forgotten that . . . again?

She heard someone clear their throat behind her. Whirling, she found her way blocked by a body. Still on edge from the earlier confrontation, she flung herself backward, unsheathing the cane sword in one swift move. The point ended up even with O'Fallon's left breast.

He blinked in stark surprise, staring at the line of steel gleaming in the streetlight. "Damn, you're more pissed than I thought."

She left the sword in place. "What the hell are you doing here?"

"Just wanted to give you an update," he replied.

He got points for style, especially with sharp steel aimed at his heart. She sheathed the weapon, too tired to bitch him out for his abandonment earlier in the day.

"Go away, O'Fallon. I'm not in the mood to talk," she said. "Go home. You blew it this morning."

His eyes swept the interior of the car as if looking for some hidden clues as to where she'd been tonight. They came to rest on the fairy wand right before she slammed the door.

Maybe he won't see the—

"Hey, what happened to your mirror?" he called after her.

Damn!

"Where have you been?" he said, moving toward the rear of the car.

She tromped toward the front door. "Go away, O'Fallon. I don't need this."

"Holy Jesus." He'd found the bullet holes. "What the hell have you been doing?" he demanded.

If she left him on the street, he'd raise a ruckus until he found out exactly what had happened. She had no other option—Gavenia turned and beckoned to him.

"Bring it inside, O'Fallon. I don't need the neighbors calling the cops."

O'Fallon watched as she limped into the condo and disengaged the alarm. Shifting his eyes back to the car, he squatted by the Miata's rear quarter panel, fingering the trinity of bullet holes one by one.

"Good God, woman." A cold shiver drove through him. What the hell was she trying to prove? Did she think this was a game?

* * *

O'Fallon lurched to his feet and marched toward the condo, anger warring with gut-twisting worry. He caught up with her in the half bath off the kitchen where the vanity light revealed tiny cuts dotted her left cheek and forehead. Bending over the sink, she splashed water on her face. Her right hand shivered so violently she had difficulty pulling the hand towel from the towel ring.

"What happened to you?"

"How about some hot chocolate?" she countered, gingerly patting her face with the towel. "I'll put some Irish cream it." Dropping the towel on the washstand, she tried to push past him in the doorway. O'Fallon blocked her and angled her face upward, studying it. Gavenia winced when he tapped a finger under one of the reddened slits.

"Where the hell have you been?"

"You've been drinking," she shot back.

"Answer me."

"None of your damned business."

O'Fallon stuck his face in hers, gripping both of her shoulders tightly. The sea-blue eyes changed from mocking to fearful. "What are your favorite flowers?" he hissed.

"What?"

"Your favorite flowers—what are they?" he asked, his volume jumping a notch higher. He felt a shiver course through her.

"Why would you care?"

"Since you're so goddamned determined to get yourself killed, I want to make sure I buy the right flowers for your funeral."

The eyes seethed. He wasn't reaching her, hadn't said what it would take for her to understand how much she meant to him. Bullying her wouldn't work so he forced his anger to fall away.

After a ragged intake of breath, he whispered, "For God's sake, Gavenia, I don't want to lose you."

Her mouth parted in shock, the blue eyes losing their fire. "Oh."

O'Fallon loosened his grip. "I'm sorry I got so angry, but you scared the hell out of me. When I saw the bullet holes and . . ."

She bowed her head as if accepting his apology, laying her

forehead on his chest. He instinctively wrapped his arms around her in a protective gesture.

"I was in Skid Row, looking for Janet. There was a gang. . . ." He opened his mouth to speak, but she pressed on. "No, they didn't hurt me. The dead came to my rescue." That didn't make sense, but he let it pass. He pulled her closer and rested his chin on the top of her head. She felt cool in his arms.

"I can't work on this case and worry about you at the same time," he said, honesty burning in every word.

She looked up at him and a slight smile appeared. "I was thinking the same about you."

He placed a kiss on her forehead between the scratches and then hugged her close. A bump impacted his ankle followed by a loud meow of protest. Bastet had found them. Another meow, this one drawn out as if they hadn't heard the first one.

"I should feed her," Gavenia said but she didn't pull out of his arms. The first full kiss was tentative, as if testing the waters. The second was deeper, more urgent. Another ankle bump, along with a chorus of plaintive yowls.

Gavenia broke the kiss and stepped back, rolling her eyes.

"Let me deal with the furry tyrant."

O'Fallon shook his head. "And I thought Seamus was a pain."

Chapter Twenty-Nine

Gavenia asked him to wait in her temple while she settled the cat and made hot chocolate. O'Fallon suspected she was allowing time to compose herself. He made himself at home, removing his jacket and placing it on a chair by the door.

Unable to locate a light switch, he scrounged a box of matches from the bookshelf and lit a few of the candles scattered throughout the room. When he found himself in front of the altar, he backed off.

Witch stuff. Something familiar caught his eye, and he leaned closer. His business card sat between two white candles. *What the hell?* After a quick glance toward the door, he knelt in front of the altar, careful not to touch anything.

Taking his pen from a pocket, he scooted the business card closer, wondering why it was there. Underneath the card was a piece of cream parchment with flowing writing. It had a Saint Bridget's cross in one corner. He bent nearer, struggling to read the inscription in the dim light, his heart thudding.

Goddess Brigit, grant Douglas Patrick O'Fallon protection from all harm. Make him strong in the face of his enemies, cunning and wise so that good will triumph and evil fail.

"I'll be damned," he said. He scooted the card back in place on top of the parchment, his mind in a tumult. She'd asked her goddess to bless him once again. When would he learn to trust her?

He heard a noise in the doorway and turned, stuffing his pen back into his pocket as he did so. He must have looked guilty as the witch arched an eyebrow, moving her eyes from him to the altar and back.

O'Fallon gave a repentant sigh. "Sorry. I was . . ."

"Nosy?" she asked. He gave a nod. "And what did you find?"

"That you consistently amaze me."

"I find the same of you."

Rising to his feet, he pointed at the business card. "You really think I'm one of the good guys?"

She nodded, handing him a cup of hot chocolate. "You're also an arrogant pain in the ass and don't know when to back off."

He thumbed his way through that statement. "Do you want me to leave you alone?"

The witch shook her head. "No. You just need to know that you're not the only one who can solve mysteries."

"I can't solve you," he replied before he thought.

To buy time, he took a swallow of the hot chocolate. As promised, it was liberally laced with Irish liquor. Without missing a beat, she took the cup from him and set it aside. Gently placing her hand on his cheek, her palm warmed the skin beneath. "You're going to have to learn to trust me."

"I'm working on it." He took her hand and kissed the palm. It smelled of chocolate. "You're going to have to do the same."

"Trust in myself?" she said, flipping the question in a direction he'd not intended. Her brows furrowed in thought. "You know, maybe you have a point."

"We'll work on it together," he said. He caressed her unblemished cheek, keeping his touch light. "You are so soft," he said. "And your eyes . . ."

Gavenia smiled. "My eyes . . . ," she prompted.

"Fiery blue to midnight dark. They have such depth." *Like your soul.* "Okay, I admit it, I'm an eye guy." His gaze trailed down her chest with the hint of a roguish smile. His hand followed, moving down the side of her neck, stopping just above the swell of her breasts.

* * *

She felt his heartbeat through the tips of his fingers.

His kiss was a curious blend of beer and chocolate. Her mouth parted and his tongue lightly touched hers. The kiss deepened and she leaned into it. His right hand cupped a breast and the sensation shot through her.

O'Fallon broke the kiss and pulled back, studying her with an intensity that made her pulse accelerate. "If I stay any longer," he whispered, "I'll want to make love to you."

He'd drawn the line. If she stayed on her side, there would be no chance of hurt, no hidden secrets that might destroy her heart. If she let him go out the front door, she could preserve the status quo. Tomorrow would be like today. And tonight she'd sleep alone.

If she stepped over that line, her heart and her future were up for grabs. She exhaled slowly to buy time, searching around the room. No sign of Bart. O'Fallon's Guardian was missing as well. What did that mean?

O'Fallon pulled back with a sigh of disappointment. "I've pushed too soon, haven't I?"

"I'm not sure. I . . . it's been a long time since I've been with someone."

"Winston?" he prompted.

"Yes."

"I swear I'm not married," he said. "And I fancy you."

The line grew thinner. Just a step over and . . .

"Why do you want to be with me?" she asked, searching his deep-brown eyes. "Why not . . . well . . ."

"Why not one of my own kind, you mean?" he asked, a tinge of hurt in his voice.

"No. . . . I've . . ." She pulled completely out of his arms, putting some distance between them. "I've dated guys who just wanted to brag they'd bagged a witch and lived to tell the tale."

The hurt in his eyes grew. "You should know me better than that," he said.

"Do I? One minute you're sure I'm going to carve your heart out and sacrifice it to some demon, and the next moment you're trying to seduce me. Color me confused, O'Fallon."

A petulant frown appeared. "I'm sorry to be a problem. I don't usually mess with—" He stopped and shook his head. "No, you're not a heathen. . . . You're . . ."

She took a step toward him, sensing he was teetering on a line of his own. "Go on. . . . What am I?"

He gently positioned his hands on either side of her face.

"A godsend," he said, leaning forward and brushing a kiss on her lips.

"Goddess-send, you mean," she whispered.

"Whatever . . . You are one of a kind."

The next kiss wasn't rushed, but savored like a fine cognac. His hand sought her left breast and he rubbed until the nipple pressed back through her sweater. The intimate sensation helped her decide.

"Stay with me tonight," she said, voice barely above a whisper.

He didn't answer, but hugged her close, stroking her hair.

A jolt of reality intruded. "Ah, damn." She abruptly retreated from his arms.

"Now what?" he grumbled.

"We need to make a pharmacy run," she said, embarrassed to even mention it. She'd been so furious at Winston's infidelity, she'd tossed out her condoms.

A smug grin. "No problem. I have three rubbers in my wallet."

"Three?" Another nod. "Wishful thinking?" she joked.

He pulled her into his arms again and nipped at her neck, sending heat lightning racing through her body. "You can tell me in the morning."

This time there was no pause, only point and counterpoint. She helped him remove his shirt, careful not to touch his bruised ribs. He pulled off her sweater, revealing her lacy white bra. He ran his hand down both her breasts, rubbing the nipples to life. His hands had a slight tremor as he fumbled with the front hook. Gavenia found that endearing. He was as nervous as she was. That told her more was at stake than a night's pleasure. She placed her hands over his, halting his progress for a moment.

"I've not been with anyone since the accident," she said. "I'm not sure how this will go."

His eyes softened. "You set the boundaries tonight. I'm here for you."

Her heart melted. "I've never had a man say that before."

"Then I'm happy to the first." He resumed his efforts to unhook her bra, leaning close. His citrus cologne scented every breath she took, his arousal pressing hard against her thigh. "Need any help with that?" she joked.

"Not since I was sixteen," he replied, the garment complying at the last moment. He removed it, dropping it to the floor. She waited for his reaction. It came immediately, his mouth falling open in astonishment.

Gotcha, she thought as he stared at the twin gold goddesses that hung like fine gems from her nipples.

"Oh, those are so . . . ," he said, and then fell silent. He rubbed a finger over one of them. Before she could say anything, he carefully lowered her onto the mound of floor cushions and began his worship of the right goddess.

A tentative flick over the nipple, then a stronger one. She hummed in response. A strong suckle. She arched upward.

"Like that, do you?" he said with a wicked chuckle. "How about this?" He wet the nipple with his tongue and then blew on it. Cold fire coursed through her. Gavenia couldn't help but moan in response.

He grinned in obvious delight. "This is going to be an evening to remember."

Surprises lurked under his clothes—he wasn't a boxer-shorts kind of guy but wore bikini briefs. They hugged every curve and bulged with promise.

As she ran her hands over his tight buttocks, savoring the sensation, he continued his exploration of her breasts, lavishing attention on each in turn.

"I've never made love to a woman who wore these," he said, deftly flicking one of the rings with his tongue. She responded by nipping at his neck, earning her a deep growl of pleasure.

She ran her hand over his chest, finding a small bump near the right shoulder. A scar, pale white against his skin. Before she could ask, he covered her lips with his, his hand kneading her left breast. She slid her palms down the side of him until she reached his hips. Racking her nails up his back produced a moan that escaped from his mouth into hers.

He pulled away and descended on her body, kiss by kiss, feathering them with increasing frequency, across the tattoo on her right arm, down her chest to her belly and finally to her thighs. Gently, he parted them. A kiss to her inner thigh made her quiver, then the other side, then one in the middle, as if he was performing a holy rite. Then he touched the part of her she'd long believed dormant.

The scent of her arousal was heady and fueled his desire. She was so different from the others, enticingly erotic, with those golden-haired goddesses who'd silently commanded he satisfy her.

God help him, he'd do his best. He touched her with his tongue and her hips moved upward in response. When he looked up, he saw her eyes were closed, waiting for his next move. Trusting him implicitly. He knew the measure of that trust and he swore he'd not fail her. He slowly moved his hands under her soft buttocks, raising her hips slightly, and let his tongue speak to her of ecstasy.

She called out once, then again, her hands tightening on pillows. Her body arched upward, tensing. Deep moans wove around her cries of pleasure. He paused only long enough to tear open the wrapper and pull out the condom. He rolled it on, testing it, and then took his place next to her on the pillows. Pulling her onto her right side, he carefully placed her left leg over his hip. With deliberate care, he moved inside her, watching her reaction. Her body tensed, then relaxed, and then tensed again as he moved deeper within.

"Oh, that . . . ," she started, and then sighed.

"Feels good?"

"Ummm-hummm."

He kissed her, deep, as he began to move, slow shallow strokes to begin with. Her body responded, pulling closer to him, her hand grasping his hip, guiding him toward her more forcefully.

"Oh, Goddess," she whispered. He felt the cold metal of the

nipple rings on his chest, her hair tickling down his arm. Her mouth sought his and she thrust her tongue deep.

Somewhere in the middle of their tandem tumult, he rolled her onto her back, hesitating only a moment before driving back into the depths of her. She cried out as an orgasm overtook her, her hair flowing around her like a halo.

God help him, he was feeling heaven with every stroke. She tightened around him and the sensation of raw heat grew, making him grit his teeth. He concentrated on the joy he could bring her before his own burning need was met.

As she rode out another orgasm, Gavenia opened her eyes. Her lover was moving faster now, his face set in concentration, bringing her the pleasure first.

She pulled herself up, nibbled at his ear, and said, "Your turn."

He groaned and then his thrusts grew harder, more urgent. He pulled her toward him, wrapping his arms around her as his release caught him. She closed her eyes, savoring the sensation of their intimate union. As his orgasm ebbed, it caught fire within her, as if transferred from one body to the other. She called out at the peak of her ecstasy, clasping him tight to her, and then fell silent.

In time, he rolled to his side, pulling her with him. She nestled on his chest.

"Stay with me all night," she whispered. "Don't leave."

"I'll be here, whenever you want," he said, kissing her tenderly on the cheek.

"I—" Gavenia stopped, unable to verbalize what she felt. She wasn't sure herself.

"I know," he said. "This was more than . . . we expected."

He did understand. She laid her head on his chest, listening as his heart steadied its pace and returned to normal.

Eventually they collected their clothes, blew out the candles, and retreated to Gavenia's bedroom. There they made love again, this time with less urgency, but more passion. She'd rolled on top of him, arching upward as she moved to her own rhythm. This time he'd come first, crying out her name to the heavens before she succumbed to the fiery pleasure.

"It just keeps getting better," he said, kissing her as she curled up next to him on the bed. "Practice makes perfect."

Gavenia nodded her weary agreement. As she fell asleep in her lover's arms, she thanked the Goddess for her life and the man who had reminded her that she was a woman.

Despite his tiredness and the pleasant after-sex reverie, O'Fallon couldn't sleep. He listened as Gavenia fell into a deep slumber, her breath tickling the hairs on his chest. They're found more joy than he'd believed possible.

Thank you for bringing her to me. His prayers had been answered in a way he'd not expected. God had sent him the woman of his dreams in a disguise that he might well have ignored.

* * *

Gavenia roused to the sound of purring in her ear. She absent-mindedly raised her hand, and it connected with fur. The purring grew louder and a low meow echoed near her ear.

"Let me sleep," she whispered, rolling onto her side. A moment later she opened her eyes, staring at the empty bed next to her. No Irish guy. A pang of regret coursed through her.

She remembered him giving her a kiss sometime near dawn and whispering that he was leaving. She'd felt the bedclothes tucked around her and then was back to sleep in an instant.

Sorting through her memories of the previous night caused a lusty smile. He'd need to restock his wallet today. She'd not told him, but the Irish did make better lovers. There was no need to feed his ego quite yet.

Stretching, she felt a slight ache in her hip. A pleased hum escaped her lips.

"Maybe Viv's right. I should get laid more often," she said.

Pulling herself to the edge of the bed, she peered at the clock. Eight and some change. There was a note propped up against the clock; next to it was a folded piece of green paper. She picked up the note first.

Gold nipples beckon
You lie beneath me sated
Spring's warmth fires my blood

"I'll be damned—erotic haiku," she said. Bastet rubbed against the hand holding the note. The green folded paper was an intricate origami parrot. It smelled like her lover's citrus cologne.

"You are an enigma, O'Fallon. You're as Irish as they come, you write haiku, you do origami, and you know how to make love. Unreal." She kissed both the note and paper, returning them to their place by the clock.

A resounding hiss startled her. Bastet fluffed to twice her size, glaring at the far corner from her place at the end of the bed, her tail stiff in the air.

Quite a picture, a voice said. Gavenia struggled with her robe as she peered into the dim corner. A figure stepped out of the shadows, hands folded over his chest, shaking his head in disapproval. He was about six feet in height, clad in a natty blue suit, with lacquered hair a hurricane wouldn't budge.

Before she could speak, he gestured toward the bed. *Your choice in lovers is just not appropriate. Things have to change in that department. Actually, a lot of things have to change now that I'm here.*

"Who the hell are you?" she snapped, rising to her feet in one movement.

I'm Reginald, your new Guardian.

Chapter Thirty

"Where is Bart?" Gavenia demanded.

Quickens has been reassigned.

"Not with my approval."

Your approval isn't needed.

"The hell it isn't."

Reginald shook his head as if she were a naughty toddler.

We'll have to start with that attitude of yours. Quickens allowed you far too much freedom.

"Go away! I refuse to accept you as a Guardian."

Quickens is gone. Throwing a tantrum won't work.

She gave him a cold smile. "I'm not throwing a tantrum; I'm throwing your ass out. Either Bart comes back, or I do this gig alone. Either way, you're not my Guardian."

A strange look crossed Reginald's face. It almost caused Gavenia to back down.

You refuse me as your Guardian? he asked.

"You're damned right."

Reginald looked heavenward and then nodded. *So be it.* His form thinned out, the chest of drawers becoming visible behind him. *Pity; you had promise.* Then he was gone.

Gavenia gnawed on the inside of her lip until it bled.

"It's Bart or nothing, got it?" she said, looking upward herself. When no answer came, she headed for the shower, the sensuous memory of the previous night tarnished by bitter reality.

* * *

"Your gut was on the mark," Zimansky announced.

"So what did you find?" O'Fallon asked, shifting the cell phone to the opposite ear so that he could take notes. A cup of convenience-store coffee steamed the car windows.

"The grocery store's security tape shows a guy walk up to the car, bend down, reach underneath the car, and pull on something. He stands up, dusts off his hands, and walks away. When the maid comes back, the car doesn't start."

"Were you able to ID the guy?"

"Nope. Too far away."

O'Fallon's mounting euphoria evaporated. "Did you talk to the repair guy?"

"Yup, and we picked up the list from Alliford. We got one from Mrs. Foster as well, just in case there was crossover."

O'Fallon gave a nod of approval. "I'm trying to track down Janet Alliford, see what she can tell me."

There was a chuckle, and then, "Can't get away from it, can you?"

"Couldn't if I wanted to."

"Keep in touch, and we'll do the same."

"Thanks, Zimansky."

"No sweat, O'Fallon."

He flipped the cell phone closed. A few more things to check, and then he'd make a pass downtown to see if he could find Janet. While he was down there, he'd swing by the Pagan shelter. Now that he and the witch were lovers, the stakes were much higher.

* * *

The shelter's dining room was nearly empty. One old guy tackled a crossword puzzle at a table by the window, muttering words to himself while another fellow napped nearby. The residual scent of food made O'Fallon's stomach growl. After this social call, he'd have to find some lunch.

"O'Fallon?" a voice called. He swung around, and it took a moment to process the face as it was out of context. He'd never seen

David Llewellyn in anything but a three-piece suit. The T-shirt, jeans, and apron made him look downright benign.

"Llewellyn?" he said, and strode forward, extending his hand. They shook warmly.

"Is that for me?" the man asked, pointing at the rose in O'Fallon's other hand.

"Sorry. It's for the pretty lady with the golden hair."

The lawyer's eyes developed a knowing twinkle. He lowered his voice. "So you're the reason she's not complaining about washing the dishes today."

"I might be," O'Fallon allowed, returning a manly grin.

"Come on, she's this way," Llewellyn said, waving him forward. "So how's retirement going?"

"It goes. More sleep, less money. It's a trade-off."

* * *

Her lover stood in the kitchen doorway, in one of his infamous suits, a single pink rose in hand. Gavenia's heart did an embarrassing lurch.

Oh, Goddess, get a grip.

"Why didn't you tell me it was O'Fallon you were sparring with?" Llewellyn asked.

Gavenia looked from one man to the next and then groaned. "You two know each other?" she asked.

O'Fallon nodded. "He's hammered me in court more than once." The flower-bearing Irishman crossed the room, planted a kiss on her cheek, and delivered the rose. Llew took the hint and the coffeepot and headed toward the dining room. Once the doors closed, Gavenia bent forward and delivered a more welcoming kiss on the Irish guy's lips.

"Mmmmm . . . that's nice," he said, his hands gliding around her waist, tugging her close.

"So what brings you down here, besides the rose?" she asked.

"Dinner. My place. I'll cook. How's that sound?"

"Sounds delightful," she said, her voice instinctively falling into a sultry timbre. "Should I bring dessert?"

"Actually, I thought you would be dessert."

"Hmmm . . . Then I'll bring a treat for Seamus."

"Just bring yourself. Then he'll stop nagging me about Tinker."

"Co-opted his affections, have I?"

"Big-time."

"Should I pack a toothbrush?"

His eyes sparked at the question. "I'd say that might be a good idea, unless you want to use mine."

The door swung open, interrupting another lengthy kiss. Aunt Lucy this time. She picked up a plate of cookies and vanished without a word.

"I'd better go. You're busy," he said. The tone of his voice told her he'd prefer to stay.

"What time?" she asked, easing out of his grasp. It felt better in his arms.

"Make it nine. I've got a few more things to track down."

"Be careful."

"I will. Same to you," he said, playfully tapping her nose.

Once he was gone, she inhaled the flower's rich scent. It filled her mind like a sweet balm as the memory of their vibrant lovemaking overtook her. He'd gone out of his way to bring her a rose. *Serious brownie points.*

"Damn," she muttered. She was losing control of her heart. No, that wasn't right. She'd lost it the night before, in the heat of their passion when he'd whispered how beautiful she was as she climaxed in his arms.

"Oh, Goddess, I hope this isn't a mistake." Sticking the rose in a glass of fresh water, she returned to the mound of dishes. Only after she finished scouring the last pot did she realize he'd not mentioned a word about the Alliford case.

Gavenia turned her mind to other problems. Ever since Reginald had departed, raw fear had coursed along every nerve. She felt like a newborn lamb surrounded by a pack of ravenous wolves. The fear had diminished when she was in the shelter and more so when encircled in O'Fallon's arms. That made sense; the shelter had a number of spiritual protections in place, courtesy of the witches, and O'Fallon wore Brigit's cross. Now as she stepped outside the shelter, the feeling rose exponentially.

"So this is how it's going to be without a Guardian?" she asked no one in particular. "I'm still not backing down. It's Bart or no one," she declared, as if someone might actually be listening.

Goddess how she missed him, costume changes and all. "I wish I could have said good-bye." Now she'd have to learn how to cope on her own.

She'd just reached her car when Bernie called her name as he huffed his way across the parking lot, face red from exertion.

"They still have some pie inside if you're hungry," Gavenia said, placing the rose in the seat next to the fairy wand.

Bernie leaned again the car's trunk to catch his breath. "No, thanks." Another deep inhalation. "I found her. She's turning tricks on San Julian and Fifth."

"Goddess, Bernie, she's lost it all."

"Yeah." He uncorked his bottle and took a lengthy swig. "It's easy to lose."

"You want to come with me?"

He was shaking his head before she finished the question. "I'm going to the VA meeting. A bunch of us vets get together and bitch about life."

"You need me to drop you?"

Bernie's face brightened. "Yes, ma'am, I'd like that. It'll save my poor knees."

* * *

Bradley's mother was exactly where Bernie had said she'd be. Despite the early-evening chill, Janet was wearing a short skirt, no hose, and a flimsy halter top—all the better to display her wares. She appeared wraith thin and strung out, just another drug addict hunting a fix.

An idea crept into Gavenia's mind and, for once, she acted on her intuition. She dialed O'Fallon.

"Hey, lady," he said, apparently recognizing the number from the caller ID. "So what's new?"

"Well, I'm telling you what I'm up to so you won't yell at me later."

"Such as?" he asked, his voice tightening immediately.

"I've found Janet Alliford and I'm going to ask her a few questions."

"Where?"

"Corner of San Julian and Fifth." She waited for the explosion.

"Oh, God." A low exhalation came through the earpiece. "Make it quick and call me the moment you're out of there, okay?"

"You're not going yell?" she asked, astonished.

"What's the point? You're obviously not listening to me."

"I'll let you know what I find out." She glanced at her watch. "I might be a bit late for our date."

"That's fine, but for God's sake, be careful."

"I know. I'll be careful." She heard a faint good-bye, and the line went dead. He was probably cursing her to high heaven. "Don't worry, I'll make it quick," she said.

Gavenia dropped the phone into her jacket pocket and jammed her purse under the seat. No reason to write *Mug me* on herself in bold letters.

She walked to within ten feet of Bradley's mother, unsure of her reception. Janet was scanning the street with bloodshot eyes, a cigarette in a shaking hand.

Dusk was falling, but there was no one near enough to threaten her except the dead child's mother, yet Gavenia still felt another surge of raw anxiety. She studied the street. There were no ghosts. If her previous experience was any indication, this part of town was loaded with them. Why wasn't she seeing them?

This is weird. She turned her attention to the wretched figure in front of her.

"Janet?"

Haunted eyes swiveled to study her. "Who are you?" the woman asked, and then took another puff of the cigarette.

"I'm Gavenia Kingsgrave. I'm the one who helped your son."

A faint flicker of understanding. "Is he okay?"

Odd question. "He's at peace."

A half smile. "Lucky him."

Janet's cold indifference nauseated her. If she'd been closer, she would have slapped the woman. Gavenia retaliated in the only way she could. "You sound just like your mother."

Janet glared. "Leave that bitch out of this."

Gavenia shrugged, trying to dampen her own anger. *How would O'Fallon play this?* The answer came quickly. *He'd run a bluff.*

"You knew your son was going to be kidnapped, didn't you?" Gavenia asked.

The eyes returned her, redder now, as if lit by demon fire. "Yeah. Taylor said it was the only way."

Oh, Goddess, she did know. Gavenia swallowed and pressed on. "Trying to extort money out of Gregory?"

"Yeah." Janet took a couple tentative steps closer. "You fucking him?"

That was blunt. "No. I just helped Bradley go home."

The woman's face twitched and she puffed on the cigarette in earnest, as if it would replace the fix she craved.

"So what happened?" Gavenia asked.

The cigarette butt spun to the ground and Janet mashed it with her heel in a jerky motion. "Bradley got frightened. He ran. Taylor said it was an accident."

Ram it home. "The cops say he was killed on purpose to cover the crime. They're looking for this . . . Taylor . . . right now."

Janet's facial twitch escalated. "No, that's not right. It was an accident. . . . Taylor said the damned dog bit him. Bradley got scared and . . ."

"Merlin bit him?"

A grotesque bob of the head. "On the leg. It got infected. Taylor was way pissed." Janet wrapped her arms around her chest, rocking on her heels. "You're lying. Taylor wouldn't have—"

"Goddess, you're pathetic," Gavenia spat, no longer able to keep her revulsion in check.

Janet glowered at her. "You don't understand. I had to—"

"You had to have the money. You'd risk your child's life just to keep that high coming."

Janet glared and sniffed, wiping her hand against her nose. It came away bloody.

Gavenia went for the jugular. "Right before he crossed over, Bradley asked about you. He loved you. It's a pity you weren't the mother he deserved."

Janet winced as if backhanded. "Fuck you," she snarled.

"The feeling's mutual."

Turning her back on the woman, Gavenia strode to her car at a furious pace, ignoring her protesting hip. She disengaged the locks with repeated angry jabs at the remote, slung her cane inside, and then leaned against the vehicle, her heart bleeding in time with each beat. Janet had known Taylor was going to kidnap her son and had done nothing to stop it. The drugs had been more important than her only child's life. Her karmic debt would be monumental.

"Goddess, forgive her," she whispered. On impulse, she opened the door and pulled out the fairy wand. Gavenia blew on the feathered top and it danced in the breeze. What a pity she couldn't just tap the ground and all the pain would disappear.

Bart came to her mind. She leaned the wand against her forehead, recalling how he'd badgered her until she bought it. *Rituals have reasons*, he'd said.

A jolt of warning darted through her. She raised her head, hunting for the source. Janet was talking to someone and the man leaned in close and handed her something. Probably a trick. Then Janet pointed, and the man began limping toward Gavenia.

Janet's words hurtled through her mind. *The damned dog bit him.*

"Taylor," Gavenia said. Her gut churned. Fortunately, the man was moving slow enough she still had plenty of time to escape and she began to climb inside the car. Something grabbed her and there was a whoosh of air as she was forcibly wrenched away from the vehicle. She cried out, landing on her knees on the cement, pain rocketing into her left hip. Brittle ice shot down both arms, numbing them. The flash freeze accelerated throughout her body, dulling her senses.

Gavenia felt herself lifted and then slammed against the car. Pain erupted across her upper shoulders, fiery hot in sharp contrast to the glacial cold in her limbs. She flailed, desperate to fend off her assailant, but her hands met nothing but air. As her eyes focused, she saw the face.

It wasn't human.

Chapter Thirty-One

Going somewhere? the entity hissed, exuding a mass of gray-black specks into the twilight air like a noxious cloud. It pushed hard on her shoulders, and again she fell to her knees. Icy talons wrapped around her throat. She continued to struggle, unable to connect with anything solid.

If she could reach her cane . . .

The roar in her ears redoubled. Stars danced in her eyes, pulsating like quasars. Desperate, she clawed for the fairy wand where it had tumbled at her feet. Grasping it tightly, she thought of Bart, of his strength, how righteously furious he would be at this moment. A roiling ball of white light formed in her chest and she stabbed at the entity with the wand to set it loose. It shot along the wand's length and embedded itself deep inside the gray figure.

A supersonic howl pierced her ears, and the pressure released instantly. The figure staggered backward a few steps, hands seething in flames. It spit at her and howled again like a rabid wolf baying at the moon.

The rush of air into her lungs brought clarity and a terrifying revelation.

It's a Guardian.

It howled in response, beating at the flames on its hands. As she turned away, intent on escape, cold metal jammed against her neck. The gun was real.

A man's face moved close to hers. "Thanks for waiting," he said, the smell of liquor on his breath.

Bradley's killer.

Gavenia moved her gaze toward the Dark Guardian. Its hands

were no longer on fire and it had murder in its eyes. It had served its purpose: it had slowed her long enough for Taylor to catch her.

In her mind, she heard Reginald's patronizing voice: *Pity; you had promise.*

* * *

O'Fallon was on his second beer at McCrea's Pub, the cell phone strategically placed next to the pint of Beamish. Every few seconds he peered at the screen, drumming his fingers on the tabletop in a steady staccato. By his watch it had been seventeen and a half minutes since Gavenia called.

"She's fine, she's fine," he said like a mantra. "Probably took Janet for some food. That's what I'd do."

O'Fallon jumped when someone slid into the booth across from him, a beer in hand. He'd been so distracted he'd not realized Adam was in the bar.

Come on, focus. "Good evening," O'Fallon said, dumping the cell phone into his coat pocket to avoid staring. He had it set to ring and vibrate—no way he'd miss the call when it came through.

Adam didn't reply to his greeting, but glared at the foam on the top of his beer as if it were the cause of all the world's difficulties.

"So . . . what's going on?" O'Fallon asked. More silence. He had no patience for this. "Come on, you asked me to meet you here. What the hell is going on?"

The young cop's eyes snapped upward, incensed. "IAD me paid a visit today. They told me if I don't roll on Glass, I'm going down with him."

"Oh, shit."

"Yeah, oh shit." Adam took a deep drink of his beer and then wiped the foam off his lips in an agitated gesture. "Problem is, I don't have anything to give them."

"Nothing?"

"Just suspicions."

"Damn." O'Fallon sucked on his beer and then set the pint down with a clunk on the table. "I'd say they're bluffing. If they had anything, they'd be talking to you downtown."

"That's what Carey said. Glass just doesn't do jack in front of me. He even steps out of earshot when he gets a call from one of his snitches."

There was no reason to keep that sort of information from your partner.

Unless your snitches are doing your dirty work.

His phone came to life in his pocket. "About damned time," he growled, pulling it out. That garnered him an odd stare from his companion. He answered the call, not bothering to check the caller ID.

"Where the hell have you been?" he said.

"Doing my job. How about you?"

O'Fallon grimaced. It was the bloodhound, not the witch. He mentally cursed himself. "Sorry; I thought you were someone else."

There was a slight pause and then, "The SUV surfaced and it's in one piece."

O'Fallon's heart leaped. "Where was it?"

"In a parking lot at LAX. The owner was in Europe for the last three weeks."

"Well, I'll be damned."

"The guy thought it odd his SUV wasn't in the slot where it should be. He finds it five spaces away. He's willing to chalk that up to jet lag, but then he gets inside. The seat's out of position and that bugs him, and then he notices the foot pedals."

"Foot pedals?" O'Fallon asked, extracting his notebook and clicking the pen against his chest.

"The foot pedals are adjustable, but these are too close for him to drive. We did some measuring and we'd guess the killer is about five nine."

"Go on," O'Fallon said, scribbling notes, his head cranked sideways to trap the cell phone against his shoulder.

"By now the owner is spooked, so he does a walk-around and finds the dented front bumper, the crushed grille, and what looks like dried blood. He freaks and calls the cops."

"Chalk one up for an honest citizen."

"They're processing the SUV right now. We found the kid's picture under the passenger seat. Larsen admits you won the bet."

O'Fallon gave a long sigh. "That had to hurt."

Zimansky chuckled. "Serves him right."

"Does the SUV's owner live in Bel Air?"

"Nope. Brentwood. He's giving us a list of service companies so we can see if there's a match with Alliford's list. We're having the parking lot pull the security tapes."

"This is great news, Zimansky."

"Yeah, it is. I'll let you know what we find out. Any luck with Janet Alliford?"

O'Fallon checked his watch. It'd been twenty-six minutes. "I have a lead on her. I'll get back to you."

"Sounds good. Later, O'Fallon."

"Thanks, Zimansky."

He disconnected the call and dialed the witch. It rolled to her voice mail as his nerves sizzled with apprehension. He flipped the phone closed, sucked down the remainder of his beer, and asked, "How about we go for a ride?"

Adam nodded, downing the rest of his brew in a swallow. "I'm game, providing you tell me what that call was all about."

O'Fallon nodded his agreement. "It's time you were in the loop."

* * *

Her kidnapper didn't talk while they drove. When she'd tried to make conversation, he'd jammed the gun into her ribs and told her to shut up. She took the hint.

When he finally did speak, the sound made her jump.

"Over there," he said, waving with the gun toward the curb. She pulled up in front of an abandoned lot.

"Where's your purse?" She dug under the seat and he snatched the bag from her, dropping it onto the floor at his feet. "Get out and leave the keys."

"Look, the car and the purse are yours. Nothing else is negotiable," she said, staring straight ahead, her hands clenched around the wheel.

The gun jammed into her ribs, making her wince.

"Get out."

As she pulled herself out of the car, she instinctively reached for her cane, the only weapon she had.

"Leave it!" was the terse command.

"I can't walk without it," she bluffed. Her captor hesitated, but before he could change his mind, the Dark Guardian appeared next to him, whispering so quietly Gavenia couldn't hear the words.

Taylor came to a decision. "Leave it."

Gavenia's panic escalated. To combat it, she picked up the rose. Holding it somehow gave her strength, as if O'Fallon were standing next to her, keeping her safe.

As her kidnapper exited the car, she took time to study him. He was about five eight or nine, brown hair with blond roots, perhaps in his early thirties. He had a tattoo on one arm. She could see the bottom of it, a mermaid's tail fin, just below the T-shirt's sleeve.

He pointed across the street. "That way."

The structure seemed incomplete, as if a child had thrown the pieces together and then abandoned the project. No Trespassing signs hung at regular intervals from the tattered fence that encircled the property.

As her eyes adjusted, heaps of broken masonry and burned timbers became apparent. Some of the exterior walls slanted ominously, and birds settled into the exposed rafters with fluttering wings. A nearby streetlight clicked on, illuminating the soot-kissed sign above the main entrance.

CUTLER AND SONS PRODUCE

"Move it!" Taylor ordered. She held her ground, debating her options. O'Fallon was expecting her to call, and when she didn't, he'd hunt down Janet Alliford. If Gavenia could buy enough time, maybe he'd find her before . . .

"No one knows this place," Taylor said. She eyed the Dark

Guardian again. It was feeding him information.

Gavenia clutched the rose tighter, and a thorn dug into her palm. She focused on the pain, blocking out all other thoughts.

Taylor gave her a shove and she stumbled. "I'm getting there."

"Not fast enough," he said.

Her stomach roiled. She knew that tone; she'd heard it the last time a man had her under his control. The Dark Guardian trailed behind them. In her heart, she knew she should fear it more than the mortal it guarded.

I don't guard him; I rule him, was the swift answer.

Guardians can't do that, she retorted.

A chilling hiss returned. *What else didn't they tell you, Shepherd?*

Her cell phone rang and she automatically reached for it. The gun slammed into her ribs.

"Don't touch that."

She figured he'd take it, but he didn't. *Why not?* The answer chilled her. A cell phone was only useful to the living.

As they approached the building, Taylor hobbled ahead and peeled back a section of the fence. He'd apparently been here before. As she ducked into the wreckage, the rank smell of smoke, mixed with the stench of charred electrical wiring and rotten produce, struck her nose.

Gavenia moved cautiously toward the gaping front entrance. As she crossed into the building, Taylor shoved her. She fell to her knees, scraping her hands in an attempt to brace herself. The rose disintegrated at her feet, silky petals raining on the cinders.

"Stop it!" she snarled. "I'm moving as fast as I can."

Swearing, her captor grabbed her braid and pulled her upward. Gavenia grimaced at the pain and struggled to find her footing. As she regained her feet, her hand curled around a piece of brick. Once she reached her feet, she spun around, slamming the brick into Taylor's face before his Guardian could react. Taylor spit out more obscenities, lurching backward as blood blossomed from his forehead.

Run!

It sounded like Bart's voice and she heeded it without thinking.

Skittering farther into the building, she dodged around broken timbers and debris. Her steps were unsure, the floor treacherously uneven. As she ducked under a wide beam, her hair caught, strands ripping out. She swore, pulled hard, freeing the braid.

"You bitch!" A shot went wide, striking a support beam nearby, ricocheting brick fragments around her. Gavenia kept moving, instinctively heading into the shadowy recesses of the building. Behind her she felt the Dark Guardian's presence. It called to her, but she noted it kept a respectful distance. It still feared her, at least for the moment.

A shot whined by her ear and she jiggered sideways, but not before another grazed her arm. Gavenia cried out, grabbing at the wound. She swung to the right, but found that path blocked by a mound of debris. Swinging back, she clambered over a large iron beam. The floor felt spongy and it slowed her flight. Another shot; she lurched sideways. A timber slewed downward, clipping the side of her head, and brilliant pain mushroomed behind her eyes. She struggled forward, unable to see clearly until her feet found nothing beneath them.

Gavenia flailed in the air and then rolled into a ball as she plummeted downward into the darkness. She collided with the debris, and broken bricks gouged her left side. As her momentum abruptly halted, her head struck a piece of broken concrete.

Reginald's snide voice edged its way into her mind. *Oh, bravo! Well done.*

Before she could reply, oblivion claimed her.

Chapter Thirty-Two

Janet Alliford had died alone, resting against the side of an old building, a packet of cocaine spilled on the ground in front of her. A thick line of blood curled out of her nose, passed her capped teeth onto her chin. Her eyes stared heavenward as if begging forgiveness.

"Oh, damn," O'Fallon said, kneeling beside her. "What a waste." He checked her pulse anyway and wasn't surprised to find her skin cooling rapidly in the night air. Behind him, Adam called it in, requesting a crime-scene team and paramedics. Standard procedure: until the cops knew this was an overdose, it was considered a potential homicide.

O'Fallon rose and stepped backward, jamming his hands into his pockets. The usual dense urban carpet of spent needles, candy wrappers, and broken bottles surrounded the body. Nothing indicated a struggle.

"OD?" Adam asked after he'd completed the call.

"Looks that way. First her kid dies, and now her." His mind went to Gregory Alliford. *How do you carry on after you've lost everything?*

The thought jolted him hard. What it would be like without Gavenia? Had he been granted a glimpse of heaven only to have it torn away from him? He looked away to compose himself.

Where is she? Why hasn't she called?

He fumbled with his phone and dialed her number again. Voice mail. He slammed the cell into his pocket and pulled the Saint Bridget's cross from under his shirt. Closing his eyes, he let its healing sensations enfold him. He had to trust that everything would be all right. God would watch over her.

When he opened his eyes, he realized that Adam was waiting silently beside him. The young man had an uncanny ability to read the moment.

"Sorry, I . . . ," O'Fallon stammered. A movement across the street caught his notice. He took a few steps forward and then broke into a run.

"O'Fallon?" Adam called from behind him. He ignored the summons, keeping his attention on the nebulous ghost under the streetlight. When O'Fallon skidded to a halt, Benjamin Callendar pointed toward the ground and then vanished.

"What the hell?" O'Fallon found a familiar object in the gutter. "The fairy wand." It was the one he'd seen in the back of Gavenia's car and had meant to chide her about until he'd seen the bullet holes. He knelt and reached for it, but instantly snatched his hand back. Sensations bled off the thing even without physical contact. He had to prepare for this vision or it might prove more than he could bear.

A pair of tennis shoes came into his field of vision.

"You okay?" Adam asked.

"Yeah." O'Fallon gazed upward. "You aren't psychic, are you?"

"Not like you."

O'Fallon blinked in surprise at his candor.

"Dad told me God had blessed you in a very remarkable way."

O'Fallon huffed. "That's debatable." He pointed at the wand. "That was in Gavenia's car last night. Could you pick it up? If I touch it . . ." He hoped he didn't have to explain further.

"Sure. You have gloves in your trunk?"

O'Fallon nodded and dug out his keys. The young cop crossed to the car, popped the trunk, and returned with a pair of latex gloves. O'Fallon stared at them, though he'd donned them innumerable times during his career. Now they were a poignant reminder that the wand might be evidence of a crime. His stomach lurched at the thought and he swallowed to keep the beer at bay.

Adam donned the gloves, picked up the wand, and studied it under the patchy glow of the streetlight. "I don't see any blood."

O'Fallon mentally thanked him for that. "Let's go back to the car. The uniforms will be here pretty soon. I don't want to do this out in the open."

He stripped off his coat and laid it on the driver's-side seat. He repositioned the passenger seat and then settled in. Adam knelt by the open door and watched with anxious eyes.

"This could get nasty," O'Fallon warned.

"Do you, like, grow fur or something?" his companion asked.

O'Fallon couldn't help but chuckle. "No, nothing like that. Just make sure I have an open airway, and the rest will take care of itself."

Adam raised his right arm, the one in the cast. "CPR isn't an option, so don't crash on me."

"I'll try not to."

O'Fallon closed the fingers of his left hand around the fairy wand as his right hand sought the Saint Bridget's cross. He opened his heart and let the wand talk to him.

He heard a man's voice talking to Gavenia about the wand. She shook her head. A name . . . Bart. *Gavenia's Guardian.* Then the darkness descended like a theater curtain. As he sank further into the vision, he swore he saw the devil leering back at him.

* * *

O'Fallon heard a voice, but it took time to put the words together.

"I'm . . . okay," he whispered.

"Jesus, you scared the hell out of me," Adam said. When O'Fallon opened his eyes, he found the fairy wand was now in an evidence bag in Adam's lap. He didn't remember it being removed from his hand.

"You sure you're okay?" Adam asked.

O'Fallon nodded and leaned back in the seat. His skin felt clammy, and sweat pooled near the waistband of his pants.

"What did you see?" his companion asked earnestly.

O'Fallon didn't answer right away, but took a deep breath.

Finally, he found his voice. "I heard a name: *Taylor*. And I saw something else. Something . . . evil." He shook his head. "I can't really explain it."

"Anything else?"

"The strong scent of burned timbers and charred wiring."

"That's it?"

"Yeah. It's not an exact science."

"No kidding," Adam agreed.

Blue lights swept behind them as a patrol car slid to the curb.

"I suppose they'll need to talk to both of us," O'Fallon said.

"Most likely. What about this?" Adam asked, pointing toward the wand.

"Let's keep it off the table for right now."

The detective pondered for a moment and then nodded. "Whatever you say."

By the time the parade of crime-scene techs, detectives, and uniformed cops were done with Janet Alliford, O'Fallon was pacing, eager to be gone. They'd had to relate their story no less than four times, and each time his impatience grew. He wanted to be on the streets looking for Gavenia, but leaving a crime scene before they were excused would only put Adam into further trouble. The cop's career was already on the line.

When he ran out of options, he'd called Gavenia's aunt, and Lucy Merin reinforced his worst fears; there had been no sign of the witch since she left the shelter earlier that evening. She'd simply vanished like one of her ghosts.

He checked his watch—it was nearing ten thirty. They'd blown almost two and a half hours on the dead woman.

"If they'd just given her this much attention when she was still alive . . . ," he grumbled. *Seamus*. He'd completely forgotten the parrot's dinner. He dialed his housekeeper, offered profuse apologies for the late hour, and made hasty arrangements to get his roomie fed.

"Come on, guys, let's move it," he muttered, watching the detectives from a distance. They kept putting questions to Adam and he kept nodding in reply. "They're just being pricks about this.

Cut him loose and let's go."

The phone rang in his hand. It wasn't Gavenia. "Yes?" he demanded

"And good evening to you, too." It was Zimansky.

"Sorry; things have gone to hell here. Janet Alliford's dead."

A low sigh. "OD?"

"Looks like it. They're still working the scene."

"Did you get to talk to her?"

"No. But someone else did, and that someone is now missing."

"That doesn't sound good. We've ID'd the guy who stole the SUV. Name's LaRue Taylor."

Taylor. O'Fallon shivered. *Just like in the vision.*

Zimansky continued on, oblivious to the reaction he'd caused. "He's got an impressive rap sheet, mostly dealing drugs, with some aggravated assault thrown in for good measure. The lab kicked it into overdrive for us, and the fingerprints in the SUV and on the little boy's packing tube are a match. We've even got security-tape footage of LaRue in the SUV at the parking lot. He works for one of the landscaping companies, and they have contracts with Alliford and the owner of the Caddy. Before that, he worked at a place that serviced cars so he'd know how to disable one."

Bingo. "You got a lead on where he is?"

"That's why I'm calling. We're working a search warrant on his apartment. We just got here. It took time to make nice with Downtown and line up some uniforms."

"Still, that was fast."

"All you have to do is mention a dead kid, and judges take notice."

"So what have you found?"

"A key for the Escalade. He ordered it from a Cadillac dealership and had it sent to the owner's address after the guy left town. Pretty clever. He had the ransom letter all ready to go. He was going to ask for four million. And we found some bloody bandages. He must have tangled with something that cut him up pretty badly."

"The dog, maybe?"

"Perhaps. We'll have the lab work them over." A pause, and

then, "Hold on." There was muffled conversation.

Adam returned at that moment.

O'Fallon asked, "Are we free to go?" The young cop gave a nod. O'Fallon pointed at the phone. "It's Zimansky. They're searching Taylor's apartment."

Another nod.

"You there, O'Fallon?"

"Yeah."

"What's the name of the missing party who spoke to the Alliford woman?"

"Kingsgrave; Gavenia Kingsgrave."

"Well, part of her isn't missing anymore. We got her driver's license and credit cards."

Oh, God, LaRue found her. His face must have given him away. Adam shook his head and sighed expressively.

"She was driving a red Miata," O'Fallon offered. He dug out his notebook and relayed the license plate number and a detailed description of his lover.

"We'll put out an APB," Zimansky said.

"Gavenia called me right before she met with Janet Alliford and was supposed to call back the moment the interview was complete. She never did."

"This isn't lookin' good, O'Fallon."

"No, it isn't." He paused and added, "Thanks for your help, Zimansky."

"Yeah, yeah. Wait until we bag this bastard, then you can thank me."

Chapter Thirty-Three

"You sure about that?" Harve Glass asked, leaning forward in his chair. "Why the hell was Elliot at a crime scene?"

The portly desk sergeant gave a noncommittal shrug. "He even called it in. Remember that PI, the one that got in your face?"

"Yeah?"

"He was at the scene with Elliot."

Glass frowned. "Who's the vic?"

"Some woman from Bel Air named Alliford. But it gets better."

"Yeah, how?"

"The two guys that were in here awhile back? They're from West Hollywood. They're executing a search warrant over near the Alexandria Hotel."

Glass frowned. "Who they after?"

"After some puke named Taylor. They say he's good for attempted kidnapping and a hit-and-run. An APB just came across on him and a woman named Kingsgrave. They think he might have kidnapped her."

"I'm not following," Glass said, his frown deepening.

The desk sergeant gave a patronizing grin. "They say Taylor is the guy who ran over that little kid in Bel Air. You remember, a couple weeks ago?"

"So what has that to do with Elliot and the PI?"

"Well, that's where it gets weird. The OD tonight? She was the kid's mother. They think Taylor was her dealer."

He was saved from comment when someone called the desk sergeant back to his post. Glass rose and pulled on his jacket, thinking through the situation. One of the other detectives glanced in his direction.

"Callin' it a night?" Carstairs asked.

"No. I'm gonna go see what my fairy partner is up to. I don't like him out on his own. Things can happen, you know."

The other cop smirked. "Yeah, I hear you."

The moment he reached his car, Glass retrieved a cell phone from the glove compartment. Waiting for it to find a signal, he muttered under his breath, "What a fucking moron." He dialed a number and waited. He just needed to set the trap and let the fool blunder into it. Then everything would be back on track.

* * *

"I told you I took care of the problem," Taylor said, pointing to the body deep in the pit. Behind the corpse glowing rodent eyes glinted in the beam of Glass's flashlight. "See? Rat food. Now can we get outta here? This place is creepy."

"Where's her car?" Glass demanded.

"Chop shop. It'll be in pieces by morning."

"How'd you kill her?"

Taylor pointed to the gun in his waistband. "A round in the head," he boasted.

"Why'd you kill the kid?"

"He ran. I didn't have . . . any . . ." Taylor jammed his lips together.

The warehouse fell silent and then Glass hissed, "They traced you to the SUV, asshole. They've got an APB out for you and the woman down there," he said, gesturing with the flashlight.

"How the hell . . ." Taylor jittered nervously on the uneven floor. "What do I do? I got no money to run."

"You don't have to run. I'll take care of everything."

Taylor gave a sigh. "That's cool. I'd have cut you in on the boy's ransom money."

"Yeah, I'm sure." The flashlight beam cut laterally through the darkness, burning into Taylor's retinas, blinding him.

"Hey, don't do that. You—"

Glass's reply consisted of three staccato bursts of gunfire that scattered the frightened birds into the night sky like arrows. Taylor tried to say something, but crumpled to the warehouse floor before uttering a word. Positioning his flashlight on a pile of rubble to illuminate the scene, Glass pulled a pair of latex gloves out of his pocket and put them on. He stripped the body of its cell phone and gun, then pushed Taylor to the edge of the pit. The corpse teetered for a moment before landing with a heavy thud on the debris below.

"One asshole down, two to go," Glass muttered. At least now Taylor wouldn't try to sell him out to save his own skin.

He reclaimed his flashlight and wove his way out of the building.

* * *

Something brushed by Gavenia's hand. Something furry. When she jerked herself into a tighter ball, shivering, an annoyed squeak said the rodent wasn't amused. When her eyes fluttered open, for a moment she thought she was blind; the area around her was nearly pitch-black. As her eyes adjusted, she saw charred and warped timbers sticking through mounds of broken brick and concrete like ghostly trees. Strands of electrical conduit hung above her like a dismembered spider web.

Another squeak resounded near her. "Rats," she muttered. No doubt they were passing around the dinner menu at this very moment, amazed at their good fortune. She touched the right side of her face; her fingers came away sticky. *Blood.* No wonder her head throbbed like a bongo drum. As she sat upright, the pain exploded and her stomach responded. She heaved hard and long until her stomach was empty.

A concussion. Just what I need.

How long had she been unconscious? Once the nausea subsided, Gavenia felt for her watch. The lighted display was gone, smashed by the debris. She remembered rousing a couple of times, thinking she heard voices, but had drifted back into the welcome embrace of painless oblivion.

By now O'Fallon would be frantic, ripping the city apart to find her. Her left hand began to cramp and when she opened it, the palm revealed two rose petals. Apparently, she had grabbed them and they'd remained with her during her swan dive. She took a deep sniff of their faint scent. It reminded her of the night before, of the inferno ignited between her and the Irishman.

"The hell I'm going to die now," she said, glaring upward. "It's just starting to get interesting." As she tucked the petals into her jeans pocket for safekeeping, she encountered a pack of gum. She unwrapped a stick and savored it. The peppermint overcame the sour taste in her mouth and seemed to ease her thirst.

Gavenia rose very slowly, testing her weight on one foot and then the other. Both hips ached and her back burned in protest, but given the fall she'd taken, she was reasonably whole.

"Thank you," she said, looking upward. Past the bare rafters, a pale first-quarter moon welcomed her. It was better than no light at all. She began a careful search of her surroundings, inching forward in the debris, fearful of discovering another hole that would lead deeper into the maw of the burned-out hulk.

The situation proved grim. She was apparently in some sort of pit, and the debris that surrounded her was at least two stories high. Climbing out would require skills she didn't possess.

"Oh, this sucks," she muttered. "This really sucks." She heard multiple rodent movements, and a shiver coursed through her. "I'm not dinner," she said defiantly. She wondered how long that boast might hold. Eventually she'd have to sleep, and if no one came for her . . .

The melodic strains of Tchaikovsky's "Dance of the Sugar Plum Fairy" filled the air. She slapped both her jacket pockets, but came up empty. The ringing stopped.

"No! Call again!" she shouted. As if obliging her, the phone began again. Triangulating on the melody, her hope melted. The sound came from above; her phone hadn't made the journey into the pit. She slumped on a large piece of concrete in despair.

The night air began to burrow into her veins, causing her to shiver. Her thirst mounted despite the gum, growing stronger with each passing minute. Another round of rat skitters came from just ahead of her. How much would be left of her by the time they found her body? Would she be like one of those skeletons that Ari unearthed?

She extended her hand, palm upward as if holding a skull.

"Alas, poor Gavenia! I knew her: a witch of infinite . . . infinite . . . whatever." Unable to summon the proper word, she gave the illusionary skull a toss. "Now what?" she muttered.

A faint glow emanated from the ground. Intrigued, she moved forward to investigate. Gavenia's toe kicked the body before she realized what it was, and she jumped back with a startled squeak that rivaled the sounds of her rodent companions. As she bent over to check the body, the glow rose from it, shifting a few feet away as if unsure of her presence. It was a soul, a newly dead one, and its aura was muddy gray, the taint of a vile life.

The body was crumpled over the bricks like a discarded puppet, its chest a solid mass of clotted blood. Even in the faint light she recognized Taylor's build and the half mermaid on his arm. She suppressed a shudder.

Her hunter had become prey.

Chapter Thirty-Four

Every minute had a weight of its own, tinged with fear and regret. Though the bulletin was out and the city was looking for her, no one had seen Gavenia. Taylor remained missing as well. It was as if the earth had swallowed them up.

Adam leaned back in the seat. His face looked drawn and he absentmindedly rubbed his cast. They'd driven through Skid Row for the last three hours with no result other than a lowered gas gauge and a tenuous caffeine high from their frequent convenience-store pit stops.

A block away a fire engine rolled by, its siren shredding the night.

"I'm missing something. I feel it. If I could only get my mind to work," O'Fallon said. When had he lost his objectivity?

When we made love for the second time. That was when his heart had told him she was the one.

O'Fallon closed his eyes and prayed, asking Bridget for a miracle. Why would God give him this damned gift only to have it fail to save the woman he loved?

In the distance another fire engine wove its way through the downtown maze.

Fire. . . . Charred timbers, the smell of burned wiring.

"Where's the closest firehouse?" he demanded, startling his companion.

Adam thought for a moment. "Station Nine's over on East Seventh, and Station Ten's on South Olive. Nine is closer. Why?"

"I need to talk to a fireman."

* * *

Gavenia retreated to the island of concrete and eased herself into a sitting position. Carefully trying to rub the grit out of her eyes, she waited. The dead man's soul stood next to his body, waving his arms as if trying to signal a taxi.

What the hell is going on? the spirit demanded of no one in particular, staring down at his crumpled form.

Perhaps he'd move across without her intervention. She immediately discarded that notion. Sudden deaths often caused the soul to follow the same emotional curve as the terminally ill, the classic five stages of death and dying: denial, anger, bargaining, depression, and, finally, acceptance. Some took longer than others. Some never crossed, too fearful of what awaited them on the other side.

The ghost began flailing in all directions, kicking debris and swearing. Some of the rubble shifted from his kinetic energy. As his anxiety rose, so did the flying debris.

"Great," she muttered. He'd jumped directly to *anger*. If he kept it up, he could bring the whole building down on her. He careened around the pit's interior, a whirling dervish of energy.

"Stop that," she said.

The soul jerked around and stared at her.

What the hell is happening? he repeated.

"You were shot."

So get me some help.

Gavenia wasn't feeling very charitable. "Gee, you tried to kill me, remember?" The form glowered but didn't answer. "Anyway, it doesn't matter now."

The soul blinked, and she thought she caught a look of understanding. He gazed down at the body and then back up. *I'm dead?*

"As the proverbial doornail. I'm sorry, but that's the truth," she said. She gingerly rose to her feet, rubbing her thigh through the ripped blue jeans. A large patch of blood stuck the denim to her leg.

You're lying! I'm not dead. I can't be.

"Denial," she murmured to herself. This one was moving along at a rapid pace.

You have to do something, the soul demanded.

Gavenia eyed the spirit, her patience gone. "See that light," she said, pointing to where a subtle luminescence hovered in the air. "That's where you need to go."

No way, I ain't goin' to hell.

She shrugged and hunted around until she found a reasonably stable piece of rubble and sat. The ground around her feet was a mélange of charred wood, broken bricks, and twisted metal. A breeding ground for tetanus and Goddess knew how many other lethal diseases.

What can I do? I don't want to be dead.

Gavenia mentally ticked off *bargaining* on the checklist. She held her silence. He was making swift progress on his own.

The soul knelt beside his body and began to cry.

I don't want to roast forever.

Gavenia looked back and sighed. "Once you're across, you'll work things out. You'll see what you did wrong and how you can do it better the next time."

I won't go to hell?

The soul sounded so pathetic she couldn't help but sigh. How could she explain that hell would be of his own making? She shook her head. Best not to try. "Once you cross, you'll find peace in your own way."

The soul looked down, trying to put a hand on his former physical shell. It passed through the bloody chest.

A sad whimper. *I didn't think he'd do it.*

Gavenia perked up. "Who?" The ghost didn't answer. "You killed Bradley, didn't you?" she asked. A slow nod. "Why?"

It's the dog's fault. I had the kid in the car, but the damned mutt wouldn't go away. It bit me. The ghost rubbed his calf as if the leg still ached. *The kid ran and I had no choice. Kidnapping's a federal rap.* He gave an anxious look toward the luminescence as if fearing what lay in store for him.

"The Dark Guardian," Gavenia murmured. *It said it ruled*

him. Why did it have that kind of power? She looked around. It was noticeably missing. What did that mean?

Not all of us are the good guys. Now you've learned that firsthand, haven't you? a smug voice observed.

Gavenia whipped around. "Bart?"

Reginald appeared in the far end of the pit, distastefully wending its way through the wreckage, his suit impeccable despite the destruction around him.

He delivered a disdainful look. *Well, you've gotten yourself in a peck of trouble, haven't you? I do wonder what Quickens saw in you.*

"Are you here to help?"

No, I'm here to gloat.

"Then go away," Gavenia said.

They've given you a second chance, he said, gesturing upward.

"Meaning?"

Accept me as your Guardian and I'll get you out of here.

It sounded like a Faustian bargain to her.

"No deal."

True to form. He chuckled, adjusted a lapel, and then vanished with an annoying pop.

"You're not getting it," she shouted, glaring toward the dark sky above her. "It's Bart or nobody!" There was no response.

Gavenia returned her attention to the new soul, trying to recall where they'd been before the interruption.

"What about Janet?" she asked. "Is she okay?"

Probably dead. It'll look like an OD.

She thought for a moment and then jumped up again. Crunching her way warily across the uneven debris, she knelt next to Taylor's body. The soul surged toward her instantly, as if guarding the remains.

What are you doing?

"Did you carry a cell phone?"

Yes.

"Cool." Taylor's face was mottled, his limbs stiffening. She swallowed to keep from being violently ill and searched around the dead man's waist.

He took it.

"Who?" she asked.

No answer. Sickened by the smell of the corpse, Gavenia retreated. "You know the way. It's your choice what you do next," she said, pointing toward the light again. The ghost made no move. "So be it. I've done my Shepherd thing."

Picking up a stout piece of wood, she cleared a wide circle around the concrete island. Ignoring the soul, she inscribed a circle, calling the quarters while invoking divine protection. Once the circle was complete, she raised her hands into the darkness above her and called down the power of the God and Goddess.

"Watch over me, protect me. Send me help." She rethought in light of Reginald's visit and added, "Mortal help."

She eased herself down to the damp concrete and huddled tight into a ball to conserve heat.

Taylor hadn't moved from his body, his head bowed.

I didn't think he'd do it.

"I can't help you if you don't tell me the guy's name," she said.

The response was muffled sobs. Gavenia closed her eyes and willed herself to sleep. When morning came, she'd have a better notion of what her odds were. If Taylor was still present, she'd try again to cross him over. If not, he could spend eternity in the rat pit just as long as she wasn't there with him.

* * *

It was nearing dawn when Station Nine's crew returned from their call, and O'Fallon hadn't been very gracious about the wait. He'd paced outside the car while Adam napped.

Once the firefighters had stashed their equipment, he went in search of the person in charge. True to Adam's prediction, it was a she, and a lieutenant to boot. O'Fallon posed the problem: he needed to find a particular building, possibly a warehouse that had burned in the last year or so. Fortunately, Lieutenant Bradley didn't seem inclined to ask any embarrassing questions, especially after Adam displayed his badge.

She spread a map on the kitchen table while a couple firefighters watched from the sidelines. Adam took notes as the lieutenant indicated locations. As she talked, O'Fallon knew none of the buildings had the right vibe. Maybe he was way off. . . .

He drifted away from the conversation, pulled toward a memorial wall that honored Station Nine's fallen heroes. One man's photo pulled him closer.

Firefighter Timothy Anderson

"Excuse me," he said, cutting across the conversation at the table. "Where was this fire?"

The firefighters traded looks. Lieutenant Bradley traced down the map and tapped on a location.

"Here. Old produce warehouse. Top three floors collapsed into the basement. Three of our guys were trapped. We got all out of them out alive . . . but Anderson." The loss echoed in the room.

O'Fallon gazed back to the photo and gave a nod of respect. "Rest in peace," he murmured. "You had more guts than I'll ever have."

"Turned out to be arson," one of the firefighters said in a taut voice. "They haven't caught the SOB yet. I hope the hell they do."

"From your lips to God's ears," Adam said as nods made the rounds.

"This one feels right," O'Fallon said.

Lieutenant Bradley raised an eyebrow. "You planning on going there?"

He nodded.

"Then watch yourself. The structure is very unstable."

O'Fallon acknowledged the warning and was headed for the door even as Adam thanked the lieutenant. His mind was already on the hunt.

"Stay alive a bit longer, Gavenia," he said as he cleared the firehouse door. "I'll find you, I promise."

* * *

The sky lightened above as they stood outside the charred warehouse. Dawn would be here in a few minutes. O'Fallon knew this was the place. He tried to steel himself against the worst, but his heart couldn't handle that. He could still hear her soft sighs as they'd made love, smell the intoxicating scent of her perfume. He wanted years to plumb the depths of those mysterious blue eyes, that intelligent mind, that sensuous body.

"You two are more than friends," Adam observed.

Once again the young cop had read him correctly.

"Yes. I thought we might have a future together."

"Then let's go bring her home," his companion said, placing a comforting hand on his shoulder.

O'Fallon's throat tightened. *Would the angels weep at Gavenia's funeral?* God, he hoped he wouldn't have to find out.

He followed Adam through the fencing and toward the building, each step thunderously loud in his ears. Adam halted, pointing. O'Fallon knelt near the wilted rose, the one he'd given his love at the shelter. She'd kept it with her, even as she walked to her . . .

"She's here," he said, standing up, pushing aside the dark thought. "Do you want to call for backup?"

Adam shook his head. "Not yet. Let's make sure before we call in reinforcements. I have enough explaining to do as it is." He peered toward the interior of the building. "You armed?"

"No."

Adam blew a puff of air out through pursed lips. "Two for two," he said, and picked a path through the debris as O'Fallon trailed behind.

* * *

Gavenia woke to the soft twittering of birds in the rafters. For a moment she thought she was in her bedroom at Aunt Lucy's estate, the birds serenading her awake. She rolled onto her back and groaned. Reality swiftly returned as every inch of her body dutifully filed its protest, in triplicate.

As she dismissed the magic circle, she allowed herself a pleased grin. Witches cast circles for a number of reasons, but using divine protection to keep rats at bay hadn't ever occurred to her before. Nevertheless, it had worked; no gnaw marks. A glance toward Taylor's body outside the circle proved that wasn't the case. She shuddered. His ghost was absent, so hopefully he'd crossed over sometime during the night.

"Time to get the hell out of here," she said.

Now that there was a modicum of daylight, she examined her surroundings. To her right was a debris channel, a narrow tunnel that led out of the pit. Gavenia crept to it and lowered herself in front of the hole. She swore she felt a cool breeze brush against her face.

"Promising," she said, chalking that up as an option if all else failed. The rest of the pit wasn't as promising, its treacherous sides too sheer to climb and interlaced with twisted beams and broken panes of glass.

Gavenia froze at the sound of footsteps above her. What if Taylor's killer had come back? She was too far away from her original position to return to it and play dead.

A faint voice. She listened intently, trying to sort through the words over the sound of the birds. More conversation. A relieved sigh escaped her. It was the Irish guy. He'd found her.

"Why am I surprised," she said, struggling to keep the tears inside. O'Fallon could find anyone if given enough time.

"Yo, baby!" she hollered, startling the birds which took flight in a rush of wings.

There was a pause and then hurried steps above her.

"Gavenia?"

"In the flesh," she called back, taking a few steps into the open. She looked down at her clothes and rolled her eyes. Definite *wrath of the Goddess* material. If O'Fallon could handle her like this, he was a keeper.

"Gavenia?" he called again.

"Down here. Tell me you brought a bag of cinnamon rolls," she said. Out of the corner of her eye she saw Taylor's ghost rise from the rubble. He stared upward, frowning.

O'Fallon's face appeared at the edge of the pit.

"Oh God," he said. "It's her!" he shouted to someone behind him. "We found her!" He turned back and blew her a kiss. The smile on his face seemed brighter than the dawn. A young man appeared and gave a satisfied smile. He looked vaguely familiar.

"Hi," he said, "I'm Adam," and waved the hand that wasn't in a cast.

"Good morning. Welcome to my humble . . . pit," she ad-libbed while executing a sweeping gesture to encompass the mess.

"Very nice. I love what you've done with the decorating," Adam said, grinning in O'Fallon's direction. "The rats are a very . . . interesting touch."

O'Fallon chortled as if it was an inside joke. Gavenia didn't get it.

"Well, the dead body is a bummer," she said, pointing toward Taylor's remains.

The humor up top withered.

"Oh, great, another one," Adam grumbled. "Two in a night. This will really piss off the crime-scene techs."

"Is it Taylor?" O'Fallon asked, squinting in the dim light.

"Yup. How'd you know his name?"

He ignored the question. "You kill him?"

That earned the Irish guy a stadiumful of brownie points. "No. Someone else."

"Well, don't go anywhere," O'Fallon said, winking. "We'll get some help to get you out."

"How'd you find me?"

"I used my God-given talents."

She nodded approvingly. "About time."

Taylor's ghost surged upward, his kinetic energy rising.

"What's wrong?" she asked.

It's him! he shouted.

"Who?"

The cop who killed me.

She flipped her gaze upward to find that only her lover remained in sight. Could she have been wrong about O'Fallon? Had he played her like Winston had?

Maybe Taylor meant the one named Adam.

Which cop? she demanded.

Taylor halted and a grim smile formed on his face. He pointed. *That one.*

A man stared down at her from the rim of the pit, his eyes widening in surprise. Like Taylor's, his aura was muddy gray, and Gavenia couldn't see his Guardian.

I told him you were dead, Taylor said. *Now what's he going to do?*

Who is he?

The ghost moved upward, hissing a name in anger. *Glass.*

Chapter Thirty-Five

O'Fallon gave Adam a warning glance, then addressed the other cop. "Your timing is good. We need to get the lady out of there."

Harve Glass kept staring into the pit, fixated on the witch. O'Fallon's hackles rose. *Why is he here?*

Gavenia she stood on a mound of concrete, frowning in concentration. He knew that look; a ghost was talking to her. His eyes moved to the body. *Taylor.* What did Glass and the dead dealer have in common?

"How'd you find us?" Adam asked, keeping his attention on O'Fallon while he asked the question.

"Heard you were at that OD scene. Wanted to know why," Glass murmured. "I saw the PI's car outside so I thought I'd find out what you two were up to."

How do you know what my car looks like?

Adam opened his mouth to ask a follow-up question but halted when O'Fallon shook his head.

"Did you call it in?" Glass asked, his tone clipped, his attention still in the pit.

"No, we just got here," Adam replied, shifting uneasily.

"Hello! Thanks for finding me," Gavenia said, her voice tighter than normal. "I'd really like to get out of here."

"What happened to him?" Glass asked, pointing toward Taylor's body.

A telling hesitation, and then she shrugged. "No idea. He just came with the place."

O'Fallon clenched his jaw. He heard the lie and he wondered if Glass did, too. The detective turned his back on the pit as if no longer concerned with the occupant.

"I'll call it in," Glass said. He reached for his cell phone, punched in some numbers, and reported the situation.

Adam remained near the hole. He knelt and then gave a nod as if some message had passed between Gavenia and himself. As he rose, Glass hung up the phone and clipped it onto his belt.

"They're coming. Now why don't you tell me exactly why you're here."

Adam took the lead. "O'Fallon's been investigating a hit-and-run in Bel Air. The guy in the pit is LaRue Taylor, and West Hollywood is looking for him on kidnapping charges."

"So you found him. How convenient. What about the woman?"

Adam glanced downward. "Taylor carjacked her last night. We've been trying to find her."

"And you just knew she'd be here?"

O'Fallon jumped in. "Just call me psychic," he said in a joking tone, and spread his hands. *Come on, come, let's take it outside.*

Glass frowned and then gave a quick look into the pit as if something had just occurred to him.

"You're the psychic that's been in the papers, aren't you?"

"Yes? You want your fortune told?" was the swift reply.

"Can you really talk to the dead?"

O'Fallon's gut lurched. *Oh Jesus, he made the connection.*

"Not on your life," Gavenia shot back. "But I make a good living off those who think I can."

The lie was better, but would it convince Glass?

The detective sighed and shook his head. "Just my fuckin' luck."

He reached under his jacket, pulled a gun from the small of his back, and pointed it into the pit.

"What are you doing?" Adam demanded, taking a few step closer.

"Got a rat problem," was the curt answer. "I'll take care of it," Glass added.

Instinct took over and O'Fallon charged across the debris with a bellow. At the sound of his charge, Glass turned and fired, the first shot catching Adam in the shoulder, hurtling him backward. Glass was out of position when O'Fallon tackled him. They wrestled for the gun, rolling across the brick-strewn floor. O'Fallon's injured ribs caught a solid blow, allowing Glass time to regain his feet, the gun in his possession.

"Wonder how the papers will spin this one," he said, pointing the gun directly at O'Fallon.

"No! Stop him!" Gavenia commanded. Another shot. The air filled with soot as the pit birthed a windstorm and she staggered backward, covering her eyes from the onslaught.

Pummeled from all directions by bits of wood and brick, O'Fallon fought his way to Avery's son. A piece of timber sailed toward him and he ducked at the last moment and it impacted behind him with a jarring crash. Adam lay on his side, blood seeping down his arm and around his fingers as he clutched at the wound.

"Glass," he said.

O'Fallon sought their enemy. He hung in midair in the maelstrom, flailing at an unseen opponent. Could it be Taylor's ghost?

In the pit below, debris seethed as if alive. O'Fallon couldn't see Gavenia and he forced down a cry of despair. He gave a tug and pulled Adam to his feet. "Come on!" he shouted, and dragged the injured man toward the entrance in staggering steps. Behind him, he heard Glass shriek like a tormented soul.

Adam collapsed near a concrete barrier just outside the fencing. O'Fallon helped him sit upright and pressed a handkerchief against the shoulder wound. The blood soaked through, anointing the cast.

Adam's face paled. "Glass . . . killed . . . Taylor," he said in hoarse gusts.

"Gavenia told you?"

The detective nodded.

O'Fallon looked back toward the building. Brick dust billowed out the entrance in torrents. Before he could thread his way through the fencing, the east wall leaned inward and, with a dull roar, collapsed in a hailstorm of broken bricks and snapping timbers.

"Sweet Mother of God." He shoved through the fencing; it tore at him, ripping his pants near the right knee.

As he reached the entrance, a figure appeared in front him, forcing him to halt.

Don't go in there, Benjamin Callendar warned.

"Get out of my way!" O'Fallon shouted as he tried to push past the ghost.

You must trust me, Benjamin said. *Don't go in there; not yet!*

O'Fallon jammed his eyes shut and clenched his teeth. Inside the building he heard a woman's scream. He shoved past the ghost in blind fear.

Chapter Thirty-Six

Kinetic energy ran rampant inside the pit, like a demented toddler. Taylor's anger powered a hellish dance of bricks and timber shards. His laughter rose above the ambient noise as he swirled in the center of the chaos above the pit, Glass entombed in his arms. Gavenia tried to shelter her eyes, her hair swirling around her, electrified.

Run for it! a voice urged.

"Bart?" she called. A low growl ensued from the remaining walls as the ground around her trembled.

"Oh, Goddess." She scrambled for the debris channel, crawling on all fours as the ground heaved beneath her as if made of molten lava. Masonry flooded downward, tumbling and bouncing like a child's blocks.

As she reached the channel, she gave one last upward glance and gasped in horror as the remaining three walls arched downward, bending like the petals of a dying flower. A massive roof timber hurtled toward her and she screamed as she dove into the tunnel, kicking her way inside like a squirrel fleeing an owl's talons. Dust flooded the cavern after a jolting impact. She crept forward, hand over hand. Something landed across her knees, pinning her, and she fought herself free. Elbowing her way down the narrow passage, she choked on the fetid stench of scorched wiring and rotten produce. A rat clawed its way over her shoulders and ran ahead, fleeing the symphony of destruction.

* * *

As the building collapsed, O'Fallon retreated to the street, near his injured companion. Tears flowed down his face, leaving thick tracks in the crimson brick dust. He crossed himself and murmured a prayer for his lover. When he'd finished, Benjamin's ghost appeared next to him, his powder-blue eyes calm and reassuring.

Have faith, he whispered. *It's a day for miracles.*

A racking cough pulled O'Fallon back to the present. Adam was leaning over, spitting up dust, his face contorted in pain. There was nothing O'Fallon could do for Gavenia, but he could help Avery's son. His police training kicked in. Dial 911. "Explain the nature of the emergency," the voice said.

"Officers down; repeat, two officers down." He gave the address and his name and then explained the situation. Then he flipped the phone closed. All business, no emotion, no sense of loss. Not yet. Later the loss would strike like a sledgehammer blow.

As he dug in the car trunk for a blanket, his voice recorder fell out of his pocket and landed with a thud. He picked it up to find it was recording.

"Dammit." O'Fallon started to turn it off and then hesitated. He rewound it and held the device to his ear and he heard his own voice, followed by Glass, then the sound of gunfire. O'Fallon clicked off the recorder, fiddling with the settings until the LCD display asked him if he wanted to password-lock the file.

"Yes," he said, tapping in a numeric code, the same one that unlocked Seamus's cage. For half a second he thought he'd done it wrong, then the screen blinked FILE LOCKED. He let out a whoosh of pent-up air and dropped the recorder into his coat pocket.

"Insurance, for when the shit hits the fan," he muttered. His gut told him it was going to be a virtual monsoon.

After he'd nestled the blanket around the shivering young cop, he dialed Avery. The man deserved to hear about his son from someone he knew.

"It's . . . Easter," Adam said as the phone rang. "He'll be . . . at mass."

O'Fallon looked up at the sunrise in wonder. *That's what Benjamin meant—a day for miracles.*

To his surprise, Avery answered, and O'Fallon delivered the news. The line went dead immediately. After seeing to the wounded man, he removed his rosary from his pants pocket.

"I'll have faith you'll do the right thing," he said, kissing the crucifix and then crossing himself. God had wrought a miracle for his Son; perhaps he'd do the same for the woman O'Fallon loved.

It quickly became a sea of uniforms, and O'Fallon did his best to stay out of the way as paramedics swarmed all over Adam. Soon the young cop had oxygen flowing and an IV in place. The care did wonders; his color improved and he even managed a smile when one of the paramedics joked about his broken arm.

Guided by a firefighter, O'Fallon cautiously made his way into the remnants of the building, edging up near the pit. Taylor's body was gone, buried under the rubble. O'Fallon's eyes picked across the landscape, but he saw no sign of his lover. He suppressed a shiver and took his place next to Lieutenant Bradley.

"I know, you warned me," he said.

She gave a quick nod, but didn't chastise him. "We were told there are three victims. Is that right?" she asked.

"Yes. One was dead before the collapse. The other two—"

A firefighter called out and pointed. In the midst of the debris an arm moved feebly. O'Fallon leaned forward expectantly, then swore under his breath.

"Glass. The bastard's alive."

"Where do you think the third might be?" the lieutenant asked, remaining all business.

That was the problem: O'Fallon hadn't seen Gavenia since the first shot was fired. He closed his eyes and let the impressions flood him, moving his arm as if guided by another source. "I think she's somewhere over there," he said, pointing opposite where Glass's body lay.

"Thanks. Leave it to us. We'll find her," the lieutenant said. He took the hint and departed the building before she ordered him out.

The moment he was back in the sunshine, O'Fallon leaned against one of the concrete barriers, feeling exhausted and useless. A comforting hand touched his shoulder, and he looked up into the anxious eyes of his best friend; Avery had beaten the homicide detectives to the scene. O'Fallon wondered how many stoplights he'd ignored.

"How you doing?" Avery asked.

"I don't know yet. How's Adam?" O'Fallon asked.

"The bullet didn't hit an artery, so he should be all right. He said you pulled him out of there. I owe you."

Their eyes met. "No, you don't. You saved my ass enough times." A firefighter trudged by toting a power unit. Behind him, another carried a cutter. The rescue was moving into high gear.

Avery leaned closer. "Adam said Gavenia's in there."

For a moment, the world seemed to shift under O'Fallon's feet. His friend grabbed his arm to stabilize him.

"Maybe you should sit down," Avery suggested.

"No, I'm okay."

"The hell you are," the priest said in a lowered voice meant only for his ears.

O'Fallon clamped his jaw tight to fight the raging despair, the growing awareness of loss. *One night.* That's all they'd had.

"What in the hell is goin' on here?" a voice demanded. They turned in tandem. It was a plainclothes detective. O'Fallon caught the look of warning in Avery's eyes.

"I'm . . ." He hesitated. He'd almost said *detective* out of habit. "I'm Doug O'Fallon." He paused and then asked, "And you are?"

"Detective Carstairs." The guy angled his head toward a tall black man. "My partner, Detective Price."

Avery moved forward, offering his hand. "I'm Father Elliot."

A frown. "Some relation to that Elliot?" Carstairs said, pointing toward the injured cop.

"I'm his dad," Avery replied, shaking each cop's hand in turn. That earned him a puzzled stare. "I wasn't always a priest."

"What's this about Glass being in there?" Carstairs asked.

O'Fallon gave them the *Reader's Digest* version, minus the

information about the recording and the fact that Glass had killed Taylor.

"This Kingsgrave woman still in there?" Carstairs asked.

"Yes."

"Alive?"

"God, I hope so."

Carstairs frowned. "Why does that name sound familiar?"

"She's the psychic that's been in the paper the last couple of days. Remember, that old murder case?" Price offered.

"Oh, yeah, that one. What the hell is she doing here?"

O'Fallon took them farther down the road as he described the botched kidnapping attempt and Gavenia's encounter with Taylor.

Carstairs and Price exchanged looks and then huddled a short distance away to discuss the situation.

"Now it begins," O'Fallon murmured. He tapped his jacket pocket to ensure the voice recorder was still in place. He hoped their "Get Out of Jail Free" card would do the trick.

Chapter Thirty-Seven

As Gavenia's ears stopped roaring, terror rose in her chest. The air seemed solid and the dust caked in her nose and mouth, while the debris around her shifted like a ravenous python, eager to envelop its prey.

Shivering with fright, she huddled in the fetal position on a hard surface. Tears muddied her face, running into her mouth and leaving a salty, gritty taste. Her legs cramped as the shivering intensified. She cried out, but no one came. This time Llewellyn wouldn't save her.

She sensed the chill presence and knew it to be Taylor's Dark Guardian.

Agree to serve me and you'll live.

"Go away!"

Why should I?

"Why did you let Taylor die?"

It was time to move on.

The blazing eyes filled her mind. Cold enshrouded her, tucking her into its hellish embrace. She fumbled for the rose petals, clawing them out of her pocket to hold them close. Little scent was left, and it was no match for the stench of the sooty tomb around her, but she rubbed the petals against her lips and kissed them, envisioning O'Fallon's handsome face, his bright brown eyes, his tender kisses as he'd moved within her. She felt his powerful love. A blossom of white light bloomed around her, and chill abruptly ceased.

Tucking the rose petals into her bra, she blinked open her eyes. The hollow was completely dark.

Indistinct voices played on the edge of her hearing. These

weren't in her mind, but sounded like someone calling to her. She shouted, but there was no response.

Save your strength. They can't hear you, a voice said softly. She found herself staring at a firefighter. He'd materialized a few feet away from her, leaning against some of the debris, clad in full gear. He was about thirty, African American, with sad eyes.

I saw your light, he said, pointing at the glow surrounding her. *It's been so dark and I didn't know which way to go.*

"How did you die?" she asked, moving so that she could see him fully. Behind her another timber sagged inward and then collapsed.

The firefighter pointed upward. *I was trapped when the upper floors collapsed. My buddies came for me—they never leave anyone behind—but it was too late.*

Gavenia searched around her while trying to blink more of the grit out of her eyes. Other than the glow enveloping her, there was no other light, no way to guide the soul to where he needed to go.

"What's holding you here?"

I didn't get to say good-bye to my wife and little daughter. I missed her second birthday party.

Oh, Goddess. "You need to go across. You'll be at peace there."

He shook his head. *I can't. Not yet.*

A deep shiver overtook Gavenia and she bent over to try to mitigate the whirlpool of nausea in her stomach.

I'll help you get out, the firefighter offered.

"What?" she asked, looking up, not sure if she'd heard clearly.

I'll help you get out. I won't leave you behind, he said.

She didn't move, her lungs on fire and her head pounding. It would be so easy to just let go.

Come on, crawl forward a little ways.

The voice sounded so calm, so in charge. She wiggled onto her knees and cried out when a piece of metal cut into one leg.

Follow me, he said, crawling ahead of her. She followed, each movement pulling on her dwindling energy reserve.

Watch this beam, it's unstable. Stay to the right of it, he cautioned. She did as ordered, feeling the beam shift. She held her breath and the board halted.

Keep moving; that's it. You're getting there.

She halted after what seemed an eternity. The cold was taking its toll.

No, you can't stop. You won't make it if you stop. Keep going.

"I'm too tired," she whispered. "Too tired."

It's the lack of fresh air. Keep going. You're almost there.

She curled up again, just wanting to shut her eyes and let it be over. Death wasn't so bad; she'd seen what it was like.

If you die, you'll never know if he loves you.

She blinked her eyes open. That had sounded like Bart, but she couldn't see him, only the firefighter a few feet ahead, still gesturing her forward.

"Bart?" she called.

Move it, Gavenia. Time's a-wasting. You're stronger than this. By now your sister would have dug herself out and discovered a lost civilization in the process.

It was Bart. She couldn't see him, but it was his chiding.

"She's a damned mole. I'm a witch," she groused.

Excuses, excuses. Now follow the nice firefighter and stop complaining.

His voice gave her hope. She rose to her knees and pulled herself through the tunnel, concentrating on one inch at a time.

* * *

Avery played peacemaker between O'Fallon and the detectives, but once he left to follow the ambulance to the hospital, the situation rapidly deteriorated.

"Not happening," O'Fallon said firmly, shaking his head at Carstairs's request that they go to the precinct so he could answer some questions.

"They'll let you know when they find her," Carstairs said. He angled his eyes toward the mangled building. Word was that they'd dug out Glass and were winching him from the pit at that very moment.

"I'm staying," O'Fallon said, "until they pull Gavenia out."

"Hell, that could be days."

O'Fallon glared at the man and shook his head brusquely.

"We can cuff you and haul you downtown," Carstairs warned.

"I'll do whatever you want once she's out of there. But until then, I'm staying here. You got that?"

The blow behind his knee caught him off guard and he pitched forward. Shouting his indignation, O'Fallon felt his hands pulled roughly behind his back and the cold sting of handcuffs encircle his wrists. When he struggled, he was slammed to the ground, the side of his face kissing the gravel. A heavy foot planted itself in the middle of his back.

Carstairs said, "Now you see, we could have done this nice—"

"Is there some reason you have your foot on my client's back, Detective?" a sharp voice demanded.

O'Fallon smirked, though the gravel made it difficult. The voice belonged to a very pissed Llewellyn.

"He wasn't cooperating," Carstairs replied.

"Is he under arrest?" was the quick retort.

"We asked him to come to the station. He refused. I was expediting the matter."

"So he's not under arrest?" Llewellyn pushed.

"No. Not yet."

"Then get those damned cuffs off him."

Carstairs swore under his breath and pulled O'Fallon up by the handcuffs, wrenching the sore ribs in the process. Llewellyn stepped between the men, no doubt sensing how close O'Fallon was to assaulting a cop.

"Easy," he said. "This bullshit is going to cease now that I'm here."

O'Fallon gave a short grunt. He gestured toward the building with his head. "I don't want to leave until she's out."

"I know," Llewellyn said. "But we might not have a choice."

O'Fallon felt a rough hand unlock the cuffs. He rubbed his wrists, brushed off his coat, and verified that the recorder still sat in his pocket.

"She's alive," he said, eyeing Llewellyn. "I feel it."

The lawyer put a hand on O'Fallon's shoulder and nodded. "So do I." He turned toward Carstairs. "Give us a little while longer. If they haven't pulled her out in a half hour or so, we'll go with you."

The two detectives exchanged looks. "Works for us," Carstairs said, scowling at O'Fallon.

"Come on," Llewellyn said, guiding him away from the scene and the temptation to kick Carstairs in the ass. "I've got some coffee in the car. While you drink it, you can tell me what the hell happened."

Chapter Thirty-Eight

Gavenia swore she could smell fresh air. It had to be a hallucination. Another draft, and she sucked it in with big gulps. She arched forward like a dog hanging its head out a car window. Another deep breath. A coughing fit ensued.

"Maybe not," she muttered. Her tongue tasted like cement; her eyes burned. Even if she did get out of here, O'Fallon would probably disown her. It'd be easier to find a new girlfriend than clean her up.

You're just about there, the firefighter reported, and gave her cheery smile.

"I better be. I don't have much more—"

She heard voices, real ones.

"Hey!"

There was a pause, and a shout returned. She heard more voices and the grating sound of debris being shifted.

"We're coming!" she heard. Behind her the tunnel began to cave in, foot by foot, advancing toward her, shoving dirt and dust forward.

A sudden burst of light erupted above her, beaming down like a light from heaven.

"Oh, whoa, that hurts," she said, shielding her eyes. They teared immediately, washing out some of the grit.

"Hello?" a male voice called.

"Yo," she shouted. She immediately thought of Seamus. "Spring me!" she called. The blood on her face cracked as she grinned. She just might live long enough to feed that parrot a few more blueberries.

A pause, and then more noise. The light grew brighter, and once Gavenia's eyes adjusted, she realized she must be in some sort of coal chute. She looked around for her guide. He was behind her now.

You'll be okay. They'll help you out, he said, clearly pleased with himself.

"But what about you?"

I don't know what to do.

Gavenia thought for a moment and then motioned. "Follow me. It's my turn to rescue you."

He gave her a big grin and a thumbs-up. She matched it and waited for his living comrades to figure out how to bring her above ground.

The firefighter who helped her maneuver out of the coal chute was a hunk. Absolutely drop-dead gorgeous.

"Never fails," she muttered as she wiggled her way out onto the pavement like a beached red whale. She only met guys like that when seriously indisposed. Like the car accident in Wales. One of the rescuers had been Scottish, quite handsome, with an accent that would have melted any woman's heart and made her catapult into his bed. He'd talked to her the entire time they dismantled the car, telling her jokes, keeping her calm. She could still hear his voice as plainly as if he were standing next to her.

"Backboard!" someone called. She felt something hard slide underneath her and then she was moving away from the building at a quick pace. It didn't make much sense until the low rumble behind her.

"Get clear!" someone shouted, and there was a scramble.

When they finally set her on the ground, she looked back over her shoulder. The coal chute was buried under a mountain of broken bricks.

"Too close," she whispered, and then relaxed on the backboard. It felt oddly comfortable after her night in the pit. The fresh air delivered a high, like a toke of good pot or three strong martinis. She'd felt this before: the bliss of survival.

A paramedic knelt at her side. "Any allergies?" he asked.

"Falling buildings," she retorted. That got her a chuckle.

"Open your eyes for a second." She did as ordered and promptly got a light shone in them.

"How do they look?" she asked.

"They're a really nice shade of blue," he said. "I don't see any sign of a head injury, but they'll make sure at the hospital."

"Of course they will," she said.

He rattled off a series of questions, examining her neck, chest, arms, and down both legs.

"Nothing feels broken," she said.

"That would be amazing. But they'll make sure—"

"At the hospital," Gavenia recited. She knew that drill all too well.

An oxygen cannula wedged itself into her nose. A few deep breaths gave her even more of a high.

Her ethereal firefighter leaned over and gave her another thumbs-up. She returned it. The paramedic, not realizing it wasn't meant for him, gave her one as well. He turned his back on her, extracting tubing and a needle out of his kit.

Knowing she had only a brief moment before he returned, she pointed with a trembling hand. "You see it?" she whispered.

The firefighter's soul looked into the distance, and a calm smile spread over his face. *I do.*

Thank you for saving my life.

Tell my wife and daughter I love them.

I will. Be at peace.

He strode away into the light as Gavenia closed her eyes.

She felt the cold sting of fluid as the paramedic vainly tried to clean a place on her arm. The needle stick barely registered.

A hand touched her opposite arm, and her aunt leaned close to her.

"Good Goddess, girl, what have you been doing?" Lucy asked with a mock frown. The chiding was for Gavenia's benefit, as there were tears hatching in her eyes.

"Not much. How about you?" Gavenia said.

Lucy leaned over to hug her and then apparently thought better of it. "You okay?"

"Yeah. Not bad."

She didn't see the Irish guy. What if Glass had shot him? What if he was buried in there and she hadn't known it? "O'Fallon?" she asked, the euphoria vanishing in an instant. "Please tell me he's okay."

"He's with the cops. They took him to the precinct. They wouldn't let him stay."

She frowned at that. "But he didn't do anything."

"Don't worry; Llew's with him."

"What about. . . Adam?"

"He's at the hospital. He was shot."

"Is he going to be okay?"

"From what I hear."

"And the other bastard?" Gavenia asked coldly.

"He's in bad shape. They're not sure if he'll make it."

"He won't," Gavenia said. *Taylor will make sure of it.*

"Ari's on a plane back from Portland. The flights were grounded until an hour ago. She's in a . . . bit of a state."

Gavenia rolled her eyes. "I can only imagine."

The paramedic posed a couple more questions and, after Gavenia answered to his satisfaction, he turned his attention back to the IV.

Her aunt hit speed dial on her cell phone. "Here, tell Llew you're okay," handing the phone over to Gavenia. She fumbled until she got it near her ear.

"Gavenia?"

"In the flesh."

"How are you?"

"Filthy, cranky, and seriously in need of a sugar fix," she said. A hearty laugh echoed down the phone. She heard him repeat what she'd said to someone. That person laughed as well. It was O'Fallon.

"Hold on. Someone wants to yell at you." There was a pause, during which Llew must have handed the phone over to the Irishman.

"Gavenia? What the hell took you so long?" O'Fallon demanded.

"Sorry, I'm not a really great mole."

His voice shifted in an instant. "Are you all right?"

"I'm bruised and battered, but I'll make it."

"Anything broken?"

"Don't think so."

A long sigh came through the phone, as if he'd vented hours of tension in one breath. "Thank God."

"Are you okay?" she asked. "I heard shots and . . ."

"No, I'm fine. Just a little dusty."

Gavenia blurted out, "Come see me sometime, okay?" She winced. That sounded pathetic. Fortunately her aunt was talking to the paramedic and missed the degrading moment.

O'Fallon didn't hesitate. "You can count on it."

"I need to talk to Llew."

"Okay. I'll see you later. No more falling down rabbit holes, you hear?"

"I promise." When Llewellyn returned to the phone, she told him, "The other cop, the one named Glass . . . he killed Taylor."

"Did you witness the murder?"

"No. Taylor's spirit told me. I know it's not admissible in court. Just wanted you to know."

"Anything else?"

"Do whatever you can for O'Fallon. He's—" Now wasn't the time.

A low chuckle filled her ear, as if Llew knew exactly what she'd intended to say. "Don't worry, it'll be okay. Just work on getting well."

"I will." She handed the phone back to Lucy, who rose and walked a short distance away. Gavenia knew they were comparing notes, ensuring that she was as uninjured as she sounded.

"We're off the see the wizard," the paramedic joked as he and his companion pulled the stretcher up and clicked it into place.

"Whee! Now I know how that witch felt when they dropped the house on her." That remark earned a round of laughter.

Once they reached the ambulance, the paramedic smiled down at her. "Probably didn't get to see this morning's paper, did you?"

he asked with a grin.

"Nope. Delivery's been a bit spotty," she said. "What did I miss?"

"You've been vindicated. Seems that reporter lied. Someone sent the paper a copy of the police report. You hit it right on the nose, lady."

Gavenia's mouth dropped open. "Oh, Goddess. Mrs. Jones . . ." She felt no sense of triumph, just immense sadness.

"So you really see ghosts?" the paramedic asked.

"Yes, I do." She closed her eyes, hoping that would end the conversation. He took the hint, and after the back doors shut, the ambulance headed toward the hospital, siren piercing the morning air.

Chapter Thirty-Nine

"Nothing broken, but lots of skid marks," the young ER doc announced. He looked all of eighteen, if a day.

"Yeah, I noticed," Gavenia replied. Her aunt stood nearby, on what appeared to be her fourth cup of coffee.

"I want you to have a shower before we start bandaging some of this. If not, we'll just embed the dirt in the wounds, and life will get really bad."

"I'll endeavor to pick a cleaner place to get buried the next time," she said. A million cuts and scrapes screamed at her from almost every part of her body. Her hair was a tangled mass of rust-coated knots.

He eyed her. "Good idea. When was the last time you had a tetanus shot?"

"Six months ago." *After the last time I did something really stupid.*

"Good. We'll give you another one anyway."

Gavenia groaned. *Then why ask?*

The doctor flung orders at the nearest nurse. She looked to be three times his age, and that fact earned her Gavenia's immense gratitude.

Once Dr. Dude was gone, the nurse told her what to expect.

"Do you want the pain pills before or after the shower?"

"After."

The nurse's eyebrow marched upward as if questioning Gavenia's sanity.

The shower was hellish. Gavenia bit her lip as long as she could and then wept openly from the pain. All the wounds burned in throbbing waves. Her mind tried to process each individual ache.

The result was overload. Shivering, she sat in a shower chair, a nurse's aide at her side. Though the girl was as tender as she could be, it felt like being flayed alive.

To mark her progress, Gavenia watched the water swirl around her toes as it spiraled down the drain. It started blood red, full of brick dust, then gradually faded to a light rose. Finally it ran clear.

Hell was followed by heaven: fresh bandages and ointment, a clean bed, two pain pills, and the supreme satisfaction of knowing the worst was over. As she sank down into the narcotic haze, her mind kept nagging her about the Irishman. Would he be okay? Surely they couldn't charge him with anything.

"Watch over him, Brigit," she murmured, and fell into a deep slumber.

* * *

How long Gavenia slept, she wasn't sure. She remembered the occasional flutter of activity around her bed: the checking of blood pressure, shining of lights into her pupils, and asking of inane questions to ensure her brain wasn't doing bad things. But for the most part they'd left her alone, as if the entombment and the shower were penance enough.

Soft sobs pulled her from her sleep. Gavenia managed to open her eyes and found her sister at the end of the bed, tears rolling down her cheeks. The moment Ari knew she was awake, she shook the bed in a furious gesture. The movement made Gavenia's head spin.

"Are you crazy?" Ari demanded.

She rolled her head over and checked to see if her roommate was present. Out for a stroll. *Good timing.*

She rolled her head back and ignored the sensation of light-headedness. "Didn't do anything," she replied, trying to string words together despite the fact she felt like a hot-air balloon cruising high on the jet stream.

"What the hell were you thinking?" her sister demanded again.

"Trying not to . . . wimp out," Gavenia said, and screwed a

crooked smile onto her face. She slowly inched a hand out from under the covers and scratched the end of her nose. It appeared to be the only part of her that wasn't sore.

"You could have died," Ari sobbed.

"Really?" Gavenia said, and then gave another lopsided smile. The pain pills were fabulous. Nothing bothered her, not even her sister's wildly careening emotions.

Ari glared at her, shaking the bed again with a furious rattle, as if it would knock some sense into Gavenia.

"Come here, Pooh," Gavenia said, waving a hand with broad swipes. "I don't need a lecture. I need a hug."

Ari hesitated at the side of the bed. "I'd hug you, but I don't know where. You're all chewed up."

"Comes from playing tag with bricks." Gavenia thought and then pointed to her nose, missing it twice before she managed to touch it with her finger. Yup, she was legally over the limit. She giggled. "No driving for me." Ari bent over and tweaked her nose and then smoothed back her hair. Tears dropped onto Gavenia's face.

"Don't do that. Makes the ouchies burn."

"Sorry. Tinker . . . I . . ."

Gavenia reached up to pinch her sister's cheek like she used to when they were kids. "I'm fine. Come back tomorrow. Go get some sleep. You look like hell."

"I feel like hell."

"You can take me home in the morning."

Her sister acquiesced. "You got it." She took something from her purse and clipped it to Gavenia's braid just about shoulder level.

Her eyes just wouldn't focus that close. "What is it?"

"A Pooh Bear. I bought it at the airport so you'd know I was thinking of you."

Gavenia stuck out her tongue, and Ari returned the gesture.

"Go home and make peace with Bastet."

Another kiss on the nose, and Ari was out the door. Paul Hansford's ghost lingered at the end of the bed.

"Hey, guy. Thanks for watching over my sis," Gavenia said.

Paul's spirit blinked in surprise, and then a hesitant grin came to his face.

Glad to see you made it. He swirled out the door in search of his wife.

Gavenia beamed. "He talked to me. Cool."

What is this fascination you have with hospitals?

. She hunted around and found Bart standing on the other side of the bed, dressed in scrubs, complete with beeper and stethoscope. He looked more like a real doctor than the kid in the ER.

"I just like being babied." Dare she hope? She awkwardly crossed the fingers on one hand, despite the discomfort. "Are you just on rounds or are you back for good?"

I'm back.

She sighed in relief. "I could have used you in the ER to hold my hand."

I was there. You just didn't see me.

"I really missed you," she said.

His expression changed instantly, and he looked down as if embarrassed.

"No, I really did. I'm sorry I've been such a pain in the ass."

I've missed you, too.

"So where have you been?" she asked. "First you disappear, then Reginald appears, and then Reginald goes. For a while there it was Wheel of Guardians."

I was working.

"With who?"

A batty old widow with too damned many cats.

She gave him a puzzled look. She'd never heard him swear.

He continued, *Twenty-seven at last count. Of course, given the number of them that were pregnant, it might be in the low two hundreds now.*

"But you like Bastet," she protested. At least she thought he did.

He nodded. *Bastet, I like. Dozens of them . . .* He shuddered. *Some of them ignored me, others hissed and spit at me. Constantly. It was like having dozens of furry hand grenades going off all the time.*

"Poor Bart," she chided. "They're going to let you stay, aren't they?"

I hope so. You raised a heck of a stink on my behalf. No other Shepherd's ever done that.

"I'll do it again," she said, glaring upward at the tile ceiling. "You hear me?"

Oh, they heard you all right. Then there was that encounter with Taylor's earthbound. That made them take notice. You stopped that thing cold.

"You mean the Dark Guardian?"

He nodded.

"He said he ruled Taylor. Is that possible?"

Another nod.

"Why the hell did they do that to me? I can't be a Shepherd if I'm dead."

A half shrug. *Not everything they do makes sense.* He sighed. *As below, so above.*

Gavenia frowned. He'd gotten that wrong. It was the other way around.

Their eyes connected. His face had that expression he used when he wanted to tell her something without actually speaking the words.

"As below . . . so above," she repeated. The truth bulldozed its way through the narcotic mist. The temporal plane was a chaotic mess. If the ethereal plane mirrored it . . .

Now do you understand? he asked.

"Goddess, we're screwed," she said.

He gave a quick nod. Before she could follow up, he announced, *Incoming!* and turned toward the door.

A knock, and the door swung open. She could tell they were cops by their suits. Apparently they all shopped at the same store

"Ms. Kingsgrave?" the taller one asked.

"What's left of me," she said.

"I'm Detective Carstairs, and this is Detective Price. We have a couple of questions."

"Oh, I just bet you do." As they took their places on either side of the bed, she could hear Llewellyn's voice cautioning her. "Just so you know, I've had some pain pills. I want that noted."

Carstairs shot a look over at his partner. "Are you a lawyer?"

"Nope, but I used to work for one."

"Which one?"

"David Llewellyn."

"Oh, lord," Carstairs muttered.

Go get 'em, girl, Bart observed as he sat on the window ledge. *Wait until I tell them who killed Taylor.*

Chapter Forty

O'Fallon leaned back in the chair trying to ease the cramp in his neck. If not for Llewellyn, he'd be in worse shape. All the usual cop tactics—a full bladder and no food—were nonissues. A member of Llewellyn's staff had delivered subs and sodas, and regular trips to the restroom were demanded and received. Updates flowed from the hospital: Adam Elliot's shoulder wound wasn't life threatening, and Gavenia was sleeping tight, with no major injuries to her credit other than a minor concussion. Benjamin was right—all he needed to do was trust in a miracle.

O'Fallon studied his hands. They were rock solid, the nails stained crimson from the brick dust. As he saw it, he had one big problem: no way to tie Glass to Taylor's death. Unless Forensics was able to connect the dots, Glass would walk.

Llewellyn stretched and rolled up his shirtsleeves. He had a page full of notes on a legal pad on the table in front of him. When O'Fallon had asked how much he charged an hour, he'd been curtly informed this was on the house.

Another miracle.

"So where are we on this, guys?" Llewellyn asked. "You've talked to Ms. Kingsgrave and Detective Elliot. My client has told you what he knows. Unless you intend to press charges, I think it's time we wrapped this up."

"We have a couple more questions."

"Such as?" O'Fallon asked.

"Why are you and Elliot suddenly so chummy? You two . . . ah . . . buddies?" Carstairs asked.

"IAD has its sights on Glass," O'Fallon replied. "Since Adam's clean, we've been trying to figure out the best way to keep him from getting sucked down the drain when they pull the plug on his Glass."

Carstairs blinked a couple of times. A look toward Price and then back again. They hadn't known about IAD.

"Why do you give a damn about Elliot?" Price asked.

"Because his dad gave a damn about me when I was coming up. I owe him."

"What is IAD looking for?" Carstairs asked.

"You'll have to ask them. Or better yet, ask Glass." There was silence, and O'Fallon read it clearly. "Is that bastard still with us?"

A quick shake of the head. "He didn't make it out of the ER."

"Pity." O'Fallon had purposely held off playing the recording as it was his coup de grâce. Now it didn't matter since Glass was pleading his case to a higher authority. O'Fallon looked over at his lawyer. "Time to put this to bed."

The voice recorder appeared out of Llewellyn's pocket, where'd they'd stashed it for safekeeping. He handed it to O'Fallon, who tapped in the security code. "This thing has a habit of turning itself on. This morning it recorded the events at the warehouse, so get your popcorn, gentlemen, and listen up."

He let the recording run as it retold the tale from the moment he and Adam arrived at the warehouse. As it played, he leaned back and closed his eyes, visualizing the scene. Listening to it proved as hard as living it.

When the recording ended, he clicked it off.

"Does it match the other witness accounts?" Llewellyn asked.

A grudging nod.

"Then my client is free to go?"

Price threw his pen on the table and gave a deep sigh.

"We have no more questions," Carstairs growled.

O'Fallon rose and took his jacket off the chair. A large footprint resided on the back. He eyed Carstairs. "Next time, a little more respect, okay?" he said, pointing.

"Go away, O'Fallon. I don't want to see you anymore."

"Works for me."

* * *

In O'Fallon's opinion, the woman on the bed looked like she'd been mugged by a hiveful of enraged bees. A myriad of scrapes and red spots dotted her face and arms, and a dressing nestled on her forehead and nudged into her golden hair. The hair was surprisingly clean and fell in one long braid down the side of the bed. Someone had clipped a tiny teddy bear holding a honey pot onto the braid. It watched over her with benign eyes.

God, she looks beautiful.

He stood quietly near her bedside, not wanting to wake her, gently touching her hand on the one place that wasn't red. Those magnificent eyes slowly opened. She grasped his hand, though he knew it had to hurt.

"Hi there," he said, keeping his voice light. "Sorry I'm late."

Gavenia raised her hand, bringing his with it. "What, no cuffs?"

He played along. "You didn't tell you were into the kinky stuff."

She smirked. "Llew got you off?"

"For the time being. There'll be more questions, I'm sure."

"And the other cop?"

"Avery's son?" he asked. "He's doing okay. He's a few doors down from here."

"Oh . . . that's why he looked familiar," she murmured, and then yawned. "Sorry. They gave me more pain pills. I'm having trouble staying awake."

"Then go to sleep. I can talk to you tomorrow."

"No, no . . . I want . . . to thank . . . you."

"Thank me for what?" he asked. She smelled of antiseptic soap and ointment.

"You . . . gave me a . . . reason to live," she said as her eyes blinked at irregular intervals.

He leaned back, caught by the weight of her words. *You gave me a reason to live.* Would she have said that if she hadn't been drugged out of her mind?

"Gavenia, I . . ."

"Stay with me . . . until I go to . . . sleep," she whispered, her lashes fluttering closed, hiding those brilliant eyes.

"I will," he whispered. "Every night if you let me." Only her deep breathing came in response.

As he bent down to give her a kiss, a young man appeared in the door bearing a bouquet of flowers. After a quick glance at the name, he handed it to O'Fallon and then scurried away. O'Fallon set the flowers on the nightstand, eyeing the card.

Praying for you—Gregory, Emily, Merlin, & TJ.

Perhaps Alliford would survive his personal hell after all—he just needed a strong woman in his life.

O'Fallon moved a wisp of hair off Gavenia's battered face. After another kiss on her cheek, he left the room, silently closing the door behind him.

You gave me a reason to live.

"Just like you've done for me."

* * *

It didn't rain the day of Janet Alliford's funeral; the weather was perfect, a light breeze with vibrant sunshine. Gavenia felt overly warm in the black suit she'd borrowed from Ari, but given the bruises on her body, it was best she was covered. She shifted her weight and felt O'Fallon's arm slip around her waist in a protective gesture.

"You okay?" he whispered. He was in black as well, with a crisp white shirt and a dark-gray tie. An Irish flag pin nestled on his lapel.

"Yeah, it's just hard to stand." He removed his hand, made his way through the mourners, and collected an empty chair, toting it back to her. She sank into it wearily. Only four days had passed since she left the hospital. Maybe she was pushing it too fast.

A brilliantly hued butterfly floated through the air and landed on the handle of her cane, its wings gently fanning. That made her smile. So many things to savor. So many things she would have lost if she'd died in the midst of the rats and bricks.

She felt her lover's hand on her shoulder. His Guardian twinkled next to him. The twinkling faded away as a young man appeared, one with vivid blue eyes and brown hair.

I can see you, Gavenia said. *Why is that?*

It was time. I'm Benjamin Calendar.

Doug told me about you. Are you at peace now?

He nodded solemnly.

"Gavenia?" The butterfly flittered away at Gregory Alliford's approach

"I'm so sorry, Gregory," she said as he knelt by her. Standing nearby was Janet's sister, her eyes red and cheeks puffy, a handkerchief knotted in her fingers. Mrs. Pierce was noticeably absent. "How are you doing?"

"I am . . . okay. Em's helping," Gregory said, gazing up at the woman beside him. Emily's face softened.

Gregory sighed and returned his attention to Gavenia. "Is . . . Janet . . . ?" He stopped, apparently unsure of how to phrase the question.

"She's with Bradley. He'll watch over her."

He nodded, catching her meaning. "He was always far wiser than either of his parents."

"Thank you for the flowers. They were very beautiful."

"Thank you for everything you've done for us," he said, and then rose and offered his hand to O'Fallon. "Both of you." They shook firmly.

"I'm sorry about how this played out," O'Fallon said.

Gregory loosed a long sigh. "Same here." He put his arm around Emily's waist and guided her toward the funeral tent.

"They're falling in love," O'Fallon said quietly as he knelt next to Gavenia.

"They'll do well together."

"What about us?" he asked.

The question caught her off guard so she hedged. "What do you think?"

O'Fallon looked away for a time as if composing his thoughts. He began speaking before he turned back toward her.

"I was so afraid I'd lost you," he said in a low whisper.

She leaned forward and placed a kiss on his cheek. "I'm hard to kill, O'Fallon. Especially if I have a reason to hang around." She took his hand and caressed it. "Just promise to be honest with me. If you find this isn't working, tell me. Don't let me hang."

A solemn nod. "I've got a bad track record, and that makes me . . . skittish."

She chuckled. "My record's not much better."

His eyes moved to the top of her cane, where the butterfly had returned. "Gran says butterflies are the Wee Folk in disguise."

"Your gran's an interesting lady."

O'Fallon's face grew pensive. "I'm leaving for Ireland in a few days. Come with me."

"But what about the police investigation?"

He shook his head. "With Glass dead, the matter's settled. They found the gun he used to kill Taylor in the pit next to him. They traced Taylor's cell phone calls to Glass. He used one of the throwaway phones. Probably figured he'd ditch it and no one would be the wiser. Since IAD doesn't have anything on Adam, his transfer is moving forward. It's over."

"All the bad guys get away?" she asked. "That doesn't seem fair."

"Not really. They're dead. They won't hurt anyone else."

She wasn't so sure. What had become of Taylor's Guardian? Or Taylor for that matter?

"How about Ireland?" he pressed, unaware of her concerns.

"I'm not ready for that, but I'll visit Seamus while you're gone."

He gave a shrug as if it didn't matter, but she could tell he was disappointed. Rising to his feet, he straightened his jacket but made no comment. To distract herself from her growing guilt, she moved a finger close to the butterfly. It walked its way onto her hand, gently tickling her with its feather-light feet.

"Hello, little fairy," she whispered. "I wish I had pretty wings like yours."

* * *

O'Fallon proved as good as his word—he called the moment

he reached Ireland, though clearly exhausted. Subsequent e-mails were short and to the point: his gran was in good health; Ireland was breathtakingly beautiful; wish you were here. Five days into his visit, he closed an e-mail with a quote from a dead king.

"I would you were in my arms, or I in yours, for I think it long since I kissed you."

King Henry number eight, Bart remarked, leaning over Gavenia's shoulder as she read the message. *Lots of wives. Sorta fits, don't you think? But then, third time's the charm, as they say.*

"Go away."

Okay. Her Guardian vanished.

She looked around uneasily. "That was too easy."

An ethereal chortle. *Should I start packing for Ireland now?*

"No."

The Irish assault continued during one of her routine drive-bys to check on Seamus. The bird was in fine spirits, spoiled by the attentions of Gavenia and O'Fallon's housekeeper.

"Yo, more berries!" the parrot commanded.

"You sound just like a cop," she said, shaking her head.

After polishing off a blueberry, the bird cocked his head. "Where's da cop?" he asked.

She realized what he was asking. "Da cop is in Ireland."

"*Éirinn go brách!*" Seamus squawked.

"'Ireland forever,'" she translated. "You got it, Seamus me lad." Setting the bird on the back of the sofa, she hunted through the pictures on the wall until she found the one with O'Fallon and his grandmother. Did she dare meet the woman? What if the old lady couldn't handle a witch?

"Toil and trouble," Seamus retorted. She gave him a quizzical look. Bart stood next to him, apparently priming the parrot.

"Cute."

Give me another week and I'll have him singing "Rule, Britannia."

"Don't you dare! O'Fallon would never forgive me."

Bart turned serious. *So what are you going to do?*

"I don't know."

The phone rang twice and then rolled over to the answering

machine.

"Yo, Seamus. It's da cop and this is your daily call. How's it going, old buddy? Is Rosa spoiling the hell out of you?"

Gavenia's face split into a grin. Apparently O'Fallon called his bird once a day.

"Yo, dude!" Seamus called back. "Yo, more berries!"

On a whim, Gavenia picked up the phone.

"Hello!" she said. There was a decided pause while Seamus racketed in the background.

"Gavenia?"

"Hi there. Seamus said I should answer the phone for him. He's having trouble grasping the receiver in his talons."

Another long pause. "Really."

"Yup. You want me to put him on?"

"Ah . . . no, I can hear him well enough." Another pause. This one was longer than the others and made Gavenia wonder if she'd done the right thing. What if he was trying to avoid her?

"How's Seamus?" he asked.

She walked the cordless phone to the picture of O'Fallon and his gran.

"Very well. He's running LA out of blueberries, one sack at a time."

A chuckle, then more silence. Gavenia fidgeted, ill at ease.

"I miss you," O'Fallon said. "I'm being bombarded by widows and divorcees. They bring me baked goods and offer to go to the movies with me."

"Oh. Any of them cute?"

"No. Not a one. But they're wearing me down. Now if you were here . . ."

"O'Fallon . . ."

"Ah, guilt isn't working, is it?"

Yes. "No."

"Damn. Well, I won't keep you. Give Seamus a scratch for me and let him know I'm thinking of him."

"I will."

More awkward silence. Gavenia chewed on a nail, trying to

figure out what to say next.

"I really miss you," O'Fallon said, and then sighed. "I'll see you in a couple of weeks." The phone buzzed in her ear.

She returned her attention to the picture. Fiona O'Fallon's eyes were like those of her grandson: intelligent and honest. Would she give a witch a chance? There was only one way to find out.

"Bart?"

Yes?

"Pack your shillelagh. We're headed to Ireland."

Chapter Forty-One

After yet another day of unrestrained attention from various widows and divorcees, O'Fallon retreated to Brogan's Last Stand, his favorite watering hole. He watched in awe as the pub's namesake prepared a proper pint of Beamish. The publican was a stickler when it came to beer and refused to top off the pint until the required ninety seconds had passed. He even timed that minute and a half with a stopwatch.

"So how's your gran?" the man asked, keeping an eye on the second hand. Ironically, he was American and his accent reflected that.

"Very well," O'Fallon replied. His Irish accent was thicker now; no way he could prevent it.

"How long are you staying?" Brogan inquired.

"Another fortnight. I don't get home that often."

Brogan topped off the beer and handed it over as O'Fallon pushed money toward him.

"Just give a wave when you want another," the publican said, wiping down the bar with a towel.

"I will. Thanks."

O'Fallon settled into a booth and worshipped the Beamish, the thick cream tickling his lips. His mind wandered through the conversations he'd had with his gran. At first, he'd tried to act nonchalant, as if nothing was amiss. She'd seen right through that. Finally he blurted out everything that had happened between him and Gavenia, even that they were lovers. His gran hadn't batted an eye, though he was committing a mortal sin with an unbeliever.

"Ye two are fine pair," she'd said. "Ye'll bed with each other but not speak of what's in your heart. Makes no sense to me."

"I'm not sure yet," he'd hedged.

"Ah, that's a load and ye know it. I see it your eyes. This woman's got your heart in her hands. The question is, do ye hold hers as well?"

That he couldn't answer. Just because Gavenia was looking out for Seamus didn't mean she gave a damn about the bird's roomie.

A figure slid into the booth across from him and O'Fallon groaned to himself; his quest for silence had just ended. It was Doyle, a man with the gift of gab, so he put on his game face and waited for the man's opening salvo. He wondered what it would be tonight: the weather, the ponies, or the current state of the Irish government.

The older man took a sip of his Guinness and smacked his lips approvingly and gave a wide smile. "Damned shame about that pony in the fourth race."

Ponies it is.

* * *

Please let this go well, Gavenia prayed as she stood in the doorway to the sitting room. Her gut was knotted like a pair of kid's shoelaces, and her right hand shook despite her attempt to hold it in check.

Just be yourself, Bart advised from his place behind her.

I hope that's enough.

Fiona O'Fallon sat in a chair near the sunlit window, clad in a cardigan and a long wool skirt. Her features were delicate. High cheekbones, glowing silver hair, and bright eyes. Just like someone's grandmother. Problem was, she was *his* grandmother.

"Mrs. O'Fallon, I'm Gavenia Kingsgrave." A strange expression appeared on the old woman's face, and Gavenia's gut flipped over in response. *Oh, Goddess, she's going to throw me out.*

Fiona waved her forward and pointed to the chair. "I figured ye'd show up."

What does that mean?

Stop reading things into the situation, Bart grumbled. He sat on the piano bench. Behind the old woman was a hazy figure of a monk, her Guardian. He observed Gavenia with a benevolent gaze.

Gavenia took her place in the chair, not bothering to remove her cloak. That'd save time when she was shown the door. She hooked her cane on the armrest and waited while the housekeeper puttered into the room.

Fiona asked, "When do ye think Douglas will be back?"

"Couple hours, I suspect," the woman replied. "He said he wanted to stop at the pub for a pint or two."

"Good. That'll be more than enough time. Give us privacy, if ye will, Agatha?" The housekeeper nodded and left the room, closing the door behind her. Gavenia's gut did another flip.

Fiona O'Fallon fixed her gaze on her guest. Was this was how a mouse felt right before a cat went for the kill?

"Douglas said ye two are lovers."

Straightforward. I like that. Now we know where O'Fallon gets it, Bart observed.

"Yes, we are," Gavenia replied.

"He said ye're a witch and that ye talk to the dead."

"Yes."

"So why are ye interested in my grandson, then?"

Gavenia frowned. "Why wouldn't I be?"

"He seems a bit ordinary for ye."

"Ordinary? O'Fallon? You've got to be kidding," she blurted, her nervousness getting the best of her. "He's a brilliant investigator; he writes poetry and does origami. He's as psychic as I am. I'd hardly consider that ordinary."

The older woman's face lost a bit of its harshness. "Are ye willing to become Catholic if he decides he wants to marry ye?"

Instant irritation. Gavenia shot back, "Would he be willing to become Wiccan if I pop the question first?"

The old lady frowned, pushing wrinkles in all directions. "If I asked ye to leave now, would ye promise never to see him again?"

Gavenia stared. *Oh, Goddess. She's going to fight this.* She tried to keep her voice from trembling. "He's capable of making his own decisions."

"What if it came down to choosing between ye and me?"

Gavenia's resolve faltered. "If it came down to making him choose between us . . ." She hesitated, and the old woman leaned forward, eyeing her. "I won't drive a wedge between you. You are the most important part of his life. He'd hate me for making him choose. I'd doom our relationship."

Silence.

Fiona's face softened. Then a chuckle. "No, Seamus is the most important thing in his life. I run a close second."

"Which makes me a very poor third," Gavenia muttered without thinking.

The woman gave an approving nod. "By all the saints, ye're a feisty one. No wonder Doug likes ye. He can't stand simple women, the ones without a brain." She gave a quick nod. "Well, ye'll not have to choose who ye worship. Ye're okay by me."

Gavenia's jaw fell slack. *What just happened?*

"Have ye ever seen the Gentry?" she asked eagerly, leaning forward again.

Gavenia's mind reeled. They'd gone from a tense confrontation to discussing fairies in a matter of moments. "Yes, on a midsummer's night on a hill in Wales many years ago."

Fiona nodded as if that didn't surprise her. "Well, I've seen 'em, too. Ye've got some of their blood in ye, all right. I'd wager on it."

Gavenia shrugged, not knowing what to say.

"I suspect ye're keen to see my grandson. Ye'll find him at Brogan's. Agatha will give ye directions."

Short and to the point. I really like this lady, Bart announced, rising to his feet.

Fiona continued, "Do ye have a place to stay?"

Gavenia nodded. "I have a room at a bed-and-breakfast."

"Well, then, go collect my grandson, and I'll see ye in the morning at eight sharp. Tell him not to come back tonight and wake me up."

Their eyes met, and Gavenia couldn't help the smile that appeared on her face. They both knew what would happen the moment she and O'Fallon were alone.

Fiona winked. "I was young once myself and known to indulge a bit of . . . tomfoolery."

"Why do I think you were a handful?" Gavenia asked as she rose from the chair.

A wry grin mingled with the wrinkles on Fiona's face. "Me? No, no. I'm just a sweet old Irish lady. Now off ye go."

Gavenia straightened her cloak. "Thank you for giving me a chance."

"It wasn't that hard. It's plain ye love him."

"I do. Now to convince him of that."

"Well, he's stubborn, but he's not stupid. He'll get it," Fiona said, "eventually."

"I hope so."

* * *

Doyle's nonstop chatter had ended when his wife called the pub and demanded he come home, a joint of mutton in hand. O'Fallon welcomed the solitude. He could brood in peace now.

Another body slid into the booth across from him. He frowned instantly, aggravated. Why the hell did everyone think he wanted company?

He blinked, then stared. Two slim hands dropped back the hood of the emerald-green Kinsale cloak, revealing two fiery sapphire-blue eyes.

"*Dia duit*," the woman said in lilting Irish. *Hello.*

O'Fallon's mouth fell open. "Gavenia . . . how . . . ?"

Her eyes danced in the dim light, mischievous. "What, no widows keeping you company? From what I heard, you were hip deep in them."

He leaned forward and pushed his beer out of the way. Grasping her two hands, he asked, "When did you arrive?"

"A few hours ago. It took me a while to drive here. You live in the middle of nowhere, do you realize that?" Her voice was warm, full of joy, the cuts on her face completely healed.

He gave a short nod, still stunned by her presence. She'd flown all the way from Los Angeles to see him. It was what he'd hoped for, but never believed would happen.

A thought speared his heart. "You've met Gran?" he asked.

"Yes. We had a nice chat. She's a character. She reminds me of Aunt Lucy—very blunt."

"Everything went . . . well?" he asked, his throat suddenly dry. He let loose of one of her hands and took a quick sip of beer.

"Very well. She's okay with us, provided we're okay with each other."

"Ah . . . good." He sighed heavily and he kissed her palms. They smelled like her perfume. The sounds of the pub receded. "We'll need to find you a place to stay. Gran's only got one spare bedroom, and while you may have passed muster with her, there are the neighbors to contend with." He kissed her hands again and then released them. "Some of them are a bit old-fashioned."

"Problem solved. I have a room at a B-and-B." She leaned toward him again and he followed suit. "One with a big comfy bed and a fireplace."

He knew his smile had to look lecherous, but he couldn't stop it.

"Well, now. Perhaps I should let Gran know I'll be a bit late tonight."

"No need. She says she'll see us tomorrow morning and no sooner."

Did she just say . . . ? "You're kidding."

"Nope. Besides, the goddesses have been replaced by something new."

"With what?"

"Best to find out in person," she said, grinning mischievously.

O'Fallon downed the remainder of the Beamish in a single gulp and was out of the booth like an arrow shot from a crossbow.

"Let's go, my lady. I need to officially welcome you to Ireland."

* * *

The trail of clothes led from the door to the bed, his and hers intermingled, tossed aside in frank haste. There had been few words spoken, but reams had been said. They had cried out together as one, souls united, bodies entwined.

Still nestled deep inside his lover, O'Fallon tipped her chin up and gazed into those blue depths. How close he'd come to losing her, losing himself.

Tell her, you fool. Just tell her.

"*Gráim thú*," he whispered. *I love you.*

He waited, wondering how much Irish she understood.

Her eyes widened. "*Tá grá agam duit*," she said, more formally. *I love you.*

He moved his hand down and caressed the closest nipple, marveling at the silver harp that hung from it.

"The harp is the symbol of Ireland," he said. "Did you know that?"

"Really? I wouldn't have guessed," she said in a teasing tone.

He was moved by the gesture. "You're enslaving my heart with everything you do, Gavenia," he said.

"You've done the same to me."

He puzzled on that. "How so?"

"You thought enough to bring me a rose, one that gave me light in the middle of the dark. You fought to stay at the warehouse for as long as they'd let you. You never gave up on me. I'm not used to man who cares that much, Doug."

"Well, you'd best get used to it. I'm yours, for good or ill."

He tilted her face toward his and kissed her nose. Then his eyes drifted down to her breasts. "Maybe we can find you some parrots." She gave him a mock glare. "Or maybe little handcuffs . . ."

"We'll get those for you," she said, reaching up and pinching his closest breast.

He winced and shook his head. "Oh, no. I don't think so. They'd look better on you."

"I think it's time for more harp music," she said, deflecting the conversation.

"Really? So soon?" As Gavenia nodded, she raked her nails

down his side, causing him to take a sharp intake of breath. "So how many movements are in this harp concerto of yours?"

She gave him a smoldering smile. "Don't know. It's a work in progress."

"Those are the best kind."

The End

About the Author

A resident of Atlanta, Georgia, Jana Oliver admits a fascination with all things mysterious, usually laced with a touch of the supernatural. An eclectic person who has traveled the world, she loves to research urban legends and spooky tales.

When not writing, she enjoys Irish music, Cornish fudge and good Scottish whisky.

Find Jana at:
Website: www.JanaOliver.com
Facebook: facebook.com/JanaOliver
Twitter: @CrazyAuthorGirl

The Demon Trappers Series
by Jana Oliver

U.S. Editions

The Demon Trapper's Daughter
Soul Thief
Forgiven
Foretold

St. Martin's Press

U.K. Editions

Forsaken
Forbidden
Forgiven
Foretold

Macmillan Children's Books

BRIAR ROSE

by Jana Oliver

Briar Rose's life is anything but a fairy tale. She's stuck in a small Georgia town with hovering parents, small-minded gossiping neighbors and an evil ex who's spreading nasty rumors about what may or may not have happened in the back of his car.

So when, on the eve of her 16th birthday, Briar learns that she is cursed to die at midnight, she says her good-byes and falls asleep….only to wake up cold, alone, and in the middle of a dark and twisted fairy tale, one created just for her.

Now Briar must fight her way out of this deadly story, but she can't do it alone. She's always believed in handsome princes, and now she's betting her life on one, or there will be no happily ever after.

Macmillan Children's Books

Time Rovers Series

by Jana Oliver

Time Travel, Shape Shifters and Jack the Ripper

Sojourn

Virtual Evil

Madman's Dance

5748050R00205

Printed in Great Britain
by Amazon.co.uk, Ltd.,
Marston Gate.